Janette Griffiths was ⋯⋯⋯⋯⋯⋯⋯⋯⋯⋯
nineteen she left for ⋯⋯⋯⋯⋯⋯⋯⋯⋯⋯
States and stayed ⋯⋯⋯⋯⋯⋯⋯⋯⋯⋯
waitress, telephonist and airline ticket agent, she
travelled from California to Toronto before settling in
Chicago. In 1979 she decided to return to Europe and
moved to Paris where she worked as a stewardess for
Air France. When she was made redundant, she went to
Florence to learn Italian, and then settled down to do
what she'd intended to do all along: write novels. She
has moved nine times since returning to England four
years ago but, at the time of going to print, is living in a
Surrey farmhouse. *The Courtyard in August* is her
second novel, her first novel, *The Singing House*, is also
published by Black Swan.

Also by Janette Griffiths

THE SINGING HOUSE

and published by Black Swan

THE COURTYARD
IN AUGUST

Janette Griffiths

BLACK SWAN

THE COURTYARD IN AUGUST
A BLACK SWAN BOOK : 0 552 99611 4

First publication in Great Britain

PRINTING HISTORY
Black Swan edition published 1996

Set in 11/12¼ Linotype Melior
by Phoenix Typesetting, Ilkley, West Yorkshire

Black Swan Books are published by Transworld Publishers Ltd,
61–63 Uxbridge Road, London W5 5SA,
in Australia by Transworld Publishers (Australia) Pty Ltd,
15–25 Helles Avenue, Moorebank, NSW 2170
and in New Zealand by Transworld Publishers (NZ) Ltd,
3 William Pickering Drive, Albany, Auckland.

Reproduced, printed and bound in Great Britain by
Cox & Wyman Ltd, Reading, Berks.

For Aggie

'Don't worry – dance'

Mrs Lilian Griffiths

PROLOGUE
THE COURTYARD

There are more beautiful courtyards in Paris. There are courtyards with more greenery, courtyards with more elegance and symmetry than the jumble of buildings that crouches this hot July dawn in the shadow of the Eiffel Tower. There are more enchanting and mysterious courtyards.

The wide green enclosures of Neuilly with their great trees fit for a forest and their obedient banks of geraniums and impatiens are more beautiful than this square of cobblestone in the seventh arrondissement. A walk along the rue des Francs Bourgeois in the Marais reveals secretive, ornate courtyards with soothing shadows and splashing fountains.

This courtyard exists almost by default. The building on its north side was standing when Louis XVI stepped out of his carriage to be beheaded on the Place de la Concorde just across the river. It was surely standing more securely than it is now. The foundations have slipped over the centuries and the building now leans into itself, its grey mansard roof resembling a cap that has been put on crooked.

A man in a pilot's uniform is leaving the other, more elegant, building on the south side of the courtyard. He is wearing a gold-braided peaked cap that has never been crooked. He is as handsome and dignified as the building from which he has just emerged – built in the nineteenth century and only joined to the other messy affair by the concierge's lodge on one side and by a long, low baker's kitchen that extends from the boulangerie that occupies the ground floor on the street. Other buildings from neighbouring courtyards fill in the spaces that remain.

The man wheels a suitcase and a pilot's fat black attaché case through the hall to a small door that has been cut out of the great oak doors that once let coaches into the courtyard but are never opened now. In his other hand he is clutching an unopened letter from his employers, and a copy of the works of Nostradamus. Several page corners have been turned over, and once he has positioned his cases and opened the door to watch for his taxi the man flips the book open and starts to read. He is interrupted by the concierge who has already started to distribute the morning's mail. They have never had a book in common before but the concierge has read the old seer's predictions in *Ici Paris* and is anxious about threats of spreading war from the Balkans and invading hordes from the south, even though she herself is from Oporto. Before the pilot can reply, his taxi appears and he steps out of the courtyard and heads for New York.

No-one has invited Nature into this courtyard. Nobody has set out a trellis and trained ivy to weave through it. There is no gardener to plant geraniums, there is no proper lawn to mow. Nature has, however, invited herself. A plane tree seeded itself a century ago; a small patch of grass has grown around it. A long-forgotten concierge once put a cherub fountain in a corner but could not afford to attach it to a system of running water. The cherub stands, nose chipped, its plump backside covered in moss, last year's leaves from the plane tree clogging the scallop-shell basin. The present concierge has provided an orange tree that no longer produces oranges, several terracotta pots of geraniums and a plumbago that has hung indolently along the walls of her lodge for years, never producing more than a dozen pale blue blossoms.

Any other beauty that the courtyard can claim is by association. Tenants in the lopsided older building can see the Eiffel Tower if they lean a long way out and ask a close friend to hold on to their ankles. Tenants in the 'better' building can see the left end of the Arc de Triomphe if they squint or use binoculars, which several of them possess, kept close to the window and usually trained on the building opposite.

The gutters are inhabited by the usual malformed city pigeons, many of them with shrunken pink stumps for feet; sparrows pass through and are fed by the concierge. Ducks occasionally fly over en route for the ponds in the Tuileries or the Luxembourg gardens, swifts are visible whirling high in the July sky, and a redstart has taken up residence above the older building. But the only tenant capable of identifying the bird or feeling any pleasure at its presence will not arrive in the courtyard for a couple more days.

Any sitting tenant hoping to rent his flat out for a summer sublet will not mention the building as much as its location. Most ads placed in the *Herald Tribune* or on postcards in the language schools will read:

Appartement sur cour (côté jardin); vue magnifique sur Tour Eiffel. Ensoleillé. Métro: Invalides.

Mort Engelberg is reading one such advertisement in his cramped middle seat on a charter flight from Chicago to Paris on this July morning. He takes out his pen, smiles to himself and underlines the first three words: *Appartement sur cour.*

11

CHAPTER ONE

As the 747 from Tokyo flew over the North Pole, Nell took her handbag out of a cupboard in the galley and felt inside it for her front door key. She always checked for her keys long before the plane started its descent. On some of the lonelier journeys, she was already fumbling for them as the crew bus crossed the runway at JFK or Bangkok or Rio. She needed to touch the reassuring cool steel and know that soon she would be surrounded by her own furniture, her own views from her own window – even her own smells. But today she was interrupted by François, the steward from the first class galley, who put his head round the curtain and said that the passenger in the back row of first class had died.

'Are you sure?' Nell let the handbag fall back into the cupboard.

'They're bringing him in here.'

The back row of the first class cabin was just yards away from the galley, and as François spoke two younger stewards struggled into the cramped space between the curtains carrying a tall, well-built man in a navy blue suit.

'I'll try mouth to mouth on him anyway,' said François and knelt down.

'But he's a bit yellow,' said Nell, peering down at the

13

man's face. 'I mean, even from here it's obvious that he's dead.'

'All the same, I must try,' said François, and closed his mouth around the pale lips. As Nell and the two stewards cringed, he breathed deeply into the dead body.

'He could have died hours ago,' said one of the stewards. 'Just out of Tokyo even. He said he didn't want any food, he just wanted to sleep. So we haven't been near him until now when I took him an immigration form.'

Nell had remembered that her duty was to call for medical help and she reached for the microphone and asked if there was a doctor on board.

Within minutes a Japanese paediatrician arrived, relieved François of his hopeless task and certified the man dead of a heart attack. Once the captain had been informed and the various forms filled in, once the co-pilot, the flight engineer and other members of the crew had come along to the galley to peer down at the dead man, there was nothing to do but cover him with a blanket and wait for him to be disembarked along with the suitcases and the cargo at the airport in Paris.

He had been travelling alone. As Nell and François went through his papers, they learnt that he was American, divorced with a grown-up son, and presented nature documentaries for television.

'I thought I'd seen him somewhere,' said Nell. 'It must have been on television.'

'You've probably seen everyone on television,' said François.

'I don't watch it *that* much,' said Nell.

François raised an eyebrow at her, then looked down at the man and said: 'You do realize we can't leave him here during the descent?'

'Why not? We can't put him back in his seat – his neighbour won't want that.'

'But if we leave him here, he'll roll – he could even roll out of the galley and down the aisle. And I don't think any of the passengers would like that.'

Nell studied the dead man's bulky form through the blanket and said: 'Do you think we could fold him over and wedge him into an empty food trolley?'

François opened the door of a food trolley and looked back at the man.

'We could get his feet and legs in—'

'But what if he stiffens while he's in there?' said Nell. 'I mean, how long does rigor mortis take to set in?'

'Longer than that, I think,' said François. He frowned and banged on the side of his head with his fist. 'We're supposed to know these things, Nelli my dear. Don't you have a medical manual? Or can't we ask the doctor?'

'I don't think he'd like it if we folded a patient,' said Nell. 'Even a dead one. Look, why don't we put him in one of the crew seats behind the curtain?'

'But what if a passenger opens it and sees him?'

'I'll sit with him during the descent,' said Nell. 'I'll wrap him up well in a blanket and say he's had a malaise.'

The two stewards carried the man to a crew rest seat behind a curtain next to the galley. Nell took her handbag out of the cupboard and went to sit beside him. She was fumbling for her keys when François pulled back the curtain and knelt down beside her.

'You OK there, Nelli?'

'I'm trying not to look at him,' said Nell, who had found her door key and was clutching it more tightly than usual.

'Look, in the light of what has happened' – François was whispering as if to avoid disturbing the dead man – 'we were wondering, the rest of the crew and I, if we could not bother collecting the passenger blankets.

We're a bit behind on closing up the galley and there is going to be a directive around soon that bans blanket collection for ever, so—'

'I'd need to see that directive before I change the rules,' Nell whispered back to him.

'Oh, come on, Nelli,' sighed François. 'Lots of crews have already stopped. Too many crew members have caught unpleasant skin complaints from handling them. People puke on them, Nelli – they spill sticky drinks on them and wrap them round moist, nasty bits of their body—'

'I think it's better if we stick to our usual procedures,' said Nell, and this time she leant as far away from her silent companion as she could, anxious that he, too, might suddenly rise up and say that blanket collection was unhygienic and unnecessary.

François closed the curtain on Nell before she could repeat her sentence. She heard him ripping open the black plastic bags that would contain the discarded blankets. She looked away, looked past her neighbour to the window and the west coast of Ireland. Nell noticed that it was as parched and brown as North Africa. She tried to soothe her feelings of unease, about the blankets, about the hot weather, about death, by telling herself that this was what you did when faced with a crisis: you kept to your routine, you respected the rules, you didn't allow yourself to be thrown off course.

François ignored her for the rest of the flight. Nell was sorry, for on this trip the two of them had spent a happy day in Nara, feeding the deer in the park and visiting a couple of temples. She looked over at her dead neighbour, tried to wonder about his life, failed and felt her attention wandering to the plane's progress across the Irish Sea and over England to France. England, her England, was so blistering brown and so dry that it scared her, this unrelenting summer. The once green island looked from the sky as if it might suddenly crack open into a million weeping sores.

When they landed in Paris, Nell, François and the captain waited with the dead man until a medical team boarded and unloaded him. Nell scowled at the brown dry fields around the runway and noticed that the hundreds of rabbits who fed at dawn and dusk were out in the mid-morning sunlight.

'That took no time at all,' she said as the man was put into a coffin and driven away. 'I don't know why – I thought it would involve more.'

François and the captain were deep in conversation about rumours of redundancies and did not hear her.

'That's it – somebody dies and then . . . nothing,' said Nell but no-one answered her.

At the air terminal, Nell wanted to say goodbye to François, but he had been delayed at crew customs and after a few brief farewell kisses to her other colleagues she found herself alone in the concrete car park.

CHAPTER TWO

Nell's pilot husband, Luc, had lent her his Citroën. Nell found it a baffling car. There were superfluous buttons all over the dashboard. Nell switched on the engine and tentatively pressed a few. When she drove away from the airport a few minutes later and headed towards her house in Chantilly, the heaters were blowing, an extra wiper was wiping, the electric windows were opening and closing and the tape deck was playing Yves Montand in a medley of Frank Sinatra songs.

She managed to control the windows as the car approached the forest of Ermenonville. Here the air was cooler. Nell shivered. The fatigue of a long-haul flight often left her shivering and with a feeling of nausea. Despite the cold that she felt inside, she set the windows on open and slowed down so that she could smell the green coolness of the forest.

Soon the Château of Chantilly appeared through a clearing in the woods. Nell turned the Citroën into a quiet street lined with pollarded plane trees and stopped at the last house. She wheeled her suitcase up the path and felt for the third time for the key in her handbag.

When she went to insert it into the lock it didn't fit. She tried pushing and jiggling the key and when that failed she knelt down and dug at the lock with her fingernail. When this failed, she decided with a lurch of panic that she'd picked up a colleague's handbag. But the British passport was unmistakably hers, as was the neatly arranged pack of Kleenex and the notepad where she wrote her lists.

'*Qu'est-ce que vous faites là, Madame Marchand?*'

The postman was standing at the end of the path.

'I'm trying to get into my house,' Nell started to say. Panic had made her revert back to English. Seeing the postman's blank look and praying that he would be her saviour she got up off her knees and told him in French that her key had swollen.

'It must be the heat,' she concluded.

'But you don't live here any more, madame,' said the postman. He walked up the path and pointed through the front window.

'What?' Nell moved to stand next to him and peered inside her house. The room was empty. Only the appalling brown carpet with the big orange spots that she'd inherited from Luc's first wife remained.

'Of course!' she cried. 'Oh, it's the heat, monsieur, it's fried my brain.'

The postman nudged her. 'Madame can get herself all over the world but she can't get to her new house.'

'My new house isn't ready yet,' signed Nell. 'We're stuck for the summer in Monsieur Marchand's old bachelor apartment in Paris.'

'Paris in summer!' The postman screwed up his face in disgust. 'I haven't been to Paris in August in ten years.'

'Me neither,' said Nell. 'I think I'd be better off back in Streatham.'

'Straitum?'

'South London – you wouldn't like it,' said Nell. She was suddenly too tired to stand up, so she sat down on what had once been her doorstep and closed her eyes.

'*Un malaise?*' asked the postman, sitting down next to her.

'No, I'm just tired. One of my passengers died on the plane this morning—'

'*Oh, là!*' said the postman. 'That happened to me once.'

'You don't have passengers,' said Nell.

'Customers — one of my customers died. I'd been delivering letters for about three days and they weren't falling to the ground as I put them through the box. You get to know the sounds of envelopes on carpets and tile when you deliver to a house for years. I called the police and they found the old man dead in front of the door. My letters had been dropping onto his face — one had even fallen into his open mouth. Turns out he always waited for me because he was hoping for a letter from his son in Guadeloupe. It never came—'

'Oh, that reminds me!' cried Nell, recalling that she too was waiting for a letter. 'Has my mail been forwarded or would there be any stray letters that might still come here? If they'd come from abroad, for example?'

'All forwarded as of last week,' said the postman.

'To Paris? We did have them sent to Paris and not to the new house in the Languedoc?'

'To Paris,' said the postman and sat back and stretched so blissfully that Nell was worried he might be about to curl up and take a nap alongside her. 'Monsieur Marchand showed me the photo of the house in the Languedoc,' he said. '*Oh, là là.*'

'Mm, yes, *oh, là là*,' said Nell, hoping that the letter she awaited would not fall into Luc's hands. 'It is beautiful. I still can't quite believe we'll ever get there—'

'A swimming pool, and that terrace with the grapevine looking out on the *garrigue*. Still, I suppose most captains have houses like that—'

'We might have had one even sooner if Luc hadn't had two children to support all these years.'

'Jean-Louis is my friend!' cried the postman, clapping his hands on his thighs and smiling at the mention of Luc's big, doughy, amiable son. 'Is he going to do your garden down there?'

'Probably,' said Nell. 'Luc certainly won't. I think he's thinking more on the lines of strolling down to the café and playing a game of *pétanque*.'

'*Quelle belle vie*,' sighed the postman.

'*Quelle belle vie*,' agreed Nell, getting up and wheeling her suitcase towards the car. 'Though God only knows when we'll get down there . . . I'd better be going before the traffic picks up. *Au revoir, monsieur*.'

'*Bonne chance, madame*.'

Fatigue overcame Nell as she crossed back through the forest of Ermenonville. She pulled into a side road, locked all her doors and, sitting very upright with her hands clasped in her lap, she closed her eyes. After twenty-four hours without sleep, her body was so desperate for rest that she felt it plummeting at full pelt into unconsciousness. Jumbled, tumbling images rained into her brain – the dead passenger under his blanket in the galley, deer in a Japanese park, her retired father in his Sainsbury's jacket and his 'I'm here to help' badge, loading passenger blankets into a supermarket trolley. Then Nell slept. She woke at noon, thinking that she had heard a phone ring but realized that she had been roused by the sun blazing through the windscreen of the Citroën.

As Nell drove back towards Paris she wondered if she should call Luc and see how the house purchase was progressing. But she couldn't remember where he was. She should have paid more attention. She had paid attention. At the time she had noted the destination, wondered something vague and mundane about the weather, who might be on the trip, and thrown the note in the bin.

Now she was driving Luc's car towards the Place de la Concorde. She twiddled more of the buttons on the dashboard, trying to locate the horn. She would need the horn at the Concorde. By the time she found it the inside of the car was lit up like the Eiffel Tower at night. Luc had installed extra headlights, an alarm system, extra speakers for the stereo, an alarm for the stereo. The tape deck was still playing; water squirted in rhythmic spurts up the windscreen; three wipers washed it away; the electric windows had taken to opening and closing again; her seat was getting warmer and warmer; all manner of lights reminded and remonstrated.

Nell ignored them all. She had to concentrate on crossing the Place de la Concorde. The trick, she had learned in her twelve years in Paris, was just to go and assume that the other drivers would adapt. She put her foot down and fixed her eyes on the columns of the National Assembly across the bridge in front of her. As always, she noticed the horse chestnut trees on the Champs Elysées side of the great square near the Seine. They had turned brown and it was only July. Like Luc's lights and buzzers they served as a reminder – a reminder that time was passing, that life had hardly got going and it was gone. Why did they do this? she wondered as the Citroën whisked her past them. Summer is hardly here, you fools, she wanted to cry at the rusting brown leaves and the forlorn naked branches, and already you are leaving.

The phone rang. This astonished her because she'd forgotten that Luc had a phone in his car. Eyes still on the Assembly but with those miserable chestnuts in her peripheral vision, she fumbled for the reciever. It was her mother in London.

'Is that you, Eleanor?' Her mother sounded old and uncertain.

'Of course it's me, Mother.'

'Are you at home? I mean the Paris home? Or is this the number on the Riviera?'

'We don't have a number on the Riviera, Mother. We don't live on the Riviera. We are moving to the Languedoc.'

'Never heard of it,' mumbled her mother. 'Where are you, then?'

'I'm in a car. I'm in Luc's car.'

'But you're not driving . . . are you?'

'Yes! Yes! That's what you do in cars. I'm halfway over a bridge across the Seine.'

'The Seine? Ah . . . ah.' Her mother's voice relaxed. 'Look, if you're in your car, I'd better call back – this really isn't the time—'

'It's certainly not the time for small talk – you know Paris traffic.'

'Oh, this wasn't small talk.'

'What then?' Nell drove past the Air France terminal, past the too-gold dome of the Invalides church, towards her street on the other side of the esplanade. 'What, Mother? What is it?'

'Oh, I don't know. I didn't mean to tell you like this – it's your father—'

'What about him?' Nell felt the panic cells in her brain organizing themselves, amassing their forces and surging to the surface.

'I'll call you back when you're at home, when you're sitting down.' Again her mother sounded old and tremulous.

'I'm sitting down now.'

'Then stop the car.'

'I can't just stop – oh, hold on a minute – there's a

space in front of the café.' She pulled over and switched off the engine. 'Now, Mother, tell me!'

'He's dying, dear. He collapsed in Sainsbury's car park this afternoon. The doctors say he won't last the week.'

Several numb minutes later, Nell found herself looking at the people in the café. It was the time of the afternoon when the following day's edition of *Le Monde* came into the news kiosks and most of the customers' faces were hidden by the pages of dense black print. Only one man was looking out at her. She was suddenly aware that she was crying. She had told her mother that she would be on the first plane out the next morning and then she had sat and cried. Now this man was staring out at her and she was embarrassed and wanted to say: 'I don't do this often but my father is dying and I'm not really sure how I feel about the old boy but death is death and I'm shocked and—'

The man turned away, lit a cigarette and walked towards the door. She hoped that he was coming to her to offer comfort. She wanted comfort from a stranger, and in those jangled moments after her mother's announcement she fixed all her hopes on the unknown man in the café. He paused at the door, turned his back and walked towards the curving green arch of the Métro entrance.

An hour later she wheeled her suitcase into the front building on the courtyard and rode the lift up to the fifth floor. She found a message from Luc behind a fridge magnet. It said: 'I waited until the last minute. Was your flight delayed? Am in NYC, PTP and back in NYC until Saturday – Luc.'

He had closed the shutters in the living room before he left. Nell hesitated before she opened them, unsure whether the greater, fiercer heat would come from an electric lamp or the light in the courtyard. She decided that, after all those hours in the enclosed plane, she needed some air. But when she opened the shutters and looked across at the humble building opposite, she sat down and wept.

CHAPTER THREE

Mort Engelberg paid off the taxi, looked hard at the great double doors that led to the courtyard and his new apartment and decided that he wasn't yet ready to move in. He wanted a cup of coffee first and a croissant and the time to relish the idea of crossing the threshold to his summer in Paris.

He put his bags on the pavement and squinted at the street in front of him. The only café open was the one that he had found the least appealing when he had scouted around the neighbourhood after being shown the flat by M. Dupuy, the permanent tenant. The café was the most spartan in the street; the interior had stark strip lighting, dingy yellow walls and an orange formica-topped bar. There were a few tables outside but, as in so many narrow streets, they were cramped onto an uneven pavement that in any other month would have been so closely skimmed by passing traffic that Mort would have risked finding a wing mirror in his morning bowl of coffee. He shuffled around the four chrome tables and chairs, rattling them slightly to test for stability and studying the view that each afforded.

Mort shouldn't have been in Paris at all. He should have been working through a trial period of forecasting the weather on American national television. As he rattled the café seats and gazed anxiously up at the hot sky for signs of rain, a guilty, jubilant, remorseful Mort thanked those heavens for the hurricane that two weeks earlier had literally swept his old life aside.

When Hurricane Horace hit the coast of Florida, Mort's first words had been: 'Who the hell gave it such a dumb name?'

Now he thought guiltily that Horace was the noblest name he'd heard in a long time. He had been settling into his job at the national network when the hurricane season had begun. He was still amazed that he had the job in the first place since, until then, the TV people had never quite taken to him. They would explain in their effusive, intimate way that while there was nothing wrong with him there was nothing in his personality that they could build an image around. He was just Mort – a nice-looking, medium-sized, studious man from Skokie, Illinois, who was passionate about weather. He had no gimmicks, no eccentricities, no endearing little personality traits that could attract a following amongst viewers. He had once been encouraged to 'clown it up' for a local station in New Hampshire and had almost fainted from embarrassment.

Mort often wanted to tell these people that his passion for weather, for the sight of angry lightning over mountains, the white silence after a blizzard, the smell of a wood in a summer shower, should suffice the watching millions. He couldn't tell them that his true desire was to paint that weather. Like Turner lashed to the masthead in a storm, Mort wanted to paint the swirling winds, the shifting sunlight, the raging tides. Unlike Turner, Mort had no genius, not even a small talent, but he returned to his easel again and again because it was his way of *loving* the weather.

He had explained this to his wife before she had left him for a sports reporter. His wife had said that she was embarrassed by his dreadful canvases and refused to return his calls until his appearance on NBC.

Then Horace had hit. Mort had just made his debut on national news when the reports came in from Florida. The network booked him onto a plane and into the best hotel in Fort Lauderdale.

Mort was thrilled at the prospect of studying Horace in person, so to speak, and decided to take along his painting equipment. Without a word to anyone at the network, he cashed in his plane ticket and set about assembling his canvases, sketch pads and paints for the long drive down the east coast. Part of him had known that this prolonged journey could result in his missing the hurricane but he had continued to plan his drive, packing slowly and methodically as the wind started to rattle the shutters and the palm trees began to bow their tips to the Florida ground. Part of him also knew that if he missed this assignment, Mort Engelberg, already a rather insubstantial figure on the weather map, might well be blown out of the picture.

And although all the practical, reasoning parts of Mort that had got him sensibly through to his forty-second year told him that he must hold on to his job, his feet led him out to his old Buick and his hands turned the ignition key, and soon he was off on a circuitous saunter down the eastern seaboard.

The Buick's engine had failed near Hilton Head and Mort had been fired over the phone when he had called the network to say that he was waiting for a replacement. He had taken the news with equanimity, checking himself into a local hotel and taking himself out to dinner, where his only memorable thought was that he'd had seven minutes of national attention which was more than most people got. It seemed enough to Mort and he decided to spend the next day painting on the peninsula.

Then the TV news had come on in the bar where he

was dismembering his lobster. Mort had sat back preparing to enjoy the sight of palm trees bending to the ground and twenty-foot waves crashing over sea walls when he saw the mournful expressions of those who had been, briefly, his former colleagues and heard that the local newsreader who had done the report in his place had been killed by an advertising billboard that had blown loose during filming.

'Tan don't burn use Coppertone,' had been the lethal billboard's message. Mort had been surprised by this since he'd always associated that slogan with his childhood and was amazed to hear that it was still around. Part of his mind had latched onto the slogan in the way that it had attached itself to a thousand banal song lyrics and, even as he found the one stable chair and table in the Paris side street, part of him was declaring: 'Tan don't burn use Coppertone.'

Mort must not blame himself for his substitute's death, his ex-bureau chief had emphasized when Mort had spoken to him. The man was a former actor and had been more concerned with showing his good side to the camera than with reporting the lethal weather. He had stood where he'd hoped the light would flatter his ageing profile and he'd been whacked by the billboard instead. Vanity, not Mort, was responsible.

Mort felt overwhelming guilt, but he had also come to believe that the billboard was responsible for his presence in Paris. He'd abandoned his lobster in the bar, walked to the seafront and, in the swiftest decision of his life, decided to come to Europe. He'd chosen Paris in a vague, romantic way because of painters and bohemians and because he'd found a brochure in a travel agency the following morning that advertised schools of French language and culture in Paris. His brief appearance on national television had proved its value when he had met M. Dupuy and informed him, with the aid of a dictionary, that he had been a star in the weather forecasting firmament.

It was going to be hot. Mort had no Coppertone but he did have a straw sunhat. He pulled it over his forehead, then realized that this obscured his view, restricting his landscape to the cobbles, the gutter and the discarded racetrack and lottery tickets that trailed from the café entrance to the pavement. The day was set to be dusty and uncomfortable. He could feel the red spreading across his eyes and knew that his allergies had followed him to Paris. He wondered for the first time whether he had been wise to come to this city in the summer.

The word 'Paris', the idea of 'Paris', had been devoid of pollen, pollution and dust. The Paris he had studied in the glossy brochure had been as two-dimensionally beautiful and free from warts as a studio photo of a film star. But when he had walked around the Champ de Mars, the formal park closest to his apartment, the dust from the gravel paths had whirled around his ankles, and even in the early morning the smell of petrol hung in the air.

Mort decided to keep a careful watch on his eyes. His logical mind made him smile at this thought as he ordered a *café au lait* from a waiter who did not smile back. Then Mort himself became despondent as he realized that there was no-one else in his new world who was remotely interested in how he looked. The combination of loneliness, heat and dust led him to the conclusion that if his eyes got any pinker he would sub-sublet for a couple of weeks and head for the south. He removed his glasses and examined his left eye in the wing mirror of a parked taxi. Already the red veins were dilating around the brown iris.

Another pair of eyes appeared in the mirror behind his. They were brown too and, judging by the surrounding creases, had been looking out at the world for almost as long as his. They belonged to a woman at the next table who was peering into the same mirror as she removed her lipstick. It was a sloppy gesture, thought Mort, and doomed to failure. She was too far away to see what she was doing and she was so absent-minded in her movements, stopping to order coffee and simper at the waiter, that she succeeded only in spreading a thinner layer of pink around her mouth. Also, thought Mort, women didn't usually remove their make-up in public – especially Parisian women who, it seemed to him, were forever dabbing and powdering and re-finishing their chic, plain faces.

He turned to stare at the woman who raised her coffee cup in acknowledgement. She had very big, sun-tanned hands, Mort noticed. As he stared at them, she ignored his gaze and started removing the rings that had encircled each finger. The two of them were the only customers at the outside tables.

'*Que chaleur,*' said the woman in a French that Mort sensed was as mangled as his own. 'Hot! Hot! Hot!' she continued in English, plucking at her blouse repeat-edly so that the rapid movement of the fabric ventilated her breasts. Mort didn't like to look but he couldn't resist replying.

'You speak English, huh? Where are you from?'

'Brésil – you know?'

'No I don't know,' said Mort. 'I'm from – well, I'm originally from Chicago but I've been working in New York.'

'I worked there!' cried the woman. 'Five years ago – that's where I learned my English.'

'Oh really?' said Mort, shifting his chair towards her table, aware now that he was lonelier than he had wanted to admit. 'Whereabouts in New York?'

'Oh . . . maybe down near 42nd Street.'

'42nd Street, huh? What were you doing down there?'

'This and that,' said the woman and turned to order another coffee from the waiter.

'I'll get that,' said Mort and ordered one for himself. 'Mort Engelberg.' He held out his hand.

The woman did not extend one of those large hands. She had folded them on her lap under the table. This gesture was so coy, so Jane Austen, so far from 42nd Street that Mort found himself staring under the table and not listening when she said her name: Marina Flor de Paraíso. She repeated it.

'Huh?' said Mort.

'Flor de Paraíso: Marina Flower of Paradise.' The big woman blushed.

'Not really? said Mort.

Marina shook her head. 'I make it up.'

'Well, it's a beautiful name,' said Mort. The invented name seemed to him to be redolent of oceans and gardens and sky, of everything that was missing from the dusty street. Again he contemplated the possibility of leaving Paris for a month and making his way down to the Mediterranean.

He was now sitting next to the woman and could look closely at her as long as he maintained enough conversation to give him an excuse to study the dusky face and voluptuous body.

'Are you working in Paris?' he asked.

'Yes,' said Marina.

'And you're not going on vacation?'

'No, no vacation for me.'

'And do you work in the neighborhood?'

'No. I work in the Bois de Boulogne.' Marina had leaned back in her chair and was looking hard at him. She was expecting some reaction to this statement. Mort felt that he'd failed her somehow for he couldn't remember which of the Paris parks the Bois de Boulogne was. He'd been to one years earlier with Peg, his ex-wife, where he recalled the most exquisite rose garden, but he'd also visited another vast park with a zoo. Could she be a keeper? That would account for the hands, he thought.

Marina unclipped her earrings, put them in her bag and said: 'I only do four nights a week. And I never do arse-fucking – just hand jobs and maybe a blow job.'

'And you live in the neighborhood?' Mort was amazed to hear his voice continue a conversation that he had just deserted. His thoughts had stalled and concertinaed into each other like cars on a freeway but somehow his mouth and tongue were able to continue on their track with no help from him. He heard himself discussing the difficulty of finding apartments, the scurrilousness of estate agents, and all the time his brain was sifting images of those big hands . . . that faded pink mouth . . .

'Now I have to go and get out of my work clothes,' said Marina. 'Thanks for the coffee.' She squeezed his shoulder as she passed.

'Do you live in my building?' said Mort, nodding his head in the direction of the elegant stone façade of the more prosperous apartment block.

'Sometimes . . . sort of . . .' Marina hesitated. 'I have a friend, Mademoiselle Sofia. I live maybe with her . . . but she is . . .' She scowled as she sought the word. 'Unstable, you say, right? She is unstable.'

'Which floor?' said Mort, quite sure that Sofia was on the same cheap side of the courtyard as him.

'Fifth,' said Marina. 'I invite you, maybe, for a *caipirinha*? You know this Brazilian drink?' Mort didn't. 'Maybe if it's my apartment I say come up for a *caipirinha* but Sofia is . . . what's the word? You never know how she's going to feel about things.'

'That's OK,' said Mort. 'I may be headed out to the ocean for a week or two if this heat keeps up.'

'Ocean?' sighed Marina. 'But this is the wrong side of the ocean. I saw it once from here and it doesn't look like it does from there. The ocean here is not worth it.' She sighed again and was gone across the street and through the large wooden doors that led to the courtyard. Mort stared after her, noting that her feet were big and her shoulders broad, and recalled that she had referred to three sexual practices of what he now knew was her trade but had omitted the most obvious. She was a man, he concluded and was relieved that Sofia was unpredictable and unwelcoming and that he wouldn't be drinking any *caipirinhas* on the fifth floor. If Paris was anything like New York, he comforted himself, he would hear no more from the demoiselles Marina and Sofia. Nevertheless, when he returned to his building an hour later, he examined the mailboxes and discovered that Sofia lived immediately above him. Hers was the only other window to be open, along with his, and as he crossed the courtyard a copy of *Vogue* was thrown from that window and would have hit him had he not been staring up at that particular apartment and seen it coming.

CHAPTER FOUR

Nell saw to her relief that the postman had been right and that her mail had been forwarded to the Paris address. She sorted rapidly through the pile of bills and magazines and saw that the awaited letter from Jameson's Private Detective Agency in London was not in the pile. Nell was not sorry. She was embarrassed by her association with Mr Jameson and had resolved to tell her oldest and dearest friend Claudine of her absurd and secret undertaking. Now, her father's illness would delay that confession.

She switched on the answering machine and heard from the messages that filled the tape that even if she had forgotten about the move to Paris, Claudine had known where to find her.

'Ma chérie, ma cocotte, ma vieille.' Her friend's three terms of endearment echoed round the small apartment. 'My dear, my stewpot, my old girl, the bunions are receding but varicose veins threaten. The bowels are ever unreliable but one must not succumb.' Had these words not been uttered in Claudine's dark French contralto and had the face behind the voice not been that of a stunning, albeit artificial, blonde beauty, Nell felt that she might have been being addressed by an Old Testament prophet.

She let the machine run on while she unpacked her

suitcase. 'Once again I am leaning towards nipple realignment,' announced the machine. One of Claudine's breasts was higher than the other, and at the beginning of their twelve-year friendship Claudine had amazed Nell by unbuttoning her blouse in the toilets of the Ritz and asking Nell if she thought surgery was necessary. Nell had averted her eyes and said that she thought not, but from time to time, when life offered no other conflicts or challenges, Claudine would reconsider the question of her nipples. Many of their conversations had run to a halt over the years when Nell had caught Claudine staring down at her chest, apparently debating the merits of surgery.

Nell had intended to call Luc. She had intended to clean up the mess in the kitchen and unpack her suitcase but instead she stood in the middle of the living room and listened to her friend.

Claudine's monologue moved from nipples to a day spent riding the cable cars in San Francisco. Luc often complained that her calls took up most of the machine's tape and had told Nell to ask her to talk a little less. Nell had never mentioned this to Claudine. She liked the messages and often wished that she had kept them as a spoken record of their years together.

Nell waited until Luc would have arrived in New York, but when the time came she chose instead to call Claudine. When Claudine picked up the phone in the small, draughty château that she had inherited from one of her lovers, Nell said: '*Papa va mourir.*' Claudine said that her car had broken down but that she would come in a taxi. Nell said that nobody could take a taxi all the way in from the Loir-et-Cher but Claudine hung up and appeared two hours later.

'I'll pay your taxi fare,' said Nell.

'I won't let you.' Claudine was wearing black silk trousers and an electric blue silk shawl. Nell was as astonished by Claudine's blond, elegant, French

beauty that evening as she had been all those years earlier when they had first become friends. This beauty
might have daunted Nell completely had Claudine not
been plagued by bunions, rheumatism and tinnitus.

Nell like to tell people, particularly those who
would never meet Claudine, that she had met the two
most important people in her French life – Luc and
Claudine – at her first ever company medical: Luc in
the waiting room for ECG's – examinations of the heart
– and Claudine when both women were handing in
their urine samples through a hatch in the corridor
wall. The symbolism of the encounter with Luc was
obvious and charming but, Nell used to say to
strangers, what was the meaning of her first meeting
with Claudine? In truth, and Nell had long since forgotten this truth, the meetings had been reversed.
Claudine had been waiting very nervously to have her
heart checked and Luc was handing in his pee.

'You were going out this evening?' Nell asked as she
sorted through her soiled uniforms.

'It doesn't matter. I can see him any time.'

'Why is your car in for a service when you've only
just bought it?' Nell was wondering who 'he' was but
chose to ask the safer question.

'Because it's not a new car! Because I bought a
second-hand car from somebody who will probably
turn out to be *louche*! Nell, what is up with you? Is this
what Englishwomen do when their fathers are dying?
Load up the washing machine and talk about servicing
cars?'

'Depends on the father, I suppose.' Nell measured
out the fabric softener.

'But you love the old boy – you've always talked
about him affectionately—'

'Oh, I love him. I don't know him. He was hardly
ever there, but I suppose men of that generation
weren't. He's always an agreeable presence, smells of

37

whisky and tweed, is big and cuddly in a bristly sort of way – all the usual clichés about English fathers . . .'

Claudine opened a cupboard near the door and took out one of Luc's better bottles of Bordeaux.

'I don't want to go tomorrow, Claudine. I'm terrified of deathbed scenes.'

'Isn't everybody?'

'Oh, you'd be good at it,' sighed Nell. 'You'd hold the old boy's hand and tell him you love him and weep. I'm scared that I'll just peer at him quizzically and say something inappropriate like "Who on earth are you, old man? And what have you been up to for the past three decades?" Do you know, I almost told my mother that I couldn't get out of the flight tomorrow and would come at the weekend?'

'You wouldn't have done that.'

'I'm capable of it,' said Nell. 'But I'm going because it's my duty. That's all.'

'Luc said that in New York last month!' Claudine cut them both some bread and cheese and set it out on the counter.

'Said what? What did Luc say?'

'He said that you reduce everything in your life to work and duty. Or did I say it to him? One or the other. In any case we both think it.'

'Where were you when you said that?'

'What does it matter where we were?' Claudine poured herself a second glass of wine and forgot to serve Nell.

'Where were you? I want to know.'

'In the coffee shop across from the hotel on Broadway and 57th.'

'Were you having breakfast or dinner?'

'Breakfast, of course! Nobody would eat dinner in that place! Why? What does it matter?'

'Was it six o'clock in the morning?'

'Six thirty and most of the cabin crew were there and

I had two eggs over easy and the hash browns. Why?'

'I don't know.' Nell burst into tears. 'That's an awful thing to say about someone—'

'At first glance I suppose it is, but Luc said that's what he loves about you.'

'Luc said that to you? At six thirty in the morning?'

'Well, you have to take the time change into account – it was really twelve thirty p.m. Paris time. You see, we were the oldest ones at the table. There was a bunch of young girls from the summer student intake and Luc and I were feeling so old. You know what it's like when these students come in to work the season – never tired, always wanting to go up the Empire State or share taxis to SoHo, never a shadow under their eyes and all that irritating enthusiasm. Well, Luc looked at them and for no reason – we hadn't been talking about you or him – but for no reason he said that you were his anchor—'

'Old and rusty?'

'Yes, but reliable and unchanging. I felt envious of you when he said that. Nobody will ever say it about me . . .'

'What's wrong with work and duty?' Nell asked, but she knew she would get no answer because Claudine's attention had strayed as it always did at this time of the evening to the Eiffel Tower, visible if she leaned far out of the living room window and looked to the left.

'There! They just lit it up!'

Claudine said this every time she visited Nell in the evenings. Next, Nell knew, she would say how much better the new system of lighting was. In the comfortable manner of old friends Nell was aware that she could safely ignore the next few minutes of Claudine's conversation – sodium lighting, the wonderful folly of the tower, how they must ride it along with the tourists one day soon – and ruminate on the statement made in the New York diner by her best friend or her husband.

39

What is wrong with work and duty? How could she explain to Claudine or Luc that when she had landed this flying job back in the days before mass transport was mass transport, back when travel was still elusive and romantic, the biggest shock had been the discovery that the world consisted more of people than of places? And what better way to avoid baffling, unfathomable people than through work and duty? Oh, the Taj Mahal had been right there where they'd said it was, floating white and exquisite, as had the Golden Gate Bridge, red and audacious, the snows of Kilimanjaro and the towers of Manhattan, but everywhere Nell had turned people got in the way and littered things up.

Nobody had told her how much of the world would clamber up the stairs of her plane – the forlorn boat people, the defiant deportees, drunken film stars, exiled monarchs, deposed tyrants, separated lovers and all the mundane disappointed holidaymakers. They swarmed onto the plane and filled the clean, empty spaces with their clatter, their tears and their odours.

How else to deal with all that clamour and confusion, all that pain and loneliness and need, but with work and duty? Make sure that the meals are served warm, the blankets collected up, draw a nice, efficient route map to tell them where they are and where they've been – hold the whole unruly, unpredictable world together by reducing it down to a thing of small routine tasks.

She needed a small routine task now to fill this summer dusk hour in Paris. It was a good time to call Luc. The low phone rate had come into operation just minutes earlier. In New York it was early afternoon and Luc would be lying fully clothed on a double bed in a green and white painted hotel room that looked out on the busy windows of an office building. His suitcase would be open; his gold-braided jacket would be hanging with his peaked cap on a hook behind the door. Purchases of various Manhattan discount stores would be lying in plastic bags on the other double bed – computer games, a Patricia Highsmith novel in English that he would never get round to reading, a half-dozen packets of Pepperidge Farm cookies that would go in the pantry with all the other 'ethnic' foods that he brought home and forgot about.

Calling Luc was not the routine task she needed, she decided. She would call him when she was sure he had gone out to dinner and leave a message telling him not to call her back – she needed her sleep to cope with the crisis in London.

'Did he mention the rumours about the early retirement packages?' Claudine had withdrawn from the window and had, apparently, been sitting opposite Nell while Nell's thoughts had been in Manhattan.

'They're just rumours,' said Nell, who had heard nothing from Luc but had eavesdropped on the same story being told by François and the captain on the runway at Roissy. 'He would have said something to me if he thought he was affected,' she added.

'Of course,' said Claudine, and pouring them both another glass of wine turned her attention back to her breasts.

CHAPTER FIVE

When the head of the news bureau had fired Mort, over the phone while Mort was sitting in a pair of denim shorts and a T-shirt, gazing out at the Atlantic from the immobilized Buick, he had said: 'The trouble with you, Engelberg, is you don't worry enough.'

Mort had thought at the time that he should be worried about not worrying. He hadn't really worried when the replacement newscaster had been killed. He had felt sorry and more than a little guilty but he hadn't been worried – it was too late for that.

'You don't worry enough,' his ex-wife Peg had said when he had failed to become a weather 'personality' on local television.

His widowed mother in Skokie had first accused him of not worrying when he was eleven and failed to make it into any sports teams. Throughout Mort's adolescence, his mother had viewed this lack of angst as a virtual betrayal of his people. You couldn't be Jewish and not worry, she'd tried to tell him, any more than you could be a polar bear and not eat blubber. Mort hadn't worried about his mother's concern, and as he grew towards manhood even his lonely mother started to see the advantages of having such an untroubled son. Compared to his driven physician brother, Mort was soothing. When a French teacher had complained to her that Mort had an 'abnormal capacity for enjoyment', his mother had almost burst with pride and love for her handsome young son.

Mort wasn't looking very handsome as he poured himself a glass of champagne from the quarter bottle that he had saved from his flight. He hadn't shaved and had not yet located a laundromat. His clothes were crumpled and his socks were beginning to smell. But, he reasoned to himself, like the old question of whether a tree falling in a forest made a sound if nobody was there to hear it, did his socks really smell if there was no-one there to smell them?

Mort was experiencing the first pangs of loneliness. He picked up the phone, took out his credit card and put through a call to Frank, his physician brother.

'I'm looking out on a genuine European courtyard,' he told Frank when the receptionist transferred the call. 'Cobblestones, pots of geraniums, chipped stone statues with moss growing on them—'

'You called me in my office to tell me that?' said his brother. 'Why don't you stay at the Crillon? Ruthie and I stayed at the Crillon last time we were in Paris. Pavarotti stays at the Crillon—'

'But I don't want to be a tourist,' said Mort.

'You have a French passport now? Suddenly your name is Marcel? Don't give me that crap about not being a tourist. If you don't live in a country and you visit it you're a tourist, period. When you coming back?'

'I just got here,' said Mort.

'Did you reconfirm your flight home?'

'I haven't even booked it—'

'Well do it today,' said Frank. 'Those transatlantic flights fill up in September. And wear a tie when you travel – that way they might upgrade you.'

'I don't want to think about coming back yet,' said Mort, gazing out at the courtyard. For a second he thought he saw a flash of blue and a shimmer of light. He put the receiver on the table and leaned out the window, where he saw only the square of sun-baked cobble.

'You'd better not stay away long,' Frank's voice said on the formica table. Frank had never been away from his hospital for more than two weeks. 'And try to keep your hand in while you're over there. I got to go – my other line is ringing.'

'It's not like playing golf,' Mort started to say to a dead phone line. 'How am I supposed to keep my hand in at the weather?'

The afternoon was very hot. Mort did try to think as a weatherman for a few minutes and concluded that this heat must shift soon. It belonged down in Madrid or Rome, not this far north in Paris. Even sitting bare-chested in front of the open window, he was sweating and uncomfortable. Still he looked with pleasure at the first courtyard that he had ever lived above. Already he loved the angles and shadows of the Parisian stone, and the hum of the city as it was sucked into the square emptiness between the buildings, rattled idly around and drifted off into the summer sky. Mort felt himself drifting off in the heat and again he felt a sense of blueness, of coolness, of water.

He shook himself awake. The phone was still on his lap and, hardly conscious of what he was doing, Mort dialled his ex-wife's number.

'I'm in Paris, Peg,' he said when the phone was picked up. 'Remember Paris?'

'Never been,' said a voice that Mort guessed belonged to the cleaning lady.

'Get off the line, Primrose,' said Peg's voice. 'I've got this in the bedroom.'

'I'm in Paris, Peg,' Mort repeated.

'Nobody goes to Paris any more, Mort,' said Peg. 'Prague is where people go now. Or Budapest – not

Paris. And never ever Paris in summer.'

'Well I'm here, and I like it, so I guess that means that by your standards I don't exist—'

'You can't exist for me any more, Mort,' sighed Peg. 'And I can't sit here and talk to you now. I have to get to the office—'

'I'm about to sign on at school,' said Mort. 'Landscape painting and French language.'

'You'll never learn French, Mort,' said Peg.

'Why not?'

'You're too old and too . . . too . . . feckless.'

'Feckless?' Feckless was not one of Peg's words. Mort was about to say as much to his ex-wife when he heard music in the courtyard. 'Now there's music in my courtyard, Peg,' he said instead but she too was muttering something about another line and Mort found himself back on the phone with Primrose.

'Well I'd go to Paris if someone gave *me* a ticket,' said the cleaning lady. 'Prague is such an ugly word. Praaague.'

Mort didn't bother to question her presence on the line throughout the conversation. The music had lured him back to the window. He didn't yet know that many of the building's inhabitants had left and for the final hour of the morning he imagined the life that would return to those blind windows with the coming of the twilight. There was, after all, vibrant, noisy life in the apartment above his. One of the demoiselles, Marina or Sofia, had lobbed a flower pot out of the window shortly after the descent of the magazine.

And now music was issuing from that same window. It sounded like a country and western song. Mort strained to hear the title which seemed to be 'My life is at a railroad crossing and God won't lift the gate'. Mort couldn't have said why, but he was sure that the music reflected the taste of the invisible Mlle Sofia.

Then came the sudden silence of a summer's

45

afternoon. Mort was supremely happy. His was the joy of the traveller who has just arrived at his destination and is filled with his own happy imaginings of what the as yet unseen streets contain.

And should those streets disappoint, he still had the option of going down to the Riviera until the heat had abated and the summer pollution had lifted. 'Going down to the Riviera.' He smiled as he realized that he, Mort Engelberg, had actually entertained such an urbane, European thought. He wasn't quite sure how you went 'down to the Riviera', or what you did once you got there. He thought he'd read in F. Scott Fitzgerald or Somerset Maugham about blue trains and flower-festooned cliffs tumbling into wine-dark sea. But such good reading had been so long ago that the images were jumbled and incoherent.

Besides, his first mission was to go to the school of language and culture and find out about signing on for his course. The brochure had mentioned year-round courses that combined Painting with Art History, Figure Drawing with French Language, excursions out to Van Gogh's Auvers and field trips to Millet's Barbizon. When he had phoned the school, they had taken a long time to answer and had passed him on to a man with a thick smoker's bass who had said in mangled English that he could do any course he wanted as long as he paid in advance. Mort had felt a twinge of suspicion and compromised by sending a deposit. In return he had received the same brochure with its colour photo of a quaint geranium-filled court-yard in St-Germain-des-Prés. An arrow pointed to a doorway that was the entrance to the school.

Now on this warm evening, Mort planned to walk over there, perhaps catch the bass-voiced man before he left and sign on for landscape painting and French language. He consulted his map of Paris. He was an efficient map reader and had a sure sense of direction and it took him just a few minutes to calculate that he could save time by riding the 63 bus from in front of the American church by the Seine.

The bus took him past the great columns of the National Assembly where it had the good grace to get stuck in a jam at the lights on the bridge and allow Mort time to take in the sweep of the river in the twilight. Mort felt that frustration of disbelief so common to a traveller when confronted with sights that have occupied his imagination for weeks.

Now, of course, travel was banal. Everyone did it. Everyone was everywhere. Still, Mort thought, this is only my second time in Paris. And even though he was over forty and his dark, lined face remained impassive, he felt a lurching sense of excitement as he stared through the bus window at the string of lights that lined the river under the generous summer chestnuts, the silhouettes of the Grand and Petit Palais and the vast, symmetrical turmoil of the Place de la Concorde.

Mort squinted across the river at the elegant symmetry of the Hotel Crillon and the Naval ministry and saw an elegance that would forever elude an American like himself. He thought that Frank must have looked pretty silly in such a place and was glad of his courtyard.

Once the bus was out of the jam, it took only minutes to make its way down the Boulevard St-Germain. Mort jumped off in front of the pugnacious figure of Danton at the Odéon and made his way back towards the Seine until he came to the small passage that had been marked on the brochure. The exuberant geraniums glowed orange in the summer twilight; the name of the school was next to the door but the interior looked abandoned and dusty. In the window was a sign that said '*Bail à céder.*'

Mort rattled the door of the school and shouted through the letterbox. Even though he could not begin to translate the sign, he knew that the bass-voiced man and his glossy brochures were long gone, taking with them his hundred-dollar deposit. 'Tan don't burn use Coppertone,' popped into his head and, as he turned away from the iron gate and realized that he had been relieved of the chore of learning French, Mort muttered to himself, 'It's an ill wind.'

Then it occurred to him that this was the first time he'd dared to ponder the wonderful, literal truth of the old proverb when applied to his life. 'Oh my God – it really was an ill wind,' he said out loud, and an elegant matron and her Yorkshire terrier crossed the street to avoid his path.

He made yet another instant decision: he didn't need a teacher or a school to make him paint. He would go home, pick up his sketch pad and draw what he was coming to think of as 'his' courtyard. He hoped that as he sat at his window he might glimpse Mlle Marina Flower of Paradise. She or he was, after all, the only person he knew in Paris. She was the only person he knew on this side of the Atlantic.

But when he entered the courtyard it was shadowy and silent. The demoiselles Sofia and Marina were out and, Mort thought glumly, he knew just what they were doing and where. Hand jobs, blow jobs but no arse-fucking out under the leafy chestnuts in the Bois de Boulogne.

Mort let himself into his flat, picked up his sketch pad and thought that Paris would never look as beautiful as it had in that first flush of excitement as he had ridden towards the boulevard in the bus. He started to draw. The shadows were so broad that he could glean nothing from the courtyard itself so instead he turned on a light and worked from memory.

Mort struggled with his pencil for two hours. At first his ineptitude overwhelmed him and he was tempted to stop and let himself be lured out into the city. But the surprising silence of the courtyard kept him at his post. He had decided to work until the evening activity of the apartments got under way, when, like James Stewart in the Hitchcock film whose name he'd forgotten, he could gaze into the lives of the Parisians around him.

When nobody came, when the courtyard remained silent and dark, when not one light was lit in the windows across from him, Mort was so unsettled by the stillness that he resolved to work on until someone appeared. From the moment that he set himself this goal, his inhibitions and nerves seemed to fall away and he found himself drawing something. He couldn't be sure that it resembled the darkened quadrangle, but it filled the paper and for those brief hours Mort could delude himself that he was a painter in Paris. He fell asleep still clutching his pencil and was woken at dawn by the same music echoing from the apartment above: 'My life is at a railroad crossing and God won't lift the gate.'

CHAPTER SIX

When Nell arrived at her parents' small house in Streatham she found it full of strangers.

'I don't know who they are,' said her mother, forgetting to kiss Nell in greeting. 'They all want to see your father. I thought the first one to arrive was the locum but she's some Lady or other—'

'You mean Lady with a big L?'

Her mother nodded.

'Where did he get her from?'

Nell's mother shrugged, pushed the door to the living room open and pointed to an elegant bearded man in a scarlet turban, a middle-aged blonde woman with bouffant hair and a royal blue silk dress, and a diminutive Indian woman in an ivory sari, all sitting on the sofa while a half-dozen equally unfamiliar people stood around drinking coffee and helping themselves from plates of biscuits.

'Where did he get him from?' Nell's mother looked at the scarlet turban. 'Or her? Or her?'

'Don't ask me. Perhaps he sold them a car, got talking and they became friends?' Nell backed out into the passage. 'It looks like a cocktail party in there, Mother.'

'No, there's an American word for it – I heard it on *The Golden Girls* – a coffeeklatsch? Something like that. It means a group of friends getting together for morning coffee.'

'But they're not our friends,' said Nell. She was grateful for these strange, unexpected obstacles who had put themselves between her dying father and herself. For a careless moment she imagined sitting down with the colourful group on the sofa, eating biscuits and talking about their travels. But her mother was leading her towards the stairs.

'How is he?' said Nell.

'Dying,' said her mother, and started to cry. 'No doubt about it. He's so ill, so old and so . . . so ill I haven't dared to ask him about all this.'

'Do they go in to see him? Or do they just drink our coffee?'

'My coffee, Nell,' sobbed her mother. 'Oh, yes, they go in. One by one. I made that a house rule when they all started arriving. One by one, I said. And they do. And they talk and laugh. I hear them from out in the passage. I suppose it's about business. So much of a man's life is business . . . so much more of it than you realize . . .'

The thought of her mother standing in her own passage in her own house listening to the laughter of strangers reduced Nell to tears. Her mother thought that they were for Nell's father and took her daughter into her arms. Nell withdrew after a polite embrace and said: 'I must go to him.' It was more of a question than an intention. She hoped that her mother would say he was sleeping, or with the doctor and couldn't be interrupted, then she remembered Claudine's words of the previous evening and knew that she had, as always, to do her duty.

When she entered the bedroom, her father was sitting up looking directly at the door and, as a consequence, at her. Because she'd been told he had a tumour that was now eating through his heart, she expected him to be breathless, lifeless, pinned to the pillows and gazing blindly at the ceiling. She had not expected those sharp blue eyes to be staring at her.

'I've been waiting for you to get here,' he said. He was breathless and as she drew closer to him she saw that even the soft light of the summer morning couldn't warm his waxy cheeks. 'I've got a job for you to do.'

Work and duty, thought Nell. Always work and duty. What 'job' could she possibly do for him? Shift a few more Fiats off the lot? No, nowadays there were only the endless supermarket trolleys to be loaded and unloaded.

'But give me a kiss first, Nell.' Her father had never been very demonstrative, had always been too busy and preoccupied to need affection. She dreaded approaching those waxen cheeks but, as she did, was reassured to smell whisky and cigarettes on his old, dying skin. He grasped her hand and would not let go.

'There's someone who will want to see me, Nelly. Your mother knows about it but I don't want her to be upset, so arrange a time when she's out of the house—'

'Who wants to see you? Who will upset Mother?'

Nell's father reached for a pencil on the bedside table and wrote a phone number and address at the top of the racing page of the *Daily Mail*. 'Don't play naive with me, Nelly. You're a worldly girl – with your air-line pilots and your fine hotels – all those fine hotels . . .' His eyelids drooped. He forced himself to open them. 'This afternoon I was trying to remember all the ones you took your mother and me to: Oriental in Bangkok, Mandarin in Hong Kong, Princess in Acapulco, Hilton in San Francisco – if my dad could know that his boy has been to all those places—'

'For somebody who's supposed to be ill you certainly remember them very well.' Nell squeezed her father's hand.

'I used to recite them to myself when I was pushing

the trolleys round Sainsbury's – just to remind myself I'd done all that.'

'But all you ever did when you got there was stare out of the window. You stared out of the window for five hours in Hong Kong – mother and I timed it. We had time to have tea, get her fitted for a dress and ride the Star Ferry four times.'

Her father's propensity for staring out of windows had been a source of irritation to Nell and her mother on five continents.

'Is he still there?' had been the question from mother to daughter on icy blue afternoons in the Canadian Rockies and on foggy evenings in San Francisco. 'Is he still there?' was asked first with amusement, then with irritation and finally with anger when her mother had refused to take any further trips, claiming that it was a waste of time going anywhere with a man who wouldn't leave his hotel room.

'I couldn't get over it,' her father said.

'Couldn't get over what?' said Nell.

'Being there. Me, Wilfred Turner from Kentish Town, being in Hong Kong, or the Hilton in San Francisco – a Hilton!'

'You might have been a bit more there if you hadn't just sat,' said Nell.

'Oh, I intended to,' replied her father. 'Once I'd got over the shock of being in the place I intended to . . . I was sorry when we stopped travelling.'

'We thought you didn't like travelling.'

'I loved it. I loved the hotel rooms. Big windows and no clutter. I'd hoped to go on another journey—'

'Well, perhaps you will. Where would you like to go?'

'Oh, I know exactly where I'm going next. No Hiltons there, Nelly.'

'Perhaps I could get us some tickets and we could all go on a trip.' Nell squeezed her father's hand, glad that he seemed to have forgotten that 'someone' wanted to see him. 'Where would you choose?'

'Taj Mahal,' said her father.

Nell was astonished by this choice, and found herself trying to remember if there was a hotel window where the old man could sit and stare out at that monument to great love.

'Monument to great love.' Her father spoke her last thought and Nell nearly fell off the bed. 'I thought I could take your mother there one day.'

'What?' Nell clutched at the candlewick bedspread.

'Never will now,' sighed the old man. 'Never will.' He reached for the *Daily Mail* and waved it towards Nell. 'Now remember, Nelly, call this number and have her come here but make sure your mother's not around.' Nell took the paper. 'Wonderful thing, all that cheap airline travel,' muttered her father. Then he fell asleep.

Nell was standing in the hall, studying the number and wondering whom she would be ringing and where she should go to make the call, when her mother touched her elbow.

'I know what that's about,' she said. 'Now, I don't want him getting upset – it makes his temperature go up – so make sure he thinks I'm ignorant of the whole thing and get her over here while I'm out shopping. And do it soon – he's only got a day or two.'

'I don't know what this is about.' Nell found herself crying again. 'You might! He might! But nobody told me!'

'Wherever did you think he was on all those weekday evenings?' Her mother's loud whisper echoed down the hall. They both looked at the bedroom door but heard only the sound of uneven snoring. 'Well, where did you think he was?' her mother repeated.

'Selling Fiats?' Nell shrugged. 'Oh, I don't know! I didn't like to ask. Because it was always that way, I didn't wonder. Children accept whatever their lives are—'

'But you weren't always a child—'

'By then I didn't like to disturb the status quo – but why didn't you say something?'

'Couldn't think what *to* say. I just didn't know what I thought of it all. I still don't. Anyway, I'd better make tea for that lot downstairs.'

'Why should you? Who are they?'

'I told you – they're his people – from the other life.'

'Ghosts? Spirits? Come to get him, have they?'

'Not afterlife – *other* life.'

She left Nell standing in the passage and went into the dining room which hadn't been used for years but was now full of more strange people. The name Harry came up a lot. Well, thought Nell, at least they're not talking about Father.

Her mother's phone was by the front door. There was no-one around. She could have performed her distasteful mission swiftly and in private but out of deference to her mother she went to a phone booth down the road. It was one of the old-fashioned red kiosks. Somebody had urinated in it and the smell was so overpowering that she had to hold the door open with one foot while she tapped out the number.

A man answered the phone. When Nell asked to speak to Ivy he said: 'Are you from the estate agents?'

'No,' said Nell.

'If you're from the residential home, I deal with all that. I'm her son. She doesn't understand much these days.'

'I'm calling on behalf of a friend,' said Nell. 'It's personal – if I could just have a few words.'

'Well, she is having a good day today,' said the man. 'You might get somewhere.'

The voice that came on the line sounded older than Nell's mother. And the speaker was obviously very deaf. Nell had to shout that she was Wilfred's daughter. This did not seem to surprise the old woman on the end of the phone, who just said: 'Oh . . . air hostess.'

Nell told the facts of her father's impending demise as crisply and precisely as if she were announcing the sale of duty-free goods. She didn't want to share any emotion with this stranger. But even when she said that appalling line: 'He won't last more than two or three days,' and felt her stomach lurch and shudder and her hands slip on the sticky receiver, the old voice said: 'He's not going to die, is he?'

'What?' She heard her anger echoing out of the booth and down the street.

'He's not going to die, is he?'

'What did I just say? I just said he's going to die within three days.'

'But he can't die,' said the old voice. 'Will he?'

'Can you hear me? Why are you making me repeat this? He's going to die. My father – your . . . friend is eaten up with cancer. It's in his heart.' Nell was amazed to hear herself say that – amazed to find that her mind gave her the image: cancer in a heart. It didn't seem possible – the tumour should have had the courtesy to go round an organ endowed with such potent symbolism. 'It's eaten up his heart.' Now she wanted to shock the hateful old woman at the end of the line. 'He can't breathe properly – you should get here by tomorrow at the latest.'

'Oh, I couldn't come. I can't go out.'

'But you must – you must see him before he dies!'

'I don't think I'm up to it – the journey across London and seeing Harry like that.'

'Harry? Harry? Hold on, are we talking about the same person? My father is called Wilfred.'

'Oh no, he's Harry,' said the voice. 'He's always liked Harry better . . . I don't go out in the street, you know – not in the street.'

'If I send a taxi for you . . . look, put your son back on and I'll explain to him.'

The son was reluctant to release Ivy into the outside world but once Nell had promised a taxi, and emphasized that she would pay both the outward and return journey, he relented.

The next morning Nell watched her mother's small, white-haired figure make its way towards the bus stop for some unnecessary shopping in town. Five minutes later she saw a taxi pull up and a frailer figure with sparser white hair climb out. As Nell walked down the drive to greet her, she saw that the old woman had a big cardboard label attached to the sleeve of her white cardigan.

'What on earth?'

'Daughter-in-law did that,' said the driver. 'It's got her particulars in case she wanders. I've been told that you're paying and that I'm to wait and bring her home.'

Nell was reading Ivy's name and address on the label.

'Like Paddington Bear,' she murmured, then remembered what Ivy had been to her father. 'I can't be doing with this,' she said. 'It's too pathetic,' and she unpinned the label and put it on the back seat of the cab.

There were more strangers in the house – an MP and his mistress, an Indian faith healer, a duchess and a district nurse who had come in a professional capacity but been whisked into a corner by the Indian who seemed to want to compare notes. Nell shooed them all into the dining room and Ivy up the stairs. She was glad that the old girl was quite deaf since this precluded any conversation. Besides, she seemed to know instinctively which room held Nell's father and went straight towards it, forgetting Nell who glimpsed his bald head lift up in greeting. Then the door closed.

About five minutes later, her father's bedside bell

called her from the kitchen where she had hidden from the strangers on the pretext of making an urn of tea. When she entered the bedroom, she found the old man groping for a flask of whisky that had been put out of his reach on a chest of drawers. Ivy was slumped forward in an armchair with her grey head between her legs.

'She took one look at me, said I had death written all over me and passed out,' said her father. 'She always was a frivolous little woman – she didn't have your mother's strength – couldn't cope with life's big themes. And now she's getting a bit senile it's ten times worse.' He gave up his struggle for the flask. 'Pass me the whisky, will you?'

'What *was* she to you?' asked Nell. They both stared at the balding head in the armchair.

'Not that much in the end,' said her father, taking a swig of whisky and holding the flask out to Nell.

'Aren't we supposed to be pouring this into her?'

'Oh, she'll come round of her own accord. She does this a lot. No backbone, you see. Great fun at parties or the races but there's never been much to her.'

'But you and her – this . . . this relationship of yours. It's poisoned our family.'

'That's a bit dramatic, isn't it?'

'Well, it's . . . it's cast a shadow. All my life I wondered where you were. I felt . . . forsaken.'

'Don't you think it's a bit late to bring all that up now? Oh look, she's coming round. Here, Ivy – have a swig of this.'

Ivy accepted the whisky and asked Nell to take her home. Nell wanted to ignore the old woman's sorrow. She didn't want to enter into any kind of exchange with this person. She didn't want to judge her or have to dislike her. Most of all she feared that she might open and soften towards her. If she had no feelings about her, perhaps she would not exist.

'I'll come back tomorrow,' Ivy was saying. 'I didn't know he was that bad.'

Nell looked at the blue ropes of veins and the brown liver spots and wondered how so much colour could fit onto such thin hands. Her mind started to youthen the hands, to imagine them caressing – but she stopped, reined in her appalling imaginings and said: 'I'll take you back to your taxi.' She didn't offer to support the old woman as she hobbled down the path.

Next day while she was out shopping for a box of tea bags – the strangers had drained them of tea – her father died. She came home to find him being carried out of the house in a black zip-up bag. At first she didn't realize that it was her father. Then she saw the black unmarked van and beyond it her mother standing in the doorway.

'Why didn't you wait for me?' Nell had grabbed her mother by the collar of her cardigan. The mottled skin on the old woman's neck reddened and wrinkled. She tried to withdraw but Nell's grip was too tight. 'How could you let him go without me being here?'

'But you are here. I waited and waited. I called the doctor, couldn't call you – you were gallivanting around town. In the end he died all on his own with me. He died in my arms saying he was sorry for any inconvenience – silly old fool. Then his teeth fell out – that was the worst part!'

'I wasn't gallivanting—'

'But you stopped for coffee – I guessed you had and I know how busy that Italian place gets. You'd have to queue and wait to pay—'

'I had to stop for coffee. I had to collect my thoughts.' Nell knew that she wouldn't even begin to collect her thoughts until she was back in the quiet of her Paris bedroom. 'Don't make me feel guilty about stopping for coffee.'

'Oh, I'm not, dear. I'm not. I'm glad it was just him

and me – it was like all those years ago before you happened. I didn't want you here.'

'But I'll never see him again.'

'No, you won't. Not alive.' Nell's mother stood at the front door and wept. Nell watched her and tried to take in the enormity of 'never again'.

'But you can go down and see him at the undertaker's,' her mother was saying. 'When they've smartened him up.'

Nell offered to stay for as long as she was needed but her mother seemed resolved to send her away and it was with relief that Nell boarded the eight thirty flight back to Paris the following evening. Once she had settled into her seat, turned on the reading light and ascertained that she didn't know any of the crew and would not, therefore, have to talk airline shop, she realized that all she wanted was to get home, sit in her old dressing gown and watch television.

Nell had a secret passion for television. She knew, but never told anyone, that it was the most constant element in her life. Entering a hotel room anywhere in the world, her first act was to turn on the television. She like the way the room filled with people at the press of a button. She recalled her mother's home in Streatham currently filled with strange people and thought, not without pleasure, that in Houston or Tokyo or Rio or Dubai she would at least see familiar faces, suffering their own bereavements, getting over broken love affairs, betraying and being betrayed. She was particularly fond of American television because people went through all manner of trauma and managed to remain slender, handsome and perfectly groomed. Nell knew that this was absurd but a big part of her found it laudable.

However, once she was sitting on her old sofa in front of the optimistic, vibrant technicolor of *La Loi de Los Angeles*, all she could think of was her father. This was not yet grief. She knew that would come when both her mind and her heart had grasped the idea of 'never again'. For the time being they were just words and she thought, instead, of her father's life, of how little she had known about it, how little she had wanted to know. Thinking about her father's life involved thinking about Ivy and she found herself feeling glad that the wretched little woman had not had the chance of a return visit. And this thought led, inevitably, to thoughts of her mother who had known about the 'frivolous little woman' and never said a word. Her mother had still chosen to see the old man's dying moments as a brief if somewhat black second honeymoon. With all that had happened in between, her mother chose, and this seemed to Nell to be the important word, her mother chose to accord only a minimal importance to the woman with the sparse white hair and the ropy, thin brown hands.

But what had her father said in response to her own question 'What was she to you?' 'Not that much in the end.'

Nell thought and thought about all this, her small tidy face pursed and bunched with the effort until she realized that she was literally suffering from faceache and had to lie back on the sofa with cold tea bags on her eyes. As the Los Angeles lawyers resolved their dilemmas in the familiar dubbed French, Nell thought about how little we consider the lives of those we love. Now she remembered the Fiat showroom where her father had worked after his leg injury had forced him out of the army. She thought about her industrious, sensible, pretty mother, poised all those years ago to become an army wife and finding herself married, instead, to a car salesman. She could see the showroom – not far from the A3 and with a Pirelli calender of naked women on the office wall. Was this a clue to her secret father? she wondered, but she knew it wasn't

61

and fell asleep no wiser about the feelings of any of these strangers whose lives ran alongside her own.

At three o'clock she awoke on the sofa and felt her brain floundering around to slot itself into the usual routine of orange juice, exercises, a cup of coffee. But with each lurch her thoughts came up against a great black wall: my father is dead. 'Never again' had come sooner than she expected. While she slept her heart and mind had been at work and were waiting with the truth when she woke.

She called Luc in New York and was astonished to find herself sobbing down the phone to a Manhattan hotel receptionist. The receptionist was sympathetic, knew the name of the restaurant where the cargo crews often dined and gave Nell the number. Nell was even more astonished to find herself dialling it and begging the maître d'hôtel to call Luc to the phone. While she waited, listening to the small-hours hum of Paris in the background and the crash and chatter of an Italian restaurant in Manhattan at the end of the phone line, she realized that she had not spoken to Luc for weeks and that Tokyo, Delhi, Moscow, London and New York had filled their combined lives since then.

Then she heard his voice from the other side of the Atlantic. He listened as she sobbed: '*Papa est mort.*' He said: '*Ma pauvre petite Nelli. Il faut pleurer, tu sais. Tu ne pleures jamais.*' Nell stopped sobbing and told him instead of funeral arrangements. She didn't mention Ivy and the Streatham house full of strangers. When she started to tell him of the tumour and express her own indignation that it had eaten away at the old man's heart, she sensed a silent change of key from the Manhattan restaurant.

'You know, Nelli – it is so strange. Something happened to me at about the time your father was dying. I was going to tell you when I got back – it wasn't urgent – but I'll tell you now . . . I was struck by lightning over Labrador.'

'If you'd been struck by lightning you wouldn't be here to tell me,' said Nell, unsurprised to see her own stolid common sense sail calmly through all the stormy emotion.

'Of course I wasn't truly struck. But the plane was – a real sledgehammer from the heavens came at us. We dropped a few hundred feet, a ball of light shot through the cabin—'

'But that happens a lot this time of year – spring and summer storms—'

'I know that, Nelli. Of course I know that, but this was different. I felt it, you see—'

'How could you? The fuselage is a lightning conductor – if you felt it you'd be dead, or at least very scorched.'

'I felt it, Nelli – for just a moment it riveted me – literally bolted me to the controls and the body of the plane and the cold air outside. I felt a sudden surge of energy! New energy! As if my molecules had rearranged themselves! And all this at twelve noon! Twelve noon Paris! Don't you see, Nelli? Just as your father was dying. Strange, don't you think?'

'Father died at eleven o'clock Paris time.'

Luc hadn't heard her. At the New York end of the line Nell could hear a group of people in the restaurant singing 'Happy Birthday'.

'It has changed everything, Nelli. It has changed me. I don't yet know how but I know that it has. Oh, I'm so sorry – I shouldn't be talking about this now, but when you told me of the time of your father's death it all seemed to come together . . .'

The New Yorkers were finishing their song. The transatlantic line was so clear that Nell could hear the name of the person whose birthday it was. 'Happy birthday to you, happy birthday to you. Happy birthday dear Davy,' they sang, 'happy birthday to you.'

CHAPTER SEVEN

Claudine was moving into a bedroom on the first floor of her small, dilapidated château when Nell arrived the next morning. Nell found her dragging her old Samsonite with the faded hotel labels up the staircase to the new bedroom. It was the third room she had occupied since moving into the building two months earlier. She had used a light and airy green room that faced south over the unremarkable countryside for four weeks and ventured into a cold damp north room for a second month, but had made such a mess of them both that she decided to move once more when she could no longer find her uniform shoes.

'*La confiture aux cochons*,' Luc had said when he and Nell had first driven out to visit her.

'But Claudine's not a pig,' Nell had responded, although she too secretly felt that the potential of the grand house was lost on her friend. The two of them had sat in envious resentment of all that Claudine had acquired so easily. For half an hour they had been unable to enter the ill-kept grounds as they discussed all that they could have done with such a property.

Nell recalled that early summer day with Luc as she parked his Citroën in front of the entrance. She had rarely felt so united with her husband, so in harmony with his desires, as on that May day when they had sat together, gazing at the château and seething. And, she now reassured herself, he had labelled the lovely Claudine a 'cochon'. As she pushed open the back kitchen door, Nell felt more well-disposed towards Luc.

'Don't go up and down stairs in those flip-flops!' she cried when she came through what had once been the servants' quarters and saw Claudine in her slippers and dressing gown pulling on the battered suitcase. 'I mean it,' Nell persisted when Claudine failed to acknowledge her. 'Those backless things are a menace on stairs. You don't realize the danger because you've always lived in apartments, Claudie, but one slip with those on a dark night and you might find yourself lying at the bottom for days. You could starve to death if all your men are out of town and I'm on a long flight.'

'Always you bring joy with you,' said Claudine, but turning to look at Nell's drawn face she left the suitcase on the top step and ran to her friend. 'Oh, you funny little thing. You are quite serious, aren't you?' She put her arms around Nell and drew her to her. Because Claudine had such long legs, Nell found that her nose was pressed hard against Claudine's perfumed left breast.

'A fall at forty isn't like a fall at ten.' She gasped for air. 'You haven't fallen in decades, Claudie, but if you do you'll jar your system for weeks.'

'And Papa? How is he?' Claudine released Nell and led her to an armchair.

'He died,' said Nell. 'He died and all sorts of strange people appeared in the house, and he seems to have had a kind of double life – well, not double – more like one and a half lives. And Mother seems to have known and I'm not sure that she cared. And Luc got struck by lightning and seems to think it's transformed him—'

'Luc! Luc! Trust him to do something dramatic when you have a crisis in your family. We'll get to Luc later,' said Claudine, waving his name away towards the unremarkable countryside. 'Tell me about your father. I liked the old man. I only met him once but he was fun and flirtatious—'

'Was he?' said Nell. 'I never noticed.'

'Yes you did. Remember at your house that Christmas? He danced the tango with me, wearing one of those hats in paper that the English put on at Christmas.'

'Oh, he always danced the tango at Christmas,' said Nell. 'I don't think that was flirting – just tradition, really . . .' Nell shifted away from Claudine and looked out of the window, where a linden tree's late blossom was sending wafts of honey into the cool room. She didn't want to talk about her father because she felt guilty that her short-lived grief of the previous night was already receding. She also knew that she would have to tell Claudine about the old woman and that Claudine would be unshocked, accepting, too sophisticated in her response. Claudine would see the Fiat salesman and the frivolous little woman through her worldly French eyes and not understand how incongruous such a situation appeared in Nell's tidy life.

'Tell me about your father,' Claudine repeated. 'How did he die?'

This was the easy part, thought Nell, and told Claudine of her father's death in her mother's arms, of the falling false teeth and her mother's pleasure in those last intimate moments.

'What about the extra half life?' said Claudine.

As Nell told the story she thought, but of course, Claudine will see herself as the other woman. She will be more sympathetic than I can stand because repeatedly, throughout her life, her role has been, unbearable thought, the same as Ivy's. Claudine had never married. She would laugh and say 'I'm *trop dissipée* for domesticity.' And the men, married and unmarried,

66

had filed through Claudine's various Paris flats for the twelve years that Nell had known her.

With this realization, Nell wanted to stop speaking, but Claudine had taken out a handkerchief and was listening intently, the tears streaming down her face. Claudine's tears brought on Nell's own. When she came to the end of the story, she omitted to mention how jubilant she had felt that the old woman had not been able to bid a final farewell to the old man.

'How lucky your mother is!' said Claudine.

'What?'

'How lucky for them both to have such a rich . . . *tapisserie*? Do I mean *tapisserie*?'

'Tapestry?'

'Yes. Such a rich tapestry of emotions still weaving around them in their old age. I always think of oldness as empty and thin and grey. But all those intense feelings . . .' She sighed and stared out at the linden tree. 'Jealousy, mystery . . . I hope I die like your father.'

'Then why are you crying?' said Nell, who thought that Claudine's tears had been shed out of sympathy for her bereavement.

'Those two old, decrepit people protecting each other,' said Claudine. 'That's love.'

'My father and that old woman?' Nell could no longer hide her disgust.

'No, your father and mother.'

'My mother is hardly decrepit. She's busy and birdlike.'

'Well, maybe. But such tenderness they showed for each other. When you said that he didn't want to upset her and all the time she did not want him to be upset and become more ill. That is love, Nelli.' She raised an eyebrow and Nell knew that the time had come to talk of Luc.

'Luc was very helpful,' she started to say.

'He was? What did he do?'

'Well, he couldn't do much. He was in New York but he was sympathetic. He came to the phone from his table in the Primavera—'

'Are the cargo crews still going all the way up there for dinner?'

'Well, they're less tired than us. They get to stay in New York for over a week, remember, so they aren't so jet-lagged. Anyway, he came to the phone and told me to have a good cry—'

'And? *Et alors?*'

'Well, that's it. What else could he do? He's three thousand miles away.'

'But he managed to tell you he'd been struck by lightning?' The summer day had died on its feet. Grey clouds and a fierce wet wind whipped past the linden tree. Claudine got up and closed the window.

'You are an infuriatingly good listener,' said Nell. 'Yes, he did – over Labrador. He says he felt it – it riveted him and reorganized . . . oh, I don't know exactly, but he seems to think that it has reorganized his molecular structure in some way. At least I think that's what he said. People were singing "Happy Birthday" in the background and it *was* transatlantic.'

'Is he coming to the funeral?' asked Claudine.

'I hadn't considered that,' said Nell. 'I never gave it a moment's thought. How strange. I can't imagine Luc at a funeral.'

'I was wondering how he looks with his molecules rearranged.'

'Usual craggily handsome self, I suppose,' said Nell. 'I'd like you to come, Claudine.'

'I'd love to!' said Claudine. 'Oh, I don't mean it like that. Not in a morbid way.'

Nell knew that Claudine was delighted to be needed for something as sober and respectable as moral support. She knew that Claudine would sort through her vast, messy wardrobe for something black and serious and turn up in crimson or saffron and fill the gloomy London chapel with a perfume that nobody in Nell's family could afford. Nell was immensely glad to know that Claudine would be there, not only for the generous comfort that her friend promised but also because Claudine's presence was a way of carrying the life she had fought for and studied for into the life she had fled. Of course, Luc – craggily handsome, airline captain husband Luc – would be an even more potent symbol of her Parisian life, but Luc would be flying cargoes of clothing and canned foods from New York to the Caribbean and could not be brought home at such short notice.

When Nell got home that evening, she found that the concierge had pushed a telegram under her door. She ripped it open and saw that crew scheduling had already acted on her bereavement and cancelled her upcoming trip to Bangkok in order to allow her to attend her father's funeral. Between now and the funeral they had fitted in a flight to New York.

'The bastards have managed to squeeze in a New York!' she said to Claudine when she called her five minutes later.

'Call in sick,' said her friend. 'You don't want to be going to New York in your state. They try it on, Nelli. They expect you to refuse. If you do they'll give you a day return to Tel Aviv or Athens. They've always got a few of those lying around.'

'Oh, I'll do the New York,' said Nell.

'Hoping to bump into Luc?'

'Why should I need to bump into my own husband?'

'Don't snarl at me! I meant for some comfort, you know – a . . . what is it in English? *Câlin?*'

'A cuddle?' said Nell. The thought of cuddling up to the recently galvanized Luc with his newly arranged molecules seemed so incongruous that she started to laugh and Claudine, who was primed for proffering handkerchiefs and a damp shoulder, got angry and hung up. Nell called her back and apologized, saying that she was feeling light-headed having drunk a neat whisky and couldn't control her emotions. Claudine, who had never attempted to control her emotions, seemed to find this acceptable and set about reorganizing her own working flights in order to accompany Nell to London.

While Claudine pored over her schedule in the draughty salon in the château, Nell wondered for the umpteenth time whether her friend, who had slept with so many men, had ever slept with the craggily handsome Luc. She was sure that she knew the answer and wondered if there was something unhealthy about wanting to be comforted by arms that had perhaps offered comfort of another kind to her husband of over a decade.

A summer evening had settled over the mansard roof while she had been on the phone. Nell had a sudden urge to lean out of the window, Claudine-fashion, and gaze at the Paris night but decided to wait until she had cleared away the washing up and swept the kitchen floor. Then she set about packing her case for the flight to New York that would fill the days before her father's funeral. She had ironed her uniform blouses, polished her shoes, and was packing her bedsocks, earplugs, tea-maker and packets of instant soup when the square of navy blue sky in the window suddenly seemed too velvet, too warm and too full of the great city's sounds and smells to be ignored. She sat on the floor, looked out at the night and wondered, with a not unpleasant sorrow, where her father now was in all that clamour and heat.

She didn't wonder for long, reminding herself in the stern headmistress voice that she'd heard in her head for so many years that Father was in the chapel of rest at the undertaker's, next to the building society and across from the new Waitrose where her mother refused to shop because you had to get your produce weighed before you got to the check-out. Father was there, lying in white satin, in a part of town that he'd never cared for and managed to avoid for the past three decades since it contained no betting shop or pub and seemed devoted only to the tedious practicalities of existence: saving money, buying food and cleaning products, and dying.

Nell stared at the velvet night, screwing her small dark face up in her struggle to sense something mysterious and hidden out there in infinity. Thoughts of infinity made Nell's brain ache. Once on a night flight to Santiago in the early days of their relationship, Luc had called her into the cockpit, pointed out various constellations and talked as he often did about the beyond and what lay beyond the beyond. And she had seen the passionate curiosity in his blue eyes and felt the beginnings of a polite, manageable passion for this man. And he had seen that early passion and thought that it was the same as his and that they were bound to be united. On such lies is love founded, thought Nell as she failed to find any sense of mystery in the busy summer heavens. All she could see was a plane headed for Orly, the glorious excess of the Eiffel Tower and a sudden whitening of the night sky over by the Seine as a *bateau mouche*, prying spotlights blazing, sailed past.

She tried again to think of her father and found that stern inner voice of hers saying: 'He's well out of it all.' And she leaned back against the warm wall and envied her father the oblivion that enveloped him as surely as the white satin inside the undertaker's coffin.

But I can fly away, thought Nell, as she had thought a million times in her life. That headmistress who resided inside her had warned that when you fly away, you take yourself along – that all the frustration and loneliness and self-disgust will be sitting there next to

71

you on the white sand beach, swimming swift behind you like a shark in the turquoise waters of the Caribbean, clinging to your ankles as you gaze down into the Grand Canyon or up at the dome of St Peter's. Even though that headmistress inside her head persisted in this view, Nell had her own very secret proof that she was wrong.

For when Nell had been a sensible twenty-eight-year-old bi-lingual secretary in Mayfair, she had fallen deeply in love with a struggling actor, encountered on the escalator at Waterloo and seven years younger than herself. She had never told anyone of this early passion, not while it was happening and not when, after a mere three months, it was over, for by then it had seemed to her to be such an embarrassing cliché – the young indifferent artist and the stable, unexciting older woman – that she hid the tale even from Claudine. She had also never told anyone that the actor had been her first sexual experience, convinced as she was that nobody in the world, except perhaps the Pope, could live that long before making love. And she had certainly never told a soul that when after eleven sexual encounters – and she had counted them – she had broached the subject of feelings, of a future, of love, the young man had withdrawn and grown cold. She had vowed never to tell even her most intimate friend that when she had gone to the young man and told him what she felt, she had left with her face red and stinging and wandered the streets of the West End for hours with his last sentence resounding in her ears.

Riding the same escalator only days later, Nell had seen the first advertisements for the new 747 and known that her salvation lay in the lumbering great planes that nobody quite believed could fly.

'I can fly away,' Nell had said to herself. And she had. She had perfected her French, she had spent her savings on a new hairstyle and lessons in make-up and she had decided to apply to fly out of Paris. To her astonishment, the French airline, which was in desperate need of native English speakers, had accepted her. And Nell, the perfectly groomed woman whose polished pumps walked daily through the skies, had emerged and sewn up all those ragged ends of her life and secreted them away out of sight.

Any stray strands of feeling that she had failed to harness, she directed instead towards places. Nell had always sensed that she loved places more than most. A bridge couldn't turn its back on you; a mountain or river wouldn't mock your love for it. Places abide, Nell still believed. There wasn't a forest or ocean in the universe that would slap her face repeatedly and tell her that she was a plain, dull woman whom no right-minded man would want.

And when Luc had come along and did want her, she had wanted him in return because he represented all those places that she had come to love so deeply. Sitting in his cockpit, surrounded by clouds or stars or sky, he seemed in his gold-braided suit like a heavenly emperor bestriding the storms, the oceans, the cities and the forests. For years she had been as astonished by Luc's love as she had been by Claudine's friendship. His arrival in her life had felt to Nell like coming across the Grand Canyon in the middle of Streatham High Street. He was a big man, an old-fashioned aviator with the confidence, the arrogance, that Nell no longer saw in the prudent mathematicians who flew the new planes.

One July day in the Languedoc during their first summer together they had stopped for a picnic at the base of a cliff overhanging a small ravine. Nell had remarked on the vertiginous drop to the water and Luc had set down his glass of wine and plate of *saucisson sec* and scaled the cliff in a matter of minutes. He made love with the same drive and the same certitude. Nell was impressed but had never really known whether she liked it. Now he was flying through the American skies talking about rearranged molecules and Nostradamus. Nell couldn't help wondering if it wasn't her fault in some way.

She went into the living room, hoping to find some comforting American television to lull her into her own brief oblivion. The room was so stuffy that she had to open the windows and look out over the courtyard. The elderly Portuguese concierge was wheeling the dustbins back into the shed. She heard Nell open the window and looked up, eager to converse across the five storeys that separated them.

'*Ma pauvre madame!*' she cried, and Nell knew that commiserations were on the way. She headed them off by asking the old woman to keep her mail during her absence in New York.

'Not me, madame. It is time for my departure to Oporto,' declared the concierge in her stately if limited French. For a moment Nell thought that the woman was retiring. Then she uttered the phrase that Nell had heard but paid no attention to throughout her day in the city: '*Les vacances.*'

But of course, in the first exodus of the summer, Paris was about to secure its shutters, roll down its blinds, hand the keys to the tourists and head off down the autoroute. This explained the silence from the estate agent down in the Languedoc, who was probably packing his own bag and would not now make any more progress on their house purchase until the second week in September.

Down in the courtyard, the concierge continued her side of the conversation. She had, apparently, described the problems of travelling by road to Portugal with both the mynah bird and the old tom cat, and had moved on to describe the various holiday destinations of the other residents of the two buildings that were under her supervision. Nell didn't know any of the people she mentioned. Luc's old bachelor flat was on the more expensive side of the courtyard. The building had been renovated years earlier and had lifts and thick carpeting in the corridors, while the other side had been a victim of the landlord's lack of money. This obvious financial superiority had been an occasional comfort to Luc who was peeved at his own failure to move down to the Midi years earlier. He took a small pleasure in watching the travails of his neighbours as they lugged their groceries up five flights of stairs over cracked linoleum under lights on timers.

Nevertheless her poorer neighbours seemed to have exotic holiday destinations, thought Nell as the concierge said that M. Dupuy had gone to California and two sisters on the first floor had gone on a cruise to Alaska. Nell had never exchanged a word with any of these people but now she begrudged them their innocent desire to move across the planet. '*Les vacances*' meant only full cabins and congested airport approaches to Nell, but this impromptu catalogue of destinations had catapulted her back to the days of her adolescence when the name of a faraway place could comfort and colour her inner world for hours at a time. Her own travels, those terse little three-letter codes that filled her diary or slipped under her door in a telegram, had been diluted by work and duty – those two again.

'And we've had a new arrival!' cried the concierge. 'An American television star.'

Nell had been about to close the shutters and retreat into the dark of the apartment. Now she turned back and stepped out onto the balcony.

'Who? Who is it?'

'I haven't met him.' The concierge shrugged. 'He sublet from Monsieur Dupuy. He arranged it all through him.'

Nell's mind raced through the hundreds of television shows that filled her rooms at the Hiltons and Meridiens and Sheratons of the world: *Mash*, *Fawlty Towers*, *L.A. Law*, *I Love Lucy* reruns, Oprah Winfrey, David Letterman, the Dick Van Dyke show. . . on and on the list went. Any one of a thousand famous or slightly famous faces could walk into the courtyard and Nell knew that they would be as familiar to her as Claudine or Luc. She saw Oprah and Lucy more than she saw Luc but she did not like to dwell on this fact.

'Who is it? What show is he in?' She was leaning out over the small balcony now. The concierge had turned her attention to some withered flowers on her old geranium.

'Who is it? Tell me his name – what show is he in?' Nell repeated.

The concierge shrugged. Pleased that she had tantalized she shrugged a second time and went into her lodge.

'Funny time to move in,' Nell called after her, hoping to draw her back out. But the concierge was gone inside for the evening, leaving Nell to retire to bed where she continued to run through all her favourite shows: *Cagney and Lacey*, *Hill Street Blues*, *Northern Exposure*, *NYPD*. She drifted through locations – Manhattan, Torquay, Alaska, Los Angeles, Dick Van Dyke's immaculate Fifties suburban home, the Cheers bar – until she fell asleep lying hot and naked on top of the bed. At three a.m. she awoke and wept for her father.

CHAPTER EIGHT

The concierge was delivering the last letters of the summer. Nell watched her slow progress, up and down stairs, across the courtyard cobbles, and hoped that the letter from London would arrive that day. In imaginary conversations with Claudine, with her mother, never ever with Luc, she tried to justify this extraordinary search for someone she wasn't sure she wanted to see again.

Had Mr Jameson himself not boarded her London flight one autumn night and had they not got talking in the galley while fog prevented them from taking off, she would never have known a private detective or dreamed of such an undertaking. But when Mr Jameson had given her his card, after telling her of 'some of the amazing things people get up to', Nell had decided to get up to one quite 'amazing thing' of her own.

She had asked Mr Jameson to find out what had become of the actor. 'I just want to know what happened to him,' she told the small, discreet Englishman. 'I don't want to see him. I wouldn't be interested in him now,' she told herself each time she scanned the post for a letter. 'But I just want to know if he became an actor, if he succeeded or failed, if he is happy – what happened to him.'

Mr Jameson had offered her a discount. In her career, Nell had received discounts on Algerian dates, Norwegian salmon, even a supposedly miraculous Bulgarian anti-wrinkle cream. In the half-light of the evening galley, Mr Jameson's offer had seemed normal.

Now she watched as the concierge approached her building and hoped that she wouldn't bring the letter – then hoped that she would.

Mort had decided not to look at his first attempt at drawing. He had awoken with a resolve to resist the lure of the courtyard. Whenever he was in his little apartment, he would be drawn to the window. Today he was determined to do some unpacking and attempt to make the two small rooms, bathroom and *'coin cuisine'*, as M. Dupuy had called the unit of sink, fridge and cupboards in the corner, feel like his home.

The room that M. Dupuy had referred to as his bedroom was what Mort would have called a walk-in closet with no window, just a ventilation hole near the ceiling. M. Dupuy had a small, neat French body but Mort, possessing an altogether larger American model, could only sleep in the closet if his feet poked out into what M. Dupuy had called the *'salon'*. Mort decided to sleep in the *'salon'* and unrolled his sleeping bag and lay down on it with his feet towards the window. When he had worked out where the compass points were situated in his *'salon'* he would sleep with his head facing north.

As he stood up, he heard birdsong in the courtyard and, allowing himself a brief detour to the window, he recognized a redstart on a gutter above an open window across the courtyard. He watched it for a few minutes, surprised by its presence in Paris and intrigued by the bird's lack of fear. It seemed to stare right at him as it sang.

When Mort turned his attention to the bathroom, he

discovered that M. Dupuy had not removed his own belongings, but had stored them in a cupboard under the sink. Mort found a bottle of hair dye. The instructions were in five languages. Mort read the English, trying to recall the exact shade of M. Dupuy's hair and wondering whether it would suit him. He had wrapped a towel round his neck, as advised by the instructions, and was about to start dabbing at the grey spots on his temples when 'Tan don't burn use Coppertone' leapt into his thoughts. Vanity, thought Mort, and put the brush down.

Later in the morning when the heat forced him to take a second shower, Mort did use another bottle that promised to give the effect of thicker hair. Mort's hair was thick, predominantly black and wiry and didn't need thickening but, adopting a 'more the merrier' philosophy, he emptied the bottle over his head. He saw no difference and turned his attention to a half-empty bottle of Eau Sauvage which he sprinkled over his naked body before sitting down to eat the remains of an ageing sandwich for lunch.

Thus occupied, Mort missed the activities of the morning courtyard. He did not know that the summer exodus from the capital was almost complete. He didn't see the concierge making her final preparations. He didn't see Nell, sitting at her window, watching the emptiness below.

She had always been baffled by the annual mass stampede out of the city. She'd watched the departure day on the TV news one year, seen the queues of cars sweating on the ring road and listened in wonder as each driver interviewed shrugged in jocular acceptance of 'les vacances'. She and Luc had long since agreed that they were all idiots. But now she almost understood the child's sense of a journey that such shared departures aroused.

She had hours to go before her own departure. As

she made herself some toast and more coffee, she heard the last apartments empty themselves. She heard the sounds of doors being double bolted, of cases banging clumsily against walls and steps, of the concierge's mynah bird and tom cat waiting noisily in the courtyard sunshine while the old woman distributed those final letters.

Nell felt suddenly lonely for all these strangers to whom she had hardly spoken. The silence in the building and the street below left room for thoughts of her father. But confronted with such a big, baffling subject Nell became overwhelmed and turned once again to the world outside. Since the concierge had not come up to her floor, she decided to watch for a glimpse of the American television star in the courtyard, and taking her coffee cup back to the courtyard window she set a cushion on the floor and lay down on her stomach. The summer day was already very hot and she knew from years of fire safety training that the coolest air was on the floor. She remained there for over an hour, her face pressed against the cool iron grille. A few anonymous people left the building but nobody entered.

Nell dozed and dreamed hazily of being in the cockpit of a plane taking off in a very black night. This was a familiar dream to Nell and even as she dreamt it a detached part of her was aware of its familiarity. The dream always involved a plane crash that was not remotely dangerous. The plane would alight on a great monument – St Peter's dome, the Empire State building, St Basil's cathedral – and she would lead the passengers in a stately procession to the safety of the Italian or American or Russian soil. She usually carried an open umbrella for this purpose and looked serene and unruffled – rather like Deborah Kerr, another detached part of her dreaming self had once decided.

This morning she dreamt the abridged version in which the plane, piloted by Luc, took off almost vertically and sitting behind him, with her head flung backwards and her feet pointing towards the heavens, she soared away from the earth in a cockpit that blazed with light – she woke up as the dream Luc lifted them both upwards through the dense, black, starless night.

Nell awoke to see a woman with very broad shoulders and an obvious wig crossing the cobbles to the other building. She rummaged for Luc's binoculars in a drawer by the window and tried to focus them on the woman, but she moved too quickly.

Dallas? wondered Nell, thinking that this must be her American TV star. She pulled herself up to a position where she could see the new arrival, gripped the bars of the grille and peered through, aware that she resembled a wax inmate of Newgate prison glimpsed years earlier in Madame Tussaud's.

The woman was wearing cheap shoes, Nell saw. Hers was not a face that Nell recognized. And there were flakes of dried mud on those synthetic pumps. Nell stayed at her post at the courtyard window but no-one else appeared. After two disappointing hours, Nell pulled herself wearily to her feet and went into the kitchen to make some tea. As she poured the boiling water into the pot, she remembered her dead passenger. What if he had been destined for her courtyard? What if he had written airmail letters and sent references to M. Dupuy and had been foiled in his desire to live in Paris by death itself? Perhaps the concierge hadn't met him because he had never arrived.

The more she thought about it, the more sense her theory made. Soon she was convinced that it had to be the truth. Nell was thrilled and comforted by this extraordinary coincidence. It would not change her life one whit, she knew, but the idea of life forging such mysterious links reassured and exhilarated her. This is

how life works, she told herself, there is a sense to it –
if we will only look hard enough.

A cuckoo clock that Luc had insisted on buying in
Geneva chirped eleven and Nell realized with relief
that she had to sign in for the New York flight within
two hours. She was going round the flat, closing
windows, drawing shutters and setting timers, when
the concierge knocked on her door. She was already
dressed in the wool jacket and black lace-up boots that
Nell knew were her travelling clothes.

'Lift got stuck – had to come up the stairs,' she said,
and held out a brown envelope. 'You got the last letter
of summer.'

'Of your summer, madame,' said Nell. 'Mine is going
to go on and on.'

Nell bid the woman '*Bon voyage*', and started to tear
at the envelope. She had got as far as unfolding the
single page and ensuring that it came from Jameson's
Private Detective Agency in London when she decided
to save it to read during the long, slow hours over the
mid-Atlantic.

I'm just curious to know what happened to him, she
told herself again, as she rode the lift to the street and
a waiting taxi. I don't want to see him. I wouldn't be
interested in him now, she told the phantoms of Luc
and Claudine and her mother as they thronged around
her. Nell resolved not to think of 'him' or the letter
until she was well out beyond Greenland.

Instead she made a mental list of her New York
chores. She would return the inoperative electric
toothbrush that she had bought on discount the previous month. She would buy support hose in the
drugstore across from the hotel. She would have a cup
of coffee in the diner where Luc and Claudine had
decreed that she was dull. This thought had appeared
unbidden in the list but she ignored it because the cup
of coffee was necessary to keep her conscious through

82

her shopping. And she couldn't change diners because . . . well, because she'd always gone to that one and didn't have the energy to explore somewhere new.

Nell got into the taxi and continued her list. She would walk over to the Met and browse in the gift shop. Fatigue would envelop her in Central Park and she would visit the museum shop in a fog before making her way gratefully back to the hotel, stopping only for some take-out soup and cheesecake in the deli on Seventh Avenue. Then she would collapse on the bed clutching the TV remote control and hope that sleep or a chat show would fill the hours and keep Father and his funeral at bay. Or perhaps the letter would tell her something that would change her whole perception of the world. But of course that was impossible and not what she wanted at all, she remembered, and told the driver to take the route that avoided the roadworks on the *périphérique* and followed the course of the Seine.

CHAPTER NINE

As Nell's taxi approached the grey stone and glass rectangle that was the Roissy crew building, she decided that like an office or factory worker she must draw comfort from her colleagues in a time of grief. For the first time in her career she would indulge in jolly workers' banter with her fellow cabin crew. Nell had no notion of how jolly banter was achieved. She'd spent too many years of her career struggling first to perfect the language, then to gain a position of superiority over those who'd tormented her because of her foreignness. She'd once overheard what she assumed was jolly banter behind galley curtains when she came down a darkened aisle on a night flight to check that no-one was drinking the company champagne. And she thought that she overheard it in the room next to hers once at the Sheraton in Djibouti. She'd spent a half-hour with a glass held up to the wall but had been embarrassed when the banter turned out to be sighs and the jolly workers the co-pilot and a married stewardess.

As the taxi pulled in to the kerb, her resolve not to open the letter was failing. She was reaching for the envelope when she glimpsed Luc's daughter Marie-France in the crew waiting room.

'Go round again,' she told the taxi driver.

'It'll cost you airport return rates now,' said the driver.

'I don't care,' sighed Nell and sat back with her eyes closed. Marie-France had been sitting with a half-dozen other crew members. Nell prayed that she was working the departing Houston or Delhi flights and would be gone by the time the taxi circled back.

Marie-France and her brother, Jean-Louis, were Luc's children by his first marriage. As Marie-France liked to remind Nell, stewardessing was not a proper job and she, therefore, only flew during her university summer holidays. Throughout the three summers that Marie-France had been with the company, a scheduling computer had programmed most of Nell's flights in her stepdaughter's company. Nell had made several long treks up to the higher floors of the grey crew building where amiable sallow-skinned young men gazed at VDU screens. There she would explain wearily that she and Marie-France were not blood relations and drew no pleasure or comfort from flying together. Still the computer maintained the bond. When Nell had found herself programmed on a two-week round-the-world with a long stay in Tahiti in the company of her stepdaughter, she had marched up the stairs, gripped one of the bespectacled young men by his thin wrist and cried: 'I can't bloody well stand the cow!' She'd said this in both English and its French equivalent – all the airline's employees priding themselves on their bilingual talents. The young man had tapped on some buttons, squinted at the screen and informed her that the computer had broken the bond and that she was liberated.

Now the taxi was pulling back in to the kerb in front of the crew waiting room. Nell closed her eyes. She'd read in a magazine that she'd found down the back of a seat on a 747 from Tokyo that one could visualize one's happiness. She wondered about the ethics of visualizing away Luc's daughter, argued that Houston or Delhi were pleasant destinations, and opened her eyes.

Marie-France was still sitting where Nell and the cab-driver had left her. The rest of the flight crew had gone but the auburn-haired, pale-skinned young woman remained.

'Go round again,' said Nell.

'It'll be another fifty francs,' said the driver.

'Just go,' sighed Nell and remembered that a Dubai, a Tokyo and a Tel Aviv were all due out before the New York. Nell always arrived very early for work and this thought comforted her as the meter ticked over.

Marie-France was still there when Nell and her taxi pulled in for the third time. The driver saw Nell poised for a fourth circuit and refused, saying that the traffic was starting to build up on the *périphérique* and he was in a hurry to find a real fare to take back into Paris.

The sight of Luc's daughter removed from Nell any chance of forgetting her unhappiness through her work. She slipped past the crew room and headed towards the briefing counter where her early arrival would at least ensure that Marie-France was assigned a galley at the opposite end of the plane. Her stepdaughter saw Nell trying to duck under the window and rushed out to join her.

'*Pauvre papa!*' she exclaimed. Marie-France took after her father, was almost six feet tall and had to swoop forward in order to plant her four kisses of greeting on Nell's cheeks.

'Which one?' enquired Nell, irritated by the two additional kisses. 'Yours or mine?'

'Mine, of course,' replied Marie-France. 'I heard about the lightning. My friend said there are rumours of redundancy and that he is plunged in depression—'

'My father died this week,' said Nell and then regretted it because she got more kisses from Marie-France.

'I think about death every day,' said Marie-France, clasping Nell's hand and screwing her face into an expression of concern. 'I've thought about death every day since I was twelve and realized that I was going to die.'

Nell was backing away from her stepdaughter's grasp. She realized as she shuffled backwards that this was a gesture reminiscent of a servant taking leave of royalty. But Nell could not turn away from the young woman because of her eyes. Marie-France had the palest blue eyes she had ever seen. When Nell had first met Marie-France twelve years earlier, she had felt queasy with envy of the glimpse of flawless sky contained in the child's pretty face. Now she dreaded those eyes.

Marie-France had perfected a technique of catching a person's gaze in that glacial blue and holding it rigid until her subject's brain ached. This wasn't a hypnotic gaze – hypnotic implies sleep, release, languor – this was a steel-blue straitjacket, a scold's harness.

'Put me in first class!' cried Marie-France as Nell backed around a corner and climbed the stairs to the briefing counter. She herself wanted to work first class and had no intention of walking across the Atlantic with Marie-France for company. She signed herself in as the purser for the first class compartment and assigned her stepdaughter the post of cabin stewardess for the cramped and smoky back galley. Then she felt guilty and was about to reverse the order when the chief purser appeared and took the sign-in sheet away from her.

It's a good place to think about death, she told herself. The dark and bumpy tail end of the plane with its night view of all those sleeping bodies, its lack of oxygen and visits from sleepless passengers was the perfect spot for Marie-France to ponder her mortality.

She consulted her briefing papers and saw that she

had Princess Stephanie of Monaco and one of Brigitte Bardot's ex-husbands in her cabin.

'Why can't these people take Concorde?' she asked the chief purser, who shrugged and muttered, 'Better food in First.'

The shuttle bus out to the 747 was leaving the crew building. Nell deliberately missed her own crew's departure, climbed into a shuttle bus containing the Dubai crew and asked them to drop her at the steps of her plane. With luck she wouldn't see Marie-France until they were over Greenland.

There was no night, no darkness on this westbound flight. They just kept flying into more and more day. The French coast gave way to England and Ireland. They were out over the Atlantic before the cabin was darkened for the film and Nell could draw the galley curtains shut and help herself to some leftover caviar. She was about to open the letter when Marcel the galley steward appeared.

'With any other purser, I wouldn't hesitate to pour a glass of champagne or vodka to go with that,' he said. Marcel was bald and plump and had a rheumy left eye and a slight wheeze that would have been more suited to a one-legged sailor. He was at least fifteen years older than Nell and had apparently decided that he owed her no obedience or respect for he opened both champagne and vodka and held a glass up to her.

'I'll have one,' said Nell, pointing to the champagne.

'That's more like it,' said Marcel. 'I haven't seen you on a New York for ages. Have you left the sector?'

'Yes, I've been working the Far East for a few years,' said Nell. She pulled out a plastic galley cupboard, set it upright and sat down on it.

'What brings you round our way, then?' asked Marcel, topping up his glass of champagne.

'My father died and they had to reschedule me so that I could attend the funeral.'

'*Pauvre chérie*,' sighed Marcel. 'Is your mother still alive?'

'Yes, thank heavens.'

'It makes a difference having one of them around,' said Marcel. 'Once they've both gone you see, the barriers between you and the end are gone. That's what I found once my mother died. The road between me and death was as flat and empty as one of those American highways. The last obstacle had gone.'

'I hadn't thought of that,' said Nell, and accepted a glass of champagne.

'Have you got any kids, Nelli?'

'Just, um, just . . .' Nell nodded her head in the direction of the back galley.

'No, not her. I mean your own kids.'

'Are you going to give me the speech about kids being our immortality?'

'No, I don't think so. I was just wondering.'

'Well I don't,' said Nell.

'Didn't want them or couldn't have them?'

'No. I mean, I don't know – I suppose I could have had them but, well, Luc already had a boy and a girl and nowadays, well, that's enough for any man, really.'

'So old Luc didn't want any more?'

Before Nell could blame her childlessness on Luc a call button rang and Marcel drew back the curtain and disappeared into the darkened cabin.

Now Nell had time to read her letter. She took it from her bag, removed the single sheet of paper from the envelope, unfolded it and started to read. When she had finished, she spread herself a helping of caviar and topped up her champagne.

The letter made no promises but Jameson's Private Detective Agency had a possible lead to the whereabouts of the young man. But he's not that young any more, Nell reminded herself and smiled at the realization that she had been picturing him in the flared trousers and wide ties of the Seventies. Jameson's Private Detective Agency seemed to think that they would have more definite news by mid-August. That would give her time to etch some lines on his handsome face and update his wardrobe, Nell thought – not that she intended to see him again.

'I didn't think you allowed drinking in your galley.' Marie-France was leaning over her shoulder. Nell folded the letter and put it in her bag. 'They'll catch you out, you know.'

'Not if nobody tells them!'

'They know anyway. They always know that sort of thing.' Marie-France had seen the caviar. She picked up a spoon and was about to dip it in when Nell pulled the spoon away from her.

'That's against the rules too,' she said.

'But it's not as serious. Eating that won't leave me in an altered state where I might not be able to tend to an ailing passenger. If we don't eat it, it will go to waste.' She took another spoon from the drawer and reached for the caviar bowl a second time.

'This is my galley!' Nell wanted to shout but had to maintain a harsh whisper while the cabin slept. 'I decide what happens to the food.'

'Drinking has made you aggressive, Nelli,' said Marie-France, who had reached the caviar this time. 'Papa said you were getting aggressive – I told him we must be tolerant because you're getting near the menopause—'

'I'm nowhere near the menopause!' cried Nell.

'You should be careful.' Marie-France rinsed the caviar spoon and put it back in the drawer. 'They always know about drinking. He'll probably tell them.' She nodded towards the cabin.

'Brigitte Bardot's ex?'

'No, Marcel, the old steward.'

'What utter rubbish you talk sometimes,' said Nell. 'Marcel suggested it.'

'That won't stop him denouncing you. We French like to denounce people. We always have. During the revolution it was virtually a national pastime—'

The co-pilot had appeared at the bottom of the spiral staircase that led up to the cockpit. The appearance in a galley of any man with gold braid on his jacket usually meant that he wanted feeding. Nell was about to open the cupboard that contained the cockpit meals when she saw how pale and agitated he looked.

'Hijacking,' he said. 'There's been a hijacking.'

'Not us?' said Nell.

'Of course not us,' said Marie-France. 'Or what would he be doing here?'

'Of course not us,' said the co-pilot.

'Who then?' asked Nell.

'We don't know yet,' said the co-pilot. 'It's one of the company's planes but we don't know which one.'

Nell stared out into the soothing, neutral darkness of the cabin and tried to think. Luc was on a cargo so it couldn't be him, she reasoned. But where was Claudine? Where had Claudine been bound for? She looked across at her stepdaughter and said: 'Papa is working a cargo out of New York.'

'I knew that,' said Marie-France.

Nell left her stepdaughter with the bowl of caviar, opened a fresh bottle of champagne and went out into the cabin to check on the princess. As she passed from one row to the other, she recited the airline's destinations to herself in alphabetical order, hoping to alight on the flight that contained Claudine.

CHAPTER TEN

Nell was standing on a passenger seat in her stockinged feet when she saw the captain, the chief purser and the station manager from Kennedy airport making their way along the aisle towards her. All the passengers had disembarked except a young, muscular Dane whose backpack Nell was struggling to remove from the overhead baggage rack. The captain held out his hand and helped her down off the seat.

'*Nelli, ma pauvre,*' said the purser and took over from her at the baggage rack. The Dane who was taller and stronger than any of them scowled at his watch.

'*C'est Claudine?*' cried Nell and found herself being eased along the aisle, along corridors in the airport and into the airline office, which seemed to be full of police and security officers and airline officials, French and American.

'I can't take any more!' Nell screamed at them in both languages. 'First my father – and that poor dead man on the plane – now my best friend!'

'It's Luc,' said the captain, who had followed her into the office.

'What do you mean – it's Luc?'

'Luc has been hijacked,' said the station manager.

'But he can't be – he's working a cargo flight.'

'That's what we said,' said the captain.

Nell sat down hard on a coffee table by a window that looked out onto the runway. Concorde was taxiing to its gate. 'Why would anyone hijack a cargo flight? It's pointless.'

'That's what we said,' said the captain.

'What was the cargo?' asked Nell.

The men from the airline and the police and security officers looked from one to another and shrugged.

'I can find out,' said the station manager and picked up a phone. This seemed to satisfy everyone in the room and they all sat and watched him expectantly as if a knowledge of the contents of the aircraft's hold would explain everything.

'Several containers of women's polyester nightwear and undergarments, a few hundred cans of Boston baked beans and a dolphin,' said the station manager.

'A dolphin?' said the security men and the police.

'Yes, I had a dolphin down in the hold on a passenger flight once,' said Nell, and the captain nodded that he too had had a dolphin.

'They coat them in Vaseline and put them in a big harness like a hammock,' said Nell, relieved to talk about something she had experienced and understood. 'The Vaseline is so that they don't dehydrate.'

'Awesome,' said the security officer and whistled his amazement.

Nell scowled at him. 'Just a minute,' she said. 'The one thing nobody is explaining to me is where the hijackers can come from on a cargo flight?'

'The dolphin's keepers,' said the station manager. 'You know how they have someone to travel with the fish—'

'It's not a fish,' said the captain. 'It's a mammal.'

'Yeah, well, you know how it has to have a couple of keepers, well . . .'

'The dolphin's keepers!' cried Nell.

'We don't know anything as yet,' said the station

manager, and the other men in the office all shrugged in chorus. Nell sensed that they were all waiting for her reaction.

'Well, he can't stay up there for ever,' she heard herself say.

'We know that,' said the station manager. 'Of course we all know that.'

'Who else was in the crew?'

Nell smiled at the mention of the co-pilot's name. She had flown many times with Eric. More of a mathematician than an aviator, he had once told her over a Diet Coke on the beach in Bora-Bora that he'd made a difficult choice between the airline and IBM. After Luc's tumultuous passion for aviation, Nell had found Eric soothing.

The people in the office were talking about Concorde now. Nell wondered if that had been hijacked too, then realized that they intended to put her on the evening Concorde flight back to Paris. Nell was disconcerted. Even when they'd announced Luc's sudden change of itinerary, she had assumed that she would go into Manhattan as she always did. She'd been counting on the bus ride towards the city's great towers to give her the solitude to rearrange her thoughts. She needed the rhythms of the rush hour, the predictability of the journey past the cemeteries that clustered near the airport, along freeways, under the tunnel and out into the avenues of Manhattan to drum this new information into her brain. She had intended to comfort herself with cheesecake from the Stage Deli and lots of appalling and familiar American television. But a security officer had picked up her cabin bag.

'Why do I have to go back to Paris?' she asked the station manager. 'Isn't there a chance that Luc might come back here?'

'*Pauvre madame*,' smiled the man. 'You must be so shocked. Try to think. The one place he won't come

94

back to is here. And wherever he does go, eventually he must return home to you and Paris.'

'I suppose so,' said Nell and reluctantly followed the procession of policemen, security officers and airline employees along the corridor to the Concorde gate. Nell knew that for this French airline everything including Luc and herself had to return to Paris. A baby born in one of the fleet's planes between Bangkok and Singapore or Rio and Buenos Aires would be recorded on its certificate as being born in Paris. Paris was the great pumping heart and all the 747s, 737s, airbuses and Concordes that were even now making their way through tropical or Arctic skies were merely travelling to or from that heart along its veins and arteries.

'But why on earth would they hijack a cargo plane?' Nell repeated as she slowly gave up on dreams of cheesecake and Manhattan and started to unscramble her thoughts. A hostess in the empty Concorde lounge handed her a flute of champagne. Nell wondered whether this was appropriate, saw the sudden look of doubt on the young woman's face and smiled not just to reassure her but because she was suddenly very grateful that she did not work for a British airline where she would currently be clutching a cup of tea.

'We do think that may be a positive aspect,' said the station manager.

'Because they can only kill three people as opposed to three hundred?'

The station manager shrugged. The hostess was offering him a flute of champagne. He'd been about to accept when he saw Nell scowling at him.

'This isn't a cocktail party,' she started to say when Marie-France was led in screaming. 'I'd forgotten about her,' said Nell as her stepdaughter headed towards her, arms outstretched.

'We've booked you in two seats together,' said the station manager.

'In the smoking section, I hope?' Nell had to think quickly.

'Of course not. You don't smoke, do you?'

'At times of stress, yes I do,' said Nell, who wasn't sure that she even knew how to smoke but had just opted for the company of anonymous smokers over three hours with Marie-France.

Once inside the plane, however, she felt guilty, relinquished her peaceful seat with three smokers in the back rows and went to sit with her stepdaughter.

'They will probably stop to refuel in Thunder Bay,' sobbed Marie-France when Nell slipped into the seat next to her. 'What if they shoot him when they land?'

'They won't shoot him,' said Nell, who was quite sure that nobody would shoot Luc. 'He's the captain. He's terribly valuable to everyone.'

'Especially to us!' wailed Marie-France and slipped her cold hand into Nell's. 'Most of all to us!'

'Of course,' said Nell.

She had never been on Concorde before. The airline's travel concessions did not extend to the supersonic aircraft and Nell had long since refused the company's invitation to join the Concorde's crews because she privately considered flying above the ozone layer to be unnatural. Once Marie-France had downed another glass of champagne and drifted off into a whimpering sleep, Nell found that she was excited at the prospect of a supersonic return to Paris. She couldn't let any of the sympathetic crew see her excitement and she tried hard to concentrate on Luc's dilemma, but rummage around as she might in her emotions she wasn't able to come up with any true anxiety about Luc. She was quite sure that he would cope. And that nice, clear-eyed Eric would cope too. They made a rather good pair, she concluded, and wondered if the flight engineer would mesh in as neatly.

If Nell couldn't produce any worry, she did come up with some sorrow for her poor father who was dead and about to miss all the excitement. He'd been a dedicated follower of the six o'clock news for years and now he'd missed a personal involvement by a matter of just a few days, Nell reflected. She wondered vaguely if his spirit was on the loose and would perhaps know about such events, then she concluded that if spirits roamed they must surely have access to a nobler, better world than this one. If I were dead, I wouldn't bother with all the stupid antics that human beings get up to, Nell thought to herself, and slipped away from Marie-France and went to the galley. The three crew members behind the curtain expressed sympathy; she was hugged by one and offered a slice of pear tart and a glass of *cuvée spéciale* by another. But when they asked her if she expected to be given time off upon her return to Paris, and she replied that she had time off anyway to go to her father's funeral, it suddenly added up to too much distress for one person. She sensed their embarrassment, saw them withdraw and thought that she would have done the same in their position. She refused the pear tart, took the glass of champagne and went back to her seat.

'Perhaps I should accompany you to the funeral,' said Marie-France, who had woken up.

'Oh, I think you will be needed in Paris,' said Nell. 'If only to give Jean-Louis some moral support.'

Nell saw Marie-France wince and found herself thinking of her stepson with more affection than she'd felt for anybody all day. Luc always referred to the large, doughy Breton boy as his biggest disappointment. Jean-Louis suffered from vertigo, claustrophobia and low blood sugar that seemed to require him to sit down and eat a KitKat or a *pain au chocolat* every hour – otherwise he would faint, he claimed. Nell knew that even now Jean-Louis was sitting placidly in front of the

French television news, a barely perceptible furrow on his brow and a red chocolate wrapper in his hand.

She would have liked to take Jean-Louis along to the funeral. His bulk would provide comfort, his impassivity would soothe and the surprising combination of Frenchness and mountainous size would daunt most of the mourners and guarantee her peace and solitude. But Jean-Louis was a gardener. To the dismay of his father, he had chosen to forage in the earth instead of soaring into the sky, and July was a busy month in the earth.

The Concorde purser bent down by her seat and whispered: 'They are heading for Thunder Bay. There is talk of releasing the dolphin.'

'Just the dolphin?'

'Yes. Apparently Luc has said that he will take them where they want to go as long as they release the dolphin.'

CHAPTER ELEVEN

At four a.m. Mort was woken by a pounding that seemed to come from the heart of the building. He turned on the light and walked towards the front door – an alert Chicagoan now, convinced that something from the Paris streets was coming to get him. The corridor was silent, the stairwell was empty. The pounding continued – a great mute thumping that he could not stem by thrusting his fingers in his ears, for the sound was rather a vibration that seemed to have entered his body and throb within him. The core of the building was pumping. Mort took his fingers from his ears, lay back down on the sleeping bag and tried to identify the sound. It squelched, it squished, there was something unsettling about its mute, elusive quality – something sexual. Mort knew that it wasn't the sound of sex. He'd lived long enough in apartments with thin walls to know that this was too massive, too lumbering a sound to come from human beings.

All sleep had left him now and he sat up and tried to think lucidly. Strange buildings in foreign lands were bound to be full of mysterious noises that surely came from sources as banal as heating pipes and air-conditioners. The throbbing surged up within him. The undefined sound had aroused him. He resolved not to masturbate. This to Mort was a matter of principle. You didn't come to somewhere like Paris to sit and play with yourself in the solitude of a crummy apartment. He tried to switch his thoughts to a solution of the dilemma that had arisen below his waist. He reached for the weekly magazine guide to Paris that he'd left on the table. It fell open at an advertisement for the Crazy Horse Night Club. Women with pageboy haircuts and bare breasts gazed up at him. Too expensive, thought Mort. And probably arousing but that wasn't what he needed. He came to a listing for 'sex shows – hard'. There was a drawing of a couple copulating on a safety net. The slogan said, 'Live show in a net two feet above your head.'

Mort contemplated the logistics of such an exercise – the risks, the noise, the mess – and lost his own erection. He turned the page and found a long listing of '*Thés dansants*' which he translated correctly as 'tea dances'. He was astonished to find that Hemingway's old café, La Coupole, was listed as a venue, and he resolved to go there on a dancing day. This he decided sleepily was how men over forty should go about dealing with their sexual urges. You went to an afternoon tea dance, met a petite, vivacious Parisian, asked her to dance and forged a romance. He had a brief fantasy of walking into La Coupole and finding the more romantic, less complex world that Mort, like most people, was convinced had existed before he was born.

The building pumped on. Again he tried to locate the source of the noise, and again it seemed to have entered him and be pounding inside him. He took a beer from the fridge, gulped it down and fell into a bleary sleep as dawn rose over the more expensive building and Mlle Marina entered the courtyard, took off her high heels and walked barefoot across the cobbles.

When Mort woke up again at nine o'clock the noise had stopped. He went to the window and saw that his neighbours had returned in the apartment opposite. Mlle Sofia or Mlle Marina was obviously at home too for the country song was echoing across the courtyard again. 'My life is at a railroad crossing and God won't lift the gate.'

The song intrigued Mort in spite of himself. He sat in the morning sunlight in his shorts and undershirt, clutching the warm mug of coffee to his belly, and tried to catch the verse where the woman's life had gone wrong, but his ears always seemed to come in at the crossroads. He thought he heard a reference to 'freight cars rolling by filled with pain and hate' but these lyrics were too awful to contemplate even if they did rhyme with the title, so Mort just hummed along until he got to the familiar refrain: 'My life is at a railroad crossing.' Then he joined in, tapping his foot against the window sill and feeling as happy as he was likely to be all day.

'My life is at a railroad crossing,' he sang and jigged across the small apartment and around his sleeping bag. Again Mort was filled with the happy innocent anticipation of the traveller in a strange city. He danced back towards the open window, singing the only line of his new song. Mort's dance consisted of his holding his arms out in front of him and alternately kicking each foot out behind him. He looked like a participant in a conga line who had mislaid the rest of the group.

As he danced, he remembered the strange noise that had disturbed his night, and was suddenly delighted to have a project to fill the morning: he would find out what was going on in his building. He wasn't sure how he would do it but decided to start immediately by looking for signs of boilers, furnaces and the like on the landing. He danced out into the corridor, heading for the stairwell, and was seen by Mlle Marina who was standing in her dressing gown on the staircase above.

101

'*Bonjour, Monsieur*,' she called to Mort, who stalled in mid-kick and looked around him for a voice whose gender he could not identify.

'Up here,' called Mlle Marina. Mort looked up and saw a severe looking woman in a blue and white cotton kimono.

'Don't you recognize me?' said Marina. 'Marina Flor de Paraíso.' She smiled down at him. Mort squinted at the middle-aged woman with her hair scraped back into a bun, saw how the glamorous whore from the Bois de Boulogne could emerge under night's kinder light, glimpsed those big hands, and panicked.

'Mademoiselle Flower of Paradise,' he heard himself saying and started back towards the open door of his apartment, walking this time and, he hoped, looking sober, dignified and unapproachable.

'You got any tea bags?' She was leaning over the banister. Her kimono was pulled tight over that mysterious body. Her unadorned, middle-aged face looked stern and reassuring. She reminded Mort of a spinster piano teacher at his junior high school.

'The previous tenant left some,' he said. 'I don't know if they're any good.'

A few seconds later Mlle Marina Flower of Paradise was following him through the open door of his apartment.

'You'll have to excuse the mess,' said Mort. 'I never make beds when I'm on vacation.'

'Why not?' asked Marina.

'Because I'm on vacation.'

'This is no reason to live like a pig.' Marina looked at the corner kitchen. 'You don't do dishes neither?'

'Not when I'm on vacation.'

'You'll get roaches. And they'll travel up to Sofia's. We don't want no bugs. I wash our floors every day. You maybe better do your dishes.'

'OK. OK. I was going to do them some time.' Mort

was rummaging in the kitchen cupboard for the small jar of tea bags. Marina's arrival, he now knew, was the beginning of the end of the brand new Mort that had been bounding around Paris since his arrival. As long as he had known nobody, he could let his life run merrily amok. In the silent, empty bubble of his first days in Paris that summer, he could forget to shave, refuse to do dishes and make beds, but Marina stood before him now like a mirror reflecting his own awfulness. It was not coincidence that she resembled his old piano teacher, Mort decided, and knew that his lonely, carefree existence was already being curtailed by this puzzling person from the floor above.

'Were you waiting on the landing to ask somebody for tea?' He handed her the jar of tea bags.

'No. I was on my way to the john.' The use of this slang word in Marina's Latin accent convinced Mort that she'd made an error of vocabulary.

'Not the . . . the bathroom. You must mean—'

'Sofia's lavatory is in the corridor,' sighed Marina. 'A lot of old Paris apartments are still like that. Just two footprints and a hole next to the stairwell. There's one on your floor, but the doorknob is gone. Nobody needs it anyway. You have a john in here, right?'

'I have a permanently wet closet in here with a toilet that I can only sit on if I leave the door open and hang my feet out into this room.' Mort glanced towards the door of his minute bathroom.

'You can never have visitors.'

'I didn't expect to have visitors,' said Mort. 'I don't know anybody in Paris.'

'You know me.' Marina smiled at him. Mort remembered the flying magazine, the flower pot, Marina's own alarming job description, and had a fleeting sense that his keenly anticipated life in Paris was being defined by this first unexpected encounter. This was not the summer sojourn that he had intended.

He wondered briefly if he could pull on the reins and change direction before his new Paris life galloped away with him.

'If your john is not in the staircase, what were you doing when I see you?'

'The noise! That's right! I'd almost forgotten! There was this awful noise in the middle of the night. Did you hear it? This terrible pounding, throbbing. At about four a.m.'

'Senhor.' Mlle Marina looked glumly down at the jar of tea bags. 'I am not often here at four a.m.'

'Oh, I'm sorry – of course not. So you wouldn't know if it has happened before?'

Marina shrugged.

'Well I figured it must be a boiler or air-conditioning or something. That's what I was looking for in the corridor. I mean, if it keeps up, I don't know what I'm going to do. Nobody could sleep through that – do you sleep in the daytime?'

'A few hours,' said Marina. 'Sofia's place is small. Just a studio. I sleep on some cushions on the floor while she sleeps in the bed but she's real restless – she's got insonn – insonn—'

'Insomnia? So she doesn't sleep much?'

'No. She reads magazines and smokes all day.'

'And listens to country music?'

'Yeah.'

'Well,' said Mort, depressed by the thought of smoke and magazines and insomnia all huddled in that small room while the sun danced in the courtyard outside. 'If this heat keeps up, I may go down to the Riviera.' The phrase had tumbled so lightly off his tongue that Mort was almost tempted to say it again – just to let this poor street creature know how urbane and European Mort Engelberg already was. 'I may ride that . . . that blue train down to—'

'You already told me that,' said Marina. 'And it's *le*

train bleu. But really you should get the TGV – it takes about four hours to Avignon and only an hour or two on to Nice, and it's air-conditioned.'

'Air-conditioned? Really?'

'Maybe I make us some tea here?' Marina had gone to the sink and was scowling down at the scraps of discarded orange peel and peach skin. She picked up a coil of peel between her thumb and forefinger and held it in front of Mort's nose.

'How you going to have a chic Paris life if you got all this garbage around?'

'I don't think I want a chic life – more kind of bohemian.' Mort reflected on that last word. It didn't feel right. He scowled back at Marina as he started to realize that he had no idea of what he wanted from Paris. The sun's rays had sliced between them and made a rectangle of light on the floorboards. Mort's gaze left Marina and followed that light back out of the window and down into the courtyard.

Marina's presence made him feel peaceful. As she moved around the small corner kitchen, he sensed that she demanded nothing from his company. She was completely absorbed in cleaning his sink and preparing his tea. Her reassuring company let him think more freely and more deeply than he had done in days.

'I never lived on a courtyard before.'

'What's so great about a courtyard?' Marina squeezed a tea bag and set a cup down on the table.

'When I was at the University of Texas in Austin, I lived on a kind of quadrangle. Two low-rise buildings and a swimming pool in the middle. With all that sun, and those modern clean buildings, I used to dream of a European place like this – kind of old and mysterious and closed in with people living lives I couldn't even imagine just yards away from me.'

'Milk or lemon?' said Marina.

'One night – it was in August; I was at summer

school – well, my air-conditioning broke down. Do you know what I did?'

'Sat in front of the refrigerator like Marilyn Monroe in *Seven Year Itch*.'

'No, no. That was the movies, Marina – I don't know how well that would have cooled a body down in real life. You know what I did?'

Marina raised both carefully plucked eyebrows.

'I took out my old air mattress, floated it on the pool and slept on that – in my undershorts. It was the coolest, most peaceful night of my life. And not only that – it got me a woman. There was this real good-looking girl on the first floor. She saw me, thought what I'd done was "kind of neat" – that's the sort of thing we said in the Seventies – and the next night she took me back to her place, which was air-conditioned. So not only did I get cool – I got laid too.'

'I don't want to hear that,' said Marina and shoved his tea towards him. 'I don't talk about sex, Senhor Mort. I never talk about sex.'

'But you told me all that stuff about what you do in the park—'

'That's my job. That's what I got to do to live. I hate it when people tell about sex they have for pleasure. It's . . . it's vulgar!'

'Well excuse me,' said Mort, who had been feeling all the warmth and relief and closeness that accompanies a revelation of one's past. He couldn't think of anything else to say. 'Maybe I will sublet this apartment and head south,' he murmured after a few minutes.

'You can't sublet this apartment. You already sublet it from someone.'

'How do you know that?'

'Because I'm here in the daytime. I know you got this from the old guy Dupuy. You can't sublet it again.'

'Who will know?'

'I will.'

'Would you tell?' said Mort.

'Not if you sublet it to me.' Marina turned to look at him. 'I wanted it before you got it but the old guy won't talk to me. Oh, senhor, this is what I dream of – my own place, no Sofia, no smoke, no music. You go to the sea – it's not the ocean OK but maybe you like it – and Marina will stay here and look after your stuff.'

'I haven't got any stuff,' said Mort.

'I can't pay much,' Marina continued. She had reached out to grasp Mort's hand but recoiled as her broad palm almost covered his. 'I could give you two thousand francs a month,' she added. 'Oh, Senhor Mort, finally I'd get some sleep.'

Mort was trying to calculate how many nights on the Riviera he could buy with two thousand francs when the sound of crashing glass overhead interrupted his thoughts. The country music stopped.

'That's Sofia,' said Marina. 'She maybe hit the turntable.'

'Finally got sick of that song?'

'No. She's crazy about that song. She just mad with her . . . her *fado* . . . her *destino*.'

'So she breaks things?'

'Just small things. Maybe that was an ashtray.'

'Because she's mad with her destiny?'

'Sure. Some days she's madder than others. But her friends say that since the operation she's real mad.'

'What operation? What is the deal with you people? If you're going to live in my apartment—'

'It's not your apartment,' sighed Marina.

'What is going on? You tell me about hand jobs and blow jobs out in some park and still expect to live in this place?'

'I have to live. Sofia has to live. Many Brazilians work in the Bois, senhor—'

'What Brazilians? I mean, I know you're Brazilian, but are there more of you?'

'Hundreds. It's like a . . . what you call it? Like a circuit. You're Brazilian, you're transsexual, you come here, you work in the Bois and make some money to pay off your operation—'

'Oh, so you are . . . oh wow!' Mort hit his forehead with his fist. 'But, Mademoiselle Sofia has had the operation?'

'Yeah.'

'And she's still here? And still working in the Bois?'

'Yeah – that's why she's mad. Her life don't change at all. All those years she waits and saves money, they do it,' Marina made a snipping motion with two fingers, 'and Sofia thinks she'll just turn into a regular woman. But she don't know what to do to be a regular woman so she's mad.'

'And you?' Mort hesitated, hoping that Marina would answer his question before he asked it but she just stared down at her empty tea cup. 'You haven't had . . . um . . . the operation?'

'Not yet.' Marina closed her eyes very tight, wrinkled her nose and clenched her fists. Now that his curiosity had been appeased, Mort could study her face not just for clues to gender but with the more mundane questions as to age, health and harmony of feature. She had a strong Latin nose and a pleasing olive complexion. He thought he saw a very faint trace of shadow where her beard should be, but found to his surprise that if he looked too hard at his neighbour he felt like a traitor.

His question had provoked a deep emotion in Marina. She repeated the words 'Not yet', opened her eyes and dabbed at her cheek with the sleeve of her kimono. 'Oh, senhor, I don't know any more. I come to Paris, I think the answer is here and I . . . oh, I don't wanna talk about this.'

'OK,' said Mort, relieved to be spared a conversation to which he was quite sure he could contribute nothing. 'There's one thing I don't understand, though. Why the Bois de Boulogne?'

'You know the Bois?'

'I went there once with Peg . . . with my ex-wife. It's a big park, right?'

'And full of hookers, queens, wife-swappers.'

'Oh no, no, no. We went to a rose garden,' said Mort, 'the most amazing rose garden I've ever seen. What was it called?'

'Bagatelle.'

'That's it! See, we went in the daytime. And we had lunch in a real expensive, real beautiful restaurant. The Cascade? The Grand Cascade? I guess it must be like Central Park – a few acres of ground become a different country after dark.'

'Oh, we are there in the daytime,' said Marina. 'Transsexuals usually work late afternoons in the bushes on the other side of the wall to Bagatelle.' She shut her eyes again and intoned: 'Transvestites, transsexuals around the Bagatelle, wife-swappers at the Porte Dauphine, flashers and hookers everywhere. Maybe I take you for a tour some time?' She opened her eyes.

'Oh no, I can't,' smiled Mort, hoping that Mlle Marina hadn't just asked him for a date. 'I've got to go by the school and I wanted to look in at La Coupole—'

'Tea dancing?'

'How did you know?'

'I was taken there once – when I first come to Paris – long time ago. It's nice – tea dancing. You'll have a good time.' Marina picked up the tea bag jar and walked to the door. She paused in the doorway and cocked her ear towards the floor above. 'Sofia's real quiet.' She scowled up the stairs.

'Maybe she knocked herself out,' said Mort. 'Maybe

the ashtray richocheted. Maybe she's lying un-
conscious on the floor.'

'No, she's reading *Marie Claire*,' sighed Marina. 'You
let me have this place if you go to the sea?'

'Oh, I don't know yet. I doubt if I'll go.'

'You go! You go and I'll come down here.'

'Maybe.' Mort looked beyond Marina out onto the
stairwell and an open window to the courtyard. He saw
a small dark woman carrying a suitcase out of the more
expensive building across the cobbles. He watched her
with little interest but noted to himself that her clothes
were far too dark and formal for such a hot day. He was
thinking how absurdly Parisian she was to wear such
chic, hot, impractical clothes on such a sweltering day
when the country song started up on the floor above. He
saw the woman look up and wince, and he wondered if
she might have an explanation for the other noise that
had filled his night. If he took his leave of Marina now,
he could catch up with her, introduce himself, meet his
second neighbour in two hours and perhaps discover
the source of the nocturnal pumping.

Marina was blocking his route to the stairs. She was
looking at him with such intensity that Mort wondered
if she'd perhaps said something of great import that
he'd missed while he was gazing out at the courtyard.
Then he saw that she was holding out her hand to
shake his, and he understood that Mlle Marina had
spent her daytime life in Paris keeping those big hands
hidden primly under tables or tucked into her pockets.
She was honouring him with a physical intimacy that
exceeded anything she might share with the strangers
under the trees in the Bois de Boulogne. Mort shook
her hand and found that he felt more self-conscious
than if he had attempted to stroke her breast or slide
his fingers under her kimono.

'Sofia's OK then?' He raised his eyes to the floor
above.

'And the stereo,' sighed Marina. She pulled her kimono tight around her waist and started towards the stairs. 'I'll get no sleep before I go to work.'

'Do you have to go? Can't you take an evening off and catch up on your sleep?' asked Mort, realizing that he had forgotten about the world of work. He started to feel jubilantly happy again; a familiar twitching pervaded his feet and legs. Sofia's music had set off his desire to dance but he knew that he must rein himself in until Marina left, and she had turned round on the first step and was staring at him with surprising ferocity.

'Senhor, my work is what it is! But I have to respect it – I can't call in sick or show up late. That's no good!'

'I guess not,' said Mort, wondering how anyone could respect hand jobs, blow jobs but no arse-fucking. 'Well then, maybe you should get some earplugs.'

'Maybe,' replied Marina and disappeared up the stairs to the floor above.

Once she was gone, Mort put a shoe in his door to prevent it from closing and danced off down the stairs to the courtyard. He had expected to lose track of the smartly dressed woman when he had lingered in the hall with Marina but he could see her standing in the big double doorway that marked the entrance to the building. He guessed from her fixed stare at the street in front of her that she was waiting for a taxi. As he crossed the courtyard, Sofia changed the music to a samba.

'Oh Paris! Oh joy!' thought Mort and incorporated a wiggle of the hips into his conga step.

CHAPTER TWELVE

Nell saw the dishevelled man dancing across the court-yard towards her and realized that her deepest fears were being confirmed. Whenever poor weather or an early flight had obliged her to spend a night in Luc's bachelor apartment, she had feared that a day would come when she would be stranded there amongst its marginal people for ever. The dilapidated building on the other side of the courtyard, with its lopsided walls and outside toilets, had stared sullenly back at her for ten years and never made an attempt to improve its looks. And Nell had harboured a secret conviction that it remained there just to remind her that her journey from the humble terraced house in Streatham to the elegant villa in Chantilly was much, much shorter and more of a round trip than she had ever wanted to believe.

Throughout the previous night she had lain awake in her bed and thought: I will get stuck here. I will be punished for running away from the life I was given and Chantilly will slip away into the past, the Languedoc will disappear into a future that is not mine and I will be marooned in the purgatory of this poky flat on a courtyard. Then she had felt guilty for worry-ing about herself instead of Luc and had become even more convinced that she would be punished.

Luc and his crew had made a brief appearance on the TV news. Their plane had landed in Thunder Bay to disembark the dolphin. A local resident with a camcorder had made a grainy recording of their brief visit. Nell had just walked in the door from her Concorde flight from New York when the French TV channels broadcast the sequence. Still in her uniform, she sat down on the edge of an armchair and frowned at the television. She saw the dolphin being carried very gently down the steps of the plane by volunteers from a local animal protection league. Apart from refuelling crews, these were the only people allowed near the aircraft, the French newscaster had announced solemnly.

The camcorder had focused on the cockpit and Nell had slid onto the floor and pressed her nose to the TV. Because the local resident was filming from the right-hand side of the plane, she could see the profile of Eric, the co-pilot, but Luc was just a blur behind him. The blur looked as though it was peeling a large, juicy fruit.

Nell had found herself instinctively backing away from the television. The frown lines above her nose deepened as the newscaster said that once the plane had refuelled it would take off for an unknown destination. The aims and desires of the hijackers were as yet unknown, said the newscaster. At that point the television news broadcast a brief glimpse of an intense young American with thin blond hair and wire-rimmed glasses who represented Return Our Relatives to the Seas, the organization responsible for moving the dolphins. The young man had denied any connection with the hijacking, said the newscaster, but was being questioned by the FBI.

Then the calls had started to come from colleagues of Nell's who had been victims of previous hijackings. A steward who had been diverted to Teheran three years earlier called with his sympathy and invited Nell to stay with him and his wife until the crisis was resolved. Nell thanked him but said that her step-children needed her. When he hung up, she stared at the phone and knew that she should take it off the hook. She had her arm outstretched towards it when it rang again. Roland Artigue, a purser who had 'spent a week in Entebbe, courtesy of Idi Amin', as he put it, had called to warn her of the aftermath of such an experience.

'Of course it will be resolved happily, my Nelli,' said Roland. 'But the shot of adrenalin that such fear injects into the system is so massive that I had dreams every night for months after I got back. Luc is a very solid man but you must be prepared for a temporary change of personality.'

'I'm already prepared for that,' Nell heard herself say and listened as Roland told her again of his own fear and how it had poisoned his system and had taken months to be passed out of his body like a toxin. Roland had told her this story two years earlier on a night flight from Delhi. He had repeated it on a short hop to Athens, and on a longer trip to Tel Aviv. Nell had always listened patiently. He told the story well, without vanity or embellishment, and Nell had always been sympathetic to his need to expel the drama from his system. Now she just wanted him to go away. But when he did, a stewardess who had been hijacked to Algiers called. Before she could express sympathy or understanding, offer a bed for the night, a cup of coffee or a friendly meal, Nell cut the conversation dead with a mention of her father's funeral. Once again this proved too much misfortune for one woman and the stewardess's sympathy faltered and stalled.

Now Nell stood in the cool shade of the double door-way, looking for a taxi to take her to the airport. A small door within the great door was ajar and she stood framed inside it as she squinted down the street in search of a taxi. The narrow street was one of the most picturesque in Paris, beloved of naive painters because, in what was an optical illusion, the Eiffel Tower rose out of the slanting slate rooftops, and the street's shops with their awnings in primary colours seemed to string themselves like beads around the tower's long neck. Blue was the colour of the fishmonger's, red for the butcher, yellow for the cheese shop and green, of course, for the greengrocer's. This childlike sense of order had thrilled Nell in her first months in Paris but she had long since ceased to notice the tower or the shops. She had noticed that the worst café in the street would remain open all summer and she was scowling at its chrome chairs and tables and thinking that it would attract the worst type of tourist riff-raff when Mort appeared in the courtyard.

He seemed to be heading in her direction but because he was dancing his progress was slow. The sun was shining into the courtyard and must have been dazzling him, Nell decided, or he wouldn't have made such a spectacle of himself with her looking on just yards away. Then he passed into the shade of the hallway which in Nell's building was paved in marble and he blinked and said: *'Bonjour, madame. Je suis une voisine'*

'Not quite,' said Nell, making a rapid decision not to waste time with this man's teetering French. The shorts, the glasses, the excellent teeth and the dancing all announced the arrival of an American. Years of circling the globe had endowed Nell with an ability to differentiate between the high cheekbones of a Finn and those of a Swede; she could tell a Canadian from an American in the 'ou' of 'about'; she knew that a businessman was a German if he wore a belted raincoat and that an elegant brunette was an Italian by the sweep of her hair and the style of her shoes. And she could always identify an Englishman, but then so could every employee in the company. This, however, was an American and Nell needed him to know that he wasn't her neighbour, first because he had come from across the courtyard and second because she didn't consider this Paris flat to be her home.

'Oh, you speak English! Thank God for that!' cried Mort, ignoring her denial and leaving her no room to emphasize that she didn't live in the building. 'Mort Engelberg.' He held out his hand. Nell shook it and decided to call herself by the French 'Nelli' instead of the English Nell.

'Nelli Marchand,' she said.

'French?'

Nell smiled but said nothing.

'Wow! And such good English.'

'I'm waiting for a taxi,' said Nell.

'Right, well, I won't take up your time but maybe you can clear up a mystery for me—'

'Oh, I doubt it,' said Nell.

'There's this noise,' said Mort, raising his hands and parting them to indicate the size of the noise. 'A real big noise,' he added – unnecessarily, Nell thought. 'I hear it at night – no, more like the early hours of the morning. Four a.m.?' Mort studied Nell's face for a sign of recognition. When he saw none, he tried to elaborate. 'It pounds, it kind of pulsates, it gets inside you and—' Mort stopped. He had been about to say that it starts to throb within you and kind of turns you on, but stopped himself in time. Here, he thought, was another stranger come to hem him back in. He'd just adapted to the fastidious transsexual and now here stood this severely dressed woman with her small, neat good looks. Why was she wearing black? Mort wondered and decided that Europeans obviously had no idea that black absorbed the heat. Look at all those wizened widows down in Spain and Sicily, he reasoned to himself, and started to endow Nell with their austerity. He certainly couldn't describe the true nature of the noise.

'Do you know what I'm talking about? Is it a boiler? An air-conditioner?'

'There are no air-conditioners on your side of the building,' said Nell.

'Then what the heck is it? Can you think of anything?' Mort heard himself modifying his vocabulary to suit Nell's clothes. He hadn't said 'heck' since before Austin, Texas. What a dumb word it was, he decided, and tried to think of another excuse to use the sentence so that he could say what he really meant. Better still, he'd find a reason to say something like 'what the fuck' so that he could reassure himself that he was a free agent and not restricted by the values of unsolicited strangers.

Nell was thinking. She had bunched her neat features up so tight that her eyes and mouth had almost disappeared. My God, that makes her look homely, thought Mort, and wondered why no-one in this woman's life had ever bothered to tell her how plain such solemnity rendered her reasonably pretty face. Still, she was obedient, he concluded. He had told her to think and she was certainly thinking.

'It's the *pétrin* . . . the kneading machine,' she said, and satisfied with her own answer her face relaxed. Her brown eyes and small mouth reappeared and she started to smile but the sudden presence of a taxi distracted her.

'The what?'

'The baker's kneading machine! He turns it on every morning at four o'clock. His kitchen runs alongside the courtyard between the two buildings. The kneading machine must be at your end.'

'So that noise, that throbbing, that almost *erotic* pumping,' there, he'd made a start, 'is some old guy making croissants and baguettes?'

Nell had stopped the taxi and opened the door to climb in. She hadn't been listening. Mort didn't have

117

time to repeat the reference to 'erotic pumping' so he just said, 'It's Mr Bun the baker?'

Nell nodded.

'Oh well then, what the fuck?'

He'd said it but the phrase sounded stilted and incongruous and she'd been giving her destination – 'Roissy' – to the driver and didn't seem to have heard. Now she scowled at him and said: 'Have you ever been in that baker's?'

'No, no I haven't. But I guess I'll go. In fact I guess I'll go now.' Mort was relieved to have an excuse to slink away down the street. He followed her out of the courtyard and turned left into the baker's shop door.

CHAPTER THIRTEEN

When Nell got to the airport, she realized that she didn't have any money. She was standing at a cash machine tapping in her pin number when she smelt Claudine's perfume behind her.

'I thought it was you, Nelli.' Claudine bent down to hug her.

'I thought you couldn't get time off,' said Nell, surveying the crimson and yellow silk suit that Claudine wore and the small overnight bag she carried. Claudine looked wonderful. Claudine looked as though she was headed for the Rio carnival, although Nell would have been quick to point out that the carnival was in fact in February. Still, she smiled at Claudine's luxuriant colours. I knew you'd wear that, she thought. I didn't even know you owned such an outfit but I knew you'd wear that. And even though she herself was sweating and stifled in her mourner's black, she was glad that Claudine had chosen crimson.

'I called in sick – it was only a ten-day thing down to Rio and Buenos Aires.' Claudine saw Nell's scowl and squeezed her arm. 'Somebody will be glad to go in my place – they fight for that rotation over on the South American sector.'

'But if you've called in sick, we'll have to go on British Airways so that you don't get seen by someone,' said Nell, whose attention was divided between her irresponsible friend and the cash machine which was refusing to give her any money. She tapped in her pin a second time. 'It won't give me my money.'

'All the more reason to go to Terminal One. We can try the machine there.'

Nell was happy to follow her friend down the stairs and onto the shuttle bus that carried them towards the giant concrete camembert that was Terminal One. On British Airways she would be anonymous and far from the sympathy of her colleagues. As the shuttle made its way across the blanched, baking asphalt, Nell looked up and saw the armed CRS guards who patrolled the roof of the terminal. She tried to superimpose an image of Luc onto that distant scene of guns and menace but instead she kept thinking of her father. And, as on the night of his death, she found herself wondering about his life, that mysterious life that had run alongside hers for so many years.

The cash machine at Terminal One also refused to give Nell any money.

'I must have forgotten to transfer anything from the other account,' she told Claudine. 'I'd better get one of the clerks to do it,' and she started towards the counters of the Société Générale.

'I've got money,' said Claudine. 'Don't waste time in there. Let's have coffee instead.'

Over coffee, Nell told Claudine of her flying visit to Kennedy airport, of the journey home with Marie-France and the night of sympathetic phone calls.

'I know, I tried to get through several times – then the phone was off the hook.'

'Should I be worried about Luc?' Nell asked Claudine. 'I know I should be. I know that I should be panic-stricken but I feel quite serene and detached about the whole business.'

'Well, you and Luc are so, so . . .'

'So what?'

'I don't know. So . . .' Claudine sought her words and when she found them her French accent was pronounced as she said very slowly, 'So refreshingly free from passion.' She emphasized the word 'refreshingly'.

'I must make a quick stop at the duty free shop,' Nell said. She didn't want to hear anything else that her friend might say about her husband.

Claudine reached down to move Nell's cabin bag out of her path. 'What have you got in here?' She peered into the half-open bag and pulled out a foil-wrapped ball. 'It looks like, like *boules*, you know, *pétanque* balls.'

'It's pastry dough,' said Nell. 'I made it this morning.'

'Why?'

'Because I woke up early and didn't know what to do. And I kept thinking about poor Mother in Streatham with all those strange people. And I thought that at least we could show them that we're not complete peasants—'

'Why do you care about what they think?'

'I don't. I don't really, but it's for Mother. I wanted her to – oh, I don't know.'

'But why the pastry?'

'Oh, I thought I'd do the dough here because Luc has always said how wonderful my *pâte brisée* is, and then I'd make up a *pissaladière* and a roquefort and walnut quiche, and pick up some good salmon, some decent cheeses at the duty free . . .' Nell turned away from Claudine's astonished gaze and fixed all her attention on the duty free shop in the distance.

'*Nelli, ma pauvre*,' Claudine started to say.

'I'm not your poor Nelli,' said Nell. 'I know it looks like a pathetic thing to do but it's not – it's a kind of . . . of power game. Rich, horrible people must play versions of it all the time.'

121

'I wasn't going to say that. I was going to say that if I'd known I could have picked up some *petits fours* from *Le Nôtre*. Perhaps even a *feuille d'automne*.'

'A *feuille d'automne* would have melted in this heat,' said Nell, thinking that the rich dark chocolate cake with its layers of meringue was too closely associated in her own mind with happy teas in Versailles with Claudine to be brought to her father's funeral.

Grief had confused even Nell's sense of timing. The funeral was at four o'clock and at two thirty Claudine and Nell's mother found her rolling out an increasingly greasy slab of pastry on the kitchen table and crying fat salty tears into the dough.

'We don't need quiches or those pissy things,' said her mother, who had been drinking tea in the living room with Claudine and enjoying her first ordinary conversation since her husband's death. Nell's mother was secretly thrilled with Claudine's appearance. She had thought to herself but couldn't say to her daughter that Claudine in her crimson and yellow silk was like a mythical phoenix come from across the sea to promise rebirth after this death. Nell's mother secretly hoped for her own rebirth. At seventy-five she wasn't quite sure how this could come about but the sight of Claudine on her sofa had seemed to her like a glimpse of other worlds, landed in her living room to remind her that 'it' – whatever 'it' may be – was never too late.

Now Claudine rolled up the crimson silk sleeves and helped a swollen-faced Nell spread onions, anchovies and olives over the slab of dough. The quiche shells were rolled out, the filling was poured in. The smoked salmon was removed from its wrapper and arranged on a platter. Nell ignored her mother's concern for her tears and stared intently at the work surface. Neither her mother nor Claudine dared to make any further mention of her distress.

122

When the big black Daimler from the undertakers arrived, Claudine stepped back and looked forlornly around for another car but Nell's mother pushed her in with them.

'What am I doing in here?' Claudine whispered to Nell.

'I suppose it's a bit like when you go to a bad play and the management invites the audience to move closer to the front so that the players won't be discouraged. This car would feel as big as an aircraft hanger with just Mum and me.'

'And we cannot discourage the player?' Claudine nodded towards the coffin in the hearse that was pulling out from the kerb in front of them.

'Better not,' said Nell and squeezed her friend's hand.

At the crematorium, her mother rushed forward to greet a vicar that neither of them had ever seen before. While the other cars discharged her mother's lone sister and her three sons, and while Claudine surveyed this sudden and unexpected profusion of manhood, Nell's mother shook the unknown vicar's hand. Nell tried to listen to the exchange between her mother and the eager-looking, ginger-bearded cleric but the older woman turned away and all Nell heard was the phrase 'Wilfred known as Harry', which her mother repeated twice, emphasizing 'Harry' each time.

Once inside the chapel, Nell looked around for Ivy. There was no sign of her. No substance, thought Nell and was surprised at her own malice, and then suddenly saddened by the idea that the old woman might not even know her father was gone.

She recognized the other mourners from those dreamlike last days at Streatham when these same people had filled what had always been empty spaces in her mother's home and life. She saw the man in the scarlet turban and the woman who her mother claimed was 'some Lady or other'. The Indian faith healer was there and the district nurse, and other less immediately recognizable faces who had, she was sure, swallowed her mother's tea and consumed her Digestive biscuits. They didn't look quite so numerous in the more spacious chapel, and when Nell saw that the only other members of her father's family were his three spinster sisters she was grateful for the presence of these strangers.

We are a family that has ground to a halt, she thought as she looked around her. Her cousins had no children; her father's sisters had not even produced any cousins. She, Nell the only child, was, she realized for the first time, the youngest member of the family. Everything in this family, the full lower lip, the tendency to knock knees, the fierce dark eyes, the obsessive tidiness, the capacity to bear a grudge for years, everything would stop at her. Why have we stopped? Nell wondered. Is there some weakness, mental or physical, that has stopped us from flourishing? Has some higher power decreed that we're not worth continuing with? Or is it all just hazard and muddle? Then she thought of nothing more because the coffin was being carried down the aisle.

She heard her mother say, 'I can't believe he's in there.' And she tried to look at the pale wooden box but found that she couldn't. A greyness had submerged her – a plummeting greyness of the unknown, the unpredictable, the uncontrollable. It swirled and lurched within her, blotting out all the old familiar landmarks: Luc, the house in Chantilly, the dream of the Languedoc, and her profession's endless promise of flight. But most of those comforting landmarks had themselves shifted out of her reach, Nell reminded herself as the congregation recited the twenty-third psalm. There must be something that I can fix in my mind, somewhere unmoving that I can retreat to . . .

'In pastures green,' sang the mourners and Nell had a sudden memory of a descent with Luc into the airport in the lush mountains of Quito. She started to remember how difficult the descent had been and how the sweat had seeped across his armpits and down to his midriff like ink on a blotter as he had piloted the plane down into . . . Then the plummeting greyness returned, she could no longer avoid the coffin as it passed within feet of her and she found herself echoing her mother's cry: 'I can't believe he's in there.'

'And so we say a farewell to Harry,' she heard the ginger-bearded vicar say, and she realized that she had missed the beginning of his address, that minutes must have passed, for the pall bearers were seated, the coffin was now settled on a stand at the front of the chapel, her face stung from tears that she hadn't been aware of shedding and her nose felt thick and red and congested.

'Who's Harry?' she heard her Aunt Aggie say to her Aunt Win.

'Harry who?' said her Aunt Win to her Aunt Flo who was stone deaf and just smiled back through a few tears.

'We're at the wrong funeral, Win,' said Aunt Aggie, and Nell turned to see her clutching Win by the black sleeve of what she called her funeral coat.

'It's all right, Aunt Aggie,' whispered Nell to the aunts in the row behind her.

'Course it's not all right,' said Aunt Aggie, who always had been the bossiest of the sisters. 'I knew it was wrong when I saw that bloke in the turban. Where would your dad know him from?'

'I don't know but he did,' hissed Nell. Aunt Aggie ignored her and clutched at her sister's sleeve.

'We've got to get out of here before they notice. All of our lot. We've got to find the coffin with Wilfred.'

'This is Wilfred!' said Nell, reminding herself that

she was a purser and used to giving orders to people the world over.

'It's a Harry!' said her aunt, who had never been impressed by Nell's profession and secretly referred to her as a 'glorified waitress'.

'That was what he liked to be called,' said Nell. The congregation was reciting the Lord's prayer.

'He never told me that,' replied Aunt Aggie.

He wouldn't have dared, thought Nell as the oldest sister started to get up.

'Well, that's the name he liked. You must admit Wilfred's a bit—'

The congregation was coming to the end of the Lord's prayer. Nell knew that she had little time left.

'Anyway, it's like a pen name or something. Mother told the vicar both names but he must have forgotten. Trust me, Aunt Ag – you won't find Dad anywhere else today.'

Nell wanted to add that she wouldn't find him here either but the chapel had gone suddenly quiet at the end of the prayer and even her aunt seemed daunted by the silence. She remained in her place.

When the coffin slid away between the curtains, Nell heard her three aunts weeping and wanted to weep herself but all she could think was: my father went out of this world under an assumed name.

When they all filed back outside into the sunshine, Nell's mother asked, 'What happens next? Do we wait here while – while . . .' She couldn't finish her sentence and was rescued by a crematorium employee in a long blue robe who explained that they need not return unless they wanted to see where the ashes had been scattered.

'Where would you like them to go?' she asked Nell's mother, who said: 'I can't think about that now,' and climbed into the Daimler.

Back at the house, Nell's French food and French

friend were the success she had planned. All her father's 'other' people thronged around Claudine and recited their own numerous trips to Paris and the Riviera as they crammed *pissaladière* and smoked salmon into their mouths. When she saw her mother sitting on the couch drinking tea with the man in the flame-red turban, Nell felt that she could slip away.

She went into the kitchen and turned on the television. She sat down on a high stool and flicked through the channels until she came to *L.A. Law*, in English this time and an episode that she had seen two weeks earlier in Tokyo. She was lost in envy of a woman lawyer who was involved in a tender passion with a much shorter male colleague when her mother and the Sikh came into the kitchen.

'You must be watching for news of your husband,' said the Sikh, coming to stand alongside her and donning a pair of glasses.

'My husband?'

'Yes, your mother has been telling me that he is being the hero of this terrible hijacking drama.'

'Oh, I don't think he's doing anything heroic. I think he's doing what they tell him to do.'

'So much worry it must be for you.'

'Well no, not – I mean, I have faith in Luc to survive anything.'

'Then you do secretly think of him as a hero!' The Sikh clapped his hands in glee. 'But you are too modest to admit it.'

'I suppose so.' Nell frowned at the television, trying to remember the times of the news broadcasts in England. She did not have to wonder long for the lawyers had disappeared and the well-groomed head of a solemn black man with good diction had taken their place.

'Turn up the volume!' cried the Sikh. 'Turn up the volume!'

127

The other guests wandered into the kitchen, attracted by his voice and the sudden boom of the television. Nell noted with relief that the lead story involved a political scandal and the 'French hijacking' got second billing.

When the image of the 747 was flashed onto the screen, the guests all turned to scan her face for emotion and muttered more condolences. The 747 was still in Thunder Bay but now, said the newscaster, they were expecting a new demand from the hijackers at any moment. He went on with the rest of the news and was about to introduce the weatherman when his phone rang and he frowned out at the nation and said they had a newsflash from the hijacking scene. There was a gasp of excitement in the Streatham kitchen and through her own sudden fear Nell felt indignation that Luc had managed to take over even her father's funeral.

The newscaster read out the hijacker's latest demand as the screen flashed the now familiar photo of the 747 on the runway. Nell couldn't take his words in because she had expected an image to accompany them. Then there was another flurry of phone calls and agitation in the newsroom as they did get a picture. The hijackers had secretly negotiated with the authorities in Thunder Bay to release the plane, the cargo and two of the three crew members in return for the loan of a small aircraft to take them and their hostage out of the country.

'Who is their hostage?' said one of the mourners.

'Which one have they kept?' said the woman who was a Lady something.

'The captain, of course!' cried Nell. 'Who do you think they would keep? What's the point of a flight engineer or a wet behind the ears co-pilot? What pull would they have?'

'Oh, but he's a 747 man,' said the Sikh smugly. 'What will he do with a bush plane?'

'Fly it, of course!' snapped Nell. 'Of course he can fly light aircraft. Luc can fly just about anything.'

The camera had focused on a small plane, parked, in an obvious attempt to elude the media, at the distant end of the runway. The picture zoomed in on the cockpit. Through the window, a shadowy figure could be seen adjusting its seat.

'Are those Luc's knees?' asked her Aunt Win.

'Are they, Nell?' asked her mother.

'I don't know,' said Nell.

'But you must know your own husband's knees,' said her Aunt Aggie.

'Well I don't! Not from this distance – and in uniform trousers . . .'

'What a brave man,' said the Sikh. 'You father would have been very proud of his son-in-law.'

For the first time that evening the flame-turbaned stranger was right, thought Nell, as the weatherman appeared on the screen, predicting more heat, and the guests sighed, avoided Nell's gaze and drifted back to the smoked salmon. Perhaps Luc was a hero after all, she pondered, and felt a sudden flush of ridiculous pride as she leaned forward to turn off the television. Then she saw her mother standing by the stove.

'Luc has rather taken over Dad's funeral,' said Nell.

Her mother shrugged. 'That's all right. It gave that lot a bit of a surprise. And from your end of the family—'

'And yours,' said Nell.

'Thanks, dear.' Her mother smiled but seemed to be smiling at something a long way behind Nell. 'No sign of Ivy, then,' she said and now she looked at Nell and scanned her face as if she might find the little woman of no substance hiding behind her daughter's small dark features. 'I mean, I don't think she was in the chapel but I was a bit distracted and I didn't like to look round.'

'Oh, she definitely wasn't there,' said Nell.

'Well that's good. I mean, I suppose it's good.'

'What exactly was it all about?' asked Nell. 'Her and Dad?'

'Nothing very much – a bit of foolish fun on your dad's part . . . that went on a bit too long.'

'That's all?'

'That's all. That is all. You're a married woman, Nell. You don't have any illusions about the whole business . . . do you?'

'Oh no . . . definitely none of those. I just thought that it was something more—'

'Well then.' Her mother had turned towards the hall passage and the guests in the living room. 'Let's see what we can do about getting rid of this lot. I've had quite enough for one day.'

'I did have a thought in the chapel,' said Nell before her mother could leave the kitchen. 'I don't know. It did strike me that she, I mean Ivy, might not have known he died. I certainly didn't call her. And she's a bit gaga – what if she still doesn't know? I mean, I'm not sure that it matters, but perhaps—'

'Oh, I told her, dear. I mean, I didn't speak to her personally but I sent a card with the announcement of his death and the time of the funeral.'

Nell didn't return to the funeral. She unplugged the kitchen TV and took it up to the bedroom that, apart from the removal of a few posters of pop stars, had remained unchanged since her adolescence. The hot pink walls and bedlinen that her fifteen-year-old self had chosen made her feel slightly queasy. She turned off the lights and, with only the blue TV screen light to guide her, climbed over the camp bed that her mother had set up for Claudine and lay down on her own narrow single bed.

She had carried the letter from Jameson's Private Detective Agency in her pocket from Paris to London. And in the light of the TV, she lay on the bed and reread it. She realized that she was mechanically counting out the weeks to mid-August on her fingers, and she stopped herself and waited for the resident headmistress to tell her how pathetic her secret quest was. In what seemed like just a few moments, she felt Claudine pulling the sheets up in the bed next to her.

'You were certainly the life and soul. What time is it?'

'After midnight,' said Claudine. 'You were asleep with the TV on in all your clothes.'

'You mean they all stayed till now?' Nell yawned.

'No, everyone left long ago. I was talking to your *maman*.'

'But you talked to all my dad's mysterious friends. I saw you.'

'Do you know where they came from?'

'I'd say at least one of them was from the Punjab.'

'No, that's not what I mean. You know how he knew them?'

'I'm not sure that I want to.'

'Sainsbury's!' cried Claudine. 'He got to know them when he helped load their shopping at Sainsbury's.'

'Are you sure?'

'Oh yes. Jimmy Singh the Sikh monsieur, he used to give your dad racing tips. And your dad helped that Lady woman to buy a new car.'

Nell propped herself on one arm.

'So that's it! There was no mystery at all. Just Sainsbury's car park. And Ivy – that's how he knew Ivy?'

'No, Nelli – of course not.'

'Oh.'

'I'm exhausted,' said Claudine. 'I have to get the early flight back so that I can see what they've given me in place of the Rio.'

'I wish I were on a Rio right this minute,' said Nell suddenly.

'It's winter over there. Probably raining.'

'Who cares?' Nell glanced at the bedside clock and did a quick calculation. 'Right this minute, in first class, I'd be helping to carve the meat, then I'd check that the cheeses are out of the fridge, make sure that the children have been given toys, open the *cuvée spéciale*, ask if the pilots want to eat yet, prepare the fruit basket and the dessert tray, announce the sale of duty free goods . . .'

Nell felt Claudine's gaze even in the darkness of the bedroom.

'What are you talking about?'

'Oh, nothing. I do this sometimes instead of counting sheep. I go through an imaginary flight, step by step. I like the routine of it. It's . . .' Nell knew that Claudine was scowling across the two or three feet that separated them. 'It's reassuring.'

'You're bizarre,' sighed Claudine. 'I never think of a flight once I'm off a plane . . . Good night, mad Englishperson. Just hearing about all that has exhausted me.'

Nell *had* intended to run through the tasks of a flight. She had been doing this since she started with the company but Claudine's mockery made her wonder if she was 'bizarre'. And her father and Ivy and Luc's knees stood in the way of the galley and the food trolleys and the comfortable tick-tock of an airline meal service.

She felt all that she had ever known and relied on receding, as though she had stepped onto a beach lilo a week or so earlier for a few minutes' amusement and found herself swept out into the middle of the Atlantic. Clutching the sides of her narrow bed to steady herself she finally fell asleep, comforted only by the loud snores that issued from Claudine's beautiful nose.

CHAPTER FOURTEEN

Inside the baker's Mort bought himself a croissant, a *pain au chocolat* and a loaf of bread called a *bâtard*. He was served by a plain, mournful-looking woman with greasy brown hair and a white film over one watery blue eye. Once he got upstairs and consulted his dictionary, he found that *bâtard* translated, as he had suspected, as bastard. Weird name for a loaf of bread, he thought, then wondered whether he would be better off taking the pastries down to a café to eat with some decent coffee. He had read in one of his 'do it on the cheap' guides that it was acceptable in some cafés to bring your own croissant. The guide had emphasized the word 'some'. Mort pictured the bald-headed Breton with the wrestler's build who ran the ugly little café across the road from the apartment and was sure that 'bring your own croissant' would not be acceptable to him.

He decided to make his own coffee. Mlle Sofia had switched off her music. He hoped that his transsexual neighbours were sleeping. The courtyard was silent. He took off his shoes and padded softly to the hotplate where he heated some water in a saucepan before going to the window. He was suddenly hungry and bit into the *bâtard*. He chewed for a few seconds, screwed his face up in disgust and spat the bread out into the sink. It was the worst loaf of bread he had ever tasted. He prodded it, squeezed it and even tried punching it but the bread did not yield to his touch. He hit it on the formica table where it landed with such force that he found himself anxiously surveying the table surface for damage that might eat into his refundable security deposit. He wondered whether he should have heated it. Was this what you did with bastards? he pondered. He held it over the glowing electric hotplate for a few seconds – he had no oven – but when the sleeve of his T-shirt started to give off a smell of burning and the sweat began to pour down his face he gave up and pitched the offending loaf in the bin.

He must, he decided, have bought one of yesterday's loaves. He was surprised that a self-respecting French baker would sell such a thing but perhaps the one-eyed woman hadn't noticed. He decided to try a croissant. He heated this by putting it on a plate over his boiling saucepan of coffee water. Then he took the croissant and the coffee and sat down to keep company with the Eiffel Tower. Before he'd moved far enough to capture it in his field of vision, he knew that the croissant was worse than the bread. He gave up his search for the Eiffel Tower and examined the flaccid piece of dough on his lap. He saw a brown hair tucked in a fold of pastry.

Mort leapt up and bounded down the stairs. This was unacceptable even for Europe. He hesitated as he arrived in front of the baker's. The shopfront looked so wonderful. On either side of the main window was an engraved panel of a pastoral landscape – a mill, a stream, some cows. Mort had never seen such a beautiful shopfront. He stared, bemused, at the country scene and was almost considering going back upstairs and trying the *pain au chocolat* when a very short, very fat man came out of the baker's carrying a box of brioches. His legs were so short that the blind descent

134

from the high Paris kerb with the rolls blocking his view proved too steep for him and he tripped and let the carton slip from his grasp. The brioches spilt out into the gutter. Mort, who was the only other person on the street, felt that he had to help. He bent down and picked up the ones that had rolled his way. When he had collected an armful he dumped them in a litter bin.

'*Non! Non!*' cried the baker, for he it was. '*Non! Non! Non!*' He proceeded to rummage in the bin. Because he was so short his feet left the ground as his head and arms disappeared inside the container. He emerged with all the rolls that Mort had dumped, dusted them off, put them back in the box, sprayed a few more incomprehensible French phrases in Mort's direction and climbed into a van that said: '*P. Pouyfaucon – Maître Boulanger.*'

'Oh my God,' said Mort to the empty street. Oh my God, he thought when he realized that there was no-one to whom he could tell his story. He went over it again to himself. Those rolls had been in the gutter where the Parisian poodles pooped and the rubbish was carried away by those mysterious twice-daily streams. It was all right in Paris to throw a paper into the gutter, Mort had already learned. Water would appear from nowhere and bear it away. It wasn't all right to retrieve a couple of dozen brioches. Mort drew himself up and decided to confront the one-eyed woman.

'This is unacceptable!' he announced as he marched into the bakery. The woman had her back to him and was stacking more of the dreaded *bâtards* onto a rack. Mort squinted at them as he spoke. Newer? Fresher? Nah, he thought. He could almost hear their bullet hardness as she set them out.

'I've never tasted such appalling bread!' He pounded his fist on the marble counter top. 'I want my money back,' he said, then remembered that he had left the offending croissant upstairs.

'*Comment?*' said the woman, her back still turned to him, her greasy hair spilling over the top of her pink overall.

'*Un moment!*' cried Mort and raced out of the shop and back up the five flights of stairs to his flat. He gathered the croissant, the *bâtard*, and the *pain au chocolat* in his arms and headed back down the stairs. The baker's was still empty of customers. Come to think of it, thought Mort, the baker's was always empty. The woman was leaning up against the marble counter. Not a thought in her greasy French head, Mort snorted to himself and flung the offending croissant on the counter.

'Regar— regardez this!' he stammered. 'Just regardez! C'est disgusting! And je suis sure that c'est illegal aussi!'

'*Comment?*' The woman didn't look at the croissant but looked instead at Mort. Her ghostly, cloud-covered left eye reminded him of children he had seen with a similar condition, in remote, wretched Mexican villages. They'd had rickets too. Mort was tempted to peer over the counter at the woman's legs but he knew that he had an argument to complete. If she did have rickets, compassion would shrivel his limited supply of French insults. She continued to stare at him. It seemed to Mort that the cloudy eye did not blink. At least it didn't blink as fully as the healthy eye – itself an anaemic, unappealing blue – which gave the impression that the sullen greasy woman was winking very deliberately at him.

Mort picked up the croissant. What the hell was the word for hair? Oh well, it didn't matter. He would show her.

'*Regardez!* he repeated. He liked that word. He was almost sure it was right and it wasn't too difficult to

136

say. '*Regardez!* He picked the croissant up and peered at it. He couldn't see the hair. He flaked a few crumbs away from the centre and peered into the flaccid dough. The woman made no attempt to peer with him but just looked at him. There was no sign of the hair.

'Forget it,' sighed Mort. 'Look, it was there! This bread is disgusting! Just give me my money back!'

'*Non*,' said the woman, sweeping the abandoned croissant off the counter and into a bin.

'You can throw the bread too,' said Mort. 'Then I'd like my money back. Argent, you know? Reimbursay?'

'*Non*,' said the woman. And she smiled at Mort. There was nothing smug about her smile. There was none of the triumph of the merchant who had beaten the customer. It was an ingenuous smile and Mort realized that she was many years away from the fifty that he had given her. He could not think of another word to say. His vocabulary was too limited to pursue his argument. His evidence was in the dustbin. He was still at the beginning of his vacation and didn't give a damn about the ten francs he had spent. And the woman had gone back to stacking her bastards. He turned and left the shop.

He bumped into Mlle Marina on his way back into the building. Her face seemed to be in a strange nowhere land between male and female. There was a slight shadow around her jowls and her lips were bare but her long lashes still bore traces of navy mascara. Mort was already becoming accustomed to this waxing, waning face and was more interested in telling her about his experience in the bakery.

He walked back out of the building with her as he described the rock-hard *bâtard* and the hair in the croissant.

'Oh!' she cried as he completed his story. 'This is so disgusting! In Brésil we have laws against this.'

'Oh, I'm sure they do here,' said Mort.

'I'm not so sure.' Marina drew closer to him. 'Sometimes I think maybe these French are pigs.'

'Maybe just in Paris,' said Mort.

'You'd be better on the Riviera.'

'I don't know about that.'

Mort realized that he was walking along the street with Marina. He wondered where she was headed but didn't dare to ask. Then she stopped in front of a lingerie shop. It was closed for the summer but its display of silk and lace bras and panties had been left in place. Mort was already familiar with the contents of this window, having studied it regularly on lonely summer walks back to his apartment. He was particularly taken with a black silk negligee at the back of the display and had started to embroider a fantasy around it, only to realize with horror that he couldn't think of a single woman to fill it. He'd been reduced to trying to remember the blonde girl by the Austin swimming pool all those years earlier but couldn't recall her face. Since his thirties, Mort had found that a face became more and more important to his fantasies. Lots of soft flesh and mysterious hairy parts were no longer sufficient. He felt deeply uncomfortable standing in front of the shop with Marina.

'I like this place too,' she said and turned to study the display.

'I got to make a phone call,' said Mort. Despite his discomfort, he was starting to enjoy Marina's company and had just decided that this was because it was the only human contact he'd had in days. The idea of friendship with someone of such enigmatic sexuality was too unsettling for Mort. He decided that a phone conversation with one of the members of his argumentative, conventional family was in order, and when he got back to the flat he called his brother.

'Now are you keeping your hand in?' said Frank,

who had picked up the poolside phone at his lakeshore home.

'How the hell am I supposed to keep my hand in with the weather?'

'That's not for me to know – I'm not a weatherman. What I do know, Mort, is this: if I were to take even a month out of my profession, dermatology would move on without so much as a wave in the direction of Frank Engelberg. Keep your hand in.'

Mort had wanted to tell Frank the story of the baker and the brioches in the gutter. Now he decided to save it for his mother.

'How's Ma?' he asked his brother as a preliminary to ending the conversation.

'Worried about you,' said Frank.

'Oh come on now,' sighed Mort. 'She knows better than that.'

'Hey, I've got a question for you, little brother. How's the weather over there?'

'Hot,' replied Mort. 'Very hot.'

'That's it? Hot?'

'Yes. Very hot. I guess you would even say abnormally hot.'

'See – you're vague, Mort.'

'Of course I'm vague. I'm on vacation.'

'It's not just the technicalities.' His brother ignored him. 'It's presentation, public speaking, performing. Did you shave today?'

'I can't hear you,' said Mort who had heard every word. 'The line is breaking up. I'm hanging up, Frank.' He was enunciating each word syllable by syllable. 'Goodbye.'

Once he had escaped his brother, Mort studied his reflection in the mirror and decided that when it came to his appearance perhaps the time had come to 'keep his hand in'. But as he rummaged around in M. Dupuy's cupboards, trying on a felt fedora, a white silk

139

opera scarf and an Hermès cravat, he found that he couldn't forget the heat.

The evening was hot. It was abnormally hot and it showed no signs of shifting. He resolved to buy himself a *Herald Tribune* the next morning and see what the forecasts were predicting. Mort, whose ability to live entirely in the moment, never fretting about the days to come, had been the despair of his ex-wife, found himself confronted with a deep anxiety about the weather.

Because he was sleepy and not rational, he found himself musing: what if it never snowed again? What if winter were lost for ever and the land never turned white again? What if this summer stretched on and on, depriving him of his scarlet maples and the first frosts? What if the beautiful green earth just got hotter and hotter, turning brown and cracking apart? A lot of good his inept paintings would do then, he thought as he fell asleep.

Then the pounding started. Mort woke up, aware even as he opened his eyes that although he was still exhausted his sleep was finished for that night. But I know what the noise is, he reasoned to himself. It's the baker down in the basement, labouring through the night to produce the staff of life for us tomorrow. But Mort could see only the baker's legs sticking out of the waste bin and the blank back of the mournful woman in his shop. The throbbing pulsed through his body again. Within ten minutes he had made his decision. In this Parisian life there was to be no more hesitating. Since South Carolina, snap decisions were Mort Engleberg's style.

When Mlle Marina slipped into the courtyard carrying her shoes at dawn, Mort was waiting for her.

CHAPTER FIFTEEN

Nell woke up the next morning, looked at Claudine who slept alongside her and wondered if Luc had ever done the same. Then the stern headmistress's voice that had always reprimanded her for any hint of folly or excess reminded her that she had seen Luc and Claudine together hundreds of times throughout the years. There had never been any hint of an attraction between them so why should it suddenly appear now? Claudine was not Luc's type, thought Nell, and flushed with misery as she forced herself to go through the catalogue of women who had been Luc's type throughout their marriage. There were virtually no blondes and certainly none with Claudine's lightness, her nonchalance, the impression she gave of barely touching the earth as she moved across it.

Nell smiled as she thought to herself that Luc, once her emperor of the skies, liked his women to be earthbound and anchored. Anchored. The image that had appeared to be an insult when repeated by Claudine pleased her now. But as her friend stirred, murmuring and clutching the pink duvet with her well-manicured fingers, Nell thought of Ivy's ropy, mottled hands.

'*Il faut partir pour Paris.*' Claudine sat up and buried her head in her hands. '*Tu entends le vent dehors?*' She

141

looked across at Nell who had not heard the wind until that moment.

'That means the weather is breaking,' Nell replied and ran to the window to hold her hands out. 'But it's a warm wind – it's almost a hot wind! Like you get down in the Sahara. I've never felt one of those this far north before.' And as her fingers reached out to the warm air, Nell thought: a strange foreign wind has blown in to bear my father away.

'Oh, just listen to that wind!' groaned Claudine and rocked herself back and forth. 'I don't care about temperature but listen to the force of that thing – I can't fly across the Channel in this.'

'Then call scheduling from here. Perhaps they have nothing for you.' Nell had remained by the window. She was disconcerted by the arrival of such a hot, southern wind in temperate, unthreatening England. She knew that winds like the one that was blowing outside her childhood bedroom had names in their countries of origin – names like scirocco and Santa Ana – and were blamed for changes of mood, for unpredictable actions, even, sometimes, for murders.

'I'll pay your mother back,' Nell heard Claudine saying and, lost in thought as she was, she could not for a few seconds understand how Claudine could repay her mother – for Ivy? for betrayal? for her sudden widowhood? 'It must be about three pounds at this time of the morning?' Claudine was holding the phone receiver in her hand.

'Not even that,' muttered Nell and sat down opposite Claudine as she dialled crew scheduling in Paris. A call to crew scheduling invariably made the caller anxious and preoccupied. In all the years that Nell had flown, she had never been able to call that notorious number without hearing her own heartbeat. This was irrational, she knew, and had discussed it with her colleagues. Many of the people who had chosen to spend their lives travelling along the world's airlanes found the reality of such constant movement to be a painful and repeated wrenching. Claudine, in a rare serious moment, had described each long journey as being catapulted out into a void with a fear of being unable to return. Now Nell saw that anxiety on her features as Claudine waited for the scheduler to assign her a flight. But Nell wasn't looking for anxiety. She was using Claudine's preoccupation to look for signs of Luc on her best friend – as if he would imprint himself on her like some religious icon onto a shroud.

'Oh,' Claudine breathed in tight and scowled. *'Bon. Merci. Au revoir, monsieur.'*

'Toronto,' she said to Nell. 'It could be worse. Where do we stay there these days?'

'Four Seasons,' said Nell after a moment's pause. She had been staring so intently at her friend that she was disarmed to find that Claudine was staring back and asking her a question.

'Bon. They're good hotels. And it's only twenty-four hours . . . I can do some shopping, get my legs waxed, perhaps a facial . . . Oh, but do you hear that wind?' She scowled at the window. 'Why do planes even think of taking off in weather like this? Why can't people have patience and just wait until it blows itself out?'

'Because it's perfectly safe!' cried Nell, exasperated at having to repeat a conversation she had had a hundred times before. 'Because planes are built to withstand it. The hinges aren't going to become unscrewed and the wings won't drop off because a bit of wind is blowing around them. Luc has told you a thousand times that most turbulence isn't dangerous!'

Nell had deliberately planted Luc's name in the conversation in order to study her friend's reaction.

'Air Inter over Grenoble,' was all Claudine said. Nell was disappointed. She knew the upcoming monologue by heart. Claudine kept a list of planes that had broken up in severe turbulence and was given to reciting it in chronological order, starting with the most recent incident and working backwards. Nell stopped listening when she reached a Braniff plane in Texas that stretched back to the days before either of them worked for the airline. Nell knew that it was a waste of time asking Claudine why she flew when the actual business of moving at great speed through the air seemed to fill her with such terror. Claudine would say, as she'd been saying for years, that she'd been fine when she started but that her fear had grown over the years as a result of being thrown to the floor or having to cling to the galley curtain over Corsica, an hour out of Nairobi, over virtually any mountain range in spring or any of the other notorious turbulence hot spots. She would add that once she landed, like childbirth which she'd never cared to experience, all the trauma was forgotten with the joy of being in a different place. And sheepishly to Nell, her closest friend, she would confess that she had no savings and no qualifications to do anything else and was stuck.

Now, of course, she had the château, Nell thought, so why stay unless it was to have a convenient excuse to continue a liaison off in foreign parts where wives' eyes don't see?

'The wind is blowing from the south-west,' said Nell. 'You'll be too far north to get it on a Toronto. You'll be flying not far from Luc!' she suddenly remembered.

'I will?'

'I think so. I think I remember tracing that place on a route map once.'

'If he's still there,' said Claudine.

'What do you mean if he's still there?'

'Well, why did they want a small plane?' Claudine reached forward and turned on the television. Nell felt the relief that she always felt when the sleek heads of the breakfast newsreaders appeared on the screen. They were talking about music festivals throughout Europe which meant that she and Claudine had to sit in vigilant silence waiting for a flash of news that mentioned Luc.

'If nothing has happened, perhaps they won't mention him,' said Claudine.

'That won't stop them,' said Nell, who had unwittingly become an expert in the ways of television news broadcasts from all her lonely years of gazing at TV screens in hotel rooms throughout the world. 'Especially since it's August and there's no political news, the royal family are on holiday . . . oh, they'll say something.'

'Shouldn't you know before the news people? Hasn't the airline installed some sort of hotline to keep you informed?'

Before Nell could say that she'd refused the airline's offers of a leave of absence and hadn't even given them her London number, the photo of the airline's logo appeared on the screen.

'That means that nothing has happened,' said Claudine.

'Or something so terrible they can't show it,' said Nell.

Luc and his captors had taken off for an unknown destination, said the newsreader. His co-pilot and flight engineer had been released but had not yet spoken to the media, choosing instead to fly directly back to France.

'It makes Luc seem so alone,' said Claudine, and Nell forgot what now seemed like foolish suspicions of the morning as she tried to imagine her husband in the small cramped cockpit of a DC3 with what could turn out to be a psychopath.

Luc's face appeared in close-up on the screen. The

photo was from his ID badge and had been taken seven years earlier. Seven years, thought Nell. Seven is a cycle, a revolution – the whole body turns round in seven years. Where were we seven years ago? And as the news moved on to other subjects, she found that she could only remember a jumble of departure and arrival lounges – the chaos of customs in the decaying old Delhi airport, a stuffed polar bear in Anchorage, hundreds of abalone shell lamps in the duty free shed in Manila.

Claudine was crying. Luc's face was still on the screen and Claudine was crying. Then Nell's mother was standing in the doorway with a tray of tea which she set down on a chest of drawers and she too started crying.

Claudine gargled something in French.

'What's she saying?' wept Nell's mother.

'Something about life breaking up into crumbs, I think,' said Nell, wondering if she was duty bound to cry with them.

'Men are so vulnerable,' wailed Claudine, 'so lonely and so vulnerable. Your poor father—'

'My father?'

'Poor old Dad,' wept her mother.

'My father?' Nell poured them all a cup of tea.

'Men are so weak,' said Claudine.

'Poor old Dad,' her mother repeated. 'Out there in this wind.' Nell looked at the bedside clock, saw that it was eight o'clock, thought that no crematorium worker would be efficient enough to have been out there sprinkling her father's ashes this early and then she thought how cold I am and started crying too but for her own inadequacies.

'It's because they can't have children,' sobbed Claudine. 'That's why they're lonely.'

'They probably will soon,' said Nell, who had finished crying and recalled an article she'd read on the

146

science page of Newsweek. 'Anyway, you never wanted children.'

'But I could have had them if I had.' Because her nose had been cosmetically corrected, Claudine was always nervous of blowing it too hard. She was dabbing at it very gingerly with a ball of cotton wool that she'd found on the dressing table. She squinted her red eyes tight at Nell and said: 'You never wanted children either.'

'Yes I did!'

'Did you, Eleanor?' Her mother looked up from her paper hankie and her cup of tea. 'I always had you down as a contented career girl.'

'What career? Distributing plastic plates through the heavens? You thought that was a career?'

'Luc said you didn't want children,' said Claudine. 'He said you didn't want to lose out on any seniority. He said you—'

'When did he say that? Where were you for that little discussion?'

Claudine dabbed her nose again, frowned for a moment and said: 'That diner in New York, I suppose.'

'You certainly got a lot said in that bloody diner!'

Claudine shrugged and examined her nose in the dressing table mirror. 'Everyone talks a lot in that place. There's nothing else to do. Everyone wakes up on European time—'

'She's right,' said Nell's mother who had once accompanied her daughter to New York. 'Remember how I woke you up at four a.m. and we had to go for a walk up 57th Street because even the breakfast place wasn't open? There was steam coming out of potholes all over the streets and I kept telling you that we were walking across the rooftop of hell.'

'We didn't sit and talk about the most private conflicts in people's lives.'

'Yes we did,' said her mother. 'We talked to that very handsome Corsican co-pilot about his wife having a

147

child with the head of the fire department. I'll never forget that. We were having one of those peculiar American breakfasts with all those pancakes and syrup and butter. And that lovely man told us how he witnessed the birth the way these silly modern men seem to think they should, and the baby came out with bright red hair and he and his wife were true olive-skinned Mediterranean types but the fireman had transferred in from somewhere like Normandy or Brittany where people tend to have red hair. I was baffled because that poor man was so handsome – in a swarthy Latin way—'

'That "poor man" has bonked every female that has passed within three feet of him.'

'Not you, dear?'

'Of course not me!' Nell turned to Claudine. 'Luc told you that I said I didn't want children?'

Claudine nodded.

'You told me that too, dear,' said her mother. 'I remember now. When you took Father and me to Hong Kong and your father found the duck's foot in his soup in that café with the spittoons at the end of each table, and had to go to bed for the afternoon? And you took me to the Peninsula Hotel for tea? You told me that if the choice came down to making headway as a purser or having a child, you'd go for the job.'

'I never said that!'

'Oh, you did.' Nell's mother had sat down on the end of Claudine's bed. She squeezed Nell's toes through the duvet. 'It was just at the moment when a bellboy came round with a little blackboard with a guest's name on it and a bell ringing above it. I'd only ever seen that on films.' She turned to Claudine. 'Did that handsome Corsican ever bonk you, my dear?'

'Bonk?' Claudine frowned. 'Hit me?'

'The meaning's changed,' said Nell. 'Have sex, make love.'

'Ah. Corsican co-pilot? Very handsome but not tall? Jean-Claude something?'

'That's the one,' said Nell's mother.

Claudine picked at a loose cord on the candlewick.

'Then you did!' cried her mother. 'What lives you girls have! I missed out on all that. Most of my lot did. I suppose we loved our husbands but we just didn't get to try anything else.'

'What else did you discuss with Luc in that bloody diner? What other intimate little secrets? I might as well hear it now! We're sitting here with my father . . . my father—'

Nell looked at the bedside clock and thought: they are probably burning my father's body right this minute. I can't imagine it. I can't let myself imagine it. And by some strange and magical grace, Nell found that she couldn't imagine it. Her mind did not stretch to such a horror. It went as far as the curtains that had closed on her father's coffin and stopped right there. Nell knew instinctively that her own lack of imagination had protected her. A glance at her mother told her that she had not made the link between the hour and the event. She turned her gaze to Claudine.

'Well? What else did you discuss? Go on – you might as well tell us.'

'You're just trying to change the subject because we caught you lying. All this time you try to make out that you're Luc's victim when you're where you are now because of your own ego . . . egoism!'

'Egoist? Me? I always try to do my—' Nell stopped. She had almost said 'duty by people' but knew that Claudine would seize that awful word and dangle it in front of her.

'Do your duty?' Claudine had known her too long. 'Do what's expected of you? People who do their duty are selfish, cowardly people who haven't got the imagination to do something different.'

'And all these bold, brave, bohemian types are always glad to have people like me to come round and lend them money and straighten out their lives when they have screwed them up!'

'I never once asked you for money!'

'You asked for plenty of other things! We helped you to move! Dozens of times we've been there to lug boxes and load up our car when another one of your boyfriends fails to show up!'

'*Salope!*' Claudine leapt out of bed and gathered up her clothes. 'I never asked! Not once! You were always there first! Showing off your husband and your stability!'

Nell knew that all of this was true. She had not realized until this moment that Claudine had known all along. Her anger lost its energy.

'Look at you,' she muttered. 'Just look at you – your clothes are a mess. You want to call in sick on the stupid job because a bit of wind has blown up. Just look at you,' she repeated and, suddenly regretting everything she'd said, she turned to the window and stared out at the horse chestnuts being buffeted by the warm wind. She heard Claudine leave the room without saying another word and then she felt her mother's hand squeezing her arm.

'Isn't this wonderful? A good fight is so full of life! So far away from that dreadful place where we left your father. You know what must be happening right this minute, don't you?'

CHAPTER SIXTEEN

When both her mother and Claudine were gone from the pink bedroom, Nell sat on the edge of her bed with her hands clasped between her knees and her face screwed tight as she tried to persuade herself to go to her friend and apologize and admit that Claudine had spoken the truth. She clenched her knees so tight that her fingers turned scarlet and her calf muscles locked. The wind blew the bedroom window shut and she thought, that's it, Father has gone. And then she chanced upon some indignation with her friend for daring to challenge her on such a dreadful day and she grabbed it and held on to it and decided that she wouldn't apologize.

When she went downstairs she saw that Claudine was in the bathroom applying her eye make-up.

'What flight are you getting?' she asked from outside the door.

'The eleven o'clock,' said Claudine.

'I think I'll stay here with Mother,' said Nell.

'I think you should,' said Claudine.

They said no more until the taxi came to take Claudine to the airport. The wind was even warmer and stronger than at dawn.

'Poor Claudine – having to fly back in this strange storm.' Nell's mother had to step inside the door to shelter from the dust that had blown off the parched flower beds.

'There's nothing dangerous in a half-hour hop over the Channel!' said Nell. They both watched Claudine carry her overnight bag down the stairs. The taxi driver made his way up the path and took the bag from her.

'Where's yours?' asked her mother.

'I haven't packed it yet,' said Nell. Claudine had not looked at her as she passed her in the doorway. There was still time to apologize, thought Nell, but immediately decided that she couldn't on account of the taxi driver's presence.

'Aren't you going with her?' she heard her mother say.

'Of course not. I thought I'd stay a day or two with you.'

'I'd rather you didn't, my dear,' said her mother. 'I know you mean well but I must start practising this being alone business. I must gather my thoughts.'

Nell wanted to say, 'What about me? my husband's missing – my father's just died.' She wanted to say that she would have liked to stay a few more days in the pink room of her adolescence, but she couldn't bring herself to argue with her mother. Besides, Nell recognized that she herself was forever saying that she must gather her thoughts when she needed solitude. 'I must gather my thoughts,' she would say to fellow crew members when invited out on some unwanted trek to the Empire State building or the floating market of Bangkok. 'I must gather my thoughts,' she would say to Luc when she wanted to distance herself from his convictions and his passions. It's genetic, she mused. We are a long line of thought-gatherers, but what are these thoughts that must be so diligently and so forlornly gathered?

Claudine had not paused at the door of the taxi but had already disappeared into its darkness. When Nell's mother went to the garden gate to say goodbye, Claudine's blond head appeared above the rolled down window and she said, '*Au revoir, Nelli, au revoir, maman de Nelli.* See you soon.' And she was gone.

Nell went inside and made her mother and herself a cup of coffee. Her mother made little conversation. She was preoccupied with papers and kept saying that she would have to go into town to see about her widow's pension. She must have seen Nell's disarray for she invited her to accompany her. Nell had already called a taxi to take her to the airport where she would take the flight that departed two hours after Claudine's. She left her mother with a promise to return within the week. The two women hugged each other and wept. Nell's mother seemed suddenly to look at her daughter and feel pity for her. They parted with a promise to reunite in a few days when the older woman had gathered her thoughts.

When the taxi had pulled out of the street, Nell realized that she was far too early for her flight and risked bumping into Claudine. She leaned forward and asked the driver to make a detour past the crematorium.

There *was* a smell hanging over the lawns and the chapel and the semicircular sweep of stone where the recently dead's families could lay their wreaths and bouquets. Nell had feared that there would be but had told herself that the smell of burning flesh was unthinkable in suburban England. Yet here it was, hanging over the red rooftops and the pink roses and the blue delphiniums of the hot summer morning. It shouldn't be allowed, was Nell's first thought, then she wondered about the effect on property prices, and worried whether the children in those houses had to grow up and play enfolded in the smell of death.

The taxi driver had stopped between the chapel and the mass of flowers that remained from the previous day's funerals. Nell got out and went straight to the flowers that were laid beneath her father's name: Turner. She read each label and was gratified to see that some of the senders actually mentioned the Sainsburys' connection. 'From Jimmy Singh in memory of our conversations in the car park,' said a flamboyant bouquet of red carnations. Claudine had been right, she winced to herself. Then she found the card from Ivy. And was disappointed to see that it said: 'To dear Harry lots of love Ivy.' That was all.

A very thin young woman wearing a clerical robe came out of the chapel. Nell remembered her from the service. She remembered thinking that the woman was just some sort of auxiliary but was got up in a long ecclesiastical-looking outfit to reassure the bereaved. Nell had also thought that such skeletal thinness shouldn't be allowed at funerals. These kind of people should be robust, she thought again now. Robust and rosy, hale and hearty to stop us dwelling too long on the bony truth. This was the woman who had been asking where Nell's father's ashes should be scattered when her mother had waved them all away saying that she couldn't think about such things at such a time. Were these among the thoughts to be gathered? Now Nell had come, on an impulse, to solve the problem.

In the taxi on the way to the crematorium, her purpose had become clear to her: she would take her father's ashes and sprinkle them in the ornamental water basins in front of the Taj Mahal. Her father had dreamed of visiting the Taj and now, thanks to her, he would go. She had rummaged in her hand baggage and made room for his urn next to the French baking equipment and a leftover ball of pastry wrapped in foil that she hadn't needed. Just before she had smelled the crematorium, she had been planning to ask for a trip to Delhi. She had imagined that Luc would be freed and they would ask for the trip together and stay in the wonderful Sheraton in Agra, and visit the Taj not by moonlight but at dawn when it is pink and cool and silent in those few seconds before the millions of Indian crows wake up.

The thin woman looked like a crow, Nell thought now as she watched her scraggy form in the thick navy garment make its way towards the lawns. From where she stood, Nell could see that here and there on the grass were white crosses, made, she now recalled, from the ashes of the dead. The woman was clutching an urn and looked purposeful. Nell ran after her.

'Cuckoo!' she started to cry, then stopped herself, realizing that this was a French means of gaining attention and sounded absurd in English. She thought for a minute and switched to 'Oo-oo!' which wasn't much better but did result in the gaunt, dark figure turning around.

'I was here yesterday,' Nell puffed. 'For my father's funeral. And I've come to collect his ashes.'

'What's his name?' asked the young woman, and Nell looked at her sharp cheekbones and thought that if she got too close she would cut herself on them. Still, she was pleased to hear that father still merited the present tense.

'Turner. Er, Wilfred Turner . . . or Harry. No, Wilfred Turner. Definitely Wilfred Turner.'

'He's under the great oak by the lily pond,' said the crow.

'What do you mean he's under the great oak? Who told you to put him there?'

'Agnes Turner. A lot of people choose that tree for male deceased. Women tend to be put under willows or rose bushes.'

'Agnes Turner!' yelled Nell. 'Aunt Aggie told you!'

The vicar had come out of the chapel to greet a funeral that had just turned into the drive. He heard

155

Nell yelling, looked at his watch and ran towards the two women.

'She saw the vicar and me afterwards and said it would be best.'

All Nell's neat plans had collapsed. In that moment she decided that her aunt and this dreadful thin woman were preventing her and Luc from ever seeing the Taj at dawn. She looked desperately towards her flight bag, still sitting in the taxi with its neat space all prepared for her father's urn. She glanced at the urn that the woman was holding and for a lunatic moment debated seizing this dead stranger and taking him or her off to the Taj Mahal. Then the rage against her aunt welled up once more and she turned on the vicar who had just arrived puffing alongside his assistant.

'Since when do you take orders from any old Tom Dick or Harry who tells you where to scatter a dead man?'

'She is his sister,' said the young woman and said to the vicar: 'She's upset about where we put Mr Turner.'

'Don't call me "she"!' yelled Nell. 'I'm his daughter!'

'Would you have preferred to put him under the beech by the rose garden?' asked the vicar.

'I would have preferred to take him to the Taj Mahal!'

'Oh, I don't think they allow that.' The young woman looked enquiringly at the vicar. 'She couldn't have taken him there, could she?'

'Stop calling me "she"!' Nell repeated.

'I'm not sure. I think some of our Hindu friends do it.' He was stroking his ginger beard thoughtfully. 'At least, they take them back to India, but would Harry Turner really want to rest eternally so far —'

'He's not Harry! He's Wilfred!' Nell heard herself repeating the words of Aunt Aggie. And she saw herself lunging towards the vicar. Without any conscious thought, her fist had shot out and was aiming for his nose. A thin arm intercepted it, dropping the urn that it had been carrying onto the grass where it landed with a thud but didn't break. All three of them looked down and noted this with relief. Nell experienced another brief moment of madness when she considered snatching it up, but her arm was still thrashing out and had reached the thin woman's lank dark brown hair and was pulling it. The woman was squealing and starting to kick her. Just as the vicar began to pull them apart, Nell realized what she was doing, turned back towards the waiting taxi, half hidden now behind the hearse from the present funeral, and ran towards it. She ran faster than she had run in the last fifteen years. The driver had been staring at the coffin in the hearse and had not seen the altercation on the lawn.

'Terminal Two Heathrow!' cried Nell. 'If you make it in under an hour I'll pay you double!'

Only when she arrived in Paris two hours later did Nell dare to look at her reflection in the window of the duty free boutique. She did indeed look like a woman who had recently been in a fight. She couldn't face cleaning herself up in a public toilet and decided to get herself back to the apartment as quickly as possible. She fixed all her dreams and hopes on thoughts of a bath and the hypnotic comfort of TV. She was about to join the queue for a taxi when she remembered that with the few francs in her wallet she could only afford a bus. When she walked over to the cash machine and inserted her card, the screen informed her in four European languages that she had insufficient funds.

CHAPTER SEVENTEEN

Nell and Mort boarded the TGV for Avignon at the Gare de Lyon a few days after her return to Paris. They did not travel together. Neither of them knew that the other was travelling. Mort had handed his keys to a jubilant Mlle Marina an hour earlier. He sensed that, had she not been carrying a bucket, a mop, a packet of Spic, a bottle of *eau de javel* and a blue thing to put in the toilet tank, she might even have kissed him. He was, therefore, grateful for her fastidiousness and not in the least insulted by her apparent desire to cleanse the studio of all traces of him. He sympathized in particular with the blue thing for the toilet. Poor old Marina must be desperate to have a toilet tank after hovering for weeks over two footprints and a hole. Mort had encountered the system the previous morning after coffee in the bald Breton's café. The shock had constipated him.

Now he loaded his cabin bag into the train and bit into a big bar of Lindt milk chocolate that he'd bought to eat on the journey. He intended to get off at Avignon because he'd read in one of his guides, and in a travel piece in the *Chicago Tribune*, that Avignon hosted a festival of theatre in the summer. Mort had decided that this would be a good introduction to his vacation in the Midi.

Nell had gone straight to the bank upon her return to Paris. There she had learned that Luc had emptied their joint account of everything but a token ten francs. She had sat in front of M. Hubert, their banker, with her mouth opening and closing like a forlorn, beached fish until he had leaned forward and squeezed her hand.

'*Strange coincidence chère madame,*' he smiled. 'But perhaps these terrible terrorists have demanded the money from your husband.'

'Perhaps.'

Nell's situation was not yet desperate. She had two secret accounts – a small savings account and a current account at M. Hubert's bank. The money in her current account would tide her over until she got paid at the end of the month or Luc's mysterious predicament was clarified.

In the meantime she decided that she must go to the Languedoc. Hoping to find news of the house purchase in the post, she had gone downstairs to check the muddle of mail that had piled up during the concierge's absence. Then she had forgotten the house for an instant and found herself sorting through the letters for an early word from Jameson's. There was not one letter for her. Back in her flat she called the estate agent who had been handling their house purchase. He was on holiday; his assistant was present but evasive when Nell asked how far the whole tedious business of papers, notary publics, etc., had advanced.

Now she boarded the Avignon-bound TGV in first class. Nell knew that she should not allow herself such an extravagance but she could never resist the promise of a journey, even one undertaken in such puzzling and potentially disastrous circumstances. 'I can fly away,' still came to Nell when pain threatened and, as with the flight on Concorde, she was ashamed to find that she rejoiced at the thought of racing through the summer meadows and villages. She had chosen her seat with care – single window facing forward. In the taxi on the way to the station she had imagined herself eating an omelette of morels for lunch on a starched linen tablecloth with a red rose in a vase, all held quite still against a racing Île de France, Burgundy and Provence. To eat a meal on a vehicle that wasn't a plane had become Nell's ideal of elegant travel.

When the train was about half an hour outside Paris – it had passed the high, old, ugly apartment buildings and seemed lost in a landscape of power lines and switching centres – Nell could wait no longer and made her way up to the restaurant car. At about this time Mort finished his Lindt chocolate and rummaged in his bag for a baguette with salami that he'd bought from a passing trolley on the platform.

Nell got to the restaurant car and found that the shutter above the counter was rolled down.

'What time will it open?' she asked a passing guard.

'It won't,' the guard replied. 'There is no-one to open it.'

'What do you mean?'

'Lack of personnel,' shrugged the guard. 'There is only one person to work this car and he didn't wake up this morning.'

'Didn't wake up!' cried Nell. The guard was disappearing down the corridor. 'But this is the TGV! I hold this up as an example in England!' Before the guard closed the door on the compartment, she tugged at his sleeve. 'What do I get to eat for four hours?'

'You should have bought a sandwich.'

'I didn't know! I suppose I could go to second class. Which way is it?'

'Not on this train. You can't cross from first class to second. There is no access.'

'Then I'll get off at the next station and run up the platform,' said Nell, inwardly reminding both herself and the guard that she was a seasoned traveller and not about to be diverted from her lunch by an oversleeping railway employee.

'The next station is Avignon, madame,' sighed the guard. 'You know that.'

'So what can I eat for four hours?' cried Nell.

'Perhaps I can find you a bottle of Evian,' said the guard and was gone into a blank, blind compartment that he locked behind him.

Fifty yards along the racing, snaking train, Mort burped garlic at himself, washed it down with beer and gazed out with immense satisfaction at the dull little houses of the Île de France. A couple of hours and a couple of beers later, golden, voluptuous Burgundy seemed to stretch and stir just slightly like a contented cat as Mort and the TGV whisked past. And then came that miraculous change from north to south. The light seemed to be infused with more light, the shape of the tiles changed from flat and square to rounded, their colour changed from slate to warm reds and oranges, the trees changed from oaks and beeches to umbrella pines and cypress.

Nell had, of course, seen this transformation many, many times before, but even as she sat hungry and angry in the frozen silence of the air-conditioned first class carriage she too was drawn to the sudden wonder of the south. She stared in loving longing at the landscape, filing it away with so many others. If things ever become unbearable, I can fly away to here, she thought. Then hunger took over. She heard her stomach groan and mutter. Her head started to ache. She rummaged in her bag in the vain hope of finding one of the little gold foil-wrapped chocolates from first class or a boiled sweet from the economy galley. At the bottom of her bag she found the remaining foil-wrapped ball of pastry dough that she had brought back from her father's funeral. She hesitated to peer inside. The dough had travelled back and forth across the Channel on some of the hottest summer days she had known in Europe. For a mad moment she wondered if perhaps it would have had the good grace to cook. She might open the foil and find a huge, crusty, shortbread-like confection. Or, more likely, she would open the foil and release into the cold, polite calm a smell of rancid butter and moulding flour. But would eating a few mouthfuls of something rancid kill you? Nell wondered. Then the headmistress's voice reprimanded her, telling her that disaster was making her slovenly. Eat something rancid? Whatever next?

Nell was so hungry that for the first time in her life she ignored the voice. She dug the foil wrapping out, noting to her astonishment that it *had* changed shape. And it felt dry and crusty, not soft and doughy. My heavens, it has cooked! thought Nell and started to tear at the paper. Outside the smoked-glass windows, the heat haze of the south hung over the brush on the hills. The intense heat always arrived outside the train round about now, Nell recalled. Even in the icy air inside you could sense the pressure outside as the heat rammed up against the train like some motorcycle maniac pursuing an innocent driver on a lonely highway.

Once she had caught a big enough strip of foil between her fingers, Nell saw that the pastry had turned into three treacle tarts, each stacked neatly upon the other, their shells broken and crumbling but the form of those shells unmistakably from her mother's old baking cases. Nell stared at them with a mixture of delight and horror. Delight because in the days before the headmistress moved into her head, a treacle tart would have been the best ever food to assuage hunger. Horror because the headmistress had moved in and was always there to remind her that no matter how hurried, how hungry, how distraught she

162

was, there was no excuse for not eating *real* food, i.e. something green, fresh, low-fat, no-sugar and a good source of protein. Delight because Nell knew that her mother had done this, that here as she tried in one last frantic attempt to escape everything she had ever been her mother had put treacle tarts in her bag to be discovered on the TGV to Avignon and bring into that sleek carriage every boring, comforting Sunday of her childhood: *Round the Horn*, Sunday roast, Father, football, the *News of the World* (just for the sport, of course) and tea and treacle tarts.

But that same delight brought shame for Nell knew that these offerings had come from the funeral buffet and that she had experienced a wince of embarrassment as her mother had laid them alongside the smoked salmon and the provençal onion tarts.

Nell looked around her, sheepish and guilty, and when she saw that neither headmistress nor mother had materialized in the carriage to scold or chasten her she ducked her head and shovelled one tart after another into her mouth.

When the TGV pulled into Avignon, she was one of the first off and into a taxi to take her up to the village where both the house and the estate agent's office were located. Mort almost didn't get off. He'd dozed just as they pulled in and hadn't seen the big blue sign until a few seconds before the train departed for Marseille. He leapt off and found himself almost blown over by a hot dry wind that was whipping along the platform. Not the mistral, he thought with relief, too warm. Because he didn't have anyone to meet or anywhere specific to go, he stood on the platform in silent contemplation of the wind, frowning as he tried to remember where it was coming from and what its name could be.

As soon as he stepped out of the station, he was aware that a festival was on in town. The crowds swept him across the street and through the great gates of the

Porte de la République that led through the city walls. Mort felt the same surge of joy that he had experienced on the bus at the Place de la Concorde.

He walked and walked through Avignon. He saw that Schiller's *Don Carlos* was being performed at the Palais des Papes. Schiller, he frowned to himself, and the idea of purchasing a ticket made him feel German and earnest. He walked on and found himself in the midst of a group of Italians who talked and laughed, oblivious of him, and swept him towards a funfair at the Place de l'Horloge. Feeling vibrant and Italian, he bought himself a ticket for the carousel, left his bag with the barker and sat on a silver horse as the turrets and mansards and ramparts of Avignon bobbed and whirled before him. Hungry and dizzy, he walked on and on, aware now of the weight of his bag, until he saw an elegant French couple walking under a canopy and over a red carpet to enter the opulent dining room of an exclusive local restaurant. Deciding that he was, after all, becoming more sophisticated and French by the hour, Mort tried to follow them. His way was barred by a maître d'hôtel who muttered something about '*réception privée*' and indicated that Mort's departure should be made not on the red carpet but on the pavement that ran alongside the gutter.

Mort shrugged and kept walking until, stopping at a fountain, he took off one of his shoes and saw that his foot was bleeding. Removal of the other shoe revealed that it too had been worn to the point where the heel and the flesh over the big toe had bled into the leather. He was more concerned for the shoes than for his feet. He had not felt any pain while they had been silently bleeding into his very expensive, albeit elderly, Italian shoes. He had bought these shoes for his first interview with the network. They were beautiful, supple and wondrously, almost erotically, smooth to the touch. Both he and his feet loved them. Now he peered inside them and wondered if the blood would stain through to the outside. 'Cold water for blood stains,' he remembered his Skokie mother saying, and without hesitating further he dipped them in the fountain. The blood was new enough to wash right out and satisfied with the result, and aware now of growing soreness in his toes, he removed the shoes and put his feet in the water instead.

'Transcendence' was a word that Mort recalled from the Sixties. It had once belonged to beads and beards and slightly vacant expressions but as his feet were enclosed by the water from the fountain Mort knew that he had found its true meaning.

He had closed his eyes and was about to drift off into a delicious brief sleep when he heard a woman's voice next to him. He looked up and saw long, rich black hair, a tight red T-shirt, eyes that looked velvet brown against their clear, creamy whites.

'Good?' said the young woman, looking at his feet in the fountain.

'Good,' confirmed Mort.

The young woman hitched up her skirt, swung a pair of brown knees over and plunged her feet in the water alongside him. Only when those knees were once again concealed under the many yards of frilly black cotton in the skirt did Mort notice that a younger woman with even darker eyes was sitting on the other side of him.

'Sister.' She smiled and held out her hand for Mort to shake.

Spanish? Mort asked himself. Italian? Hungarian? Oh, he felt so European, he hardly recognized himself. As he stared at his large naked feet between the two pairs of smaller naked feet that enclosed them, for a few wonderful seconds he believed that from now on he would speak several languages, cook elegant dishes with incomprehensible names, understand wine, shun

165

shopping malls and freezer counters, buy his vegetables in a market place, lose all interest in network television and appreciate Pasolini's films.

Wonderful, miraculous, beloved Europe, thought Mort. And as he made the sort of stumbling, dull conversation that he always found himself making with people of another language, Europe and all her splendours paraded through his brain. His brain seemed particularly fond of Jeanne Moreau, who paraded a lot and in ever skimpier outfits. Occasionally it alighted on second-hand bookstores, a cathedral or two, and lots of red-tiled rooftops.

'I'm a dancer,' said the older sister, pointing to her legs. Mort realized that he had been staring at them. 'She's a dancer.' She pointed to her sister.

'A dancer,' said Mort dreamily, still lost in so many thoughts. He thought of his happy dancing sessions in the courtyard. 'I dance.'

'Musicals? *West Side Story?* Broadway?' asked the woman.

'Oh no!' said Mort. 'Not me! I'm an amateur.'

'You from Chicago – bang bang!' the little sister was saying.

'Yeah. Bang bang,' said Mort, and turned his attention back to the older sister. 'Are there any good places to go dancing around here?' The woman shrugged. 'Maybe you don't like to dance on your day off,' Mort mumbled. 'You know any good places to eat around here then?' He was still at a point in his travels where he could afford one of the better restaurants. Perhaps he could take them both to dinner and then, perhaps, take them both to bed. At the same time. Hmmm, thought Mort. Suddenly all the anxiety he had experienced in front of the lingerie shop window evaporated. From the realization two days earlier that he had no ongoing sexual fantasy figure, he now found himself in this sensuous southern town with two

166

potentially compliant young women on either side of him. They had approached him, after all. The blonde memories of Austin were beginning to seem pretty tame.

'We must eat with our grandmother tonight,' said the older sister. The image of these brown, voluptuous young women eating a dutiful meal in a house that smelled of lavender with an old woman in black, and a grandfather clock tick, tick, ticking through the silence, made Mort desire them even more.

'Can I buy you both a drink?' he said. The older sister had moved closer to him. Now she reached forward and placed her brown hand over his.

'Grandmother lives outside the walls,' she said, as if this explained everything.

'Tomorrow then?' said Mort.

'OK.' She shrugged.

'Here, same time?' This is too easy, Mort thought to himself.

'OK.' She shrugged again. Then she kissed him on each cheek and was gone.

Something in Mort's head had told him that things had gone very quiet on the other side of his feet. And when he turned to bid farewell to the younger sister, he saw that she had disappeared. Then, of course, he saw that his bag had disappeared. A quick pat in his pocket showed that his wallet had disappeared. And a glance at the cobbles in front of the fountain revealed that his shoes had disappeared.

Nell had almost fainted when the taxi driver had announced the fare from Avignon station to the estate agent's office in Bagnols-sur-Cèze. He had seemed such a nice man until that moment, Nell thought. They had talked about gardening and mushrooming. He had said he envied her the English climate for all the flowers she could grow. She had reciprocated by declaring her envy for the sudden second flowering of a Provence autumn and the wealth of mushrooms and fruits to be found in the forests. Now he was waiting for a few hundred francs. Nell looked at the meter and realized that she had never had to take a taxi alone to this house before. Luc had almost always driven them in the Citroën. And once when they had come from the station, Luc had settled the cab fare in that brisk almost conspiratorial way that most men seemed to have. No fumbling in handbags, no rummaging for change, none of the smothering panic that overcame Nell now.

She paid the man, noting with relief that her wallet contained dollars from the American trip and yen from Tokyo that could be exchanged to pay for a bus ride back to Avignon. As the cab drove away, she saw that the estate agent's office was closed for lunch.

'If it's not sodding *vacances* it's sodding bloody *déjeuner*.' Nell said this out loud because the street at this sacred lunch hour was deserted. She decided that instead of waiting until the estate agent returned at perhaps four, or even five, she would look in every bar and brasserie until she found him. Nell had brought the small cabin bag on rollers that she used for round trips to New York or short-haul journeys in Europe. She pulled out its handle and rolled it across the cobbles. The clatter echoed through the empty street. A waiter in a nearby café stopped to stare out at the source of the noise. Nell wheeled her case past him and into the café where a brief glance at the clientele told her that her chic, elegant estate agent would never eat here. She rattled back out again, tried the brasserie on the corner, a pizzeria in an alleyway, and finally found M. Bosquet, the estate agent, in a small, silent restaurant in the street behind his office. He was about to slide a forkful of ratatouille into his mouth when he saw Nell, let it slide back to the plate and gazed at her with what seemed to be great sorrow.

He rose, pulled out a chair, shook Nell's hand and offered her a pastis which she accepted.

'You must be so worried,' he said and nodded in the direction of a small television on the bar, as if to indicate that this was now the source of Luc and all the worry that currently went with him.

'I am,' said Nell. 'But I believe in his return. I believe that within a matter of weeks he will be here with me.' Nell was amazed to hear herself make such a statement but she went on. 'That's why I want to go ahead with the house purchase – I can then take care of the move and Luc will have his refuge in the Languedoc waiting for him when he returns.'

The great sorrow returned to M. Bosquet.

An hour later, Nell finished a second pastis, refused his umpteenth offer to buy her some lunch and wheeled her bag out of the restaurant towards the bus stop.

M. Bosquet had offered to interrupt his lunch and return with her to his office in order to show her the fax that Luc had sent him more than three weeks earlier. Nell had said this wouldn't be necessary. If M. Bosquet said that Luc had decided not to buy the house, why should she not believe him? A glance in the window of his office confirmed that he had not been made a better offer. There was the house, her house, being offered for sale again.

The loss of the house was too great for Nell to comprehend so she fixed all her attention on the loss of the deposit instead. When she had broached the subject of the deposit with M. Bosquet, he had become brisker and less sorrowful.

'What would be the point of leaving a deposit if you were sure of recovering it, madame?' he had asked. The thought of all that money spent on nothing strengthened Nell's resolve to take the bus back to town. She found a machine that exchanged foreign bank notes near the shuttered tourist office. After parting with a lot of yen and several ten-dollar notes, she just had time to board the Avignon bus.

Once at the Avignon bus station, Nell decided that it was too late to return to Paris. She would book into a small hotel and set about the familiar business of 'gathering her thoughts'. The headmistress was back at her desk inside Nell's head and seemed to be of the opinion that Nell should suffer for this latest mishap. Thus Nell ignored the pleasant-looking two-star hotel on a quiet side street, telling herself it would be full because of the festival, and booked into a depressing one-star hotel on a noisy corner outside the city walls.

The hotel did have a small courtyard with a pink oleander spreading its blooms up to the rooms which were all situated on a balcony that wrapped itself around the first floor.

Poisonous, thought Nell as she dragged her bag, step by rattling step, past the tree's branches to her room. Only when she was inside and the door had slammed on her did she realize that it had no windows. The door onto the balcony served as the only source of light and air. If Nell wanted either, she would have to gather her thoughts with the door wide open. She closed it, turned on the forty-watt light bulb next to the bed and started to make a list of what she must now do to hold on to that raft of her life that seemed to have floated even further from the shore.

'1: Ask for more hours at work,' she wrote. '2: Learn another language—' A mosquito bit her eyelid. Nell jerked back, startled at its impertinence. She banged her head on the wall. I need television, thought Nell. Whenever flight delays had made her wonder if she would ever see her home again, when the earth had trembled in Tokyo and a thin crack had appeared in her hotel wall, even when she had found a two-foot-

170

long iguana in her bathroom in Cayenne, Nell had always turned to the TV for solace. There was no television in her room. She opened the door, stepping onto the communal balcony, looked past the languorous pink blossoms into the small hotel lounge and saw that there was no television there. She was about to return in despair to her list when something inside her rose up and punched her resident headmistress in the mouth, just as something outside her had tried to punch the vicar a few days earlier.

She folded up the paper and walked out into the warm wind that blew through the Avignon twilight. Nell knew Avignon well. She and Luc had a favourite restaurant in an alleyway just beyond the ramparts. She entered the city through the Porte de la Republique and made her way towards it. But when she got there the waiter winced when she said *'Pour une personne,* and said, *'On est festival, madame.'*

So much for revolution, thought Nell, and decided that a compromise was in order. She would make her list – she could not ignore the collapse of most of her life – but she would do it near the Palais des Papes so that she could enjoy the festive atmosphere of the evening and feel a part of the crowds headed out to the theatre.

She bought a slice of pizza, sat down on a low wall and started to write. '1: Ask for more hours at work. 2: Learn another language and qualify for language supplement. (Nell wrote "Portuguese" to herself and wondered why.) 3: Transfer money from savings account. 4: Keep an eye on Mum to ensure that she is coping. 5: Do something about Claudine. 6: Do something about Luc.'

She scratched this last item off the list. What was there to do about Luc? There was nothing she could do about Luc. Luc had betrayed her. Yet somehow she wasn't surprised. It is my fault for pretending to love

171

him when I didn't, she thought. It has all caught up with me now.

She put the list away, stood up and went to select a postcard from a nearby rack. She picked one that showed the famous half bridge.

CHAPTER EIGHTEEN

The advantage of being so seductively mugged, Mort concluded, was that he no longer had to lug his bag around Avignon. And the cobbles still held the heat of the day and were warm and smooth under his bare feet. He still had his train ticket and a couple of thousand francs in cash. He had lost two credit cards, his traveller's cheques and, of course, the contents of his bag and his shoes. He tried to remember just what he'd packed in his bag and could only think of one frayed pair of boxer shorts that he'd been intending to throw away for years. He hated the idea of that beautiful woman thinking that he, Mort, wore underwear like that. Of course he, Mort, did wear underwear like that but he'd been intending to do something about it, he wanted to tell the brunette with the smooth brown knees.

Mort knew that he should go to the police and report his loss but he couldn't face explaining his foolishness in a vocabulary of less than a hundred words. He wandered through the crowds, thought with relief that he could no longer afford a ticket to Schiller, and at almost ten p.m. found himself at the train station where the ticket clerk glared at him through the flexi-glass with the microphone in it and said if he wanted to go to Paris, he'd have to take 'l'omnibus'.

Mort wandered back out of the station and looked in vain for this bus. When he failed to find it, he sat down on the kerb and looked up at the night clouds. There was a storm heading this way, he decided, and felt relieved to be down in the officially hot end of the country, where the weather still behaved with a comforting predictability. 'See,' he wanted to say to Peg and Frank and even Primrose if she was listening, 'I'm not feckless. I'm a mature concerned citizen.' He felt the first fat drop of rain on his toes, looked down at his bare feet and went in search of the omnibus.

The station surroundings were full of adolescents. They drove up on noisy scooters, gathered in flocks, chattered and dispersed. In darker corners, some of them were dealing drugs, Mort now noticed. In other corners lone shabbily dressed men were huddling down to sleep out of the rain under jutting gutters. Cigarette packets and McDonald's wrappers blew across the pavements. The gates to the city which were just across the road seemed a long way away now.

Mort turned and went back inside the station. Now that he'd seen the crowd outside, he decided that the clerk had taken a dislike to him and tried to get him on an omnibus because of his bare feet. He decided to try a new tactic and ensure that his feet wouldn't be seen by approaching the ticket office from the side, like a crab.

This time a different clerk also told him that he'd have to take the omnibus.

'But I can't find the goddamned omnibus!' yelled Mort, wondering what could possibly be wrong with his torso. 'There has to be a train that goes at some time! I'll wait all night if I have to.'

'*L'omnibus* is a train,' said the clerk. 'It stops everywhere.'

'Oh, you mean like a milk train!' said Mort. 'Train au lait?'

174

The clerk raised his eyes to the ceiling. 'Platform three,' he said.

The train did stop everywhere. But it was a nice, old-fashioned train with threadbare, cushiony dark velvet seats that seemed to welcome Mort's bare feet. He had bought a baguette with camembert at the station and by the time they had reached Vienne he had wrapped the bag from the sandwich around his feet and was sleeping peacefully.

Only when the train pulled alongside the high, huddled, dirty cream stone buildings of central Paris did Mort suddenly feel guilty about Mlle Marina.

When he got to the courtyard, he saw that she had set a bunch of pink roses in front of his now spotless windows. He looked at his watch: six a.m. For the first time in months the poor creature would be sleeping off her working night with no interference from the other one. Mort sat down under the lone plane tree. He stared up at Marina's window and wondered how long she would sleep, and what he would say to her when she woke. After a while he took off his jacket and his plaid shirt and put them under his head. Then he stretched out on the scrubby patch of grass and fell into a deep slumber.

Somewhere in his sleep, a beautiful blonde peered down at him, wrinkled a perfectly shaped nose and walked away. Part of Mort thought that another part of Mort was dreaming of his days in Austin. That same part of Mort thought that it was his standard youthful remembrance dream of floating on the Austin pool and being reeled in by the beautiful blonde from the University of Texas. Then Mort realized that all of him was wide awake and had been staring up at the sky for several seconds at least. By the time he realized that he had stared wordlessly up at the blonde, she was gone.

He sat up, pulled his jacket on and raced up the stairs to his apartment, ripping the jacket back off as he climbed. It was ten a.m. and the city was already sweltering. He frowned into dark, silent corridors and even stopped once to look inside one of the landing doors that hid a two footprint and a hole toilet. The blonde was nowhere to be found but Mlle Marina was waiting for him on the landing in front of his flat.

'I see you downstairs,' she said. 'Sleeping in public!' She seemed to be barring the way to his flat. He decided not to try to pass her.

'Did a blonde woman come up here?' he asked.

'No,' said Marina. 'What are you doing here?'

'I was robbed.'

'Oh,' said Marina and softened and invited him into his apartment. 'I've been robbed in the Bois.'

'You have? Yes, I guess you would be.'

'Forty, maybe fifty times, I've been beat up and my money taken. Now I just give them the money so I don't get hit but they still do it sometimes.'

'You shouldn't carry cash,' said Mort, sitting at the table by the flowers and surveying the empty courtyard.

'What do you want me to do?' cried Marina.

'Oh yeah, right. I guess I wasn't thinking,' said Mort, whose attention was on his single Paris drawing, which Marina had unrolled and propped up on the table by the window. He hadn't dared to look at it before. Even now he averted his gaze as he turned to Marina.

'What do you think of it?'

Marina shrugged. 'It's OK.'

'You do recognize it?'

'It's one of those cheap motels you get out on the highway.'

'No it's not! It's here! It's downstairs – the view from this window!' Now Mort did turn to look at his efforts and saw that an uninformed viewer would indeed see a rectangular building overlooking a rectangular space.

He had tried to concentrate on the corner of the courtyard that was bordered by the baker's low shed-like
kitchen. In his amateurish hands, the structure resembled a million low cube-like discount warehouses,
cocktail lounges, liquor stores and motels that lined
the highways of his homeland. 'But what about the
cobbles? Cobbles are European! Didn't that give you a
clue?' Mort was proud of the cobbles. He loved the idea
of them, had worked hard on them and was sure he'd
succeeded.

'Look like water,' said Marina. 'I thought it was one
of those dirty swimming pools you get with motels.'

'They don't look anything like water!' Mort squinted
at his drawing and saw that the cobbles looked very
much like waves, and the statue that he had sketched
in the corner looked more like a high school cheer-
leader emerging from an afternoon dip. 'Oh, what do
you know anyway? What qualifies you to talk about a
drawing?'

'I have an eye!' cried Marina and pointed to her left
eye which still bore the traces of the previous night's
make-up. 'How would I paint myself the way I do
every day if I did not have an eye?'

'Forget it,' said Mort, who suspected that Marina was
right. He folded the drawing and tucked it into his
pocket. Marina patted him on the shoulder.

'You wanna coffee?'

Marina made the coffee in silence. She had brought
a percolator and fresh beans that seemed to need grind-
ing. She had also supplied a machine for this. Making
the coffee seemed to require all her concentration.
Mort decided that this was on account of her being
Brazilian. 'They've got an awful lot of coffee in Brazil,'
bounded into his brain and he found himself trying to
remember the words and tapping his feet to a rhythm
that only he heard. 'A politician's daughter was
accused of drinking water, and was fined a great big

177

fifty-dollar bill . . .' Those were the words, thought Mort with relief, but it couldn't be fifty dollars . . . that's not much at all. Inflation maybe? It was an old song.

Outside in the courtyard he thought he saw a glimmer of blond hair, then when he squinted to bring it into focus he saw only the tree, the patch of grass and the plumbago. That thing really had grown, he now saw.

'I put my own miracle mix on it,' said Mlle Marina, setting down two cups of coffee and staring out into the courtyard with him.

'Maybe, but I've only been gone a day. It wouldn't grow up like that. It's not the Little Shop of Horrors down there – well, maybe the baker's is—'

'I've been doing it since I come here,' said Marina. 'Who is this blonde you're looking for?'

'I don't know,' sighed Mort. 'I mean, I thought I saw her but I think I was dreaming.'

'That happens to me a lot,' said Marina. Mort didn't like to ask what kind of dreams hers were or who or what she longed for.

'Great coffee,' he said instead and meant it.

'I forgot the croissants,' said Marina and handed him a warm croissant that she had heated efficiently on the hotplate.

'This is delicious,' said Mort. 'How come you got such good croissants? They even look different from what that one-eyed woman gave me.'

'Everyone knows you don't buy no croissants or bread down there,' said Marina. 'I pick these up just across from the Bois on my way home.'

'Well, they're real good—' Before Mort could go on, Marina had grabbed his hand. He was surprised at how smooth and warm her hand felt and how good it felt to have his own rather grimy hand held by someone – even poor confused Marina. This could go no further, of course, but for the few seconds it lasted he resolved to enjoy it. He smiled stupidly across the table at her.

'OK then!' For the first time since he'd known her, Marina was shouting. 'What do we do now?'

'Us?' Mort cried back. 'Nothing,' he said with conviction. 'It's out of the question. Not a thing. Nothing.'

'So I gotta go back up there with her!' Marina was shouting even louder and pointing to the ceiling and the flat above. 'I got to go and try to sleep with her cigarette smoke and her getting mad and throwing things!' Mort looked out of the window, anxious that the blonde might hear this astonishing scene. 'I'm real sorry you got robbed, Senhor Mort, but I got to think about me! I cleaned this place for hours yesterday and all so you could come back and mess up and I go back up with her?'

Mort had now understood that her question involved her future in the flat as opposed to her future with him. He tried to interrupt but Marina pulled her seat closer to his, clasped her hands on the table and looked hard at him.

'You know what I never understand about this life?' She obviously wanted a response.

'I never understood much at all,' said Mort.

'What I don't understand is this,' Marina drew in her breath. 'I'm from Brazil, right?'

'Right,' said Mort.

'OK – now I'm walking by the Eiffel Tower maybe or the Notre Dame and I stop to buy an ice cream, OK?'

'OK,' said Mort.

'Now someone hears me say "*glace au chocolat*" maybe, OK?'

'OK,' said Mort, fearing that the blonde would have left the building, met another man, raised children and sent them off to Harvard before Marina made her point.

'OK, so I'm saying "*glace au chocolat s'il vous plaît*" and some woman next to me hears me, OK?'

179

'Yeah,' said Mort.

'And she hears that I'm from Brazil, 'cos like I've got a little bit of an accent, right?'

Mort smiled. He sensed that this discourse was about to round a corner and reveal the summit that it had been climbing towards in all its shining glory.

'Now she knows I'm from Brazil, 'cos she's from Brazil, so she comes and talks to me. Now maybe she's OK but maybe she's not. Maybe she's stupid, or boring, or maybe her clothes are not as clean as she wants me to think they are, right?'

'Yeah.'

'So why do I got to like her 'cos she's from Brazil and I'm from Brazil?'

'Oh, you don't,' said Mort. 'No way you don't.'

'Yes I do! Oh yes I do!' cried Marina. 'You Jewish, right?'

'Right,' said Mort, wondering how she'd known.

'Then you got to like other Jews . . . but why?'

'Well, I don't really have to. In fact in Skokie I hated Jeff Goldblatt who ran the Ford concession, but then, well, Jews are different—'

Marina wasn't listening. 'What I got to know then is why I got to like Sofia. OK, she has the same "*confusâo*" as me. You don't understand it. She don't understand it. I don't understand it. Doctors don't understand it. But why do I got to like her?'

The blonde was in the courtyard. Mort didn't even have to squint to see that she was real and beautiful and looking up at a window at the other building. She picked up a pebble and threw it against a shutter. When there was no response, she sat down on a step with her long legs stretched out in the sunlight that now filled the courtyard.

'I hate Sofia,' Marina was saying. 'I only like about four of the girls at the Bois. Why do I got to like them because we got one little problem that's the same?'

'Oh, you don't!' said Mort, rising and heading towards the door. Now he knew why he'd been brought back by fate from the Midi. Here she was. He hadn't dreamed her.

'But I don't want to go back and live with her,' Marina was crying.

'Then don't!' cried Mort. He was off to live with the blonde. They would have one of those penthouses he'd glimpsed on his walks along the Seine. Cathedral windows opening onto the rooftops, *bateaux mouches* floating past the living room, Notre-Dame visible when you sat on the john.

As he reached the ground floor and was about to step from shadow to sunlight, a pulsating, sinuous samba song issued from Mlle Sofia's window. Mort almost responded to his natural reflexes by breaking into his conga step but he pulled himself up just in time and, looking almost too dignified for a man with bare feet, walked towards the blonde.

CHAPTER NINETEEN

Nell took the first TGV out of Avignon the next morning. The restaurant car was open this time. A familiar voice told Nell that in her current uncertain situation she should save money. Nell told the voice that she'd saved money yesterday when she sat for four hours with nothing but the scenery for sustenance. As she ate her brioche and drank her coffee, Nell didn't fulfil her dream of gazing out at the passing countryside. She did her accounts. By the time she got to Paris, she had cobbled together enough money to pay off several outstanding bills and still have enough to live on until her pay cheque arrived.

She went straight from the Gare de Lyon to the crew building at Roissy. She wanted to put in her overtime request immediately and she also wanted to arrive at the building at a time when most of the returning long-haul crews had gone on to their homes and the departing crews had not yet left them. Nell didn't want sympathy or concern. All those emotions felt messy and chaotic. She wanted her life to be a clean straight line, like Concorde taking off at dawn, she thought, and slipped behind a filing cabinet as the purser from the last New York flight walked towards her.

The second floor of the crew building was taken up by row upon row of red and yellow plastic stackable mail trays. They formed a labyrinth of primary colours on the green industrial carpet. There was a mail tray for every employee, and company rules demanded that every employee empty that mail tray upon departure and return from a trip. The mail tray was the company's only way of keeping in touch with such a nomadic population. The trays were intended to receive payslips, schedules, schedule changes, and summonses to sector offices when an offence had been committed. They were also depositories for notes from passing colleagues. Over the years Nell had found recipes, gossip, invitations to dinner parties and once, at the very beginning of their relationship, a surly declaration of love from Luc, written on the notepaper of the Meridien in Rio and stuffed between a schedule change and her payslip.

Nell always approached her mail tray with dread. Life could suddenly be altered by a note from scheduling that said: 'Cancel OSA replace with JFK and IAH.' And she'd have to transform the landscape that she'd thought lay ahead of her from Japanese pagodas and stone zen gardens to Manhattan and the tangle of highways around the hotel in Houston.

The brief walk to the mail tray also involved the risk of bumping into a colleague Nell hadn't seen for years – somebody she had fallen out with over the order of meal service on a Nairobi or fallen secretly in love with over the North Pole. A decade on, this familiar stranger would walk along the corridor by the mail tray and Nell would struggle to remember just what the emotion had been.

Nell had to make her way past the mail trays of the North and South American sectors, the Indian Ocean and Africa, the Middle East and Europe, and only reached her sector, Asia, at the end of a long corridor. This late morning the corridor was empty but Nell's mail tray was full. Somebody from the sector had taped a note in front of it saying that more mail was being kept for safety in the sector office. Nell pulled the bundle of notes out and saw that they came from dozens of those strangers whom she was so assiduously avoiding. There were notes from stewardesses who had flown with her in the days when the narrow 707s crossed the planet; there were notes from pilots who recalled snorkelling in Tahiti or shopping in Bangkok; there were cards purchased in Los Angeles or London or wherever the sender had been when the news of Luc's disappearance had been announced. All of them sent warm thoughts, '*bisous*' (only the French would send little kisses at such a time, Nell thought to herself) and offers of dinners, weekends in the country, anything she might need.

'You have come for your letters, *ma pauvre Nelli*?' said the head of the sector when Nell appeared in the doorway. He was a small, fussily neat man whose steel-grey hair was plastered unpleasantly down over the left side of his forehead.

'Sit, sit.' He indicated a chair and as Nell sat down he reached in a drawer and pulled out a large bundle of mail.

'And this does not include our own most sincere thoughts here at the sector.' He smiled. Nell didn't smile back. She had last flown with this man on her yearly check flight when he had said in his report that her waist was too thick and that she had signally failed to serve peanuts with the aperitif on both the outward and return New York flights. Nell had written an angry letter stating that peanuts had not been available on that flight; the sector had replied that peanuts were always available. Nell had continued to write letters insisting that there hadn't been a peanut on board that particular day in May, until Claudine had told her to shut up about peanuts and forget the whole affair.

Nell hadn't been able to tell Claudine that her letters had really not been about peanuts at all. The slick man who sat so sympathetically in front of her now had not intended her to see the report and had added a post-script saying that, while of course the company did not want to follow American examples and penalize employees upon whose silhouettes the passing of the years and the bearing of children had had a negative effect, he just felt that it would be prudent to mention the excess weight to Mme Marchand before it was too late – petite women could not hope to get away with too many extra pounds.

Nell had read that report upside down when it had been on this desk after the check flight. Then she had locked herself in the toilets on the second floor and cried until two colleagues came in and started to discuss the problems of finding someone to mind their children when they worked the longer flights. 'The bearing of children' was everywhere that day, it seemed to Nell, and was something to be understood and encouraged. She'd put on her sunglasses, slipped past the two women and made her way back to Chantilly where she had stood naked and alone in front of a bathroom mirror and flushed with shame at the body she now inhabited. The headmistress inside her head forbade any further tears and advised a diet. Nell had denied herself everything she enjoyed and for a while the waistline had retreated.

The cause of all this distress hardly seemed to remember her as he sat in front of the wide glass window and planes taxied along the runway and took off behind his head.

'I've come about my flight schedule,' said Nell.

'Oh, don't worry about that,' said the supervisor. 'It's all been taken care of. The sector has put you on paid leave until your husband is safely back amongst us.'

'Oh, but I don't want . . .' Nell hesitated. 'What kind

of paid leave? Basic salary? What about flight allowances? Expenses?'

'Let us not exaggerate.' The man smiled. 'We'll take an average of your pay over the past year—'

'It's not enough!' Years of duty free sales in several currencies had made Nell swift at mental arithmetic.

'But madame, your husband is a captain.'

Nell could have retorted that this was a personal and insolent remark but she was too ashamed of all that lay behind those five words: 'Your husband is a captain – and alongside his salary your pay amounts to peanuts.' 'Your husband is a captain and most captain's wives would rather stay in their beautiful homes with their beautiful children than work in our wretched planes.' 'Your husband is a captain and yet you choose to fly on long-haul flights that must inevitably separate the two of you.'

'Unexpected expenses,' muttered Nell and lied: 'Luc's children.' Then she remembered that this man's wife had left him because he was never at home and she knew what to say: 'Look, Monsieur Duchamp, I can't stay at home and wait. I need to be busy. I need my planes to take my mind off this.'

'I can understand that,' smiled the supervisor. 'But don't overestimate your ability to cope with this crisis, dear Nelli.'

'I need to fly,' said Nell, 'as many flights as possible. Oh, and I'll be adding Portuguese to my languages in a month or two so I'll take any Rios or Recifes that are going.'

'Not too fast!' smiled M. Duchamp. 'I'm willing to bet that within the week Luc will be back and you'll be expecting a long leave to spend time with him. The sector will, of course, be happy to accord paid leave in the circumstances.'

'But until he is,' said Nell, 'I need to fly.'

M. Duchamp tapped a few instructions into his

computer and motioned to Nell to examine the screen with him.

'It may not be too easy, *chère madame*,' he said. 'As you can see, scheduling has already cleared your month. We acted as soon as the terrible news came through.'

'I'm sure you can fill it back up again,' said Nell. 'We all know this company is understaffed, and everyone else is flying more hours than there are in a day. Can't you give me some of them?'

'I could put you on reserve?' He raised an eyebrow at her, sure that she would refuse. Everybody hated reserve. In the rooms below them waited two or three dozen crew members, suitcases packed for a day and for three weeks, clothes inside them suitable for Anchorage or Addis Ababa. Some of them slept, some of them gossiped, waiting for the phone on the doorman's desk to ring and an anonymous voice from scheduling to give them an hour in which to leave for any one of a hundred destinations on the airline network.

'Then put me on reserve, please,' said Nell.

M. Duchamp frowned at the computer. 'I can put you on reserve at home. That way if any news on Luc comes through—'

'Perfect,' said Nell, and, forgetting to shake his hand, nodded her goodbyes. Clutching her unwieldy bundle of letters, she slipped away down the corridor.

The bus into Paris got stuck in traffic just outside Terminal One. Nell sat in the back row and watched the planes line up on the runway with so much love that she forgot about the time and the letters on her lap and let them drop to the floor. Nell looked with love at the unwieldy 747s as they took their first lumbering steps along the runway, straining and struggling to leave the earth, suddenly to become as light as the clouds they entered. She looked with love and awe at the sleek six o'clock Concorde as it followed them into the heavens. Boeings, airbuses, planes that still had propellers, planes with two engines, planes with four, planes that were bound for mysterious kingdoms that few could enter, planes that belonged to oil millionaires, dictators, film moguls and tyrants. One after another they raced along the skid-marked runway and pointed their noses to the heavens and were gone.

'I can fly away,' Nell repeated to herself again and again, until she dozed and woke when the bus pulled up at the Arc de Triomphe. Nell had stepped off the bus and was looking for a taxi when the driver came up to her with the bundle of letters that she had left lying on the floor.

CHAPTER TWENTY

The blonde was gone when Mort reached the courtyard. He decided to pursue her up the stairs of the more elegant building upon whose steps she had so recently alighted. He found his way blocked by an electronic panel of buttons and an impenetrable double oak door. He was rattling a brass lion's head handle in vain when the winking woman from the baker's came out of the door, leaving him the opportunity to slip into the building behind her.

'Eh!' cried the woman and for a second Mort found himself staring into the watery blue eye on the other side of the entrance. He expected resistance or some small protest but after her first squeak of surprise the woman seemed to lose interest in him and went on her way across the marble flooring and out through the door to the street.

Mort was inside. He was tempted to study the names on the doors and find out who the invisible residents of this elegant Parisian apartment block were. But he was in too much of a rush to find the blonde. There was an elevator on this side of the courtyard. Mort recalled countless Hollywood films where a combination of elevators and stairs had led to lost villains, lost lives and lost loves. Trying to remember what Cary Grant would have done in his place, Mort opted for the stairs, pausing at each landing to listen for the whoosh of elevator doors opening and delivering his blonde out to him.

When he reached the floor that faced his own, the floor where the blonde had been throwing pebbles, he found a note pinned to an apartment door.

'*Bonjour, ma grande,*' it said. '*J'étais dans le coin. A bientôt, je t'embrasse très fort, Claudine.*'

Claudine, so that was her name. Mort liked that name but what the hell did the note say?

He took it to the window and read it again in the light as if sunshine would translate those baffling French words for him. After several long minutes of scowling in silence at the piece of paper, Mort translated the message as: 'Hello, big boy. I was in the corner. I embrace you very strongly, Claudine.'

A dejected Mort stared out of the window, wondered who the lucky French big boy was, and realized that he'd left his plaid shirt and his empty sandwich bag on the patch of grass under the plane tree. Mlle Marina wouldn't like that, he thought, and looked up to the windows of his apartment. Marina was staring back at him. She must have been watching him as he read the letter. He wondered whether he'd unwittingly picked his nose or scratched his crotch in front of her. Before he could wave or dismiss the embarrassing moment with a banal, friendly gesture, she disappeared back into the darkness of his small room.

Mort pinned the note back into its place on the door. He stared out at his shirt, then made a sudden decision and raced down the stairs, gathered it and the bag up and climbed the other stairs to his apartment door.

When Marina opened it, he saw that she had been crying, and that all her belongings were gathered in a box by the door.

'Oh, stop it!' Mort said, and walked in past her. As proof of his intentions, he took the coffee percolator off

190

the top of the box and returned it to its place on the stove.

Marina had gone over to the window, where she stood gazing down at the plumbago and sniffing.

'Make me another coffee, Marina,' said Mort.

'I don't want to go back up there with her,' said Marina. 'I never had my own place before. In Rio, I shared with five people. I thought you were gone for the month.'

'So did I,' sighed Mort. 'Look . . . don't panic, Marina, we can come to some kind of arrangement—'

'I'll sleep in the cupboard,' said Marina.

'You won't need to, I don't think,' said Mort. 'I left my sleeping bag here. I can stretch out in that and you can have the bed when you come back from . . . when you come back from . . . from work. Half the night's over by then so you won't be disturbing me.'

'Oh no, no I cannot do that,' said Marina and folded her arms over her kimono.

'But I said it's OK.'

'No.' Marina walked to the door and picked up her box.

Mort took it off her and set it down. 'You can stay here because – well, I didn't want to go into this, but I think I've found somewhere else to stay.'

'You do? Where?'

Mort stared out of the window and down at the plane tree below.

'I can't say for the moment but why don't you stay here until it's all worked out?'

On the floor above them Sofia put on a collection of Brazilian songs. Marina put her box down and put the coffee on. While Mort sat on the couch and sorted through his suitcase for a pair of comfortable shoes, Marina made them coffee and sang along with the music in a husky contralto.

Nell heard Marina's singing as she tapped the code

191

that would let her into her apartment building. She found Claudine's note on the door. She too walked into the sunlight to read it and found to her surprise that she was crying with relief and embarrassment. She put the note on top of the stack of letters and walked into the hall. The heat that had collected in the closed-up flat during her absence almost pushed her back onto the landing. This was going to be the hottest day of the year, she now knew. She threw back the shutters in the living room and opened the windows. There was no welcome rush of cool air. The heat outside was equal to the heat within. Nell stretched her arm out over the cobbles, hoping that even the warm wind that had danced through her father's funeral had come to France, but nothing moved.

Then her attention was drawn to the singing woman across the courtyard.

How could she sing? Nell wondered. The heat was so intense that Nell felt it would be folly even to put a radio on. Sound waves would make the room hotter, she was sure. She just wanted to sit very still and wait for the phone to ring and send her off to Anchorage or somewhere in the southern hemisphere where blessed winter reigned.

Nell continued to stare into the apartment across the courtyard. The singing woman was pouring coffee into two cups on a table by the window. And behind her a man was dancing back and forth waving a sneaker in each hand. Nell recognized him as the American. He had a wife, she now saw. And a wife who sang in very fluent Portuguese. Nell sat down and remained very still, but her mind was spinning. Here was her Portuguese teacher, she told herself. Here was her chance to add a language, change sectors and earn quite a lot more money. All of this had been delivered up to her just at the time when she most needed it. But instead of feeling that life, in its usual convoluted way,

192

was helping her towards a solution to her problems, Nell could feel nothing but anger and envy for the feckless couple across the courtyard.

Mort had forgotten that he'd packed his sneakers and had been jubilant to find them and a clean pair of socks at the bottom of the large suitcase that he had left in Marina's charge. As soon as he had something on his feet, he headed out of the flat, telling Marina that he had to exchange some money but admitting to himself that he now felt like an intruder in Marina's home.

Once he'd stepped off the marble floor and through the door of the main building, Mort knew that any movements he made in Paris that day would be restricted to those stretches of the pavements that offered shade. Glancing up and down the street, Mort realized that this wouldn't be easy. So much for tree-lined Paris streets. He saw now that his old neighbourhood on the near north side of Chicago was cooler and shadier and greener than all this stone – all this elegant, refined, sweltering stone. He longed for a quiet line of brown brick houses, cool, dark patches of impatiens wastefully watered hour after hour and the blue promise of Lake Michigan at the end of the street.

He skirted the north side of the pavement but was forced out into the sun at the Esplanade des Invalides. Avenues of lime trees had been planted in the dusty gravel and in twenty years' time they would offer a small forest of shade in the hot heart of the city. But for now there was no relief from the heat for the time that it would take him to reach the Seine at the Pont Alexandre III. Beyond that lay the sweltering wide boulevards.

Baron Haussmann, designer of those boulevards, hadn't bargained for global warming, Mort mused as the heat on the Alexandre III bridge became so intense that he stopped in front of one of its ornate green cherubs and told it, 'I can't go on.' Paris was an

193

unyielding city, he now knew, glaring into the cherub's blackened eye. Nowhere did it soften underfoot. Concrete became cobble and cobble gave way to gravel or stone. Whenever he tried to find his way back to the earth and stepped on a patch of lawn in a park, a goddamned keeper with a whistle and a peaked cap appeared and chased him off.

Mort made his way to the Tuileries where he sat down on a bench overlooking the river and unfolded his one and only Paris drawing. Marina was right. It did look like a cheap motel. He tried to comfort himself with the thought that many artists, writers and painters alike, could often only portray the homeland that they had left behind. He was smiling to himself at the pretension of this thought when he recognized the scene on the sketch pad in front of him.

He had drawn the swimming pool and the apartment buildings in Austin. He had sat in front of this long-yearned-for courtyard in Paris and drawn an image of his youth.

'Poor sap!' he said to a passing pigeon. 'Poor dumb middle-aged sap!' A man who had been leaning against the wall overlooking the river smiled across at Mort.

'I just had an illuminating moment,' said Mort. 'Did you ever have one of those?'

The man lit a cigarette and shifted onto his other foot. Mort hoped that he would be one of the thousands of fellow Americans who were supposed to be in Paris along with him. He never seemed to meet any of them. But now he needed to speak his own language. He needed to tell someone that he'd just had . . . what was it called? There was a term for this in literature. An epiphany? That was it.

'I just had an epiphany,' he told the man, who smiled and flicked his wavy black hair back off his forehead.

'Not a clue,' Mort muttered to himself. He was

disappointed. He was desperate to talk to someone. The anxiety that he was beginning to experience could probably be attributed to a build-up of words inside his body, he decided. Mort had grown up surrounded by emotional, volatile people and all the beauty of this city could not compensate for what he thought of as 'the lack of talking'.

Mort imagined all his American words going round and round his body with no outlet. In his present state of loneliness, he could willingly believe that all those stranded words of joy, frustration and amusement would build up and turn themselves into toxins of worry and unhappiness. When he got back to the US he resolved to look up one of his old school friends who'd gone into the psychology business and give him his theory about 'word congestion'.

And if there had been a phone box in sight he would have called Peg, Frank, Mother or even Primrose and told them that he'd just discovered that he had come to Paris, not to find the artistic talent he had always known he didn't have, but to retrieve his youth.

He dumped the drawing in a bin, where he found a copy of the *Herald Tribune* and, folded inside that, the *National Enquirer*. This proof that fellow Americans had passed along this path brought some comfort to Mort as he helped himself to both and sat back down to read them.

'Ninety-eight degrees in New York City,' he told the dark man, who was still standing with his back to the river. Mort had decided to talk to him whether he understood or not. Mort was now convinced of the health dangers of 'word congestion' and was determined to let all his backed-up words out into the air. He turned his attention to the *National Enquirer*.

'Man rides weather balloon into LA flight path.' He read the headline out loud. The dark man moved away from the wall and turned towards him. Mort looked

195

nervously to either side of him. And he saw that other lone men were waiting under trees and on park benches. From time to time one would approach another and they would walk away together in the direction of the towpath along the river.

Oh my God, I'm being picked up, said Mort but to himself this time. His first instinct was to move away from the man but he immediately revised this plan. To move would be to show that he was insecure about his own masculinity and felt threatened. To move might imply a lack of tolerance for a group of people to whom he'd never given much thought. The gravel paths of the gardens were suddenly mined with prejudices and potential for offence. Mort wanted to be a sophisticated man in a sophisticated city. He decided that his body language must indicate his indifference. He would relax and feign a deep interest in the façade of the Musée d'Orsay across the way. The man was smiling broadly now. He left the wall and walked towards Mort. Mort concentrated on the parasols and plastic chairs of a snack bar located high up on a balcony of the museum. The man walked past Mort's bench and greeted another man with a warmth and affection that left Mort feeling lonely and rejected and deeply foolish. He feigned a yawn and put the *Herald Tribune* over his face to indicate to anyone who might be watching that he had just stopped in the park for a brief nap.

Just below his chin one of the lesser headlines on the *Herald Tribune*'s front page announced that the co-pilot, the flight engineer and the plane from the hijacking had been returned to France. The captain was still missing.

CHAPTER TWENTY ONE

Even though she knew there was little chance of the airline calling her to work so soon, Nell had packed her suitcase for any climate that may be circling the planet that summer day and was sitting by the window with the airline timetable on her lap and the telephone at her feet. She was too hot to move and even turning its pages with each hour that went by made her palms sticky and her eyelids drip with sweat as she studied each possible destination and ticked them off as their departure hour passed.

It was four o'clock now. All the flights to India and the Middle East had gone. Houston had gone, Chicago had gone, Tokyo had gone. All that remained was a New York and that left at five thirty. There wasn't time for scheduling to call her in from Paris for that, Nell knew. There was a Rio that left at ten in the evening but the crew scheduling would probably choose some-one who spoke Portuguese. Nell admitted to herself that flight was not possible that day. She was doomed to spend the evening lost and alone with her thoughts in this deserted Paris apartment building.

The shutters of the apartment opposite were thrown open by the woman in the blue and white kimono who had sung while her husband had danced with such irritating abandon earlier that day. She wasn't singing now. She was pouring a blue powder through a paper funnel into an Evian bottle. When she had done this three times, she opened her front door and was gone from Nell's sight.

She reappeared in the courtyard, hugging the three bottles to her chest, set them down by the concierge's lodge and proceeded to water a large pale blue vine that had grown up around the concierge's shuttered window. Nell started when she saw the blue flowers. She forgot about discretion and leaned right out of the window. In all the years that she'd stayed in Luc's apartment, she'd never seen that plant grow more than a couple of feet up the wall. Now it covered the concierge's door and her window. When she came back from her holiday the old woman wouldn't be able to get in. But this flower was so beautiful and such a surprising presence that for an astonished moment Nell found herself wishing that the concierge would never return.

Then she sensed that somebody was watching her watching the woman in the kimono. She saw that the shutters on the window above the flat opposite had also been thrown open. She couldn't see inside that flat – the glare from outside made the interior look very dark – but as she stared up at it a voice boomed out of the blackness.

Nell leapt back, clutching her chair for balance. She knew that she was no longer visible but the voice continued, shouting down, not at her, she now knew, but at the woman in the kimono. The voice was speaking Portuguese with a Brazilian accent. Years of over-hearing the Portuguese concierge with her friends helped Nell to make the distinction. She stood well back in the dark, watching and listening. The woman in the kimono put down her Evian bottle and shouted back at the attic window. More abuse came from above. The woman in the kimono picked up another Evian bottle and watered the blue vine with renewed vigour, making what sounded to Nell like a very dignified and controlled speech in response to the abuse from the attic.

The voice in the attic fell silent and was replaced a few seconds later by a country and western song that Nell had heard in a bar with Luc on a long forgotten layover in Houston: 'My life is at a railroad crossing . . .'

Nell continued to watch the woman in the kimono when she returned to her flat. Nell had made a decision and she knew that she must act on it now. She stood in the shadows, chewing on a piece of dead skin that was loose around her thumbnail, and waited for the country song to stop. Then she put on her shoes, switched on the answering machine and headed out of her front door towards the lift.

She was about to cross the courtyard to the dilapidated building less than twenty-five yards from her living room. Nell, who had crossed the Berlin wall when it still stood, been in Peking with the airline when most civilians were shut out, even gazed into North Korea at Pan Mun Jŏm, had never imagined that she would visit the other side of the courtyard. Even though this building was in Paris, it seemed to Nell to come from the past that she had fled. For years it had teetered on the brink of squalor, just managing to pull back when it seemed it would collapse. Nell felt her escape from her own humble beginnings to be as precarious and had trained herself to avoid even looking across the courtyard.

Now when her own background seemed set to reclaim her, she found herself obliged to enter the other building. She stopped at the door and worked at the piece of loose skin a second time. When she had bitten it off and chewed it up, she started the long climb up the stairs.

The building wasn't as squalid as she had imagined. Her worst fears had centred around the Turkish toilets that she knew lurked on every floor and were shared by the occupants. She saw the doors to these sinister little rooms but on each floor it was locked shut. No foul odours issued from behind it, and on the second and fourth floors someone had even put a jar of flowers above the small stone communal sink.

Luc had once told Nell that some of the older buildings on the street still drew their water from an underground stream that ran below the seventh arrondissement. The stream fed the Mars fountain on the rue St-Dominique near the park and Luc had once stopped there on a warm summer's evening and made her feel the icy coldness of the water. Nell felt the same icy coldness as she ran the tap into the stone sink. So this building was fed by that underground stream. There was something strange and magical about the idea of something so hidden coming up from the earth's darkness to cool its blistering surface.

On another summer's evening in Avignon, Luc had shown Nell what he said was an old Midi trick for cooling your body rapidly, and had dipped his elbows into a fountain and held them there for over a minute. Nell did this now, holding her elbows in the icy water of the underground stream that she'd run into the stone sink, and noting that as Luc had promised a sudden shiver ran through her body after about thirty seconds, and she felt cool and calm and refreshed.

Then she knew that she could delay no longer and she climbed up to the fifth floor and banged on the door. She heard footsteps approach, then silence while she was examined through the glass peephole, then the woman in the kimono opened the door and said '*Bonjour?*' She had some sort of cream all over her face. Nell paid little attention to this. She was too busy preparing her speech, and besides, Claudine and most of her French colleagues seemed to have a greater faith than she in face masks, anti-wrinkle creams and the like. Nell was accustomed to having conversations with heavily greased women.

'*Je vous dérange, madame?*'

The greased woman shook her head in reply.

'*Il me semble que vous êtes brésilienne?*'

'*Brésilienne?* Yes, yes, I'm from Rio,' said the woman. And at the mention of the flamboyant city, she ushered Nell into the flat.

Nell was resolved not to pay attention to any squalor that she might find. She had come for a purpose and did not want to be distracted. She fixed her eyes on the woman, choosing to ignore the disarray that this seemed to cause her and said: 'Good – well then, madame, I've come to ask you for Portuguese lessons. Brazilian Portuguese, of course. I work for the airlines and do know that there is a difference—'

'Lessons?'

'Brazilian Portuguese. I heard you speaking it this morning.'

The woman was backing away from Nell's stern gaze. She couldn't go far – the room was too small – so she performed a rather elegant backward semicircle. Nell followed her, still trying to ignore the flat but aware even as she pursued the woman that there wasn't much to see. She took in a vase of flowers and a pile of shirts and socks that must belong to the absent husband. 'I wasn't deliberately listening in on your conversation, but with this heat I had to have the window open and I couldn't help hearing—'

'I teach you Brazilian?'

'Yes. Conversation. I learnt some basic grammar on a course at the airline so I've got the music but not the words, so to speak—'

'How much you pay?'

'Well, I've noticed on the boards at the British

201

Council and on the postcards at the bookshop that the going rate is a hundred francs an hour. Or' – Nell had remembered her own dire financial situation – 'I could give you English lessons in return?'

'I speak English,' scowled Marina.

'All right then – a hundred francs an hour.'

'I not a teacher,' said Marina, reaching for a pencil and doing a rapid piece of arithmetic on the back of a phone directory.

'But you're Brazilian and you can speak – that's all I need.'

'When?'

'Ah well, that's a slight problem because my job entails travel, but why don't we set up a first lesson and then just play it by ear?'

'You pay in advance?' asked Marina, repeating a phrase that she knew well in three languages.

'Of course.'

'Tomorrow afternoon then,' said Marina. 'Four thirty.'

'That's fine – as long as my job doesn't call me away . . . but if it does I'll pay you fifty per cent – does that seem fair?'

Marina looked to either side of her, as if consulting with invisible financial advisors.

'OK,' she said slowly.

'Good!' Nell stepped forward to shake her hand. Marina kept her arms folded and backed clear out of the apartment and onto the landing where Nell couldn't reach her.

'Bring paper and pencil,' she said.

'Of course,' said Nell and walked off down the stairs feeling pleased with herself and her mastery of the crisis in her life. This is how life works, she told herself as she walked out of the building and into the sunlit courtyard. You had a mishap, a disappointment, but you came out of it by picking yourself up and

202

getting down to work, to a new dream, a new project.

When she got back to the flat, she ticked 'learn another language' from her list of things to do, and sat wondering whether she should work through the rest of the list in numerical order or just select the chore that most appealed. But the headmistress in her head said, 'Mother.'

Nell dialled the London number. Her mother picked up the phone on the first ring.

'Oh, Mother, were you expecting a call?' Nell had a sudden vision of her lone mother, waiting by the phone through hours of solitude for this small moment of comfort from her daughter.

'No, I just came in the door and happened to be walking by the phone,' said her mother. 'What do you want, Nell?'

'Well, just to see how you are.'

'I'm all right.'

'Where have you just been?'

'Nowhere,' said her mother.

'You can't have been nowhere, Mum.'

'Well, I haven't been anywhere, then,' said her mother.

'But you just said you'd just come in.'

'I have,' said her mother.

'Well then, from where? Where have you just come in from?'

'The tube, if you must know. I was on the tube.'

'And where did you go?' asked Nell, very slowly and deliberately, wondering if the senility that her father had ascribed to Ivy had spread to her mother.

'Nowhere. That's just it – I didn't go anywhere.'

Nell looked at her watch and found to her shame that she was calculating how much this pointless exchange was costing her.

'I applied for my free travel pass,' her mother went on. 'I never bothered with it before, but now I've got it

I decided to use it. So I went for a ride on the tube – on the Circle Line. So you see, Nell, I haven't been anywhere. I just went round—'

'In a circle,' said Nell, not sure whether she was relieved at her mother's lucidity or terrified at the thought of the old woman riding around beneath the great terrible city.

'Got it in one!' said her mother.

'And how did you get on?' asked Nell.

'Oh, for God's sake, Nell, I have ridden on the tube before!'

'Not in a long time,' said Nell.

'Well, to be honest I did find the Circle Line a bit confusing,' said her mother. 'But I finally worked out that it's rather like life: if you keep going long enough, it tends to sort itself out in the end.'

'That's not true,' said Nell. 'Life doesn't sort itself out at all. You just die.'

'Did you call to cheer me up, Nell?'

'Of course I did, Mother. I want to get over there and see you but with all that's going on here at the moment—'

'There's nothing you can do for me anyway, Nell. I'm quite – well, not happy, but, well, I'm all right – I really am. You look after yourself so that you'll be happy and healthy for when Luc comes back. You don't want to make yourself sick with worry.'

After she'd hung up the phone, Nell turned on the evening news. Luc was the fourth item, coming after traffic jams on the road to the Midi, a spat in a Central African state, and the divorce of an Italian film actress who hadn't made a film in ten years.

The TV channel showed the same photo that it had been showing for over a week now. Nell heard Luc's name while she was in the kitchen buttering herself a slice of bread and jam after gazing in despair at the empty fridge. She took her paltry supper and sat down very close to the set, as if such intimacy would draw a confession or at least an explanation from Luc's unmoving image on the screen. When the newsreader said that Luc and his kidnappers had abandoned their small plane and headed off into the woods, Nell took her bread and jam and squashed it against Luc's face. Then she put on her shoes and wandered out into the hot night, leaving the newsreader to announce the lottery numbers through a slice of wholemeal bread and butter.

CHAPTER TWENTY TWO

When Mort returned to his apartment that afternoon Mlle Marina was dressing to go to work. No matter how much he moved from one small room to the other, Mort could not avoid these mysterious preparations. He found himself walking in face powder that had settled on the floor, and when he walked away from Marina to the window he was enfolded in twin clouds of hair lacquer and Chanel. He stared down at the plumbago and the plane tree, saw neither and decided that this was his flat and that the frank approach would probably help them both to get past this embarrassment. He turned to Marina, who was applying lipstick in front of the bathroom mirror.

'So I guess this, all this,' he waved his arms in the direction of the pots of make-up and brushes, 'I guess all this has always felt quite natural to you.'

'I'm getting ready for work.' Marina blotted her lips against a tissue. 'So don't start now.'

'Start what?'

'Asking me how I got like this? Was I too close to my mother? Is it maybe hormones in the water? Would I have wanted to be a real man?'

'No – no, but . . . well, I mean, Marina, that's no regular job you're going to. I mean, I grew up in Chicago – I was at school in the Sixties and Seventies

206

– I mean we liberated everything, but . . . I don't know – when I think of you out there in that park—'

'Why you thinking about it? It's not your business. I never think about it when I'm not there. Never! That person in the park – that's not me! That's someone else. I hate that person in the park but I've got to live with her – kind of like a bad marriage when the Pope says you can't have a divorce – you know about that, Senhor Mort . . .' Marina's flamboyantly made-up face peered at Mort from round the bathroom door.

'Not really – I mean, I had a lousy marriage but I didn't have a Pope.' Mort had shifted towards the door. The frank approach had failed and now he only wanted to get out of the apartment.

'Maybe you should've had a Pope,' he heard Marina saying as he drifted out onto the landing. 'Then maybe you wouldn't be here living like—'

Mort didn't wait to hear the rest. He went downstairs and sat under the plane tree. Marina didn't see him when she left for work half an hour later. Once he was sure she was gone, he crept back up to the apartment but the sun had pummelled it all day and the mixture of hot unmoving air and Marina's various hairsprays, deodorants and perfumes was too much for him. He picked his sleeping bag up and carried it out into the courtyard where he unrolled it under the plane tree. He had just stepped into it when the lights went on in the baker's kitchen.

'*Comme ça vous dormez dans la cour?*'

Mort heard the little man's voice but couldn't see him. A window had opened in the long low kitchen and Mort saw the baker's short arms setting a small portable television onto a broad ledge.

'Too much working.' He heard the baker's voice again, this time in heavily accented, mangled English, and now he saw his face behind the television. 'Summer – all bakers in the *quartier* pffft.' The baker made a flying motion with his hand. 'Makes all working for me,' he concluded. He pushed a button on the TV. The late night news was being broadcast. 'Informations.' The baker nodded knowingly at Mort, who still had his feet inside the sleeping bag and was wondering whether to step out and engage in a ludicrous half-conversation with this mean bastard who made disgusting bread that he was willing to sell even after it had rolled through the gutter.

A photo of a man in a pilot's peaked cap was flashed onto the screen. The little baker leapt into the air and motioned to Mort that he must look at the television.

'*C'est le monsieur du cinquième étage!*' he cried at the uncomprehending Mort. '*Venez voir!*'

Mort stepped out of his bag and walked towards the television. He couldn't understand a word of what was being said but he was fascinated by the baker's agitation.

'*Monsieur le commandant!*' cried the baker and repeated his flying motion. Then he stopped and pointed up to a window in the elegant front building. 'Him – fifth *étage!*' he cried. Mort followed his finger and gazed up at the window. The guy in the peaked cap was up on the fifth floor as far as he could make out. He was about to attempt to ask the baker why the man in the cap should be on the fifth floor and what he was doing up there when the baker held his hand up in front of Mort's face and rubbed two fingers against his thumb in the universal sign for money. '*Riche,*' sighed the baker. There was nothing Mort could say to any of this and, aware yet again of the loneliness of being cut off from his own language, Mort started to wander away.

'*Tenez, monsieur!*' The baker's excitement had made the little man generous. He handed a thick slice of pizza past Luc's handsome face before closing the window.

208

All was silent in the courtyard. Even the hot air seemed to have gone away to sleep, and for the first time that day Mort felt cool. He climbed into his sleeping bag and stared up at the stars with the same joy that he had experienced on his first days of blissful ignorance of Paris. Or, and on this thought he fell peacefully asleep, with the same joy that he had experienced floating at midnight on that swimming pool in Austin.

The next morning he was woken by two dark eyes staring down at him. For one wonderful moment he thought that they belonged to his blonde but these eyes were embedded in a big, doughy, amiable face that needed a shave.

'*Bonjour,*' said the face. Mort sat up.

'*Sandwich au jambon?*' The amiable young man sitting alongside him held out a half of baguette, lavishly buttered and with fat pink slices of ham bulging out of the ends and the sides.

Mort waved it away. 'You been here long?'

'Ah! American?' asked the young man, who had cocked his head to one side and listened to this terse greeting with rapt attention.

Mort nodded.

'I don't speak much English,' said the man. 'But I understand almost everything you say.'

'I've hardly said anything. What are you doing here? You live here?'

'*Non.* I'm a gardener. I live in the country. Only crazy people live here. I am here to see my – my . . .' he frowned, groping for his word, '*ma belle-mère.*'

Mort translated this to himself as 'beautiful mother' and thought it rather touching that the big, doughy young man should refer to her like that.

'She lives in the building?'

'Up there.' The young man pointed to the same fifth floor that had so excited the baker the previous

209

evening. Mort did a quick calculation and realized that this was also the floor where his blonde had left the note to her big boy. He looked hard at his companion who was intent on rummaging through his trouser pockets. Could this be the big boy? He certainly was big. Or, and this was a more appealing theory, could the sublime blonde be his 'beautiful mother'?

Mort sensed that his Paris life might be about to tip over into excitement and glamour. He would have to tread carefully. He was pondering the form his questions about the blonde should take when the young man produced a flattened bar of KitKat from a back pocket and held it out to him.

'Chocolate?' He studied the crushed packet. 'It doesn't like the heat but it will taste OK.'

Mort waved the chocolate away. His companion shrugged and tore open the wrapper himself.

'I'm Mort Engelberg,' said Mort, sliding out of his sleeping bag and shaking his legs in the air to straighten his jeans.

'Jean-Louis Marchand.' He held out his chocolate-free hand for Mort to shake.

'If your mother is up there, what are you doing down here?'

'She is still asleep.' Jean-Louis pointed to the closed shutters. 'She is a – a – air hostess? *Non, non* she is more a chief air hostess – these air people they never sleep enough, always they are worried about sleep, so when I come here I look to see if the window is ready.'

'If the window is ready – I like that. It sounds kind of Romeo and Juliet.' Mort himself was feeling romantic, sure as he now was that the big guy's mother was the blonde. He was about to confirm this with Jean-Louis when he remembered the handsome pilot in the peaked cap.

'Was it your dad I saw on TV last night?'

'Oh yes – he is on TV every night. And in the

papers.' Jean-Louis produced a folded copy of '*Libération*' from yet another large pocket. As Mort reached for his glasses the shutters opened on the fifth floor. The window was ready. Mort put his reading glasses aside and gazed up, hoping to see the woman and almost sure that he would encounter the ubiquitous, uniformed man.

Nell leaned out over the railing. She was still in her grey silk dressing gown. Jean-Louis leapt up in greeting.

'*Bonjour, belle-maman!*'

Nell frowned at the affectionate mockery of her stepson, nodded her acknowledgement and turned her attention to the man next to him.

'Oi, you!' In her anger her south London accent almost escaped. She started again. 'You there! The American!'

'Me?' Mort pointed to himself.

'What do you think you're doing down there?'

'Getting to know your son?' Mort shrugged and smiled at Jean-Louis.

'My stepson!'

'*Ah oui!* Stepson.' Jean-Louis scowled and ate some more chocolate. 'Step . . . why step? What does this mean?'

Before Mort could think of an answer, Nell shouted down at him again. 'I don't mean that! I mean what the hell is that sleeping bag doing down there? Were you sleeping in it?'

'That's generally what you do with them,' smiled Mort.

'Not in this courtyard it's not!' yelled Nell. 'This is the seventh arrondissement! This is Paris! This isn't some doss house in the Bronx!'

'Flophouse, Madame Marchand – you mean flophouse. And I'm from Chicago.'

'All right then.' Nell drew herself up. 'This isn't

some flophouse on the south side of Chicago! See, I know your city. I know how many rundown dumps and wastelands there are behind all that fancy modern architecture—'

'But isn't that architecture astonishing?' said Mort, comforted by a sudden vision of the high-rises on the lakefront that this angry woman had conjured in him. 'You gotta admit that the place is amazing!'

Nell *had* found Chicago amazing. She and Luc had walked the length of Michigan Avenue one snowy winter's day and returned to their hotel with aching necks and shoulders from staring up at those same high-rises.

'Well . . . well, as I was saying, there are some very sordid corners, and I won't allow you to bring that kind of slovenliness over here! Sleeping out there in front of everybody! And how do you think your wife feels? Parading your differences in front of the whole courtyard!'

'My wife?'

'There is nobody home in summer, *belle-maman*,' Jean-Louis smiled up at his stepmother and waved a hand towards the closed shutters on either side of the courtyard.

'I have noticed!' Nell heard herself yelling at the large young man for whom she had always had such affection. 'Only the misfits and the – the . . .' Nell was seeking a word that would describe her own situation. The castaways? No – no, there was another frightening implication in that word. 'The stranded people who have no choice—'

'*Les naufragés!*' cried Jean-Louis. '*Les naufragés d'été!*'

'What?' asked Mort, who was still wondering why his wife should care where he slept. 'What are you guys talking about?' he asked Jean-Louis.

'The shipwrecked of summer!' cried Nell, who could

never resist a chance to show off her French.

Mort recalled his bare-footed journey back from Provence, looked across at his cosy sleeping bag under the shady plane and smiled with pleasure at his new appellation.

Nell saw the smile.

'I want that sleeping bag out of the courtyard in five minutes or I'll, I'll call the concierge!'

'She's in Oporto, Nelli,' said Jean-Louis.

'I know that! Of course I know that! Then I'll call the landlord!' Nell did not know who the landlord was. This was not her home. With every new day in the hot apartment under the eaves she was more and more aware of how homeless she was becoming. The sight of Mort in his sleeping bag had terrified her. 'You heard me!' she shouted down at Mort. 'I want you out of this courtyard immediately.'

'Madame is right,' said a voice from the other building and Nell saw her new language teacher smiling down at the two men below. 'You are making our courtyard look untidy, Senhor Mort.'

'And letting you get a good night's sleep,' Mort smiled back.

Nell watched this exchange open-mouthed. A deep furrow was settling across her forehead when the phone rang inside the flat. Despite her repulsion for the building opposite, she felt compelled to go on watching its marginal inhabitants. The phone rang on. Still squinting across at her new Brazilian teacher, she backed reluctantly away from the balcony and picked up the receiver.

'*Ma chérie!*' It was Claudine. Even though Claudine was on the list of things to do that Nell had drawn up in Avignon, calling Claudine had felt like a chore that she had hoped to postpone indefinitely. Since the argument at her mother's house, Nell had known that a confrontation about Luc and Claudine was

213

inevitable. And Claudine's next sentence confirmed this.

'Nelli, *chérie*, we have to talk,' said her oldest and dearest friend.

'I know,' sighed Nell.

'Oh, I am so glad you said that,' said Claudine. 'I've missed you so much, Nelli. I came looking for you – did you get my note?'

'Yes, I did. I had to go to Avignon.' Nell wanted to blurt out that the house had been sold out from under her, that her bank accounts were empty, that she had tried to hit the vicar at the crematorium and attacked his assistant instead, and that the dreadful people from the tatty building opposite seemed to have come out to mock her in her time of distress. But Claudine was perhaps about to become her rival, an enemy and a traitor. There was no longer any comfort to be had from what had always been a source of consolation and happiness.

'Usual place for tea tomorrow afternoon. Five o'clock?' Claudine was saying.

'Yes, yes,' said Nell and tried to tug the phone cord to bring her nearer to the balcony. But when Claudine hung up and she was free to turn back to the courtyard, Jean-Louis and the American were gone, the sleeping bag had disappeared and the window opposite had been shut.

She heard Jean-Louis's heavy tread in the corridor, and opened the door to greet him.

'Nelli!' Her big, doughy stepson always lifted her several inches in the air when he hugged her. 'Why were you so angry at that nice American?' He addressed her in French as he set her back on the floor and stared solemnly down at her.

'Because he was making this place look like a slum.'

'I think he was being a pragmatic American. It's hot inside and he can't get air-conditioning so he sleeps

214

outside. Perhaps you should move out there, Nelli.'

Nell ignored this suggestion.

'What are you doing in this city you hate so much and this early in the morning?' Jean-Louis had recently told Nell that he had gone through the previous year without once travelling the sixty kilometres into Paris.

'I came to see how you were. All this worry about Papa—'

'That was kind of you,' said Nell. 'It is a strange kind of limbo time – just seeing him moving around America on a TV screen – and yet, I have some sort of faith . . . or more of a conviction that – that he's going to be all right.'

'Of course he will be all right.'

'No, I don't just mean some empty comforting homily – I can't explain it, Jean-Louis, but I feel that he is somehow invulnerable.'

'I'm supposed to think that! He's my father.'

'And do you?'

'Yes, I must confess I do. I am quite sure that he is under no threat.'

'See? We have the same instincts!' cried Nell. 'There must be something in that.'

'Yes, there must,' agreed Jean-Louis. 'I am quite sure that he is safe and that soon you will both be down in the house in the Languedoc.'

'Oh . . . that's what you think. Well, yes, of course . . .' Nell's voice trailed off and her attention turned back to the empty courtyard as she realized how alone she really was in her inability to worry about Luc.

'And you, poor Nelli – losing your own papa in the middle of all this. I thought perhaps there I could do something for you.'

'No, there's nothing I need.'

'Nothing?'

'No.'

'And you are all right?'

'Yes.'

'Then do you mind if I tell you some good news? I felt guilty about it with all your troubles but I wanted you to know.'

'I'd love it,' said Nell. 'There is a limit to how unhappy you can be even when you're awash in unhappiness, so it would be nice to have an excuse to feel something else. What's happened? Has one of your roses won a prize?'

'I got to the finals out at Bagatelle. You can see my rose in the competition section across from Maria Callas and Princess Margaret, but that's not my news.'

'What then?'

'I'm in love, Nelli.'

He had of course said it in French: '*Je suis amoureux.*' How much more easily these people said such a thing, thought Nell. Did they feel it more easily? Or just express the feeling more freely?

Then all rational thought went from her and a flood of jealousy, envy and bitterness washed over Nell towards the big, gentle stepson who sat across from her.

'How nice,' she managed to say. 'Who is she?'

'A botany student who came to the gardens to do a summer job—'

The phone rang. This time Nell raced to answer it.

'Madame Marchand?' said a familiar voice. 'Crew scheduling here. We have a Delhi for you at thirteen hundred hours. But my boss says to say it's not obligatory. You don't have to take it, Madame Marchand.'

'I'll take it!' said Nell.

'It's only a thirty-six-hour turnaround,' said the scheduler. 'So if anything should happen – I mean, if you need to come home—'

'Yes, yes of course,' said Nell. 'I'll be there.'

I can fly away, thought Nell as Jean-Louis described

216

the wonders of his new love. I can fly away from the meeting with Claudine, from Luc's face on the television, from the squalid people in the courtyard and from the unsettling joy of Jean-Louis in love. How can you be so innocent? she had been about to cry when the phone had rung. How can you be so stupid and so innocent?

'I've just been given a flight,' she told her stepson. 'The Delhi at thirteen hundred hours. I'd better be getting packed.'

'That's OK,' smiled Jean-Louis. 'I'm meeting Jacqueline at lunch time. We've got to get some more netting for the beds. The rabbits have gone crazy in this heat and are eating everything.'

'I'll call you when I get back,' said Nell.

'Come out to Bagatelle and see my prize rose. Perhaps Papa will be back and will come too.'

'Perhaps,' said Nell and ushered him towards the door. As he kissed her on each cheek, Jean-Louis fumbled in his breast pocket and produced the remains of his sandwich.

'Do you want this, Nelli? I'd meant to bring you some fresh croissants but only the awful place downstairs was open. You should eat before you go.' He pressed the sandwich into her hand, winked and walked towards the lift.

Nell looked down at the sandwich, realized that she was hungry and raised it to her mouth. Because it had been in her stepson's breast pocket, the crusty top side was damp from his sweat. Nell smelt this odour just before biting into it. She tossed it into the waste bin. For all the differences between father and son, Jean-Louis smelt very much like Luc. This realization was almost as unsettling as Jean-Louis's ingenuous discovery of love.

217

CHAPTER TWENTY THREE

Mlle Marina had started preparing for her afternoon lesson with Nell at nine a.m. She was very nervous. During quiet moments in the Bois de Boulogne the previous night, she had recalled her own struggles to learn French. She had attended a rundown language school in St-Germain for a couple of sessions but had ceased to go when the sniggers at her women's clothes and wigs from the young Japanese, Spanish and Italian students proved too humiliating. She did remember that the French teacher at the school had made them act out scenes from daily life and talk their way through them: buying a ticket at the railway station, going to the cinema, a visit to the dentist, etc. Marina had decided that she would make Nell some of her best coffee and talk them through a 'going to a café in Rio' scene. They would pretend that they were at the Confeitaria Colombo in Rio with its mirrors and chandeliers and art nouveau decor. Marina would tell her about the elegant youth of Cariocan society who frequented the place.

Marina, who came from one of the many city slums that huddled against the Corcovado mountain, had never actually been in the Confeitaria Colombo but she had gazed at it from the outside and decided that one day, when her operation was over, she would return there and eat pastries and take tea at one of the tables on the balcony overlooking the main floor. Once or twice she had even dared to dream that she might have a companion with her but in most of the dreams she took tea alone.

Once she had planned the lesson, she turned her attention to her appearance. Marina was very daunted by the efficiently pretty Nell and had decided that she must look as demure as possible if she was to succeed as her tutor. She had been in the process of scraping her hair back in a French pleat when she'd heard the brouhaha on the courtyard. The sight and sound of her new pupil's anger had daunted her further and once the courtyard was restored to silence she decided that she must have a full dress rehearsal of how she would look and what she would say when the dreaded four thirty came. She had donned a black spaghetti-strapped dress and buttoned Mort's old black cardigan over it when there was a knock at the door.

When she opened it, she saw Nell standing there with a fifty-franc note in her hand.

'Madame, I'm so very sorry, but as I feared I've been called away on a flight.'

'You mean you're not coming?'

'I'm sorry. But here is the half rate we agreed on.' Nell pressed the note into Marina's hand.

'But I was expecting you,' said Marina, who was more disappointed than she could have expected. 'I'd prepared the lesson. I spent most of last night preparing it,' she added.

'That's the trouble with this job,' sighed Nell. 'You can never plan anything.'

'But when will you come back?'

'Come back to Paris? Or come back to a lesson?'

'To our lesson,' said Marina. Then thinking quickly she added, 'It's not good to decide to do something and

219

then not do it – you won't accomplish anything in life like that.'

'I'm never one to procrastinate!' snapped Nell. 'I always do what I'm supposed to do.'

'Well, that's good,' said Marina. 'That's very good. Then you must start your Portuguese as soon as you get back. It is a pity you couldn't do it today – even half an hour would be good—'

Marina was dangling the consolations of structure and discipline in front of Nell. Nell could not resist.

'What about now?' she said. 'I have half an hour to spare now . . . and you've already got the fifty francs.' She pointed to the sticky note in Marina's hand.

And so Marina's rehearsal became her first Portuguese lesson. Nell proved an eager and diligent pupil. Marina borrowed a sheet of paper and a pencil from Mort's sketching materials and watched as Nell wrote down useful vocabulary. They drank Marina's best coffee and discovered that Nell herself *had* taken coffee in the Confeitaria Colombo during a rare layover in the city.

Nell didn't bristle on being corrected and she even asked Marina for homework, saying that she could do it while she was in Delhi. Marina had to think quickly. Then she said: 'Next time you come, be ready to describe your family in Portuguese.'

'My family?'

Nell looked so distraught at this instruction that Marina added: 'Or your job – describe a day at work.'

Nell seemed pleased with this project and reached out to clasp Marina's hand in farewell. She frowned as their fingers met, looked hard for a moment at Marina, then shook her head to herself and walked towards the stairs, bidding Marina farewell in Portuguese.

Her half-hour lesson with Marina had left Nell with little time in which to pick up her uniform from the dry cleaner's. She walked briskly to the deserted market street where the cleaner's was situated. Only one grocer's shop was open; the other illuminated sign belonged to the pharmacy on the corner.

'Bugger these bloody holidays!' Nell pounded on the glass door of the dry cleaner's in the vain hope that someone was lurking in the darkness behind the counter and would produce her uniform.

'You're not French at all, are you?' She heard a man's voice behind her. 'You're from London.'

Nell turned to see Mort stretched out on a bench in front of the grocer's.

'I never said I was French,' said Nell.

'But you let me think that you were.'

'What you think is your business,' said Nell, trying to visualize the uniforms in her wardrobe at the flat and remembering that only her thick navy blue winter two-piece was clean.

'Forget to pick up your dry cleaning?'

'The bloody place is closed!' Nell gave the glass door one last hopeless whack.

'Everything's closed as far as I can make out.'

'Well, actually, that's not the case,' replied Nell. 'French law says that, for example, at least so many *boulangeries* must remain open – if you look in the windows of the ones that are closed, you'll see that they have to inform you of where the nearest open one is situated.'

'And in our case that would be that crap-hole downstairs,' said Mort.

'Well, yes, but just for August. There are some marvellous bakers and pastry shops here the rest of the year.'

'I don't know about that.' Mort stretched and yawned. 'So far I have to say I'm pretty disappointed in French cuisine in general.'

'I just told you that's because it's August!' Nell looked at her watch and started to walk back towards her flat. Mort got up and walked alongside her. Nell wanted to ask him what he was doing in Paris, how he'd got together with her severe Brazilian teacher, most of all why he'd taken to sleeping outside, but she was determined not to take any interest in the life of the courtyard. As long as she could keep him from sleeping in it, she would ignore these people and their baffling lives. She accelerated her pace. Mort caught up with her. 'Even if a restaurant stays open in August, you can be fairly sure that the cook is on holiday and a replacement is in the kitchen,' she continued, hoping to fill the silence that hung over the deserted street.

'Maybe, or maybe the French have overblown their own reputation,' said Mort.

'Not for food they haven't,' said Nell. And to Mort's astonishment, she grabbed him by the wrist and marched him fifty yards along the street to a closed *pâtisserie*. She pushed him into the doorway.

'That is a master baker and pastry-maker – smell that! Smell the unsalted butter! Smell the quality cocoa! The sugar, the *crème fraîche*! It hangs in this doorway all year long.'

Mort sniffed the air in the doorway. It did smell wonderful but at the same time he read the sign in front of the canvas blind. '*Fermeture 15 juillet – 31 août.*'

'It's closed!'

'Well, yes, but you can tell it's good, can't you? You can smell it.'

'A lot of good that does me! I wanted a nice fresh baguette with lots of butter and jam. What I really wanted was eggs over easy and hash browns, but even a decent croissant would do.'

'Can't help you, I'm afraid.' Nell shrugged and turned towards the big doors that led to the courtyard. 'Doesn't your wife have any ideas?'

'Why do you keep on about my wife? My wife is

in Indianapolis with a sports reporter.'

'Oh . . . oh . . . then who is the woman in your apartment?'

'Been peeking out from behind your shutters?'

'No! But you were both making such a racket with all that singing and dancing the other day I couldn't miss you . . . I just had a Portuguese lesson with Marina. I thought you two were—'

'She's my tenant.'

'Oh. Oh.'

'So where can I get breakfast?'

'I don't know. It's not my problem. If you'd stop living on the grass like some old tramp you could buy yourself a healthy breakfast and eat it indoors. Croissants are no good – too much fat. I haven't had a croissant for breakfast in at least ten years. I have porridge – every morning that I'm in Paris.'

'Porridge? Oatmeal?'

'They call it "*flocons d'avoine*" here. Do you want me to write that down for you?'

'You eat oatmeal in ninety degree heat?'

'I never thought about that,' said Nell who'd eaten her usual porridge that morning and been convinced that the ensuing wave of heat that washed over her was the harbinger of an early menopause.

'Hey – do you want to go for an ice cream?'

'I have to go to Delhi.'

'Now? This minute?'

'In about forty-five minutes.'

'Why?'

'Because it's my job.' Nell was pushing on the small door within the big door that led to the courtyard. 'I'm a purser – you know, for an airline.'

'An air hostess!'

'A purser.'

'Huh. Well, come for an ice cream – it will only take five minutes. You can explain the rules of Paris in

223

August to me. I had no idea they all packed up like this – I mean I knew that they went on vacation but . . . I mean . . . well, I didn't think that they all went – not all the tradespeople . . . in Chicago or New York it would be, well, it would be unthinkable – illegal probably.' Once Mort had realized that he was free to speak his own language with this woman, he was unable to hold it in. English words and sentences started spouting from him like the Old Faithful geyser on a good day.

'Going for an ice cream won't take five minutes.' Nell had been too disarmed by his invitation to hear anything that he said after his offer of ice cream. 'The best ice cream is on the île St-Louis at Berthillon.'

'Let's go to the île St-Louis – I'll pay the taxi.'

'Impossible!' cried Nell. 'Berthillon is closed!'

'Closed on a Friday morning? Are you sure?'

'Closed for the whole summer!' Nell smiled, triumphant. 'Closed from the end of June to September!'

'The best ice cream parlour in Paris is closed all summer?'

'Yes,' frowned Nell, vaguely aware of Mort's mockery. 'But it is very very good when it's open – all pure ingredients and just as many flavours as those Baskin Robbins places.'

'You're so Parisian!'

'No I'm not! I'm English!'

'Oh, so you admit it, Madame Marchand! Well, in some ways you're very, very French – the best ice cream, the best croissants. Can't you just relax and have a second-rate ice cream in good company?'

'I told you – I've got to go to Delhi.' Nell stepped into the courtyard. She was tempted to let the door slam on the American but he caught it and followed her across to the lift.

'But do you have five minutes for a coffee? Or just a chat? I'd really like to speak English with someone who doesn't have to think about their irregular verbs.'

'I try not to do anything on the day of a flight – at least nothing that might distract me from my work.'

'But you don't do your work until you're in the plane, do you?'

'Well, no . . . but I have to . . . to worry about it in advance.'

'Why?'

'Because, well, because that's . . . that's what you do in life – you worry.'

'I don't.'

'Then you're peculiar,' said Nell. 'There's a scientific reason for worrying. Human beings have to worry – it goes back to when we were hunted by – by . . .' Nell couldn't remember just what, if anything, had once hunted human beings. 'By dinosaurs!' she said after screwing her face up in deep thought.

'Oh yeah, right, dinosaurs,' said Mort and winked at her. He tried to follow Nell into the lift but she had pressed the button. 'Hey – do you have a friend who came by the other day? A tall blonde woman?'

'Claudine,' said Nell as the lift door closed on her.

'Claudine,' Mort smiled to himself and went in search of ice cream.

CHAPTER TWENTY FOUR

The rabbits of Roissy were still burrowing and grazing when Nell's taxi drove towards the crew building. She recalled Jean-Louis's explanation for this frenzied day-time feeding and felt sorry for what the summer drought was doing to these, the most constant inhabitants of her nomadic world. There were so many of them – how easily they reproduced themselves, she thought, and closed her eyes, pained at how easy the big landmarks of life were for these dumb creatures to attain. And for Jean-Louis, whose account of falling in love had taunted her throughout the hot ride to the airport.

The taxi drove past the dull concrete rectangle of the administration building. All I need to do is go in there and tell my tale to a social services worker and the company will help me out of this hole, Nell thought as the building slipped into the background behind her. 'But the humiliation!' She must have said this out loud for the cab driver turned briefly towards her. She waved his attention away and felt in her handbag for the list of things to do. Claudine. She had forgotten to tell Claudine that she would miss their rendezvous.

Inside the crew building she tried to phone her friend but got only the answering machine which responded with a long series of bleeps and cut her off in mid-*bonjour*. Once again Nell took a back corridor in an attempt to avoid any chance encounters with sympathetic colleagues. She found a quiet briefing room and sat down at a computer where she entered a request for the names of her crew.

François, the steward who had performed the kiss of life on the dead passenger on the Tokyo flight, was the first name on the list and had left a request to work the first class galley. Nell had intended to work in first class but, on seeing his name, knew that she had neither the energy to face up to him about blanket collection nor the humility to concede that he had been right in his refusal to touch the wretched things. She signed herself up to work the smoky cramped back galley in economy class.

She didn't see François until the crew were disembarking in the hot, wet, early-hour heat of Delhi airport. He came up to her and hugged her briefly as they stood in the long unmoving line to clear crew customs.

'I am so very sorry about Luc, Nelli,' he said and his lips, those lips that had so patiently tried to breathe life into the yellowing dead man, brushed against her cheek as he whispered: 'Why are the bastards making you work when all this is going on in your life?'

Nell hugged him hard in her relief at being forgiven. 'Oh, they didn't make me, François! I asked to keep working.'

François stepped back and frowned at her. 'You mean they wouldn't give you paid leave when your husband has been kidnapped because he works for their company?'

'Oh yes! But I wanted to keep busy. I couldn't stay home and just wait.'

'Perhaps not,' smiled François.

'What are you doing with yourself tomorrow?' asked Nell, sure now that her friendship with François was

227

restored and remembering that happy, oblivious time feeding deer in Nara only days before everything had happened.

'A few of us were thinking of getting a car and driver and going up to the Taj,' replied François. 'We've all been before – I'm sure you have – but it never stops being beautiful.'

'The Taj! But my father wants to go to—' Nell stopped herself. 'Can I come with you?'

'Oh, look, they've just opened another counter,' said François. 'Come on, Nelli, let's get there before that Lufthansa crew sees it.'

Nell didn't have another chance to mention the trip to the Taj. Outside the customs hall, she experienced the familiar shock at Indian mud and Indian crowds and Indian heat and Indian beggars and Indian noise and garish Indian lorries and rickety, spluttering Indian taxis. She and François went through the ritual of handing out airline and hotel biros to clamouring children, and when she boarded the crew shuttle the only seat left was a lone place with some cabin baggage at the back of the bus.

But Nell sat happily on her own – pleased with her ability to fly away, relieved that she and François were still friends, and looking forward to her trip to the Taj. As the bus moved towards the hotel she relaxed in her seat, sure that within minutes India would perform its habitual miracle and, with the sure touch of a woman winding a sari, would twist itself around from dirt and clamour to marble and tranquillity. Father could die, Luc could disappear, her world could be pulled from under her and still Nell knew that within minutes she would enter the foyer of the hotel and find a beautiful Indian woman in yellow silk arranging rose and jasmine petals on the marble floor in the shape of hands folded in greeting that was the hotel logo. Nell had always been entranced by this opulent and sensuous, albeit overtly commercial, gesture. The same woman had performed this task for all the years that Nell had been coming to the hotel, and her enviable beauty was gently fading now, but like the rabbits on the Roissy runway she was valued by Nell as one of the most constant inhabitants of her swirling world.

The beautiful woman in yellow had finished her task when Nell and the rest of the crew entered the hotel foyer. Nell stopped to admire the petal arrangement and when she got to the desk for her key only just had time to catch François and arrange to make an early start the next morning for the Taj.

Nell heard her bedside alarm when it rang the next morning but the relief of being in a bed so many thousands of miles from her worries sent her drifting back into a light, floating sleep that was inhabited by nothing but the sound of the monsoon rain and the distant cries of the crows on the branches outside her room. She arrived in the foyer ten minutes late, ready to apologize to the other crew members and accept the least desirable seat in the hire car.

François and his colleagues had left. Nell saw the backs of their elegant Parisian haircuts as their stately black Ambassador taxi pulled out of the hotel driveway and into the Delhi traffic.

'They must have left me a note,' she said to a Sikh doorman who saluted in reply. There was no note at the reception desk and nobody had attempted to call her in her room.

Nell slumped down on a very soft couch next to the flower petal arrangement. She knew now that she had been left behind because they had never wanted her. She told herself that she was being punished for insisting about the blankets. 'Bloody blankets,' she said to herself but in a whisper because the beautiful Indian woman had arrived with her petals and was folding her hands in acknowledgement of Nell's presence. The

229

stern headmistress was back in residence in Nell's head and was arguing that blankets had to be collected and if the same situation arose again she should do the same thing, Taj Mahal or no Taj Mahal, when Nell saw one lone steward who had also been left behind in Delhi.

She had not exchanged a word with him during the flight. He had been working up in the solitary post on the upper deck. Now she dragged herself out of the soft couch and walked towards him. He was thin and pale with wispy blond-grey hair and a very prominent, sharp Adam's apple.

He shook her hand in greeting but before he had time to make any routine conversation about how she'd slept, or if she worked this flight often, Nell asked him if he felt like a day at the Taj Mahal.

'It'll work out at about six hundred francs the round trip, including meals and tips.'

'I've never been to the Taj,' said the steward. 'I thought I heard the others talk about going during the flight, but when I asked them what their plans were last night they said they'd all prefer to sleep in.'

'Well . . . they've all been before,' said Nell. 'You have to decide now – it's at least four hours' drive.'

'Oh, yes, I'd love to,' said the steward and added that his name was Alain.

An hour after her colleagues had left the hotel, Nell and Alain were sitting in the back of another black Ambassador and heading towards the chaotic road that connected Delhi to Agra.

'Aren't you the wife of Commandant Marchand?' said Alain as their car overtook a camel caravan on the outskirts of the city. 'How awful for you.'

'You're kind to mention it but I prefer not to talk about it,' said Nell. She wanted to talk about her father. She wanted to tell someone, even this stranger, that she was revisiting this place as a gesture to her dead father.

She was looking for a way to introduce the topic without embarrassing Alain with her bereavement when he said, 'At a certain angle you look a little bit like Vivien Leigh.'

'I don't look anything like Vivien Leigh!'

'Well, just a bit, perhaps.'

'Nothing at all like her. I'd like to, who wouldn't?' said Nell, aware that the conversation was moving definitively away from fathers. 'But there isn't even a minute resemblance.'

'Oh, yes, there is – in those fine delicate features, so English, so far from the heavier, sensuous Latin traits. Her eyes weren't green, you know – they weren't brown like yours either, but they weren't green – even though she played Scarlett. They managed to make them look green by lighting and dressing her in green. Her eyes were blue.'

'You sound like an expert.' The car was on a flat muddy stretch of road between two villages. Ahead of them two elephants were being ridden by four men and a camel was pulling a hay cart and blocking the Ambassador's progress. Nell leaned forward to look more closely at the elephants but the steward had leaned forward to look more closely at her.

'My entire flat is devoted to Vivien.' He uttered her name in a whisper. 'I made it into a shrine to her after she died – in Eaton Square in your London, you know.'

'A shrine?'

'Oh yes,' sighed Alain. 'I have several thousand photos – many of them signed – and a pair of gloves that she wore in *Gone with the Wind* – I bought them at an auction during a layover in New York.'

'And here we are heading for another shrine today,' said Nell, in a clumsy attempt to turn the conversation away from Vivien Leigh, an actress to whom she had never given even a minute's thought and who

231

seemed about to take her father's place at the Taj.

'A shrine?' asked Alain.

'But of course. The Taj was built by Shah Jehan, the Mogul ruler, as a shrine to his most beloved wife.'

'He had more than one?'

'Yes – but he loved Mumtaz so deeply that on her death he built this most beautiful of all tombs to house her remains. It's one of the great love stories. The Taj is a symbol of eternal love,' added Nell, surprised by her own knowledge.

'And they never made a film about it?'

'I don't know. Perhaps the Bombay film-makers did.'

'But not Hollywood? Just think what a role it would have made for Vivien. She would have been perfect.'

The Ambassador had slowed down to pass an accident on the road. An enormous cow's body lay mangled in the mud. In the long grass by the side of the road, Nell could see a bloodstained turban and what she thought was an arm. Alain glanced back at the carnage.

'If they wouldn't let those stupid cows loose all over the place the roads would be much safer. Do you remember that scene in *Waterloo Bridge* where Vivien, a ruined woman, sees Robert Taylor her lost love, then walks out in front of the Red Cross lorry?'

The Ambassador had accelerated to a sedate forty miles an hour. Nell dozed as they passed another camel caravan and Alain recounted Vivien's career and the truth about her turbulent relationship with Olivier. When she woke up he was explaining to their driver that there was no foundation for the rumours about all those casual sexual encounters. Nell stared out at the huddled shacks of the villages and found herself wondering what was happening back in Paris.

Soon she should be hearing from Jameson's Private Detective Agency. She felt suddenly anxious that the letter would arrive during her absence. She pictured the communal letter box, and as she did so her thoughts drifted out into the courtyard. As a tenant of the better building, she told herself that it was her responsibility to ensure that the American removed himself and his sleeping bag from under the plane tree. She was even tempted to call the baker when she got back to the hotel in Delhi. Then the heat overwhelmed her and her thoughts drifted to the plumbago and her new Portuguese teacher and again the word 'tenant' slipped into her brain and she smiled to herself at her stupidity in thinking that the irritating American could be married to Marina.

When they arrived at the Taj, Nell knew immediately that her idea of a pilgrimage for her dead father had been folly. As she and Alain pushed their way past the clamouring men offering to be their guide, she found that she couldn't even recall her father's face or the sound of his voice. The heat and the crowds drowned out any time but the present. And in the present, Alain had taken to recounting the details of the evening in Los Angeles when Vivien had a funny turn and was taken to the hospital by Olivier and David Niven.

Nell sat down on a low wall by one of the water basins. She had been told by a guide on a previous visit that these once flowed with rose water. But the impact of the Taj now had no more immediacy than when she had stared at its photo in an old red-bound children's encyclopedia thirty years earlier. This disappointment had pervaded most destinations of her travelling career. Claudine had once explained such disenchantment by saying that crew travel was like standing in a *pâtisserie* and having the finest cakes aimed at your open mouth – there was never time to savour anything. Nell squinted at the Taj's white dome, then turned away, remembered Luc and went to ask a group of

American tourists by the fountains if Indian television received CNN.

On the way back to Delhi, Alain fell asleep; Nell stared into the sudden sunset and resolved to call the baker when she got back to her room. She didn't like the little man but had made a note of his number in case of emergencies during the concierge's absence. By the time their hired car had arrived at the hotel, Nell was in such a hurry to make her call that she forgot to say goodbye to Alain. She left him in the foyer where he had found a Punjabi beautician who had seen *Gone with the Wind* more times than he and was insisting that the role of Scarlett would have been better served by Paulette Goddard.

As the phone rang in Paris, Nell sat on the edge of her Delhi bed, hoping that the baker's pitiful, down-trodden wife would stop endlessly stacking her *bâtards* and her baguettes and pick up the receiver.

'Allô,' said the woman's mournful voice when the phone had rung more than twenty times.

'It's Madame Marchand,' said Nell briskly. 'In Delhi so we must be quick. First, has there been any mail for me? And second is that man still sleeping in the court-yard?'

'I'll go and look,' said the baker's wife and before Nell could stop her she had set the receiver down and begun to make her slow, sad way along the long back room of the kitchen to the courtyard. When she returned several minutes later, Nell thought that she heard the woman laugh for the first time since she'd known her.

'Oh, madame, yes, he is there. And the Brazilian lady. And your Jean-Louis and Marie-France. And madame's friend Claudine—'

'What are they all doing?'

'Just talking, madame.'

'What about?'

'I don't know,' sighed the woman.

'And letters?' asked Nell. 'Did you check for letters?'

'No letters, madame. No letters for you.'

Then the line started to echo and Nell bid her good-bye. When she hung up the phone, Nell felt too lonely to stay in her cool, lovely room. She made her way downstairs ready even to discuss Vivien Leigh with Alain. She thought she saw his pale profile in the coffee shop. He was alone and staring out of the window, his Adam's apple bobbing frantically. In her haste to talk to someone, she rushed towards him and forgot about the jasmine and rose petal logo on the marble. She was about to enter the coffee shop when she turned and saw that she had walked right through it.

CHAPTER TWENTY FIVE

Mort had met Claudine. He had found her sitting on the stairs outside Nell's flat examining the reflection of her crows' feet in the immaculately polished doorknob.

'Everyone seems to be after the folk in this apartment,' he told her.

'I'm looking for my friend,' said the blonde in fluent English. 'She's a purser — with the airlines.'

'She's gone to Delhi,' Mort told her.

Claudine hadn't looked surprised. 'Reserve.' She shrugged and turned her attention back to her crows' feet. 'You're an American?'

'Yes,' said Mort. Within seconds of entering her presence, Mort had realized that he would not relive any lost romance of his youth with this woman. As Claudine had turned to speak to him, the Mort who had drifted so blissfully in the Texan pool floated away from his life for ever. Not that she wasn't lovely. Whatever she might be thinking about herself as she studied her reflection, Mort thought that she was beautiful. He was relieved to see her crows' feet and the deep furrows on her wide pale brow. Had he felt the attraction that he had thought he would feel, those signs of time's passage would have been reassuring. He could have imagined that the girl by the pool in Austin had slipped off into her corner and done a bit of ageing of her own. But Mort was surprised and disappointed to find that he was not even slightly attracted to Claudine. As he tried to make polite conversation with her, he was experiencing a sudden panic about his libido – and his sexuality. Briefly holding hands over a chummy coffee with Mlle Marina had been more sensuous than this sudden encounter.

'She could have phoned me and told me she'd been called away,' Claudine was saying.

'She was in a big hurry,' said Mort, sitting down next to her on the stairs in the hope that proximity would kick-start his hormones. 'She couldn't get her uniform out of the dry cleaner's.'

'That doesn't sound like Nelli,' said Claudine. 'I'd hoped to stay at her place tonight.'

'Don't you have your own place in Paris?'

'I have my own place but they cut my water off.'

'Who did?'

'I don't know. Whoever it is that does things like that. I haven't had water for two days.'

'Are you sure it isn't kids playing with a fire hydrant? In Chicago they do that all the time in summer – it sends the water pressure way down.'

'Oh, no. I don't live in the city – I live in a . . . in a big house in the country.'

'I would think that would be a better place to stay in this heat.'

'I can't flush the toilet,' sighed Claudine.

'That would be depressing. What will you do now?'

'Check into a hotel, I suppose. I did want to talk to Nelli.'

'You could wait in my flat,' said Mort. 'I don't really live there much—'

Before Claudine could reply, the lift door opened and Jean-Louis stepped onto the landing, followed by a tall, lithe young woman with very pale blue eyes. The next few seconds seemed to be filled with French limbs as Claudine drew herself up on her long legs to hug the young man and kiss the air around the young woman. Jean-Louis seemed delighted to see Mort again and bent down to shake hands with him.

'This is my sister Marie-France.'

Mort looked into her blue eyes, thought that they should be beautiful but weren't and turned his attention back to Claudine. She had sat down next to him again and removed her left shoe.

'I have an onion here that gets very bad in the heat.' She pointed to her big toe.

'Bunion, you mean bunion,' said Mort, scowling down at her swollen foot.

'In French we say onion both for the thing that you eat and for the thing on your feet,' explained Jean-Louis.

'And in English,' said Marie-France. 'I've heard the English say onion. Last week I had an English passenger on a Paris–London who said her onion was troubling her.'

'I don't think so.' Mort smiled up at her.

'But you're American.' Marie-France smiled down at him. 'How would you know?'

'He would know more about his language than you, Marie-France,' said her brother.

'I don't see why. I did a *licence* in English. Did you?' She turned those pale blue eyes back on Mort.

'No, but—'

'Two nations divided by the same language,' said Marie-France. 'Isn't that what Shaw said?'

'I don't know,' sighed Mort. 'I thought it was Mark Twain or Oscar Wilde – someone with a W in their name.'

'Shaw has a W,' replied Marie-France.

'Well then it was Shaw,' yawned Mort.

'The problem with onions,' sighed Claudine, 'is that

238

your feet swell on a plane and you really need to have a second pair of shoes in a bigger size to fit the onion, but I never think to do that when I get my uniforms. Nelli does.'

'Does she have bunions too?' Mort heard himself asking the beautiful blonde. For days he had imagined the conversation that he would have with the elusive Claudine. Now he sat waiting to hear about the state of Mme Marchand's feet.

'No,' said Claudine. 'She doesn't even have cors.'

'Corns,' said Marie-France. 'They are definitely called corns in English and American.'

Mort nodded his agreement. The conversation had run to an end. Claudine, who seemed untroubled by the sudden silence, took off her other shoe and massaged her foot.

'Why are you here, Claudie?' Jean-Louis sat down next to her, relieving Mort of the need to decide whether he should stand or remain seated.

'I wanted to stay with Nelli. I have no water at the château.'

'Château?' asked Mort but the others ignored him.

'Did they, er, cut you . . . for not paying your bill?' Out of courtesy to Mort, Jean-Louis was struggling to converse with Claudine in English. Mort heard his difficulties and almost told him to go ahead and speak French. But he was very curious to hear the rest of the conversation, so he set his face in an expression of deep concern for Claudine and her water, and waited for her reply.

'What water bill?' asked Claudine.

'You have not paid your water bill, Claudine?' Marie-France brushed the floor with a paper handkerchief and sat down next to her brother.

'You don't pay water bills,' said Claudine. 'It's included in the rent.'

'But you don't pay rent any more,' said Jean-Louis.

'Water is included in Paris rents but you're a proprietor now that Albert has left you the château—'

'Château?' Mort repeated.

'So you have to pay for your water,' concluded Jean-Louis. 'You must have received a bill.'

'I get so many bits of paper – I just pile them up on the kitchen table.'

'I'm surprised Nelli didn't go through them for you,' said Marie-France. 'Doesn't she usually help you with things like that?'

'Not since Albert left me the – the . . .' Claudine looked across at Mort and said, 'The house. She and Luc were so envious they didn't even come out there for weeks. Then just as she got used to the idea, Luc disappeared.'

'*Belle-maman* has always helped Claudine with practical matters.' Jean-Louis beamed with pride at the thought of his absent stepmother. 'When Claudine couldn't find her keys and went to stay in a hotel, it was Nelli who thought to call the *pompiers*.'

'Fire brigade,' translated Marie-France.

'That's true,' smiled Claudine. 'It was wonderful. The *pompiers* were all so handsome and they brought that big ladder into the courtyard and climbed in through my window!'

'On a harness!' added Marie-France. 'Like Peter Pan!'

'The *pompiers* are always wonderful,' sighed Claudine. 'They all stayed on for a glass of whisky afterwards.'

'But Nelli didn't like that because she said they had to drive their lorry,' added Marie-France. 'And what about when you tried to pay your rent with your credit card? And the landlord wouldn't let you?'

'It was *belle-maman* who spoke to the bank and arranged an overdraft until Claudine got paid,' Jean-Louis explained to Mort.

'Oh, that's right, she did. *Elle est merveilleuse, la*

Nelli!' cried Claudine, who obviously thought this opinion too important to be expressed in English. 'But I think she is angry with me.'

'Why?' asked Mort, astonished that his concerns had moved from the absent woman's bunions to her emotions.

Claudine shrugged. 'We had a little dispute after her father's funeral. I don't remember what it was about. And yesterday we were going to have tea in Versailles, and she went to Delhi instead and didn't even tell me. I took tea all alone.'

'Well, like I said, she was in a big hurry.'

'Perhaps.'

Mort found to his surprise that he was feeling sorry for Claudine. He patted her long, slim hand, felt no desire but did feel an urge to console her.

'Look it's getting real hot here – why don't we all go and sit in the courtyard? Or better still in the park under the Eiffel Tower?'

'Why are you here?' Marie-France narrowed those pale eyes and leaned past her brother to look at him. 'What did you come to Papa's apartment for?'

Mort couldn't tell them that after Marina had gone off to sleep in the tiny back room he had felt suddenly lonely and pointless and had been wandering around the building with a vague hope of finding once more a glorious night on a pool in Texas.

'I was looking for something,' he muttered. He stood up and held out a hand to help Claudine to her feet. 'Well, shall we all get out of this hothouse?'

When they got down to the courtyard, Mort was suddenly embarrassed by his recent sleeping habits and suggested again that they all go to the park. As they were stepping through the small door in the big door, they bumped into the baker who was sweating into a tray of *pissaladière*.

'*Quelle chaleur*,' he said to Jean-Louis, who told him

that they had decided to go and sit under the trees in the park.

'*Je vous accompagne,*' said the baker, and without waiting to be invited set the tray down in the entrance to the bakery, rolled up his sleeves and fell into step alongside Mort. For the length of the street that led to the park, he kept up a one-sided conversation in French with the American. He didn't seem to notice that Mort only understood international words like 'television', 'pizza', 'croissant' and 'terrorist', and would nod in welcome whenever one of these appeared. 'Television' and 'terrorist' appeared several times and Mort concluded that the man must be talking about the mysterious 'commandant' from the fifth floor.

'What happened to that guy?' he called to Claudine.

'To Papa?' Marie-France replied. Mort wanted to talk to Claudine. He was still puzzled by his lack of desire for her. Love, romantic love, was sold by the travel merchants as a part of Paris and love with Claudine would have occupied some of his empty days and kept his mind off the blankness of his future. But Marie-France seemed anxious to speak her excellent English and had fallen in step alongside him to recount the tale of her father's disappearance.

'Wow!' said Mort when she had finished. 'All that was going on above my head and I didn't know.'

'Well, actually nothing is going on above your head,' said Marie-France. 'It's all going on thousands of miles away. That's what makes it so difficult for us, for poor *belle-maman.*'

'Oh my God,' said Mort. 'That poor woman.'

Marie-France had gripped his elbow and was looking hard into his eyes. 'Nelli, *belle-maman,* is an indomitable English woman. We are filled with admiration and awe for her.'

'And we're worried, of course,' said Claudine and

242

smiled at Mort who thought: I even like her – she is a good woman but that is all.

At the park, Mort bought them all a beer from a mobile stand and led them to a cool spot near the puppet theatre. They sat down under an acacia tree and made stiff, awkward small talk that involved translating the most trivial remark into French in order to include the uninvited baker. Everyone except the baker seemed very relieved when a brass band from Parma on an exchange visit to Paris set themselves up on the bandstand and started playing Sousa.

The band had just started to play an encore of 'The Stars and Stripes Forever' when Mort saw Mlle Marina walking towards them. She was wearing her teacher's clothes, the black dress with the spaghetti straps and his old black cardigan buttoned over it. His first thought was that only a Brazilian who was used to tropical heat could stand to have that hot wool on her skin, then he was aggrieved that she had obviously rummaged around in his admittedly messy baggage to find it, but these thoughts were swamped by an overwhelming embarrassment at having to introduce his flatmate to the elegant Parisian women with whom he was sharing his patch of grass.

'I thought I find you here,' said Marina. 'I woke up early and thought maybe I come down here before I go to work.'

'You're not on holiday?' Marie-France squinted up at her.

'Sit down, Marina,' whispered Mort. 'Claudine, Marie-France and Jean-Louis, this is Marina Flor de Paraìso.' As he pronounced first the French names then the Portuguese, Mort felt suddenly delighted with his new-found cosmopolitanism and abandoned all thoughts of returning to Skokie.

'What a lovely name,' said Jean-Louis. 'Flowers and the sea all *mélangées*.'

'*Comment?*' said the baker and Jean-Louis patiently translated the observation.

'It's an odd time to be going to work,' said Marie-France. 'You're not with an airline are you? Sometimes it seems that only we poor fools at the airlines are working in this weather.'

'And gardeners,' said Jean-Louis. 'I'll be at the Bois de Boulogne all day tomorrow showing my rose from—'

'There goes the lift up the Eiffel Tower!' cried Mort at the mention of the Bois.

'The lifts have been going up since we've been here,' said Marie-France.'

'Amazing,' said Mort.

'*Comment?*' repeated the baker. Jean-Louis started to translate for him.

'You're not going to translate every dumb thing that gets said, are you?' said Mort. 'That's what I hate about these bilingual conversations – the dumbest utterance gets blown out of all proportion because some foreign ninny doesn't understand it.'

'You're the foreign ninny here,' said Marie-France. 'We're all speaking English for you. We could just as easily speak French with the baker.'

'*Comment?*' said the baker, who seemed resolved to have every syllable of every exchange translated into French.

'Well, nobody asked him to come,' said Mort.

'It's a cheap trick to insult someone when they don't understand the language,' said Marina. 'You should know that.'

'Don't you start,' said Mort.

'What was it you said you did?' Marie-France turned her attention back to Marina.

'Maybe we should ride up to the top of the tower,' said Mort. 'It must be cooler up there.'

'Heat rises,' said Marie-France.

'I'm a teacher,' said Marina and smiled across at Mort. 'A language teacher.'

'Portuguese?' asked Marie-France.

'Brazilian Portuguese,' said Marina. 'I'm from Rio.'

'But that's wonderful!' said Marie-France. 'I've been looking for someone to have Brazilian Portuguese conversation with so that I can do more Rio flights. How much do you charge?'

'A hundred and fifty francs in advance with a seventy-five franc charge if you cancel with less than twenty-four hours' notice.'

'Can you book me in for three hours a week?'

'I'll have to look at my diary,' said Marina.

'Didn't you say you wanted to learn Portuguese?' Marie-France asked Claudine.

'Oh, I should,' yawned Claudine, who had been stretched out and dozing in the sun. 'But I can't be bothered.'

'You won't go forward in life if you don't bother,' said Marina, who was sitting next to Claudine.

Claudine rolled over to look at her. 'I've seen you in the courtyard,' she said. 'You have a friend – with very thick dark hair—'

'She's not my friend,' said Marina.

'Does she teach Portuguese too?'

'No. Do you want to take lessons?'

'Too lazy,' smiled Claudine, and closed her eyes again.

'It is not good to stagnate.' Marina was speaking only to Claudine now. She had turned her back on the others and on the tower. 'You're lucky to have your job. Lots of people would love a job like that.'

'Slave ships with wings.' Claudine pointed up at a passing plane.

'That's bullshit,' muttered Marina.

'Oh no, Marina. Do you know that on long flights your internal organs swell with the pressurization, the

245

air is as dry as the Sahara, women's monthly cycles are thrown out of rhythm and if you fly for too many years you even get the menopause earlier?'

'I wouldn't like that,' murmured Marina. 'But you get good pay, and you go to nice hotels all over the world and wear a nice uniform.'

'Well, I only go when I'm sure there's no turbulence and the plane won't be full. Do you know' – she turned to Mort – 'that Nelli and I started the same day and yet she has flown a thousand more hours than me? Where could those hours have gone?'

The band from Parma had moved on to play 'The Halls of Montezuma'. The baker had thrust his head into the middle of the group and was listening intently to each sentence, then looking over to gentle Jean-Louis for a translation. Soon they all became bored by the stilted progress of the conversation and wandered back to the courtyard where the baker handed them each a slice of the onion and anchovy bread. Mort thought that the oil in the dough had gone off and was about to ask Claudine when Marina motioned to him to come upstairs.

'What for?' asked Mort who had drunk several beers and was stretched out on his sleeping bag under the plane tree.

'You're not going to stay out here.' Marina was leaning over him again. 'It's disgusting, it makes the place look like a slum.'

Mort raised himself up on one elbow. 'Look here, Marina,' he said. 'When I first decided to come down here it was so that you could get a decent night's sleep away from whoever that nut is that you were rooming with upstairs, so you can stop trying the schoolmarm routine on me. All I want right now is for all these people to just take off and leave me and my bag in peace. OK?'

'Yeah,' said Marina. Claudine had come over to offer

her a beer. Marina ignored her and walked into the building.

As Mort fell asleep, he heard Claudine saying to him that she felt sorry for the poor one-eyed baker's wife, working away while he lazed around watching TV and drinking beer. He heard Marie-France reply that she should be put in touch with one of the Paris women's groups who would help her break out of her shackles. He heard Claudine's bored assent, and finally he heard Jean-Louis say that she could at least get her eye fixed.

CHAPTER TWENTY SIX

Nell drove Luc's Citroën out to Versailles a week after her return from India. During that week she had slept late into the day, eaten whatever food was in the freezer, looked down with contempt at the sleeping bag in the courtyard and watched television for bulletins about Luc. He was, the news services assumed, still in the North American woods with his captors. She had received several messages from Claudine. Some of them had been pleading and concerned, others had just been the usual Claudine message. 'Poorly applied lipstick is a sure sign of an ageing woman,' said the message that greeted her return from Delhi. 'Those red-stained teeth and crimson rivulets in the creases of the upper lip are abominable. Remind me to go to the Elizabeth Arden discount store on my next New York.'

Nell had wondered how Claudine had known a word like 'rivulet'. Then she had contemplated erasing the message and never contacting her old friend again. But she needed to tell someone about her turbulent summer and Claudine was the only person to whom she could talk of strange, unsettling and painful events – even if she did dread what her friend was about to tell her. When she did eventually call Claudine they arranged to meet at Versailles for tea. The outing would also prove a good excuse to get away from the wretched courtyard, Nell had told herself, as she walked down her empty Paris street towards the garage where Luc's car was kept.

Upon her dawn return from Delhi, she had found Mort asleep in his shorts on top of his sleeping bag. The blue flowers of the plumbago had multiplied and were reaching towards the door of the ugly apartment building. She hadn't needed to enter the courtyard; she could have wheeled her suitcase into the lift and been whisked up to her flat without ever glancing at the plane tree and the solitary sleeper beneath it.

But she had left her bags in the entrance hall, stepped out of her uniform shoes and tiptoed across the cobbles in the half-light to see if the stranger was still there. When she saw that the heat had driven him to sleep stretched across the outside of his bag, she stepped back in anger, but not before she noticed the line of black hair that stretched down across his flat muscular stomach. She had stared at that stomach in silence for several minutes, watching as it rose and fell with his breathing and sweated gently in the hot dawn light. Then her eyes travelled up and down his body, and she stared and stared wondering at the trust in the world, in life, that such a careless, exposed sleep implied.

This sleeping man was more foreign and mysterious than any of the continents to which her 747s delivered her. With his inability to worry and his pleasure in this place that she despised, he seemed to Nell to be the most foreign land she had ever encountered. He was a true stranger. A weary Nell had sat down next to his sleeping body and pondered the real meaning of that word. All her life she had longed for a wise stranger to whom she could tell things. But what things? thought Nell, running her fingers across the warm earth around the plane tree. She knew immediately that she longed to tell someone about her absurd and pointless search for the actor. Even now she longed for and dreaded a letter from the detective agency. If she could tell her story to someone who would soon disappear and never taunt her with it, perhaps the need to find that cruel, cold man would also disappear.

Nell started to regret not having coffee with Mort, then she tried to rouse herself and decided that all these thoughts were a result of fatigue. Still she sat on in the silent courtyard, listening to Mort's breathing and gazing in bafflement at his peaceful body. She avoided his face for fear that her gaze might wake him. She did notice that he had good legs – muscular and tanned with a light covering of dark hair.

After about ten minutes, she pulled herself to her feet, and by the time she rode the lift up to her flat she was resolved to have Mort removed from her sight by the end of the week. When she was standing under the hot shower, she tried to remember what Luc's stomach and legs looked like but could recall nothing of her husband except the ID photo that flashed across the TV screen from time to time.

Now she was back in Luc's baffling Citroën with most of its lights flashing and buzzers sounding. At the approach to Versailles, she slowed down almost to a halt and tried to separate her fear of her approaching betrayal by Claudine from her inability to think about Luc for more than thirty seconds. On the wide, dusty Avenue de Paris she stared at the château on the horizon and yearned for those few minutes of still summer dawn in the courtyard.

Nell and Claudine had walked the severe, symmetric gravel avenues of Versailles' gardens throughout the years of their friendship. They had walked along them when snow cloaked the statues, when frost rimmed the smiles of the stone dolphins and the water froze in the ornamental fountains. They had walked along those same avenues on buoyant, optimistic, green May days and in the autumn when the leaves on the trees in the dark secretive groves turned yellow and red and the October light bathed the cream stone of the château and the pink marble of the Grand Trianon in flaming gold. They had walked miles and miles as the years had traced their first lines through Claudine's tan and streaked some grey through Nell's brown hair.

Today they were to meet for the afternoon buffet of unlimited pastries at the Trianon Palace Hotel. Nell usually looked forward to the hotel buffet. Years of practice meant that she could push past any number of angular Parisian elbows and stake her claim to the *tarte tatin* and the *marquise au chocolat* that were the favourites and consequently kept at the back of the long table in front of the window. Today she stood in the hotel car park and longed to sink down into the hot red beds of geraniums and never see Claudine again.

As she delayed the moment when she would enter the great ornate salon where tea was served, she realized that she was gripping the door handle of the Citroën, reluctant to let go of this proof that Luc – the Luc whose face she no longer recalled – like his car, belonged to her.

She heard a sharp tapping on glass and looked towards the hotel to see that Claudine was knocking on the window to usher her in.

'Don't do that,' Nell mouthed to her in English. '*Ça ne se fait pas.*'

Claudine winked at her and squashed her lovely nose against the pane.

'Don't do that!' Nell repeated. 'Not in a place like this.' She entered the salon through the French window that opened out onto the formal gardens. The two women had never met for tea in summer and Nell sensed that everything about the afternoon was wrong. The room was not air-conditioned and the éclairs and gâteau St-Honoré on the long table in front of the window were sweating almost as visibly as the deeply unhappy maître d'hôtel who was leading her to her friend.

'The cakes don't look right,' she said as Claudine stood up to kiss her.

'I know,' Claudine scowled across at the table. 'The chef must be on holiday.'

'The garden doesn't look right either – it's so dusty and the flowers seem so tired,' said Nell, and sat down on one of the hard, high formal chairs next to Claudine.

'The customers don't look right either,' said Claudine before Nell could express the same opinion. 'There's not a Parisian here.'

Nell wished that the conversation, and the afternoon, could stop right there where she felt aligned with her friend, where they both could consider themselves Parisians, characteristically unhappy with their surroundings and contemptuous of their fellows.

'I've got no water,' said Claudine.

'What do you mean you've got no water?'

'Out at *le château de tous les malheurs*, I've got no water. I can't even flush the toilet.'

'Did you pay the bill?'

'No, no I didn't. I've already had this explained to me. I can't seem to find it.'

'Is this what you called me out here for?'

'Of course not, but I did think that perhaps I could stay with you for a few days—'

'You don't want to do that,' said Nell. 'It's bad enough having one sweaty body oozing around that cramped apartment. Two would be unbearable.'

'Oh, oh . . . I thought it might be fun – like being back in training again.'

'I hated training,' said Nell.

'How was Delhi?' asked Claudine, as the waiter brought them a pot of Darjeeling.

'I went to the Taj,' said Nell. 'With a most peculiar steward called Alain who has a Vivien Leigh fixation.'

'Oh, I know Alain!' cried Claudine. 'I bet he invited you back to his place after the flight – to see his Vivien Leigh portrait gallery.'

'No, he didn't,' said Nell. 'Not that I'd have wanted to go.'

'Well, who does after a long flight? But I'm surprised he didn't ask you back for breakfast – he usually does. I've known him cook for half a dozen people.'

'Well, he didn't cook for me!'

'You just said you didn't want him to.'

'I didn't.'

'Well then. But he does cook a wonderful American breakfast – just like you get in the diner in New York. You wouldn't think to look at him, with that funny nervous throat of his, that he could do anything but daydream, but he cooks very good hash browns – and French toast.'

'He didn't even mention breakfast to me,' said Nell, and thought that she recalled seeing him huddled in conversation with François as the plane started the descent towards Paris. 'Perhaps he invited the others back but not me.'

'Why would he do that?' Claudine poured them both a cup of tea.

'Because nobody ever invites me back! In all my years with the company, nobody has ever asked me to do anything impulsive or surprising!'

'*Et alors?* That's because nobody does that much after a flight. People are too tired. I've only had a few moments like that. It's nothing against you personally.'

'You told me that you used to go to Les Halles for breakfast in the old days and to Rungis when they moved the market out there. And you told me you once got invited back to a captain's house near Reims for a champagne tasting. I know that captain – he never invited me.'

'It's because you're a purser,' said Claudine. 'The French don't like figures of authority.'

'The crew ran away from me in Delhi,' said Nell. 'I saw the backs of their heads in the taxi. I felt as though I was back at infant school watching the other children run away from me in the school playground.'

'Now you're just rolling around in your own unhappiness,' said Claudine. 'That's not why I asked you out here. Let's get some cakes.'

'Why did you ask me out here?'

'Let's wait until we've had cake,' said Claudine.

'No,' replied Nell. 'You can't do that. Tell me now.'

'Let's have cake first,' said Claudine and got up and walked towards the long table. A string quartet had entered the dining room, tuned up and started to play Schubert.

'Even that's wrong,' muttered Nell as she followed Claudine.

'What?'

'The musicians. They're not the usual ones – they're students. That cellist looks as though he doesn't even shave.'

'They might be good,' said Claudine and took the last piece of raspberry roulade.

'I wanted that!' cried Nell.

'What is wrong with you today, Nelli?' Claudine pressed her thumbnail down hard on the roulade and pulled her plate closer to her chest. 'If you'd wanted it you should have got to the table first.'

The cellist played three wrong notes in the Schubert and a passing gardener's cart sent a flurry of dust into the dining room. The only cake that wasn't sweating was a *tarte tatin* that shone crisp and golden in the sunlight.

'Take some of the tart.' Claudine pointed to the *tatin*. 'It's your favourite.'

'It's my favourite in autumn, after the harvest when the air is getting cold – then it's my favourite. Nobody wants caramel and pastry in this heat.'

'Well I do,' snapped Claudine and piled a large slice of tart onto her plate next to the raspberry roulade.

'Why did you ask me out here?' Nell opted for a chocolate éclair and turned back towards their seat under the gilt mirror.

'The Darjeeling will go bitter if we don't drink it soon,' she said, resenting how small she was compared to her willowy French friend. She almost had to stand on tiptoe to say that last sentence, and she knew that this reduced her power. But why did she suddenly need power to talk to her oldest and sometimes dearest friend?

'We'll get some more hot water, then,' said Claudine.

'Hot water won't make any difference if the tea leaves are bitter,' said Nell. 'You know that, Claudine. You've known that for years.'

'Then we'll get a fresh pot of tea.'

'They'll charge us, and you know how much tea is here.'

'Oh, my poor Nelli! Have you got money worries?' Claudine bent down and scrutinized Nell's face. 'You have, haven't you? Hasn't the company helped you out at all while Luc – while Luc . . . well, you know.'

'I won't ask them,' replied Nell.

'But you must. Tomorrow you must ask them. And I'll pay for the tea – don't worry about that.'

'I can pay my part. I wasn't worried about that,' said Nell. 'What is this urgent business you have to talk to me about?'

The young musicians had moved on to a Bizet medley. Nell noticed that the young woman playing the viola had a thick rivulet of sweat running

255

from her double chin down to her cleavage.

'I know we hear it too much but I still love *Carmen*,' said Claudine.

'They play like a band of tone-deaf baboons,' sniffed Nell.

'Oh well, it is the holidays,' said Claudine. 'Let's sit down.'

'Well?' Nell sat back down on one of the high, formal, uncomfortable chairs and stared at Claudine.

'I don't know how to tell you this.' Claudine set her cake plate down and closed her hands across her face.

'You always told me not to rub my face like that,' said Nell, her own panic leading the conversation away from the subject. 'You said it's bad for the skin.'

'Ah, clever, wonderful Nelli!' cried Claudine and her hands dropped away from her face. 'You've guessed what this is about, haven't you?'

'Have I?'

'Oh, Nelli – I've been trying to tell you all summer but then I just feel so embarrassed that I don't know how to say it.'

'Tell me now. Go on, Claudine. Say it now. If you've brought me all the way out here in this heat, you had better get on and tell me.'

'If you've already guessed, can't we just move on to the practicalities—'

'Tell me now.'

'But I feel so foolish—'

'Tell me now.'

'I'm getting a face lift,' said Claudine. 'I've booked into a clinic in Neuilly to have one, and I need to use your name on the release form.'

'A face lift? That's what you wanted to tell me? You're getting a face lift?'

'I've booked it. I got an address of a very good man from one of the chief stewardesses on a Los Angeles the other day, so I decided that that's how I'll spend

256

my holidays – in the clinic. But I need to have a name of next of kin to put on the release form.'

Nell knew that Claudine had no family to sign for her. Both her parents were dead and her brother was a country curé in a dull, grey village near Lille who thought that working for the airlines was a euphemism for prostitution.

'Not that anything will happen,' Claudine continued. 'It's a perfectly safe procedure, and I'm only getting the crows' feet done – and the lines on the upper lip – they're much easier than you would imagine, he says. So there's no risk.'

Nell had screwed up her own dark eyes and was examining each feature as Claudine describe it. To Nell, her beautiful blonde friend had not changed in the twelve years that she had known her. Claudine's exuberance and flamboyance shone out from behind these treacherous and slippery bits of skin and muscle. Claudine would always be beautiful, thought Nell, and for the first time in their friendship she felt no envy at all.

'You don't need a face lift,' she said.

'I knew you'd say that, but I do, so don't argue with me. I do.'

'But you look beautiful to me,' said Nell. Now that the threat to her own situation was removed, Nell could lavish on Claudine all the love and generosity that was at the heart of her feelings for her friend.

'That's sweet. But you're seeing me with your eyes. Not with a prospective partner's.'

'But you've always had any man that you wanted—'

'Not these past few years, Nelli. You've been too busy to notice but my life has gone very quiet. Men don't turn to look at me on the street any more. Not even in Italy. I noticed that on a Rome layover last month.'

'I bet they do. And even if they don't, who needs that

sort of attention? Not these days. We're not far from a new century – you don't really want men to be wolf-whistling you, do you?'

'Yes,' smiled Claudine. 'Yes, I do.'

'But that's preposterous!'

'If I knew what preposterous meant I could agree,' said Claudine.

'*Absurde, ridicule, grotesque,*' Nell translated and noticed for the first time that two thick grooves had etched themselves between Claudine's nostrils and her mouth.

'Oh yes it is absurd, but it's all that I've got.'

'But you always said you didn't want a settled life!'

'I didn't. I still don't know that I do, but I'm getting older, Nelli, and I don't want to be alone out in that awful château either.'

'It could be a lovely château,' said Nell.

'I don't want to discuss that now, Nelli.'

'All right, but believe me you wouldn't want a routine marriage.'

'How can I know if I've never tried? You see, Nelli, I've always thought, and you're not going to like it but I have to say it, I've always thought that with so many married women, I don't mean you and Luc, but, well, that for a lot of married women status and being kept, even now, well it is a good substitute for true emotions. As long as they can have a *mari* at their side they feel that they exist, even if he is boring and flatulent and sexless—'

'You're probably right,' said Nell. 'So why want that?'

'Because living on honest emotions is all right when you're twenty. It looks ridiculous on a woman my age. I'm lonely, Nelli.'

'Even if you are, and even if you're mad enough to think that you want to be landed with someone for ever, looks aren't what matter.'

258

'Rubbish!' cried Claudine. 'Everybody says that but it's not true. Everything in our world turns around looks. I've never had anything but my looks – I'm too old to suddenly develop an intellect or a talent so I must keep polishing up the few remaining jewels that I have.'

Another cellist had joined the string players. They started to play more Schubert.

'The Quintet in C major,' said Nell. 'That's a bit ambitious for this lot, and for this place.'

'It's wonderful,' said Claudine.

'But they keep playing the wrong notes.'

'Well, try to listen past the mistakes,' said Claudine.

'There! You've just demolished your own argument!' cried Nell. 'That's what people do with a face they love! They see past the wrong notes!'

'That's if they already know the face,' said Claudine. 'Not it they're seeing it for the first time. Can I put your name on my release form?'

'Of course you can,' sighed Nell, and as Claudine kissed her cheek in thanks and turned to order another pot of tea, Nell shuddered at the loneliness of her friend and yearned to be back in the flat on the court-yard, with perhaps the comfort of television and even a fleeting image of Luc on the screen.

CHAPTER TWENTY SEVEN

When Nell crossed the courtyard for her second Portuguese lesson with Mlle Marina, the American wasn't under the plane tree, but signs of his occupation remained in the form of his rolled-up sleeping bag, with a six-pack of beer tucked in its centre, and a pair of decaying tennis shoes. Nell kicked the bag as she passed it and considered throwing it out into the empty street but, as she stood with her foot still resting on the duvet, she sensed that she was being watched.

When she looked up she saw Mlle Marina waving down at her.

'I bought you a book of irregular verbs,' she cried from the fifth floor window. 'I found it in a second-hand shop in St-Germain.'

'How kind of you!' Nell called up to the window. 'I will reimburse you, of course.'

As she shielded her eyes from the sun, Nell saw a woman's figure emerging from Marina's building. It was Marie-France.

'What are you doing here?' said Nell.

'I just had my first conversation lesson. She's much cheaper than Berlitz.'

'How did you know about her?'

'She told me herself. In the park about a week ago.'

'But you don't need to speak Portuguese – that's not your sector at all,' said Nell.

'I'm thinking of moving over to the South American sector next summer.'

'Oh,' said Nell. 'Oh.'

'Are you going out to the rose garden with Jean-Louis today?' asked Marie-France.

'Yes, he's picking me up at one o'clock. You're not going, are you?'

'Oh yes, most definitely. It will be my first chance to meet my future sister-in-law.'

'I suppose so,' said Nell. 'Well, I'll see you out there.'

'No you won't. I'm going to stay here until Jean-Louis comes by. We'll all go out there together. Jacqueline will meet us at the Bois.'

'But where will you stay until then?'

'In Papa's apartment, of course.'

Nell tried for a few baffled seconds to locate 'Papa's apartment', then realized that Marie-France intended to wait in Nell's home.

'But I haven't got a spare key,' said Nell, aware of how weak this excuse must sound when she herself would be within sight of the apartment.

'Oh, I've got my own key,' smiled Marie-France. 'I've always had a key to Papa's flat.' Before Nell could stop her, Marie-France had stepped neatly over the sleeping bag and disappeared into the lift.

When Nell sat down at Marina's table a few minutes later, she was too angry to remember the vocabulary about her job that she had studied so diligently over breakfast in Delhi. Instead she found herself asking Marina for the Portuguese for stepdaughter.

She was comforted when she heard Marina utter the Portugese for 'difficult'. And when Nell felt obliged to say something nice about Marie-France and intoned the Portuguese for 'beautiful eyes', she felt a surge of friendship for Marina when the Brazilian waved her finger sternly and pronounced the Portuguese for 'definitely not beautiful'.

The rest of the lesson was a success for both Nell and Marina. Nell absorbed the vocabulary and grammar with ease, and to Marina's astonishment seemed eager to discuss her turbulent summer. When she couldn't find a word, she leafed through the dictionary, and as a result came away knowing the Portuguese for 'dead passenger', 'wrong house', 'father's funeral', 'double life', 'hijacking', 'empty bank account', 'estate agent', 'private detective', 'first love', 'irritating American', 'sleeping bag', 'half-naked', 'deception', 'betrayal', 'confusion', 'resignation' and 'loneliness'.

Nell's need to recount the story of her summer was to Marina's advantage because the lesson spilled over into a second hour and Nell didn't hesitate to pay Marina the extra money.

They left each other at noon. Nell hadn't noticed how long she had spent in the little flat until the time had come to pay. Now she was relieved to have reduced her time in her own flat with Marie-France. But when she stepped out into the courtyard, she saw that her stepdaughter was sitting on a large, dark, man-sized T-shirt and talking to the American who was lying on his back and waving a can of beer towards the heavens. During her lesson, the American had done his laundry: three pairs of underpants and some socks were now hanging on a string suspended between the plane tree and the concierge's dormant orange tree.

'When the concierge comes back, I'll have you removed,' she said to Mort.

'Would you like a beer?' Mort rummaged in his sleeping bag.

'It looks like Naples down here.'

'I've never been to Naples,' said Mort. 'Have you?'

Before Nell could admit that she hadn't, Marie-France said: 'I have. Contrary to popular perceptions, it is a city of great charm and fascination. It has many extraordinary Baroque buildings that one can find if one is just willing to be an independent traveller and not just a tourist.'

'We're all tourists when you get down to it,' said Mort.

'I'm a traveller,' said Marie-France.

'I could probably even get the police to move you,' said Nell.

'I bet they are all on the Riviera,' said Mort, sitting up and moving along his sleeping bag so that Nell would have a place to sit. She remained standing. She was about to threaten Mort with actual physical removal by the riot police or a couple of muscular soldiers from the Ecole Militaire round the corner when Jean-Louis wandered into the courtyard.

He hugged Nell, kissed his sister and hugged Mort which astonished both Nell and Mort.

'I'm double parked,' he told them. 'That wretched baker has his delivery van in front of the door. We must get going if we are to be there in time for the judging.'

'What judging is that?' asked Mort.

'I have a prize rose in a competition out at the Bois. Would you like to come along?'

Before Nell could object, the four of them were standing in front of Jean-Louis's Deux Chevaux. Nell had always thought it absurd that such a big man should drive such a small car and for many years had expected to see her stepson's feet peddling furiously below the vehicle in the place of wheels.

The baker appeared from inside the bakery. He was clutching a tray of sinister-looking croissants.

'*Où allez vous tous comme ça?*'

'*Bagatelle – pour les roses,*' replied Jean-Louis.

'*Je viendrai bien avec vous,*' said the baker and set his tray down inside the entrance to his shop.

263

'No room – *hélas*,' said Marie-France.

'Doesn't that man ever do any work?' said Mort.

'His wife does it all,' said Nell and Marie-France in unison.

'*Belle-maman* and I are planning a campaign to liberate her from behind the counter,' said Marie-France.

'Are we?' said Nell. 'Well, we probably should.'

She started to settle into the front passenger seat but was firmly edged aside by Marie-France. Mort winked at her and helped her into the back.

'We can talk English together,' he said. 'It will give us both a rest.'

'I don't need a rest,' said Nell.

And Marie-France turned around and said: '*Belle-maman*, like me, has attained the true level of bilingualism where she is hardly aware which language she is speaking. Do you know what the tests of true bilingualism are?'

'Nope,' said Mort, clearing a place amidst a sea of chocolate wrappers on the back seat.

'Among the true tests of bilingualism are to write poetry in the other language, do mathematical calculations and, of course, make jokes.'

'I bet you do that all the time,' said Mort, emerging from the wrappers with a Milky Bar. 'These aren't all empty,' he informed Nell.

'That makes it more fun,' said Jean-Louis from the front of the car. 'Jacqueline is trying to reform me and make me clean the place up but I like surprises.'

'Chocolate goes rancid in the sun,' said Marie-France. 'You can tell because it gets a faint white hue.' She pronounced those three difficult last words with a terrifying precision.

'This chocolate was white in the first place,' said Mort, breaking off a square and putting it into his mouth.

'Disgusting!' said Marie-France. 'A true chocolate

connoisseur would only eat dark chocolate. I belong to a club called *Les Croqueurs du Chocolat* and we would not even classify white chocolate as a chocolate.'

'I love it all,' said Jean-Louis.

Nell had started to nod off during this conversation. She had not slept well since her return from Delhi and subsequent meeting with Claudine. Now she dozed as the Deux Chevaux bounced across Paris. She was aware of Mort sitting inches from her. At one point he offered her a piece of chocolate, then he seemed to be telling her stories of blizzards, hurricanes and tornadoes. When the car pulled up in front of the path that led to the Bagatelle and she was thrown towards the back of her stepdaughter's head, she heard him saying: 'Now in Kansas there was a cow named Fawn that was twice picked up by tornadoes and each time set down in a field containing a bull. How's that for serendipity?'

'What?' blinked Nell. 'What are you talking about?'

'I'll tell you again when you're awake,' said Mort and climbed out of the car ahead of her.

Jean-Louis got them all waved through the admission turnstile as his guests. They walked past the herbaceous border, past the small water garden that in spring would be filled with irises, past the gardener's lodge, and were all suddenly silenced by the sight of the enormous rose garden.

'Oh my God,' said Mort. 'We've walked into Alice in Wonderland.'

'It's not at its best,' said Jean-Louis. 'June was a moment of paradise here. Now there is too much dust and most of the roses are past their prime.'

'We won't hold that against them,' said Mort. 'I remember this place now. It's the most beautiful rose garden I've ever seen.'

'But how many have you seen?' asked Marie-France.

'I don't recall that roses were ever an American forte.'

Mort hadn't heard her. Like Ferdinand the gentle bull of the children's tale, he had charged forward to fling himself into the perfume and softness and colour of the thousands of roses that lined the paths. There were roses strung along trellises, roses climbing up poles, roses draped across pergolas and roses on round bushes that looked as though they were indeed waiting for the Queen of Hearts' footmen to give them a coat of paint.

'Which one is yours, Jean-Louis?' cried Mort, dipping his nose into a deep red rose. 'Maria Callas? Princess Margaret?'

'The roses in the *concours* don't have names yet – just numbers,' said Jean-Louis. 'But here comes my Jacqueline. Meet her first, then we'll show you.'

An auburn-haired young woman in overalls with no make-up and big healthy eyes and teeth was walking towards them. Jean-Louis picked her up in his arms as he often did with Nell, then set her down and introduced her.

'You look like an American,' said Mort.

After the introductions, there was little opportunity for any real conversation, walking as they were along the narrow gravel paths between the thousands of roses. Nell was pleased. She didn't have the energy to make any new acquaintances today, and she didn't know whether meeting a stepdaughter-in-law needed to be treated as important.

'Here is my rose: number 22,' said Jean-Louis, and stopped in front of an old-fashioned pink and white variety with a dense cluster of pale velvety petals.

They each took it in turn to bend down and smell Jean-Louis' rose. It had a heavy old-fashioned scent.

'Are you planning to name it after Jacqueline?' asked Mort, straightening up slowly and rubbing his lower back with both hands.

'Not this one,' said Jean-Louis. 'I have others in my future that will be for Jacqueline. This one I will name after Nelli.'

'After me? Whatever for?'

'Because you are *belle-maman*,' shrugged Jean-Louis. 'And because this is such an English type of rose: reserved, discreet, quietly beautiful, never flamboyant – and constant.'

Nell was almost moved to tears by the big Frenchman's first four adjectives. At the mention of constant, she grabbed Jacqueline's arm and said: 'This is such a lovely evening – why don't I take you all for tea.'

'You don't have to do that, Nelli,' said Jean-Louis.

'But I want to. There is an open-air restaurant under the trees – just beyond the gardens. It's very cool there.'

'Only impatiens will grow because it's so shady – I know the place,' said Jean-Louis. 'But you don't have to.'

Nell led them away from the roses. Jacqueline seemed to want to stay next to her, and when their pace had slackened a little she whispered in French that she was very sorry about Luc.

'We all are,' said Marie-France behind them. 'But we are confident he will return.'

'You sound like a presidential aide giving a news bulletin,' said Mort.

'But we are confident,' repeated Marie-France.

'We are,' agreed Jean-Louis. 'Papa is so resilient, so . . .'

'Indomitable,' said Marie-France.

'He is?' Mort turned to Nell.

'Oh, definitely,' said Nell. 'All those things.'

'Both,' said Marie-France. 'We only said two things so it would be "both" not "all" – isn't that right?' She turned to Mort.

'I've never given it any thought,' said Mort.

267

'I have had to think much about Papa for my psychoanalytical studies,' said Marie-France.

'What studies are those?' asked Mort.

'My real job,' said Marie-France. 'You didn't think my airline job was my profession?'

'I didn't give it any thought at all,' said Mort.

'You don't think about much, do you?' said Marie-France and Nell wondered if this was her stepdaughter's perverse way of flirting with the American. 'In order to practise my profession, I have to undergo an analysis myself,' Marie-France went on. 'This involves much thought about my past, my parents. So often the father is the unknown, the figure in the shadows. But I feel, after much thought, that my father is just what I have always known him to be – a hero. Papa should have been here to day. Then we would have been truly happy – the day would have been perfect.'

'He would never have come here,' said Jean-Louis. 'He couldn't see the point of gardens.'

Nell didn't participate in the conversation because she was feeling quite happy in a calm, unrapturous sort of way and didn't dare admit it to her stepchildren. Walking through the roses and the heat and the fragrance she felt dream-like and agreeably light and empty.

Mort had dropped back to talk to her and was repeating his story about the cow.

'Twice she got picked up by a tornado,' he was saying. 'And twice she was set down in a field with a bull.'

'Is there a point to that story?' asked Nell.

'Just that it's true. And wonderful. And it supports my theory that worrying is a waste of time. I mean there was old Fawn one minute – chewing the cud, not a thought in her empty cow brain – and then whoosh! Her whole world was transformed.'

'That was the Wizard of Oz,' said Nell and quickened her pace.

'Then there was the one about the guy in LA who wanted to float over his neighbourhood so he got his neighbours to tie weather balloons to his garden chair but when they released him he shot up to eleven thousand feet. Nobody knew how to get him down safely so he stayed up there for hours. Air traffic had to be diverted around him at LA international airport – he'd turned into a dangerous obstacle!'

'That's not possible,' Nell laughed.

'Oh yes it is, Nelli,' interrupted Marie-France. 'I was in LA when it happened. The man caused a very grave threat to air traffic. I think he should have been arrested.'

'Most definitely,' said Mort and turned his back on Marie-France. 'Then there was the guy in Minnesota wanted to fly with a flock of—'

Before he could finish his sentence, Marie-France stepped in front of him.

'I heard the irony in your tone when you said that,' she told Mort. 'I thought Americans had no irony but that was irony. And I think you should know that by laughing at silly pranks of that type you are . . .'

Nell dropped behind the two of them. She was too jet-lagged to bother with another Marie-France diatribe, and as long as she could just drift past the flowers her drowsiness was almost pleasant. They had come to a narrow lane with dense rhododendron bushes on either side and high, old oaks and lime trees back behind them. Jacquline had stopped to examine a wild flower in amongst some shrubs. Mort was struggling to change the subject and was telling Marie-France that there was something Shakespearean about wandering in midsummer through woods such as these. Marie-France replied that there was a true Shakespearean garden further back in the Bois. To which Mort replied that that wasn't what he had meant. Jean-Louis had donned his gardener's hat to keep the sun off his thinning hair and was several yards ahead of their little group.

Nell overtook Mort and Marie-France. She wasn't in a hurry. She felt almost as though she were sleep-walking but amongst fragrance and colour. Even the headmistress who still resided in her head had relaxed and was concluding that at last Nell had started to understand life. She had learnt that happiness was not based on perfection and that a truly happy day like today could just *be* – even with Luc off God only knew where and in the presence of such large, irritating flies in the ointment as Marie-France.

There was a sudden rustle in the bushes to the right of Jean-Louis. Nell thought it must be a squirrel or even, judging by the noise and disturbance, a deer. Were there deer in the Bois? she was wondering when Mlle Marina, in full make-up and a gold lamé jacket, stepped out and approached Jean-Louis. He lifted his hat to reveal his identity, winked and waved her away. Marina would have disappeared back to the bushes had Nell not caught up to her, grabbed her by the arm and, with her mouth opening and closing but no sound coming out, tripped and sent them both into the rhodo-dendrons.

CHAPTER TWENTY EIGHT

'Try to imagine we're in a Shakespeare play.' Mort was kneeling next to Nell, who was sitting on the gravel path where she had fallen when Marina had wrenched herself free and hurtled off through the bushes. 'Changed identities, even changes of gender, magical things happening in the woods in summer.'

'They put on Shakespeare plays in the Shakespeare garden on the other side of the Bois,' said Marie-France. 'And they have every flower there that was ever mentioned in any of his plays.'

'Shut up about the goddamned garden!' cried Mort. 'That's not what I'm trying to say at all.'

'Don't tell me to shut up!' Marie-France pulled herself up to her full six feet and tried to glare down at Mort who was five foot ten. 'I knew that your American vulgarity would reveal itself in time. I'm not even going to ride home with you. I'm going to take a taxi.' She turned away from them and started to walk along the gravel path.

'Did you know?' Nell called after her. 'When you had the lesson this morning did you notice?'

'Of course.' Marie-France turned to her stepmother. 'Of course I knew, but I didn't care. She is half the price of Berlitz and has an excellent accent, worthy of imitation.' She hailed a passing taxi as she finished her sentence, ran along the last lengths of path and was gone.

'Maybe I should have gone after her,' said Mort.

'Oh no, definitely not,' said Jean-Louis, who had found a bench to sit on and produced a Mars bar from his back pocket. 'She really only did that because her place is not far from here and she didn't want to waste money coming all the way back into town and then getting a taxi back out. She's always doing things like that to make us feel guilty.'

'Did you know about Marina?' Nell asked Jean-Louis. She was still sitting on the gravel and would have liked to lie back and sleep, were it not for the three people looking down at her.

'Oh yes. But you see, Nelli, I'm always digging around in mud and dirt. I find worms doing strange things, frogs in surprising positions, mating dogs stuck together – whatever humans do on their bit of earth doesn't bother me.'

'Remember when we found those three hedgehogs?' said Jacqueline, who had come to sit next to Jean-Louis on the bench.

'Wasn't that extraordinary?' said Jean-Louis.

'Not hedgehogs,' groaned Nell and closed her eyes.

As they drove back to the seventh arrondisement in the Deux Chevaux, Nell took out her notebook, studied her list of things to do, and decided that she needed her mother. 'Keep an eye on mum' had not been ticked on her list because she hadn't felt that the unsettling conversation about the Circle Line qualified as 'keeping an eye'.

Mort read the list over her shoulder and slumped into his cramped seat. He wondered whether he should keep a list but couldn't think of anything to put on it.

By the time the little car pulled up in front of the

apartment, Nell was feeling confident and resolute. She had understood what she must do – she must turn her attention away from her own troubles and go to her mother who, bereaved as she was, had far greater sorrows than Nell. As she bade a hurried farewell to her stepchildren and the appalling Mort, Nell realized that she had come close to being sucked into the life of the squalid courtyard but had been warned in time. Life, fate, destiny had sent that terrifying transsexual to show her that none of this was her world. Life, fate and destiny had also conspired to give her free airline tickets and no new flights and the time to devote her attention to her mother.

As Nell rode the lift up to the flat, she felt sure that she would sleep peacefully that night and be fresh for her journey to London the next day. Even turning on the television in search of Luc didn't unsettle her. He was still missing somewhere in the north of Canada, said the news bulletin, and didn't even bother flashing his face on the screen.

Nell didn't sleep peacefully that night. The plan to fly to London proved more unsettling than she had imagined, and as she lay awake in the hot room under the roof, she found herself brooding on Marie-France's pronouncements about fathers. She sat up on one elbow and thought about Ivy and her father and the strangers from Sainsbury's car park.

After a while, she got up, made a cup of coffee and walked over to the window. It was six o'clock and the sky was lightening. She stared down in the half-light to the plane tree and saw that Mort was sleeping peacefully, his arms flung behind his head. She saw the light in the baker's kitchen and thought she heard his kneading machine thud into action, and she saw a woman's figure slip into the courtyard, remove her shoes and tiptoe across the cobbles. The figure stopped to caress the leaves of the plumbago. Nell watched and was overcome by sadness at the quiet morning scene before her.

She turned away from the window. As the dawn rose, she understood that she must go and see Ivy. Marie-France was irritating and frequently absurd but it seemed to Nell that she was right, and that in order for her own life to continue more clearly and more cleanly she must lift the shadows that surrounded her father's past.

She had kept the piece of the *Daily Mail* on which her father had written Ivy's name and address, and when she got to London she took a taxi straight there. She had no baggage. She intended to take her mother out to tea, ensure that she was as well as could be expected, and get the last flight back to Paris. The detour to Ivy would not take too long. She did not know what she expected to glean from the old woman, but she was convinced that the poor old dear was senile enough to be garrulous about the past.

She found Ivy's home with no difficulty. It was in a group of semi-detached houses at the end of a cul-de-sac. Nell calculated that her payday was close enough for her to afford to keep the taxi until her meeting with the old lady was over. As the cab came to a halt, Nell saw that there was a 'For Sale' sign in front of Ivy's house. A BMW parked up on the kerb and in front of the gate prevented her cab from getting any closer.

She left the taxi, squeezed in through the front gate, sniffed at the overgrown garden and rang the doorbell.

She heard loud, heavy footsteps and saw a wide silhouette approaching on the other side of the frosted glass door. She'd been on the point of panic at the thought of encountering the despised old woman again, but was now curious to identify the large figure who was about to open the door.

It was a man. A very big man – not fat, not tall, but robust and broad with no neck, not much hair and a flaming red face with narrow watery blue eyes.

'I'm looking for Ivy Osborne,' said Nell.

'Why?' said the man.

'I'm a friend. Well, a friend of a friend.'

'Mother didn't have any friends,' said the man.

'Didn't? Is she dead?' She is dead, thought Nell, the wicked old cow made sure she got up there to Dad before Mother had a chance. But up where? Everyone knows there isn't any up there up there. Still, Nell was furious at being outrun by the frivolous little woman.

'She might just as well be,' sighed the man. 'What did you want with her?'

'What do you mean? Might just as well be?'

'Poor old duck has almost lost it completely.' The man's flaming face sank into several folds. His small eyes seemed to be sucked into those folds as he sought to continue his sentence. 'What's that word now? Alzheimer's. That's what they said. She doesn't know a thing – doesn't know me any more.'

'Can she have visitors?' asked Nell, not yet ready to relinquish her mission.

'What's the point? The wife and I go and sit there but she doesn't know. I didn't want to put her in there, you know. There is no profit in selling this place for me. We've got a detached house in Hayes, thank you. And all the money from this will pay for her nursing fees.'

'Which home is she in? Is it far from here?'

'But we had to put her away,' the man went on. 'First she started going down the street with two pair of tights. She'd put one pair on one leg and the other on the other. She'd have two loose legs dangling on either side of her. It would have been laughable if it hadn't been dangerous. She could have fallen, you see—'

'And broken hips are very tricky at her age,' said Nell. 'I really would like to visit—'

'Then she started roasting chickens by putting them on the gas ring. Well, it stopped being funny then—'

'She could have burned the house down.'

'The wife is still trying to get the grease out from underneath. Now she, the wife, says we have to see the humour in it or we'd go mad. But I don't know. I can't. She was my mother, you see.' He hadn't made any attempt to ask Nell into the house, and now he picked up a briefcase, stepped outside and started locking up. 'I've been told we can rent this out to the Japanese for a thousand pound a month,' he said, staring up at the upstairs windows. 'But I'd rather just be rid of it now.'

'It's probably better,' said Nell. 'Which home did you say your mother was in?'

'Queen Mary's – it's only a couple of minutes from here. Opposite the common. But there's really no point – unless, like me, you have to.'

Nell thanked him, said she probably wouldn't bother, and made her way back to the taxi. The driver knew the home well and two minutes later Nell was standing at reception, asking for Ivy Osborne.

'She's right there,' said a Jamaican nurse, and pointed to Ivy who was sitting by the window. 'We try to encourage them into the garden on days like this but she keeps coming back inside.'

'She can talk a bit, can she?' asked Nell.

'No, not really. She doesn't have many lucid moments – she just sits there on her own little planet, looking out at the rest of us like we're the aliens. Maybe we are,' laughed the nurse and added, 'She likes music. That's how that illness goes. She don't know her own son but she knows all the verses of "She'll be coming round the mountain when she comes."'

'I didn't know there was more than one verse,' said Nell.

'Me neither.'

Nell pulled a seat up in front of Ivy's chair. 'Hello, Ivy. Do you remember me?'

Ivy didn't look up.

'I'm Wilf's daughter,' said Nell. 'No, actually, no I'm not. I'm Harry's daughter. You remember Harry.'

Ivy stared at the buttons on her blouse.

'You knew Harry well, didn't you?'

Ivy didn't reply.

'Harry was one of your best friends,' Nell persisted. 'I'm his daughter.'

Nell struggled on for almost half an hour, recounting tales of her father, trying to remember friends or memories that they might have shared. When all her efforts failed she even sang the only verse that she knew of 'She'll be coming round the mountain'.

The old woman didn't look up.

'It doesn't always work,' shrugged the nurse who had brought Ivy a cup of tea.

'I'm exhausted,' said Nell. 'I flew all the way from Paris for this.'

'Have her cup of tea,' said the nurse. 'She never drinks it.'

Nell drank the tea and stared at the woman. But Ivy was looking down and all Nell could see was the sparse white hair on her pink head.

When Nell got up to go, she squeezed the old woman's shoulder.

'You're Vivien Leigh,' said Ivy.

'What? What did you say?'

But Ivy had returned to her barricaded world.

'Did you hear that?' Nell asked the nurse.

'I wouldn't complain,' laughed the nurse.

'But I don't look anything like Vivien Leigh – do I?'

'Not to me. She did once tell me that I was Jean Harlow.'

'Oh,' said Nell, suddenly crestfallen. 'Did she really?'

'I'm joking,' said the nurse.

Nell waited several more minutes, but when she saw

that Ivy was sealed back up inside her own universe she left and took a taxi to her mother's house. She sat back in the cab and closed her eyes, relieved to have some precious time to gather her thoughts before she saw her mother. She had no intention of telling her about her failed mission and told herself that she was just ensuring that Vi got over this silly business about the Circle Line. Nell would warn her of the dangers of public transport, eat a quick supper with her and be on her way. But perhaps mother will want to talk about Ivy, thought Nell and tried to think of a way to introduce the subject.

She let the taxi go at her mother's house in Streatham. Vi was in the kitchen, chopping some courgettes.

'I've never eaten these things before,' she said to her daughter in greeting. 'I decided it was time to try some new food.'

'There's nothing very exciting about courgettes,' said Nell.

'Well, I won't know until I've tried, will I?'

Vi had apparently been planning to eat courgettes and baked beans for dinner. She dished out a helping to Nell who ate in exhausted silence.

'You look terrible, Nell,' said her mother. 'When all this worry is over you must take yourself off to a health farm.'

'What a funny idea,' said Nell.

'I saw one on daytime telly. I'd go if your father had left us more money.'

'So you've stopped all that gallivanting round London?'

'I lost interest in that weeks ago,' said Vi.

'I'm glad to hear it,' said Nell. 'Public transport isn't safe at any time of day lately. You're better off staying away from it.'

'You should have said that to your Luc,' said her

mother, then leaned over and squeezed her hand. 'That wasn't a very good joke, was it? But you look so fraught, Nell.'

'I've had a terrible summer, Mum.'

'I know, we both have, but you mustn't get too glum, dear. People aren't really that sympathetic to unhappy people. If you complain too much, they just drift away.'

'I don't care about people,' said Nell. 'They can all drift away for all I care.'

'You don't mean that. You think you do, but you don't. I was so fed up with people just after your dad died – all the ones who come up to you in the street and say that they are there if you need them. And then you never hear a word. I wrote some very rude letters to the aunts, I can tell you.'

'You didn't, Mum?'

'Yes I did. I told Agnes to stick her charity up her date box. And Flo – even if I do feel sorry for her for being deaf.'

'Up her date box,' sighed Nell. 'I haven't heard that expression in years. Did they write back?'

'No, and I don't care. Just a minute. I want to show you something. Make a cup of tea if you want one.'

'I never drink tea after dinner,' said Nell.

'You used to,' said Vi and disappeared up the stairs.

While she was gone, Nell looked around the kitchen for an old newspaper to read. She didn't want to be alone with just her thoughts. As she rummaged in the cupboard where her mother kept the recycling bags, she found a diary on the top shelf.

'I didn't know you kept a diary,' she shouted up to her mother to ensure that she was still at the other end of the house. Nell leafed through a few pages, amazed that anyone would bother to record such a boring life.

'Went to market,' said the entry for 4 August. 'Changed dressing gown at C and A's.' 'Went to

279

opticians,' 5 August. 'Got new frames for my glasses.' Then suddenly in capital letters spread across two blank pages Nell saw the words: NOBODY CAN KNOW THE LIGHTNESS OF MY THOUGHTS. NO FUTURE AND BUGGER THE PAST, HERE I HANG ONLY IN THE MOMENT, LIGHT AS A GADFLY IN A SUMMER EVENING MEADOW.

'Look what I bought at the market,' said Vi, who had come back into the kitchen. She was holding out a pair of golden sandals.

Nell slipped the diary back onto the shelf and said: 'What on earth do you want with those?'

'That's what I wanted to tell you.' Her mother sat down in an armchair and started to buckle the sandals.

'I went to the ballroom dancing at the community centre one afternoon a couple of weeks ago. I stood outside in the heat for half an hour watching them – I didn't want to go in and be with all those old people – then I saw myself in the plate glass window and saw that I'm an old person too. So I went in – it's only fifty pence a session – and some old woman asked me to dance. I thought I'd hate that but it's all right really – men die so much more than women that you can't be fussy. Anyway, look what I learned!'

Nell's mother hoisted herself slowly up from the armchair. She turned on the radio and moved the dial to an easy listening station. Then she walked over to the only space in the room, between the kitchen table and the sink, and, silhouetted against the summer twilight, she started to move. She moved with grace and ease, arms outstretched, her arthritic hands looking as though they were meant to be held in their permanent half-closed position. Nell could see that she was counting out the rhythm to herself. Vi crossed the room, jutted her chin out and turned: 'Tango!' she cried triumphantly.

'Very good, Mother.'

'Don't patronize me, Nell. That was good.'

'Oh, it was, and I'm not . . . I'm just a bit surprised. I didn't think that – well, Dad hasn't been dead long, and—'

'You try,' said her mother. 'It will do you good – believe me it will.' She was walking towards Nell, arms still outstretched. Before Nell could back away those arms had closed themselves around her. The two women stood in the golden evening light. Nell, frowning and uncomfortable, gazed down at her mother and realized that the old woman had shrunk by a couple of inches and seemed, for the first time in their lives, to be smaller than she was. Her mother's lined face seemed to Nell to be full of the evening light. She was counting, one, two, one, two. 'Now go!' Nell failed to go anywhere and her mother stepped forward onto each of her feet.

'Try again,' said her mother. 'Go on the count of three.'

'Go where, Mum? I can't dance.' Nell tried to disentangle herself from her mother's grip but Vi pulled her closer to her.

'Just follow me. I'll lead. You follow. Now one, two, one, two, three.'

Nell felt herself being pushed backwards. She was disconcerted by the strength of her mother's grasp and the forcefulness of her step.

'There, you're getting the idea. Just let me lead you.'

'I can't, Mother. I can't.' Nell stopped in the middle of the kitchen floor and burst into tears.

'What on earth is the matter? You were doing very well.'

'I can't. I can't dance. And I certainly can't go backwards.'

'But you were.'

'It terrifies me. I can't see where I'm going. I hate not to see where I'm going. I panic. And anyway, I can't dance. I haven't got any dancing in me.'

'Everybody's got dancing in them, Nell.'

But Nell was sobbing too loudly to listen. She sat back down on the kitchen chair. Vi sat down next to her. She took her hand.

'You always were a tightly wound little thing. You'd hardly been in the world an hour and you had that same intense look on your face, probably already wondering what you should be doing – what your duty was. I said to your father that you'd need a lot of un-ravelling but we never worked out how to do it.'

When Nell left for the airport an hour later, she saw her mother through the gently billowing net curtains in the living room. Vi usually waited at the window to wave to her daughter but today Nell saw that she was dancing again, on her own and clutching a Digestive biscuit in one hand. On every third beat, she kicked her leg in the air and yelled, 'Whoo!'

Nell remembered that other infuriating dancer back in the courtyard and wondered for the millionth time what was wrong with people. There is so much trouble in the world, so much to be taken care of and worried about, and all they can do is dance.

CHAPTER TWENTY NINE

Nell took British Airways home in order to avoid her colleagues. But when she entered the plane the purser looked at her boarding pass and said: 'Oh, you're one of us even if it is with the competition. Come on up front.'

Nell followed him to business class where she almost ripped the welcoming glass of champagne from the stewardess's hand.

'Can I have another one?' she asked the purser as he came through. And he smiled and came back to her seat with four small bottles wrapped up in a duty free bag. This was an old airline tradition among employees. For years it had kept Nell and Luc's fridge in Chantilly full of bottles just big enough to provide a toast before supper. Nell had no intention of storing these.

She drank all four bottles in the forty minutes that it took to cross the Channel. She drank the first one because her mother no longer needed her. She felt that she deserved a second bottle for sitting singing 'She'll be coming round the mountain when she comes' to poor, batty old Ivy. Then she drank the third one as a toast to her father and again to the mother who had gone her own merry way, and she finished off the fourth to prepare herself to face the sordid courtyard in

Paris. She stuffed the empty bottles down the back of her seat, and tried to eat the tray of smoked salmon and cold chicken that had been placed before her. But it was a long way away and every time she tried to spear the salmon she missed and had to pull her fork out of the upholstery on the seat in front of her.

When it came time to disembark, she couldn't stand up. The purser saw her and came to her assistance.

'My father died,' wailed Nell.

'Oh, I am sorry. You should have said something,' said the purser and with the help of a steward he carried her down the jetway. Somewhere during the long, slow descent of that passage, Nell decided that they were both lovely, lovely men and was trying to reach the purser's ear to kiss it when she was faced with a deputation of senior officials from both British Airways and the French airline. They were all waiting for Nell.

The deputation took Nell to a private room behind her own airline's ticket counter. The deputation also now included the steward and the purser from the British airline because Nell wouldn't let go of either of them.

'Very tired and emotional,' said the BA purser and his French colleagues smiled and translated this phrase to themselves with great solemnity.

'When she sees the news it will become worse,' said the French station manager.

'Telly!' cried Nell as a wide-screen model was wheeled in.

The station manager pushed her gently onto a sofa and said:

'*Il faut que vous vous prepariez, Madame Marchand.*'

'She must prepare herself,' the BA purser translated to the BA steward.

The Frenchman turned on the television.

284

'Luc!' cried Nell when Luc's face appeared on screen. 'Wait a minute, the picture's wobbling!'

'It's not a picture – it's live,' said the station manager. 'The Commandant Marchand has asked to speak live to the, to the . . .' The station manager wasn't sure whom Luc wanted to address.

'To the world!' cried Nell.

'Shhh – he's about to speak,' said an assistant station manager.

Luc looked very tanned and slender. He was standing in what looked like a campground. There was a big statue of Smokey the Bear in the background next to a sign that said: 'Fire Danger EXTREME today!' Beyond that, Nell thought she could see a shop selling fishing tackle.

'*Mesdames, messieurs,*' he said. '*Ma femme aime beaucoup la télé—*'

'*C'est vrai!*' cried Nell. Then remembered that the two companions who had been forced onto the sofa with her were English. 'It is true,' she translated to them and for reasons she didn't understand she said the three words in a very thick French accent which so amused her that she repeated it to the whole room. 'It is true!'

'Shhh,' said the station manager. Luc was speaking again. Nell stared at his image and thought how much she loved television even with Luc on it. She tried very hard to understand what he was saying but he kept doubling up, fading, zooming up to almost in front of her nose, then backing away to the other end of the room. And he was slurring his speech. Nell gave up on him and stared at the rabbits out on the runway.

'*Lapins,*' she translated to the BA men on the sofa. 'Rabbits. Not *sapins*, that's Chriss-mus trees, but *lapins*. There's millions of them out there but nobody knows but me – and some taxi drivers.'

Nell passed out. Somewhere through her stupor, she

heard the BA men wish her goodbye. She thought that the purser bent over and gave her a kiss but she couldn't be sure. Some time later she heard the station manager say something about keeping her away from the press in her current state. Someone else said something about putting her in one of the reserve rooms to sleep it off. Then Nell felt male arms being slipped underneath her. When she woke up she was in a small bed in a dark, narrow reserve room with Marcel the old steward from the New York flight standing over her with a cup of coffee.

'I'm not on reserve,' said Nell, who had recognized her surroundings immediately even though she was still a little drunk.

'But I am,' said Marcel. 'I came on at six a.m. and they said you were down here. I've been bringing you coffee on the chance that you might wake up for three hours now.'

'Thanks,' said Nell and sat up and took the coffee. 'But what on earth am I doing here?'

'You had a big night last night, Nelli. Luc was released.'

'He was? Oh, I'm so glad! I knew he would be. When's he coming home?'

'Well, there's the difficulty,' said Marcel, sitting down at the end of her bed. 'He's not.'

'He's not?' said Nell. 'Why not?'

'Oh, Nelli, he explained all this on TV last night.'

'Why didn't I see it?'

'You did but you weren't paying attention.'

'Oh dear,' sighed Nell. 'I do remember watching telly last night. At least I think I do. What did he say?'

'Well, I don't really think it's my place to tell you all that. The station manager has left you a video of Luc's appearance.'

'I've got Luc on video?' said Nell, reaching out and patting the videocassette that was on the bedside table. 'In colour?'

'Of course he's in colour,' said Marcel.

'Did he look nice?' asked Nell.

'He looked thinner and tanned but very fit.'

'That's good,' said Nell. 'What did he say, Marcel?'

'Well, he seems to have found a new life for himself.'

'With a woman?' asked Nell, deciding that Claudine wasn't in any face lift clinic after all.

'No. At least, I don't think so.'

'Then what kind of a new life is he having?'

'Flying DC3s,' said Marcel and stroked Nell's feet through the blanket. 'You know, Nelly, I'm not surprised. I mean his behaviour is extreme and outrageous and very selfish but he had been so unhappy ever since the fly-by-wire system came in.'

'Luc's never unhappy,' sniffed Nell. 'He's too strong and resilient to be unhappy.'

'But he hated all this computer business,' said Marcel. 'Said it wasn't proper flying.'

'Did he?' said Nell, wondering whether the alcohol had muddled her memory or if she had never known about this unhappiness of Luc's.

'Well, anyway. Watch the video.' Marcel tweaked her foot again. 'He didn't say he would never come back. I mean, I don't think he actually used the word "never".'

'Hmm,' said Nell, and sat in puzzled silence looking down at Marcel's mottled hand that was still patting her toes. 'So I suppose I go home now.'

'Yes, the company said they would lay on a taxi. And they also said not to talk to the press for a day or two. Apparently they've sent them up to your old address in Chantilly so you should have some peace for a while.'

Marcel pulled Nell out of bed where she noticed for the first time that she had been sleeping with all her clothes on.

'I'll help you to a taxi,' said Marcel, and hugged her.

'Poor old Nelli,' he said, stroking her hair. 'What a summer you've had.'

'*Faut pas râler*,' said Nell and repeated the phrase in English. 'Mustn't grumble.'

'Of course you must grumble,' replied Marcel. 'You're in France. We're all in favour of grumbling.'

Nell started to cry. She sat back down on the bed and put her shoes on. 'I'm still drunk, Marcel,' she wept. 'I can't stand up straight.'

'You did drink at least a bottle of champagne yesterday. They found the bottles behind your seat.'

'I usually can't drink more than a glass or two,' said Nell.

'Well, you must have had a lot to celebrate,' said Marcel. 'Come on – there are no long-haul flights leaving for an hour or two. Nobody will miss me if I walk you to your taxi.'

Nell looked at her bloated face in a mirror above a cheap formica dressing table. She turned to Marcel.

'When I'm made up, not when I'm looking like this but when you usually see me, do I remind you of anybody?'

Marcel had crawled under the bed to retrieve Nell's shoes. He emerged, wiping the dust from his bald head, and said: 'Well, Nelli, you've always put me in mind of the woman behind the counter in the duty free shop in the Terminal One basement. You know – the one who sells foie gras and Godiva chocolates.'

Ten minutes later, Marcel bundled Nell into a cab where she sat with her overnight bag at her feet and her video tape clutched in both hands on her lap.

CHAPTER THIRTY

Mort had returned from a hot, lonely walk around Paris to find Marina untying his laundry from the line that he had strung.

'This looks disgusting,' she said.

'Mmm,' agreed Mort as she piled his clean underwear into his arms. 'Do you know that the temperature hit a hundred degrees Fahrenheit in New York, London and Paris this past week? I just saw it on a TV screen in a shop window – a hundred degrees! That's kind of terrifying.'

'I don't have time to think about the weather.'

'Oh, Marina – I am so sorry! I felt so guilty about you the other day in the Bois,' said Mort. 'I felt as though it was my fault. I should have known we might bump into you.'

'I'm fine,' said Marina. 'Do you want some coffee?'

Once Mort was seated at the table and Marina had made the coffee, she placed a cup in front of him and said: 'I've got a job – a real job.'

'How'd you get a job? You're illegal like me. You can't work here.'

'I have a skill that a French person doesn't possess,' declared Marina.

Mort raised an eyebrow at her.

'I speak Brazilian Portuguese and the language

school round the corner will take me on as a teacher. The guy there said Parisians think Rio is a very chic place to go on vacation.'

'Well how about that,' said Mort. 'When did you line this up?'

'This morning.'

'How's the money? Can you live here on it?'

'Maybe not very well. I don't know yet. I'm never going back to the Bois.'

'You shouldn't let that airline woman upset you like that. What's it to do with her what we do with our lives?'

'I like her,' said Marina. 'She's got, I don't know how you say it, she's got a kind of . . . of serious in her way of living. Not like that blonde one—'

'Claudine?'

'She's got no serious in her,' said Marina. 'She told me she don't go to work if it's windy and the plane moves around. She don't go to work if she don't like the place they send her. In Rio, girls dream of her job and she don't hardly do it.'

Mort wasn't listening. 'What is going to become of me, Marina? I guess I believed all that American talk about striking out, having the courage to change paths – you know the kind of thing.'

'No,' said Marina.

'Sure you do – don't be difficult.' Mort folded and unfolded the *Herald Tribune* as he tried to order his thoughts. 'You know the kind of talk that always comes packaged up with some success story – the guy who founded a company or discovered a latent talent for tap dancing, you know? Nobody ever mentions the guys who thought they could do something new, then found they had no talent, or lacked the energy or the courage and got nowhere, you know? You never hear about them.'

'You can go home,' said Marina. 'You got your

brother and your mother. You can live legally in America. You know how many Brazilians want to do that?'

'I don't want to be on TV any more, that's for sure – not that they'd have me. And yet I wouldn't want to leave the weather – I'd like to do something about it. I guess that's why I tried to paint it.'

'You could go to art school in the States,' said Marina, setting the percolator back on the hotplate.

'No talent,' said Mort, and swung his feet up to rest on the window ledge. He folded his hands behind his head and gazed out at the sunshine. 'Have you ever thought what an amazing journey the seasons take us on, Marina? It's better than anything the airlines can provide.'

'Not in Brazil,' sighed Marina.

'No, but where I'm from every three months or so the landscape is completely transformed. I once wrote a poem about it. Do you want to hear it?'

'Sure.'

' "The Seasons",' announced Mort and scowled as he concentrated: ' "Leaves in, Leaves out, Leaves brown, Leaves down," ' he recited, and waited for Marina's approval.

'That's not a poem,' said Marina.

'Well I think it is,' said Mort. 'Actually I'm not even sure I made it up, maybe I read it somewhere. But it is true. The world goes white, then green, then kind of dusty yellow, then red and orange, then back to white. I love it. And yet I keep having this weird thought that maybe in decades to come the seasons will disappear. Isn't that terrifying?'

'I've never seen snow,' Marina shrugged.

Mort was again preoccupied with something that he seemed to be seeing in the courtyard outside.

'There are guys I knew in school who are doing something about weather changes. Guys with names like Howie . . . dumb name . . . are studying these new weather patterns. There's a place that looks into all this in Boulder, Colorado. Guys like Howie aren't sitting on their backsides in Paris—'

'Can't do anything about the weather,' said Marina. 'God's in charge of the weather.'

'If you really believe that, then you might also say that God's in charge of gender,' said Mort, still gazing, eyes half closed, into the sunlight. 'And that hasn't stopped you—'

The silence that greeted this last comment caused Mort to open his eyes and swivel round to look at Marina. She was standing staring into the empty sink in the corner kitchen.

'That was so cruel,' she murmured. 'And I thought you liked me.'

Mort leapt to his feet and ran to put his arms round Marina.

'Oh, but I do, Marina! I do!' He guided her towards the table and pushed her gently into a seat. Then he bent down and took one of her large hands in his. 'It just slipped out. And you got to admit there's a logic to it – but I didn't mean to hurt you.'

'But you did.'

'See? That's what happens when I try to get all earnest and ponderous. I'm not cut out for it.'

Marina said nothing.

'You know, the truth is, and I'm not just saying this, but, well, if I'd had a big sister instead of old Frankie over there, well I'd have liked to have a sister like you.'

'You would?'

'Yeah, I would.'

They sat in the sunshine in an uneasy but not unpleasant silence. When Mort felt the time was right he withdrew his hand and said: 'And I keep thinking about that cow Fawn who got picked up by a tornado and deposited in a field with a bull. So you see,

Marina, a lot of my thoughts aren't worth much.'

'What cow?' Marina blew her nose and scowled at Mort.

'Oh, it's an old story about a cow in Kansas or Iowa or somewhere that was just chewing away one day when a tornado blew in, picked it up and deposited it, like I said—'

'In a field with a bull,' Marina laughed.

'The thing is it happened twice – and to the same cow. And I keep thinking about it which sounds dumb but I've lived with my brain for more than forty years and if it latches onto something there's usually a reason. Though God only knows what this is about. I've also been thinking about the guy in LA with the weather balloons—'

'What balloons?'

Before Mort could answer, the baker appeared in the courtyard and waved frantically up at them. '*Venez! Venez!*' he cried. '*C'est le monsieur du cinquième. Il va nous faire un discours! Venez!*'

'What's he all fired up about?' Mort asked Marina.

'He says the man from the fifth floor is going to make a speech,' said Marina.

The baker had set his television up on the window ledge. He turned up the volume and waved to them to come downstairs.

Mort followed Marina down to the courtyard where they sat with the baker while the newscaster recounted Luc's latest development. Then the same scene that Nell would see repeated out at the airport flashed on their screens. Mort smiled at the familiar sight of Smokey the Bear in the background.

'What a schmuck!' he said when Luc had finished his speech in both languages. 'That poor woman!'

The baker said something to Marina and signalled that she should translate.

'And her father just died,' said Marina.

293

The baker uttered another sentence.

'And she's virtually bankrupt.'

'That poor woman,' Mort repeated. 'It kind of puts us in perspective. How does he know all this?'

'He says he spends his life here on the courtyard, the mail goes through him—' The baker motioned to Marina that he had more to add. 'Oh, and he says she's virtually alone in the world.'

Mort looked up at the shutters of the fifth floor and felt a sudden admiration for the stern, dark little woman who had refused to allow her life to collapse.

'And I was ridiculing her for being so worried all the time,' he said. 'Poor old Nelli. We'll have to do something for her—'

'Flowers?' said Marina.

'No, that's like a death,' said Mort. 'We should do something fun, something . . . hell, I don't know.' Then a random thought popped into his head and he leapt to his feet. 'It wasn't the cow at all, Marina! It was the balloon man all the time! Where's the weather bureau around here?'

'They'll never give you a job,' said Marina. 'You don't speak the language.'

'Such faith you have in me,' said Mort. 'Just tell me where the meteorological guys are kept.'

Marina shrugged but translated the question to the baker who said that they were just a few blocks away on the Avenue Bosquet, and why did Mort want to know anyway?

Mort ignored him and headed towards the door. 'Oh, and some thick rope, like rope for mooring a boat?'

'What boat?'

'You'll see,' said Mort. 'Where do I get it?'

'BHV – it's a big store opposite the Hôtel de Ville – they have everything and they're open all summer.'

Mort paused and was about to ask Marina why she would know about mooring rope when he saw that he had little time to get across town before the shops closed. He turned and crossed through the cool shadows of the entrance hall, leaving Marina and the baker in front of the television screen where a young, balding, blond ecologist was defending his organization.

CHAPTER THIRTY ONE

When Nell got to her building, she slipped in through the door on tiptoe and saw with relief that the lift was waiting on the ground floor. Once she was inside the apartment, she closed the shutters on the courtyard, had a shower, pulled on her old grey silk kimono and walked towards the television. Then she paused and decided to make herself a pot of tea, and when that was made and placed neatly on a tray by the armchair she leaned forward and slipped the tape into the video player.

As soon as Nell saw Luc's tanned handsome face, she remembered her behaviour of the previous evening. But this time she was almost sober and could understand every word he said. Her finger hesitated above the stop button. If she wanted she could just erase Luc now and switch over to a daytime talk show. Or even turn off the television and just fly away. But Nell knew, although she could not have said why, that that was no longer a possibility.

She drew her legs up under her chin, hugged them to her and watched Luc's image on the screen.

He spoke first in French and then made an abbreviated version of his speech in English. When he said that opening phrase, '*Mesdames, messieurs, ma femme aime beaucoup la télé,*' Nell remained awake this time to hear him add that he knew, therefore, that she would be watching this and that he was sorry that he was not an LA lawyer, a New York policeman or Oprah Winfrey. He hoped, nevertheless, that she would stay with his show until they ran the credits.

Nell did watch his 'show'. She watched it several times, her brow creased and her whole face crumpled up in that expression that Mort had found so plain.

After her second viewing, she put Luc on pause and reached for a notepad and pen. She was still woozy from the previous day's champagne and couldn't quite hold on to her thoughts. They kept floating away from her like a child's balloon. She rewound Luc and noted each point that he made in a neat list. She omitted the statement about her love for television and went on to note down his following declaration: 'I am a dinosaur, ladies and gentlemen. Dinosaurs are, we all know, very fashionable at the moment but soon they will go the way of turtles and power rangers. Before I am disposed of I am making myself extinct.' And he had gone on to underline that this did not mean that he intended to kill himself but that he had chosen to remove himself 'from a life that I had worked many years to build but that was no longer acceptable to me.'

Luc had hijacked himself, Nell now understood. She had to watch the tape twice before she could register this baffling truth. Or rather, Luc had had himself hijacked, giving the money to Return Our Relatives to the Seas, which explained the empty bank accounts. It didn't really explain the house, but Nell had too much else to take in at that point.

'Says he is dinosaur because of change in flying methods,' she wrote down. 'Says men not computers should fly planes. Says "Like so many men over fifty, the world has overtaken me and I don't like what I see up ahead."' Nell was writing as quickly as she could but her hands were trembling and in either language

Luc spoke rapidly so she still had to put him on pause from time to time.

'Now that I've ensured that I can never be tempted to make a remorseful return to my old life, I'm off to fly DC3s. The DC3 is a wonderful old plane. And I, no matter what the company might believe, am a wonderful old pilot. For reasons of my own security I can't say where I am going. I do know that in the eyes of American justice I am a felon, but I would like to remind them that no-one was hurt and a few dolphins will lead better, freer lives. As for my old company, I don't really care that they were inconvenienced by the loss of an aircraft for a few days. They should have treated their old, experienced pilots better!'

Nell let the tape run on as she reread her list. At one point Luc had mentioned something about Nostradamus and the world's future lying in the northern latitudes, but his voice had faded at that point and even when she put her ear to the set she could make out no more. She was about to rewind the tape and watch Luc yet again when she saw that his speech was part of the news broadcast and that once his image left the screen it was replaced by the face of the blond, balding young American in glasses who had spoken for Return Our Relatives to the Seas in the first days of the hijacking. He reiterated what he had said then: that his organization was an ecological lobbying group and would never do anything as potentially dangerous and dramatic as hijacking a plane. He went on to explain that the two men who had been accompanying the dolphin were not members of his group but just marine park keepers who had been assigned to the flight. The older one of the pair had served five years in prison for grand larceny but had been taken on by the marine park as part of a social programme. Dolphin keepers didn't handle money and he had not, therefore, been considered a threat.

These claims seemed to be accepted by a representative of the airline and an American lawyer, who both agreed that not only had Luc practised self-hijacking but, in believing himself to be contributing to the ecologists' cause, was now practising self-delusion as well.

Nell switched off the video, put the notepad aside and gripped the side of her head with both hands. So much baffling information had gone into that head in the past hour, she was sure that Luc's speech must be rattling through her brain like a ball in a pinball machine, illuminating a light here, ringing a bell there.

A bell was ringing, Nell soon realized. But it was ringing on the phone that was on the table next to her armchair. She picked up the receiver. Before she'd had time to say ''Allô', Luc's voice said: 'Nelli?'

'Luc?' said Nell.

'Well, Nelli, it's good to hear you.'

'What have you done, Luc?'

'You saw the broadcast?'

'I'm watching it now.'

Luc didn't reply. His silence seemed to indicate that he was waiting for Nell's opinion of his performance.

'I can never forgive you,' said Nell. 'Even if you have gone mad, and I think you have, I can never forgive you.'

'But you do understand?'

'Of course I don't understand! You commit an enormous crime! You attract the attention of the world to yourself! You put your colleagues at risk! And you leave me alone and humiliated with no money and no house and stuck in this fucking awful dump in the middle of summer!'

'But that's the point, Nelli. Don't you see? I had to blow my life up! And not a controlled explosion but one that would send out flames in unexpected places, that would burn so many bridges that I would never have the chance of trying to find my way back to that boring retirement house in the Languedoc—'

'But you wanted that house too!' cried Nell.

'I thought I did. But it was stagnation, Nelli. I'm not yet ready to wander down to the café on the square with the other old men and read the paper and play *pétanque*—'

'But you could have said so! This is so extreme—'

'Exactly! I had to do something so extreme, so appalling, that there would be no hope of return, no chance of forgiveness. People don't often care to do that. Most of the time they'll make a big show of walking on the tightrope but there is always a safety net below. They'll throw in their unbearable job when they are sure there is another one waiting. They have insurance policies, well-padded little savings accounts stashed away in the bank. They never make a really dangerous move in their lives. I had to do this in such a way that there was no way back – there could be no chance of forgiveness and repair.'

'But why couldn't you tell me the company was laying you off?'

'Because I've always known that you married a pilot, Nelli. You married the four gold braids on the sleeves and the left seat in the cockpit. You wouldn't have wanted me moping around under your feet down in the Languedoc.'

Nell knew that this was true. She stared at the screen where Luc's face had been frozen by the pause button. She couldn't respond to his vision of the future so she tried to grasp hold of their past.

'But was our life so bad?'

'Seen from the outside it was wonderful, my Nelli. Seen from inside me it was arid, hollow, with the cuckoo clock ticking my days away.'

'You bought the fucking clock,' said Nell.

'And you moved around inside that emptiness, always just outside my reach, Nelli. The past few weeks I've had time to think and I've been wondering, is this what English women do? Are they all as distant as you?'

'Don't bring my nationality into it!'

'I'm just trying to understand. Why did you marry me, Nelli?'

Nell stared at the receiver in silence for several seconds, then she remembered her mother's words and said: 'Because I thought I should.'

Samba music coming from the courtyard below drowned out Luc's response. His voice had been fading anyway. Nell had to shout at him to speak up. For several seconds he was just crackle on the line. Again she heard him tell her that the old seer had said that the safest world would soon be in the northern latitudes. Then through the static she sat up and wept as she heard him say: 'Sorry for any inconvenience, Nelli. I know you can cope – you always do. You are a brave Englishwoman. I shall always think of you with tenderness.'

'You abandoned me!' Nell started to cry. 'You left me here in this awful flat with all these rubbishy people!'

She was shaking the receiver, slowly realizing that Luc was no longer anything more than a few blips and squeaks out over the Atlantic, when Mort suddenly loomed up outside the window in front of her. Or rather his back loomed up. He was sitting on a kitchen chair which seemed to be suspended in mid-air over the courtyard. Two helium weather balloons were tied to the rungs of the chair behind Mort's head. Another two were attached to the front of the seat.

Nell stood, unable to move, about a foot from the window, still holding the crackling receiver in her right hand. She stared at the black back of Mort's head as it hovered a few feet across from her.

Mort's idea was not going according to plan.

'Turn me round, Marina!' he called down to Marina

301

and the baker who were standing below, holding on to four very thick long ropes which were tied to the legs of the chair and had cost him what remained of his traveller's cheques. Mort was holding up a cardboard placard on which he had written in bold, red block capitals: BE STRONG AND OF GOOD COURAGE, NELLI MARCHAND. YOUR FRIENDS IN THE COURTYARD ARE WITH YOU.

But because he was turned the wrong way round, Nell could not see the message.

The baker had got his ropes tangled up and his lack of height probably contributed to an imbalance, Mort was thinking as he looked down at Marina's muscular arms as she attempted to pivot him round.

'Tell the baker not to move – he'll only confuse matters!' Mort yelled down. Nell was still standing open-mouthed beyond the window. Mort had hoped that Jean-Louis would arrive and prove an equal partner to Marina on the ropes, but when the gardener had not put in an appearance he had been obliged to settle for the baker.

Now he felt himself turning just enough for his placard to be visible. A reluctant and sceptical Marina had tied him so tightly to the chair that he had only a few inches of leverage for his arms. He held up the placard and smiled sheepishly across at Nell.

'What do you think you're doing?' said Nell as soon as Mort's face became visible and before she read the placard. 'You could kill yourself . . . or . . . maim . . .' Nell's voice trailed off as she took in the written message.

'Not with our friends down there to haul me in,' said Mort. Nell was still staring at the placard. When she glanced down into the courtyard, Marina smiled shyly up at her.

'Isn't this fun?' said Mort, who was starting to pivot away from her. 'Whoops! Back in a minute.'

'Fun?' said Nell and found herself staring at his back again.

'Yeah, fun,' repeated Mort who had turned 360 degrees and was facing her once more. 'Look, I know this may not be the right time but, well, we're going to have a little party down in the courtyard in an hour or two – whoa!'

One of Mort's balloons had burst. He lurched sharply down to the right.

'Oh, Nelli Marchand!' he cried from his wobbling perch. 'I'm here to tell you that the world is a mysterious and unpredictable place. Years of working with the weather have shown me – whoa!' He lurched back to the left.

'I'm pulling you in before you kill yourself!' Marina's voice echoed up to them.

'Have shown me that we can rely on nothing!' he persisted as Marina pulled on the ropes below.

'Come to our party!' cried Mort as he sank, lopsided like a torpedoed ship, below Nell's horizon.

She leaned out of the window and watched as he was hauled back to earth, untied and hugged very tightly by Mlle Marina. The placard was thrown aside and landed next to three mattresses that someone had spread across the ground as a precaution. Nell read the placard again, then she pulled the curtain tight against the afternoon sun and sat down in an armchair and stared at the blank wall.

CHAPTER THIRTY TWO

After Mort landed back in the courtyard, he found that he needed to lie down and, taking a six-pack of beer up to his little flat, he retired for an hour, leaving Marina to prepare the party.

Mort had suggested his plan when he had returned with his balloons and his rope. He had smiled enigmatically when Marina had asked him how he had come by the balloons and muttered something about the advantages of having appeared, however briefly, on network TV.

'We should have a party to celebrate your new job,' he said to Marina. 'It's almost Labor Day. In Chicago we'd have a barbecue, maybe string lights round the yard.'

To Mort's astonishment Marina had produced some lights which she said belonged to Sofia and which she was now stringing around the courtyard.

'Why haven't I ever met Sofia?' Mort had asked.

''Cos she doesn't like to be outside when she's not working. She doesn't like too much big air. Maybe you'll meet her tonight.'

Marina had been resistant to the balloon ascent. She had folded her arms in sullen protest at his first fumbled attempts at launching himself. Then, when he had pointed out that his safety was entirely dependent on her, she had relented and stepped forward and tied him so tightly to his chair that he felt like a hostage in a burglary. She even produced a big shot of whisky and poured it into him before take-off.

She had, however, seemed thrilled at the idea of a party to celebrate her new life. She even expressed a desire to invite four other 'girls' from the Bois. Mort had been bemused by the idea of Brazilian transsexuals filling his courtyard.

'Just because I hate the life, it doesn't mean I hate the people who have to do it.'

'But would they take the time off?' asked Mort, remembering Marina's own refusal to call in sick.

'August is a quiet month,' said Marina.

'The big gardener guy and his girlfriend could come,' said Mort, feeling that he had to contribute some guests of his own and aware that these two recent acquaintances were the closest he had to friends in Paris.

'The baker will come whether we ask him or not,' Marina had sighed. 'But I'll make a point of asking his wife.'

When she had finished stringing the lights, Marina went into the baker's shop to interrupt the baker's wife in her eternal stacking of the stale *bâtards*. The woman didn't accept her invitation but responded with a mournful smile and wrapped up two pizzas and a small stack of the previous day's *pissaladière*, and handed them to her. Marina took this offering as an acceptance. Her colleagues from the Bois arrived just as Mort emerged blinking into the courtyard. They had brought excellent savouries from the baker's next to the Pont de Neuilly Metro stop, and throwing out the stale goods set them out on the table that the baker had provided.

Jean-Louis and Jacqueline arrived to visit Nell a few minutes later. Mort pointed up to the now half-open shutters on Nell's apartment and Jean-Louis decided to go off and buy chocolate cake until he could be sure that she was awake. As he was leaving, Marie-France arrived in search of her stepmother, frowned at the coloured lights and the music but saw an opportunity for a free Portuguese lesson with the five Brazilians who were now in the courtyard. She obeyed her brother's instruction to go and buy some champagne.

'Oh course, we are celebrating Papa's release,' she said to one of the Brazilians, and translated the phrase into slow, precise Portuguese.

Marcel, who had come by to ensure that a sober Nell could cope with the news about Luc, found to his astonishment that he and his wife were invited into a courtyard filled with lights and music of celebration.

When Alain, the steward from the Delhi flight, arrived to offer an odd combination of condolences for Luc's departure and congratulations on his safe release, he didn't find Nell but saw to his delight that one of the Brazilians had modelled herself on Vivien in *Streetcar*. He forgot Nell in his amazement at finding that this exquisite creature would dance a samba with him.

Nell had risen from her armchair and was watching red-eyed through the half-open shutters. When she had first seen Marina and the coloured lights, she had retreated to the kitchen, hoping that the festive scene would disappear. But even in the kitchen, with her radio tuned to the BBC, she could hear the sounds of the courtyard. And when she crept back to the window an hour later, she had seen, not only her stepchildren, and Alain and Marcel, but François the steward who had abandoned her in Delhi, her supervisor with the unpleasant hair, several other members of the Delhi crew, the New York Concorde crew that had flown her home when Luc had first disappeared – and the baker.

She sat on in the dark and watched and wondered.

And when, an hour or so later, the isolation became too much for her, she put on some make-up and a clean dress and rode the lift down to the ground floor. The rational part of Nell was convinced that most of these people had come to see her. But why then did they not come as far as my door? she asked herself. And with no answer to this hurtful question, she stood in the shadowy marble hallway and watched Mort dance with Mlle Marina.

'Have some chocolate cake, *belle-maman*.' Jean-Louis was standing next to her in the shadows, holding out a paper plate with a slice of cake. 'Or I have a KitKat if you'd prefer,' he said, feeling in his pocket.

'What's going on?' Nell waved the cake away and nodded towards the courtyard.

'The woman from the Bois has got a new job. They are celebrating.'

'Oh,' said Nell. 'I thought that . . . but wait a minute . . . they are my friends – well, not friends, but—'

'Oh, they came to see you, Nelli – because of what happened with Papa – but we saw your shutters and, well, nobody liked to wake you.'

'How kind of you all,' said Nell and turned to go upstairs.

'Don't go,' Jean-Louis clutched at the sleeve of Nell's dress. 'Dance with me.'

'With you?'

'Come on,' said Jean-Louis. 'We'll dance for Papa.'

'But he's buggered off!' said Nell. 'What's to dance about?'

'Because he's alive and seems to be happy?' Jean-Louis shrugged and pulled her into the courtyard. For the second time in two days, Nell found herself dancing backwards. Jean-Louis was a clumsy, robust dancer and she had to move fast to avoid his wide, flat feet. He pushed her around the plane tree at such a pace that she felt giddy and breathless and could only escape when the door in her building spun past her for the third time in one direction and Jacqueline danced by with François in the other.

'Go get your girlfriend!' she cried and slipped back into the darkness, where she found Mort sitting on the marble with a bottle of champagne.

'You! What kind of a stunt do you think you were pulling, looming up on me like that! I could have had heart failure! And you could have killed yourself! What were you thinking of?'

'I thought you needed to be reminded of the fundamental lightness of life,' said Mort, and poured himself some champagne. 'Now there's a statement. Actually I just thought it would be fun. I've wanted to try that ever since I heard about it.'

'But what if something had gone wrong? Trusting your life to a couple of strangers like those two—'

'Oh, I trust Marina implicitly. Besides, what if something had happened? I guess I'd have floated away across the rooftops of Paris like in that old movie. Instead of *The Red Balloon* you'd have *The Red Mort*! Nah,' he reflected, refilling his champagne. 'That sounds too political. Would you like a glass? It's very, very chilled. The baker put it in his fridge.'

'I can't,' said Nell, looking with professional approval at the well-chilled bottle.

'Go on,' said Mort and held out his glass. 'Go on, I'm healthy. Here.'

Nell took the glass and found that for all her excesses of the previous day, champagne had lost none of its appeal.

'And whose idea was this carry-on?' she said, glad to be able to express herself in English.

'Mine,' smiled Mort.

'Oh – well, you do realize you wouldn't have any guests without me?'

'Well then, it's all worked out very well for both of

us.' He held his hand up in the air as if to call a halt to his own voice. 'Oh, I'm sorry. I didn't mean to be sarcastic with you. I mean I'm really sorry about your – um, the . . . the pilot guy.'

'Don't talk about him, please.'

'OK. Can I get you something to eat?' said Mort, standing up and nodding towards the plates of pizza.

'No. I think I'd better be going back upstairs.'

'Why?'

'Why? Because it's somewhat unseemly for me to be down here dancing the samba, given my circumstances.'

'Oh, screw unseemly,' said Mort. 'I'll get you a slice of pizza.'

Nell stepped back into the shadows and poured herself another glass of champagne. She smiled as she saw her supervisor with his unpleasantly plastered-down hair dance past with a woman in a thick black wig, who Nell now knew was a man. Marie-France wasn't dancing but was deep in conversation under the plane tree with another of what Nell had privately christened the 'woods women'. She even thought she saw Mille Sofia open her window and sing along with a Brazilian song. She did see Jean-Louis and Jacqueline dance by and felt suddenly lonely. She told herself that she was hungry and wished that Mort would come back.

Then she saw him dancing with one of the Concorde stewardesses, and she decided that her behaviour was unseemly, after all, and stood up to return to her apartment. When she got to the lift, she took a long time to push the button and stood instead, trying to make out the hazy silhouettes that were reflected in the lift's steel doors.

'I got waylaid.' She heard Mort's voice as she stepped into the lift. 'Here's your pizza. I didn't know the French could make pizza but as long as it's not our baker guy they do a pretty good job.'

Nell stepped back into the dark entrance hall alongside him.

'Maybe I should turn the light on,' said Mort, fumbling around for a light switch.

'No, don't do that,' said Nell. 'I like the dark back here.'

'OK,' said Mort.

'You don't have to stay with me if you want to get back out there,' said Nell.

'No, no, it's wonderful to speak English. I mean, not that I speak French, but it's nice to speak English with someone who really speaks it – you know what I mean.'

'Yes,' said Nell.

'Of course it's different for you. I guess you speak perfect French.'

'Yes,' said Nell.

'And you are used to French people, living among them all the time. Whereas – well, I haven't really met any except the big guy—'

'Jean-Louis?'

'Yeah.' Mort finished his champagne and poured another glass. 'Now take Jean-Louis. This is going to sound weird to you maybe but I never imagined a French guy to be so big – to look so much like a football player and then to turn out to be a gardener!'

'Why ever not?' asked Nell.

'I don't know. You just think of the French as elegant and sleek and stuck-up—'

'For God's sake stop talking about "the French"!' cried Nell. 'People like you drive me mad. You come to Paris and you go on and on about the French – "the French are this, the French are that." The French are my daily existence – my stepchildren, my colleagues, even – even my husband! I have to live with them. I don't have the leisure to stare at them through some microscope and look at their charming foibles. They

310

are my bank manager, my gynaecologist. Oh, people like you don't have a clue! You're on holiday, that's all. It's all unreal!'

Nell had no idea why she was so angry. She could see Mort's brown eyes watching her in the shadows.

'Philosophically speaking, your argument is flawed,' he said, and she saw that he was smiling. 'Your reality is real for you and mine for me. There's no way of proving that your Paris is more Paris than mine. It's not. Shall we dance?'

Because Nell couldn't think of a reply to Mort's argument, she accepted his invitation. And for the third time in two days, she danced. Mort danced well with her and she found that she could dance backwards and wondered if she should phone her mother and tell her. Instead, she stayed down in the courtyard, whispered 'Screw unseemly' to herself and danced with Marcel, Alain and even a contrite François.

If at any point she sensed that she was being seen as 'unseemly', Nell announced to her partner that she was dancing 'because Luc is alive and free'. And if any of them were astonished by her behaviour, they soon set their faces in expressions of encouragement and said: 'Yes, but of course, Luc is alive and free!'

CHAPTER THIRTY THREE

When Nell opened her eyes the next morning, she found that she was staring up at the leaves of the plane tree. She tried to move but her arms were zipped inside a sleeping bag and there was a heavy weight lying across her chest. She looked down and saw the concierge's old tom cat sitting between her breasts, staring back at her. Beyond the cat she saw the concierge herself, standing at her feet and dressed in her travelling clothes.

'*Qu'est-ce que vous faites là, Madame Marchand?*' she said.

'*Je ne sais pas,*' said Nell and tried to shift the cat. The cat didn't move. Nell sank back onto the bag. The concierge advanced the few feet that would bring her to stand over Nell's head.

'*Pauvre madame,*' she said and frowned and walked away. Nell remembered the plumbago that had grown across the door of the concierge's lodge and had looked so wonderful in the lights of the previous evening. Where were the lights? she wondered.

She tried to sit up again and say, 'Don't touch the flowers,' but still the cat wouldn't move. She had just succeeded in extracting her arms from the sleeping bag and was lifting the huge cat off herself when Mort walked into the courtyard carrying a bag of croissants.

'Nice cat,' he said, and took the cat into his arms as he handed her the bag.

'But these are the good ones – from the bakery I told you about,' said Nell, taking a croissant and a *pain au chocolat* from the paper bag.

'I was their first customer of the fall season,' said Mort. 'They just opened back up today. I think the lady in there – you must know her, a severe blonde matron – I think she told me all about her vacation. But I didn't understand a word.'

While Mort was speaking, Nell was looking up at the windows of the courtyard. At least four sets of shutters were open for the first time in weeks.

'Where did the coloured lights go?' she asked Mort. 'And the table?'

'Marina cleared all that away last night,' said Mort. 'Eat the croissant. It was still warm when I bought it.' He stroked the cat, turning it onto its back and caressing its stomach. 'Oh my God, look at the balls on this thing!' he cried as Nell was raising the croissant to her mouth. 'Don't they believe in fixing cats over here?'

'Not the concierge,' said Nell, looking across at the plumbago and wondering where the concierge had gone. Now that she was wide awake she didn't know how to behave with Mort. She wished that she could be like a heroine of an old Hollywood comedy who wakes in the morning in the company of a strange man (probably Cary Grant) and wonders just what she had done with him the night before.

But Nell knew what she had done with Mort. She had danced and danced with him. Then she had talked and talked to him, suggesting, after much champagne and dancing, that they both get in the sleeping bag because a wind had blown up in the by then deserted courtyard and for the first time in months she had goose pimples on her legs from the chill night air. Mort had been happy to comply and had squeezed in

313

alongside her in his underpants and T-shirt. Nell had been fully clothed but bare-legged because of the summer and climbing into the bag had caused her skirt to rise up above her waist. She had an agreeable recollection of the warmth and roughness of Mort's legs against hers, and of the ease and spontaneity with which he had put his arm round her while she talked on and on. She remembered that she had laid her right palm flat against his chest while she talked, and that it had felt warm and good. She remembered that she had remembered the sight of his bare stomach as he slept some nights earlier and that she had kept her hand pressed hard against his chest and thought that perhaps something more might happen if only she could dare to stop talking. Several times he had repeated how happy he was to be speaking English again. And Nell had talked on until she became sleepy. As she had dozed off she had felt the other legs untangle from hers and an emptiness in the sleeping bag as Mort climbed out.

'I'm real sorry about the old lady with Alzheimer's,' said Mort as he turned the cat back onto its feet and patted it on its way across the courtyard.

At about the time that they had climbed into the bag, Nell had been describing her visit to Ivy. Mort had obligingly sung the remaining verses of 'She'll be coming round the mountain' to her. Nell had listened carefully, trying to memorize them in case she ever decided to try Ivy again.

'I'm not,' said Nell. 'I hated the old cow.'

'No you didn't,' said Mort.

The sun had come out over the courtyard. It shone down on Nell's face and she became aware of how dry and tight her skin felt, of how her eyes were stinging and her hair was matted and tangled.

'I think it's time I went inside,' she said and unzipped the sleeping bag.

'Make some coffee? Have a shower?' said Mort who seemed to have assumed that he would accompany her.

Nell stood up, shook her rumpled clothes down around her and stepped onto the scrubby patch of earth around the tree. Now, in the first cool morning for weeks, she knew that she would never try to visit Ivy again. She knew that her mother had been right and that rummaging around in the past was pointless.

'Are you going to leave that down here?' asked Nell as Mort rolled up his sleeping bag.

'No — I think it's time to clear all this away,' said Mort, looking up at the open shutters in the courtyard. The concierge had returned, carrying a heavy suitcase and a stack of letters. As Mort went to help her with the case, the baker appeared in the courtyard. He was also carrying a letter which he handed to Nell with a smile and a wink towards the sleeping bag.

When Nell saw the envelope, she realized that she had completely forgotten Jameson's Private Detective Agency. Now she was sure that this was the letter that the baker was handing her. Now her life was about to make sense. Now she reversed the decision that she had made seconds earlier, and decided that she would understand that most important, elusive part of her past. Then she noticed that the envelope on her letter had no stamp; it didn't even have an address — just the words Mme Marchand. She ripped it open, read it and said, 'I've been evicted.'

'What?'

Only Mort had understood and he left the concierge who was uttering *oh, là làs* to the plumbago, and took the letter from Nell's hand.

'You won't be able to read it,' said Nell. 'But it's an eviction letter.'

'But who's evicting you?'

'The baker! Do you believe that? The baker was my

315

landlord all along! Or Luc's landlord. That's why he brought me the letter – smiling like that! See' – she pointed to the letter – 'It says Pouyfaucon – like on his van. I had no idea that he owned anything other than his own property.'

'What reason does he give?' asked Mort.

'A very valid reason actually,' said Nell. 'The place was Luc's. It was rented in Luc's name – and now that Luc is gone, the proprietor has the right to reclaim it.'

'Wait a minute,' said Mort, squinting at the letter. 'Is the baker's name Georgette? I mean is that a guy's name in France?'

'What do you mean, Georgette?' Nell took the letter from him.

'Look at the name on the bottom,' said Mort. 'Even I can see it says Georgette Pouyfaucon.'

'That's his wife!' cried Nell. 'It's his wife who's evicting me!'

A phone was ringing above them. Nell looked up and knew that it was ringing in her apartment. She decided to ignore it.

'Georgette,' she said to herself. 'She would have a name like Georgette.'

'What kind of a name is Georgette?' asked Mort.

'*Ordinaire*,' said Nell. 'Which would translate into what my mother would call "common". The phone rang on. 'I felt sorry for that woman!' cried Nell. 'I thought she was a victim and now she's evicting me!' The phone persisted.

'Is that yours?' asked Mort. 'Maybe you'd better answer it. Maybe it's your husband – or your mother.'

Nell felt a sudden sense of urgency in the ring of the phone and ran towards the lift. The phone was still ringing when she ran into the flat and picked it up. A man's voice said in French that he was calling from the Marly Clinic regarding Mlle Valentin, and that he needed to speak to her next of kin most urgently.

'Mademoiselle Valentin?' said Nell. 'Who is—' Then she remembered that Valentin was Claudine's last name. 'Claudine! What's happened?'

'Mademoiselle Valentin is not at all well,' said the voice from the clinic. Nell wanted to tell him to stop calling a woman as elegant and urbane as Claudine 'Mademoiselle'. It was ridiculous. Then she took in what he was saying. 'Can you come out here this morning, Madame Marchand?'

'Yes, yes. I'll come in a taxi,' said Nell. From where she was standing she could see the concierge and the baker down in the courtyard. The baker was carrying an axe now and had started to hack at the plumbago.

'I'm Doctor Mauroy,' said the voice from the clinic. 'Tell the receptionist to escort you up to my office as soon as you get here.'

Nell put down the phone. She rushed into the bedroom to find some clean clothes and was running a shower when she decided that she couldn't let the plumbago be demolished. Even though she knew she had to rush to Claudine, she was convinced that the plumbago was linked to them both in some way. She wrapped a towel around herself and ran to the window.

'Leave that alone!' she cried.

'How am I supposed to get in?' the concierge yelled back at her.

Nell didn't know.

'I can't get to my door!' the concierge shouted. 'I want to get inside and feed the cat.'

'Well, just don't let him hack it all down!' Nell yelled back. But the baker was already swinging his axe at the delicate flowers. A shower of blue blossom sifted through the air and settled on the cobbles. 'Does he really need an axe?' Nell persisted. 'Secateurs would do it.'

Claudine is ill and I am talking about secateurs, Nell thought to herself. She turned from the window, let the towel drop and walked into the bedroom. As she pulled a dress over her head, she heard footsteps in the hallway.

'Nell,' said Mort's voice. 'I brought you some coffee.'

'Put it on the kitchen table,' said Nell as she looked for her shoes. Nell had never had to look for her shoes in her life. They were always neatly aligned in her shoebag, in the wardrobe. 'Claudine is ill!' she called through to Mort, who walked into the bedroom without knocking.

'Seriously? What's the matter with her?'

'I don't know.' Nell knew that she couldn't explain the face lift so she just repeated, 'I don't know. A hospital in Neuilly called and I have to go to her. I can't face driving. Can you call me a taxi?'

'No I can't,' said Mort.

'What? Why not?'

'Because I don't speak French, Nell.'

'Oh, that's right. I forgot,' said Nell, pulling on a jacket for the first time in weeks. As she passed Mort and walked out of the bedroom, she saw her open window.

'Would you do me a favour and lock up? I must get going.' Mort nodded. 'Oh, and tell the baker to go easy on that poor flower.'

'I can't do that either,' sighed Mort, walking to the window and pulling the shutters towards him. 'Besides, I think it's too late.'

Nell made a rapid detour to the window. The baker had hacked through the main stem of the plumbago which now lay wilting on the cobbles.

'That's what I'm beginning to hate about being here,' she heard Mort say behind her. 'Without language you're reduced to being a kid again. I could have told

318

that arsehole to just cut a space for the door.'

'Oh, the hateful fucking bastard!' said Nell. 'It's almost as if he did it deliberately.'

'Well then, maybe you should be glad you're out of this place,' said Mort.

'I suppose so. I must go.'

'I'll ride downstairs with you,' said Mort, securing the windows and handing Nell her keys.

As they stood on the marble floor in front of the small door within the big doors and watched for a taxi, Nell said: 'I don't quite know how to ask this but, well, last night, um – you, well you didn't make any . . . any sort of . . .'

'I didn't try to make love to you?'

'No,' said Nell.

'No I didn't try to make love to you? Or no that's not what you meant?'

'No you didn't try to make love to me,' murmured Nell.

'Well, twenty years ago I wouldn't have hesitated,' said Mort.

'Thanks a lot!'

'No, I don't mean twenty years in your life, I mean twenty years in mine. Twenty years ago I might have taken advantage of your . . . disarray, but it wouldn't have been very elegant on my part since I'm heading back to the States in a couple of days.'

'Oh! Oh, are you?'

'Yeah. See, the truth is that little party last night was my last hurrah – I mean it was for Marina too but, well, I've turned into a slob, Nell. In a way it's your example that set me thinking—'

'My example?'

'The way you never let your life collapse. It made me think that it's time to get back to—'

A taxi had pulled up as Mort spoke.

'I must get to Claudine,' said Nell, opening the door and giving the clinic address to the driver.

'Yeah, right. Well, goodbye, Nelli. I hope she's OK.'

'So do I,' said Nell. And her taxi pulled away into what Nell now noticed was busy autumn traffic. Paris had come home from its holidays.

CHAPTER THIRTY FOUR

Nell sat in Dr Mauroy's office and looked out at the well-watered lawns, banks of impatiens and the tall trees that sheltered them and thought that the trees with their vase-like shapes looked like elms. But surely elms were dying or dead throughout the world, she recalled, and wanted to ask someone if these could be elms out in this opulent Neuilly courtyard.

'Sorry for the delay,' said Dr Mauroy, entering the office and opening a file onto his desk. 'Are you a sister? Or sister-in-law?' He looked down at Nell's name, scrawled in Claudine's childlike handwriting, on the release form.

'Just a friend,' said Nell.

'But the person closest to Mademoiselle Valentin?'

'I hope so. What has happened to her?'

'Well, as you know she came in here for cosmetic surgery—'

'But what is happening to her now? How ill is she? I know why she came in here, but where is she now?'

'She's all right, Madame Marchand.'

'Then she's not going to die?'

'Not if she looks after herself,' said Dr Mauroy. He was a handsome man, Nell now noticed for the first time. Dark and elegant – the kind of man English women imagined thronging the streets of Paris. He was the first of his kind that Nell had seen in years. 'Mademoiselle Valentin has a rather serious heart condition,' said Dr Mauroy. 'She certainly can't have surgery – not for the time being at least. And she most definitely shouldn't be flying for a living.'

'Can we call her Madame Valentin?' asked Nell, who was trying to gain time while she absorbed this information. 'I know she's not officially Madame but Mademoiselle is just ridiculous after a certain age.'

'I believe in your country they have, what is that term: Ms?'

'Yes. I don't know whether it ever caught on. I've been here too long. What kind of heart condition?'

Dr Mauroy explained that Claudine had collapsed on being admitted the previous evening. An examination had revealed a weakness of a heart valve. He added that his predecessor had not recorded any of this vital information upon authorizing the procedure. He shook his head in bafflement.

'But how has she managed to fly for all these years?'

'That's what I was going to ask you,' said the doctor. 'Perhaps you can ask her?'

'Can I see her? Is she conscious?'

'Oh yes – she's very tired but she has been asking for you.'

'But she isn't going to die?'

'Not if she changes the way she lives. She'll have to look for a new job, that's for sure. Don't people in your profession have some kind of insurance to cover this kind of eventuality?'

'Oh, yes. We have to.'

'Flying's a risky business?'

'Yes,' said Nell, who sensed that Dr Mauroy was unwittingly leading the conversation towards Luc. She didn't want to think about Luc.

'Can I see her now?'

'Of course. I'll have the nurse take you down.'

* * *

Claudine was sitting up in bed tracing a red line around her mouth with a pencil. Nell had known that she would look frail and vulnerable. As she had followed the nurse along the corridor she had prepared herself for the fact that her beautiful friend would look old. But when Claudine smiled across at her and held out her arms, crying *'Nelli, ma vieille!'*, Nell could only think that behind the shadows under the eyes and the pale skin, she was still her beautiful Claudine.

'How long have you had this?' asked Nell, pointing to Claudine's chest as she sat on the edge of her bed.

'You mean my crooked nipples?' said Claudine. 'I must get something done about them—'

'I mean your heart.'

'Well, it's been coming on for years – since almost before I started flying.'

'It can't have done,' said Nell. 'They wouldn't have let you fly.'

'You are so naive, Nelli,' said Claudine. 'I worked a fiddle! I found a crooked doctor in the company and got him to sign my papers for me. People work fiddles like that all the time. For their eyesight, for alcohol and mental problems. Even your Luc—'

'But a doctor wouldn't work a fiddle,' said Nell. 'I mean, they take oaths against that sort of thing. I mean they could be risking your life—'

'Not really – you are risking your life. If you're an adult and take the responsibility—'

'Just a minute – what do you mean "Even your Luc"?'

'He's been working a fiddle for at least a year,' said Claudine. 'When they introduced the fly-by-wire system and he hated it, hated the idea of handing control over to computers, and then they wanted to shift him out of the company within a year or two, he got so depressed he had to go on medication—'

323

'Of course he didn't. I would have known if he had.'

'You're the last person he would have told.'

'What's that supposed to mean?'

'Well, that's what we were talking about in the diner in New York all those times, Nell. Luc always knew that you married a pilot – you married the gold braid, the left hand seat in the cockpit. If he ceased to be those things . . . Well anyway, it's not an issue now, is it?'

'I can never forgive him,' said Nell.

'I don't see why you should. But at least you should know more of what was behind it. Luc and I had a bond of *hors la loi!*' And Claudine started laughing. 'All that time you were getting so worked up about the two of us – he was never my type anyway – and that's all we were: two outlaws plotting to deceive the company together. Actually, when Luc knew how bad I was he tried to persuade me to tell you and get you to help me stop flying, but—'

'*Hors la loi!* Outlaws!' cried Nell. 'It's not funny. And it didn't work for either of you, did it? Neither of you will ever fly for the company again – so a lot of good all your plotting did you.'

'Well, Luc will get to fly DC3s, and I held on for all those years. Had lots of fun in the process. Think of all the things I've done, that I would have missed if they'd caught me out that first day in the medical – where I met you, Nelli? I was so scared that first time in the ECG room and then you appeared looking so serious, so calm and efficient. See? You've been my guardian angel all these years.'

'Oh, no. When I met you, you were handing in your urine sample,' said Nell. 'Luc was having his heart examined.'

'That's the story you've always told yourself,' said Claudine. 'But it's not true. It was the other way round, but that didn't suit you so you changed it—'

'No I didn't. No, I most definitely didn't,' said Nell.

Claudine stared down at her breasts.

'Well, it's too long ago for either of us to be sure,' said Nell. 'You do have an insurance against this kind of thing, Claudine? Doctor Mauroy asked me if you did and I said we all do.'

'Of course I haven't. I've never had insurance against anything in my life. Don't believe in it.'

'What will you do?'

'I don't know, Nelli. I haven't any idea what I will do.'

'But you've got some savings? I mean, in addition to the property you've got some capital put aside?'

Claudine shook her head.

'Nothing?'

'Less than ten thousand francs,' said Claudine.

'What have you done with all your money?'

Claudine shrugged.

'But it won't be that easy to get another job. You're not getting any younger.'

'I know that – don't you think I know that! What do you think I'm doing in here?' Claudine started to cry. Nell took her friend in her arms, thought how bony her shoulders felt, thought this is what men pursue, wondered if they were disappointed, then just thought that she loved her friend as much as she had ever loved anyone in the world and that her friend was her responsibility and this was, in a way, a gift from Luc, one that she was very, very glad to have.

'I've been evicted,' she said when Claudine paused to blow her nose, still remembering to pay attention and just dab the Kleenex to her nostrils. 'The baker has evicted me. Well, actually his wife has.'

'His wife? That poor, miserable, one-eyed creature that we all felt sorry for?'

'Her name is Georgette,' said Nell.

'How vulgar,' said Claudine.

'That's what I thought, but her name is on the eviction paper.'

'Well, you've always said you hated that building,' said Claudine. 'I suppose you'll have to come and live with me in the château. You always did want to get your hands on the place, didn't you?'

'Was it that obvious?'

'I watched you and Luc through the window the first day you came out. I had a bottle of champagne ready for us and I opened it when you came up the driveway, then you both just sat and sat out there in the Citroën. By the time you came in it was tepid and flat.'

'I'm sorry, Claudine,' said Nell. 'I am so very sorry.'

'I wouldn't get that upset,' said Claudine, and pursed her lips at herself in the mirror. 'It was a free bottle I stole out of first class, so it was no real loss to me.'

CHAPTER THIRTY FIVE

'Sometimes I think you're a mutant,' said Frank when Mort phoned him that morning.

'Because I said I want to go back to school?' said Mort who had called his brother to get the phone number of Howie who he thought was doing climate research out at Boulder. 'What's so mutant about that?' Mort had only mumbled a few words about a return to academia to fill in the conversation while his brother found the number.

'You're too old. But at least you're coming back – that's a start. Did you reconfirm your booking?'

'Yes.'

'Now wear a tie. Wear a suit.'

'It's almost a hundred degrees over here!' cried Mort.

'Precisely. If you wear a suit you have a chance of being upgraded. If you're upgraded you'll be in the cooler part of the plane which is at the front.'

'Are you sure of that? How do you know that the cooler part of the plane is at the front? Planes look to me like they point a bit upwards which would mean that, since every schoolboy knows heat rises, it would be hotter at the front.'

'Trust me – it's cooler.'

'Why am I discussing this? I'm on long-distance! And besides, it's a charter. There is no first class.'

'Wear a suit anyway – it shows you have faith in your life,' said Frank and gave Mort Howie's number.

Howie was at Boulder. And he was doing research into global warming which excited Mort for about ten seconds, then he realized that he had to decide what he wanted from Howie and the Institute. He gained time by going through the formalities of establishing that he was divorced, and 'on sabbatical' from the TV business. He omitted to mention that he was in Paris because he knew that nothing anyone could say about the city would have any relevance to his life there. When he said that he was thinking of going back to school, his old roommate honked with laughter.

'Oh, Mort, you're such a pill!' cried Howie, whose vocabulary had not evolved in the twenty years since Mort had seen him. 'And you on TV and all!'

'Well we TV people are real interested in what you guys are doing out there,' said Mort, deciding to try an indirect approach.

'I know,' said Howie. 'I was on one Discovery Channel and two PBS documentaries last year.'

'You were?' said Mort, thinking that his friend had done almost as much TV as he had.

'We've missed you, Mort,' Howie was saying. 'George Axelrod – remember him? – and I were saying just last week that life is, I don't know, kind of serious and boring these days. Why does it have to change like that, Mort? Do you ever wonder about that?'

'If I'm in Boulder why don't I drop by for coffee one day?' Mort heard himself saying.

'Oh yeah,' Howie honked again. 'Like you're going to be in the neighbourhood.'

'Well, I'm planning to do some travelling during my sabbatical year,' said Mort.

'Oh, well then, sure! Come by! Come by and have coffee, dinner, whatever. You can stay here. I'll take

328

you round the Institute. Do you want to fix a date now?'

When Mort hung up the phone, he looked at his empty diary and smiled at the solitary entry: '1 October – Lunch with Howie and George.' In all the blank pages of his future it was the only appointment. This did not distress or sadden Mort – it was, he shrugged to himself, quite enough to be going on with.

That night, when Mort was sure that everyone in the apartments on the courtyard was asleep behind their shuttered windows, he crept back outside and unrolled his sleeping bag one last time. Nell had not returned from the clinic; Marina had announced that she had changed her mind and would finish off her week in the Bois. Mort had been tempted to point out that nobody would notice if she stopped working immediately but he knew Marina's idiosyncratic moral code too well to question her decision. And he had, at first, been glad to have the evening alone to catch up on his sleep and recover from his hangover in a real bed up in the apartment. But when midnight had come and the courtyard had fallen silent, he had been drawn back outside. As he climbed into his sleeping bag, he told himself that he would probably never do anything this *young* again.

There was a full moon that night. Mort put on his glasses the better to see the heavens above him. He stared at the moon for a long time, taking pleasure in the frame that the mansard rooftops in the courtyard gave to the dark square of sky with its gleaming ball of white. The sky was dark for, as Mort now knew, the Eiffel Tower was switched off at midnight and the *bateaux mouches* were moored at the pier by the Alma bridge and had extinguished their floodlights.

The moon went behind a thin cloud. In the corner of the square of dark, Mort thought he saw a shooting star. And he found himself staring up at Nell's shuttered fifth floor window and making an astonishing wish. He rolled over and reminded himself that the time had come to head for home. He fell asleep as the last plane into Orly flew between him and the moon.

Mort woke an hour later to see a wide, pale face staring down at him. At the same time he felt his arm being roughly shaken by, he assumed, the owner of the face. The face was surrounded by long, thick black hair. Mort had fallen asleep with his glasses on and his improved vision combined with the moonlight that still shone from a far corner of the courtyard gave him a frightening, minutely detailed view of the face.

'Mademoiselle Sofia?' he whispered. The face was so close that he could see the creases on the eyelids where the false eyelashes were attached. He could see some dark hairs in the nostrils. He could smell stale tobacco on the breath and a fainter odour, emanating from the body, of leaf mulch and sweat. This was too intimate an encounter for Mort. He took his glasses off and watched as the pale face softened and faded and stuttered the word: 'Si.'

'Mademoiselle Sofia,' Mort repeated, and thought that had it not been for the odours he would have convinced himself he was dreaming. 'What do you want with me?' he whispered.

'I have a letter,' said Sofia.

'For me?' asked Mort. 'From Marina?'

'No! For them!' She pointed up to the fifth floor windows.

'For who? For the pilot?'

'No, for her.' Sofia held up an envelope and read it. 'For Madame Eleanor Marchand.'

'Why are you writing to her?' asked Mort.

'Not me,' said Sofia, and took the letter from the opened envelope. 'Jameson's Private Detective Agency.'

Sofia tucked the letter in the top of Mort's sleeping bag and stood up to walk away.

330

'Wait a minute! What are you doing with this letter anyway?'

'Come to me by mistake,' said Sofia.

'When?'

'Three weeks.'

'And you opened it and read it?'

'Sure – I don't get no mail,' said Sofia.

'Why did you keep it so long?' Mort was trying to free his arm from the bag and prop himself up to address her.

'I forgot it, senhor – I found it last night inside a magazine.' She turned her back on Mort.

'Don't go, Sofia.' But Sofia was moving away. As she stepped across the cobbles, Mort heard the crunch of splintering glass as she trod on his glasses.

'Oh fuck!' cried Mort.

'I'm sorry, senhor,' said Sofia, and he saw her blurred form bend down and gather up the frame and the bigger pieces of glass and set them down next to him. 'I'm sorry,' she repeated.

'That's OK – it was an accident.'

'Goodbye, senhor,' said Sofia.

'No, don't go,' said Mort, who was wide awake now and curious about Marina's mysterious colleague.

'Yes go,' said Sofia. 'Too much outside for me here.' And she disappeared back into the building.

Mort looked at the envelope that was poking out of his sleeping bag and thought that, since it was already open, there really was no harm in reading it. Without his glasses and with only the light of the moon to read by, he could not make out much of the letter. He saw that it contained a grainy photocopied head and shoulders picture of what seemed to be a dark man. Tucking it inside the sleeping bag, Mort decided to get some sleep before dawn when he would have to move quickly to be back inside before the 'fall people', as he had christened the courtyard's permanent residents, emerged from their homes and headed for work.

He was about to fall asleep when he felt the rain on his face.

'I should have known that was coming,' he muttered to himself and squinted up at the sky. The moon was covered now and the rain was falling in straight heavy drops. Mort gathered his sleeping bag up around him and, looking like the loser in a primary school sack race, hopped inside his building and made his way up to the flat.

When he woke up the next morning, he saw Marina's feet poking out of the small cupboard-like back room. He heard her deep, even breathing and decided not to wake her. The day was raining and deep grey but even the grey had found its way through the open windows and roused him. He looked at his watch and saw that it was ten o'clock. Squinting across the courtyard, he saw that Nell was home.

When he had made himself as presentable as he could without waking Marina, Mort took the letter from the sleeping bag and set off to deliver it. As he walked across the cobbles through the blue blossoms that still covered the entrance to the concierge's lodge, he could no longer resist the desire to read Nell's letter. He could see more clearly in the daylight and by half closing his eyes and holding the paper at the right distance he managed to read that Jameson's Private Detective Agency had traced the 'party in whom you have expressed an interest'. The 'party in question' had, apparently, moved to Florida in an attempt to 'relaunch his faltering acting career'. Jameson's Private Detective Agency would need Mrs Marchand's authorization and considerable increase in expenses if they were to pursue the matter any further.

Mort sat down on the step at the entrance to Nell's building. His eyes and face muscles hurt from squinting but he was delaying his ascent to Nell's home because his brain was slowly sorting through the information contained in the foggy letter and was telling him that Nell had been seeking a lost love. As he sat and massaged his forehead, he told himself that she could also have been seeking an old school friend, or someone connected with her husband or her career, but Mort knew, although he could not have said how, that the efficiently pretty woman who never let her life collapse had been searching for something much more dangerous and elusive.

When his eyes had stopped aching, Mort opened the envelope again and took out the grainy, black-blotched photocopy. He unfolded it, held it at the right distance, squinted hard, then cried: 'Holy shit!'

CHAPTER THIRTY SIX

Mort held the paper up to the grey daylight. He turned it at an angle, turned his head at an angle, switched on the light in the hallway and held it up to that, and finally concluded that without his glasses he couldn't be sure.

Certainly the man looked vaguely like his deceased stand-in who had been so abruptly despatched from this earth by the Coppertone billboard. There again, Mort told himself, there were millions of these vacuously good-looking dark men in America. Just as, he now had to admit to himself, the world was full of emptily beautiful, even-featured blonde women. The kind of man whose image was reproduced on the photocopied paper might just as well have been run through a copier himself, considering the number of them that Mort had encountered.

There was, of course, the question of the acting career with a company in Florida, and the thought of this almost persuaded Mort to destroy the letter.

'Holy shit, holy shit, holy shit.' He was bouncing up and down on his heels in the hallway clutching the letter with one hand and pounding his fist against the side of his head. 'I killed her man,' he finally dared to mutter to himself. Then thought, no I didn't, vanity killed him. Nevertheless Mort remained in the hallway, holding on to the last chance of never giving the letter to Nell.

Marina appeared at the window. She didn't see him for her attention was fixed on the remains of the plumbago that she had nurtured throughout the summer. She stared down at the hacked-off stump, then closed the window and went back inside.

The sight of Marina confirmed Mort's conviction that he must go to Nell with the letter. He now knew that for the duration of his summer in Paris he had been held securely between the solid, if singular, moral codes of the women on each side of the court-yard. He had come seeking freedom and youth and his own lost love and had found, instead, that he had been compressed back into an acceptable mould by severe, disenchanted Marina and efficient, stoical Nell — women whose difficult, often charmless characters now seemed to have squeezed him out of his patch under the plane tree and were about to catapult him back to his home.

He knew that he had to give the letter to Nell and accept whatever followed because he admired her and could not let himself betray her. He pressed the button for the fifth floor and stepped inside the lift.

Mort found Nell, the door to her flat wide open, dragging a trunk across the living room.

'Got to have a clear-out if I'm going to move,' she said.

'Oh, of course. When are you going?'

'As soon as possible,' said Nell. 'How about you?'

'Tomorrow,' said Mort. 'My flight goes tomorrow.'

'That is soon,' said Nell, and sat down on the trunk to catch her breath. 'That really is soon.'

'It's a charter company. They only go once a week, so I decided that tomorrow had better be it.'

'Oh, well, I'm sure that's wise. Paris is a very different place after *la rentrée*.'

'When they all come back, you mean? I thought I'd noticed a difference.' Mort was fingering the letter in his pocket. This did not seem the right moment to mention it. Then he remembered why. 'How's Claudine? I should have asked you right away. How is she?'

'That's a good question,' said Nell. 'She isn't at death's door. I thought she was yesterday – I was terrified. I hope I wasn't rude to you, but the man at the clinic gave me such a shock—'

'She's lucky to have a friend who worries about her like that,' said Mort.

'I love Claudine,' said Nell and was amazed to hear herself make such a declaration. 'She is my dearest, oldest friend – if anything happened to her I don't know what I'd do.'

'But she's all right.'

'Apart from the fact that she doesn't have a penny to her name, can never fly again and has no skills to do any other work, yes, she's all right.'

'I would never have imagined the two of you being friends,' said Mort, still fingering the letter as he sat down on an armchair next to Nell.

'I think I live all the reckless, outrageous parts of life that I don't dare to live myself through her,' said Nell.

'You have reckless, outrageous parts?' asked Mort, and took the letter from his pocket.

Nell thought hard about this question. She screwed her small face up in that same intense expression of deep thought that Mort had seen weeks earlier as she'd stood in funeral black waiting for a taxi.

'Probably not,' she said finally, and stood up and pushed the trunk against the wall.

'I've got a letter for you,' said Mort. 'It was delivered to Mademoiselle Sofia by mistake. She opened it, not me, but she doesn't seem to dare to come over here to give it to you herself.'

Nell didn't take the letter but pointed to a stack of mail on a table near the window.

'It doesn't matter,' she said. 'I mean, it doesn't matter if she opened it – I've had so many letters these past few weeks, I just can't deal with them all. If you put it with the rest, I'll go through them later.'

'Are you sure?' said Mort and walked over to the table where the pile of unopened letters was almost six inches high. 'You haven't opened any of these!' he exclaimed, his own curiosity piqued by the sight of air-mail letters that even his limited vision told him came from New Caledonia, New York, Buenos Aires and Tokyo.

'I opened a couple,' said Nell. 'I know what they all are. They're from colleagues offering sympathy about Luc. I've been getting them for weeks now. They all say more or less the same thing – how sorry they are, can they help in some way? Would I like to stay with them for a while? Or can they cook me dinner? Or take me to see a film or for a weekend in the country?'

'But that's wonderful!' cried Mort. 'I never thought of the French as being—'

'Don't start that rubbish about the French again!' Nell had climbed up onto a chair and was removing an abalone shell lampshade from a wall lamp.

'You're right. But don't you see how lucky you are to have colleagues that show so much interest? I wish my colleagues had rallied round me like that,' he added.

'Why should they?' said Nell. 'No-one hi-jacked you, did they?'

'No, of course not, but really you should read these letters. They might make you feel better.'

'All right,' sighed Nell, climbing down from the chair. 'I'll have a look through them if I have time tonight.'

Mort had not yet put his letter on the stack with the others. Now he handed it to Nell. 'I think you should look at this one now,' he said. 'It's not like the others. It's from Jameson's Private Detective Agency.'

'Oh,' said Nell and looked at the letter but made no attempt to take it. 'Then you did open it?'

'Yes – I mean, it had been opened by Sofia, so there didn't seem anything wrong in, well, having a quick look.' He pushed it towards her.

Nell took the letter from him. She opened it and unfolded the two sheets of paper inside.

'I think I'll have to get reading glasses soon,' she said and glanced at the photocopied picture and the brief letter. Then she walked past Mort into the kitchen where he heard her strike a match. When he followed her over to the sink, he saw that she had burnt the envelope and its contents and was washing the ashes down the drain.

'Foolishness,' she said as she turned off the tap. 'Utter and total idiotic foolishness.'

'Maybe not,' Mort started to say. 'Everyone has some secret part of—'

Nell held up her hand. She pressed the tips of her fingers against his lips and shook her head. 'No,' she said.

Mort nodded. They stood in silence for a few seconds until Nell withdrew her fingers.

'Hey, how about I take you out for breakfast?' said Mort.

'I can't.' Nell shook her head. 'I've got an urgent appointment at the bank this morning.'

'A cup of coffee then?'

'I haven't got time, Mort. I'm sorry.'

'Well then, why don't you come with me to the airport tomorrow? I've lost my glasses – did you notice that?'

'I thought you looked better,' said Nell.

'Without my glasses I'll be in a total fog and since you're the expert when it comes to airports

338

maybe you could come along and see me off.'

'But I never go through the front of an air terminal!' Nell laughed. 'I go in through the back door, like a performer in a theatre. I hardly ever see the bits that are all lit up and on show to the world.'

'You could keep me company in the taxi,' said Mort. 'I've always thought that going to the airport is one of the loneliest hours anyone can spend. What was it Graham Greene said: "Travel is the saddest of pleasures"?'

'What an odd thing to say!' The quotation had produced the familiar expression of deep thought in Nell. Mort looked at the tightly bunched face with affection and stroked her hair. Nell didn't respond. She simply repeated: ' "Travel is the saddest of pleasures." What an odd thing to say. People spend fortunes on travelling. Why would they? I mean, it isn't sad, is it?' She sat down hard on a kitchen chair. 'All my life I've thought it was the answer to everything. I mean, I knew it wasn't really – I'm not that stupid. But I didn't – I mean, I suppose I did feel sad sometimes.' She looked up at Mort as if she'd forgotten he was there. ' "The saddest of pleasures" . . . Could he be right?'

Mort shrugged. 'If he is, then I'll need you to see me off.'

'I can't,' sighed Nell. 'Claudine is leaving the clinic tomorrow, so I'm going to stay out at her place tonight and drive out and pick her up in the morning.'

'You can't change that, I suppose?'

'Can you change your departure date?' asked Nell.

'I guess not.'

'Well then,' smiled Nell. 'I suppose we should say goodbye now.'

'Yes.'

'I'll walk you to the lift,' said Nell.

'OK. You will say hi to Claudine for me?'

'Oh, yes.'

'And you'll read those letters? You do owe them that, you know.'

'I know – I'll read them when I get this mess sorted out.' They had come to the lift. Mort squinted at the panel of buttons; Nell pushed 'Open'. The lift had remained on the floor since Mort had ridden it up to see Nell. Now he stepped back inside it.

'I do sometimes work flights to Chicago and New York,' said Nell.

'I'm not sure that I'll end up in either of them,' said Mort, 'but I'll drop my card with my mother's Skokie address into your letter box before I go. You will be coming back here?'

'Tomorrow night with Claudine,' sighed Nell. 'I'm beginning to wonder if I'll ever get away from this wretched flat.'

'And all my life I've dreamed of living in an apartment like yours – on a mysterious courtyard – with cobblestones—'

'Cobblestones?' Nell frowned out of the window in the hallway. 'What an odd thing to long for.' But, she thought, probably no odder than Taj Mahal marble or the blue of the Pacific Ocean or any of those distant foreign things that she had suddenly ceased to want.

'Well, whatever – but if I were you I'd be real glad to come back here tomorrow night. The air is getting cooler already. Soon the plane tree will turn gold—'

'And you'll be flying away from it all in the morning.'

'Absolutely,' said Mort. 'I have to be back in time for my coffee with Howie.'

'Who?'

'Long story,' said Mort. 'But in a way you're responsible.'

'For what?'

340

'I can't define it – but for getting me headed back home, getting me back on some kind of track—'

'With someone called Howie?'

'Like I said, it's a long story.'

'But you *will* have to take the plane tomorrow?'

'I can't afford to miss it. The next one doesn't leave for a week – you know how charter companies are.'

'Unreliable,' said Nell. 'Not worth the money they save you as far as I'm concerned.'

'You would say that, wouldn't you?'

Nell ignored him. Now that she had retreated safely behind professional concern, she couldn't stop talking.

'And God only knows where they get their pilots . . . And you'd better make sure you leave in plenty of time because if you should miss it, or there were any technical problem, you'd be left to fend for yourself. You could be stranded, and . . . and have to come back here.' Nell concluded more to herself than to Mort, who hadn't heard and was squeezing her on the shoulder.

'But thanks to your fine influence, Nelli, I'll be out of here bright and early and on my way, all packaged up and ready to go.'

'Well aren't I wonderful,' muttered Nell and turned her attention to the lift buttons which had registered a call on another floor. Suddenly she could think of nothing more to say. As Mort struggled to hold the doors open she added, 'You will leave me your card?'

'I'll slip it under your door so that no bakers or concierges or mysterious transsexuals can intercept it,' said Mort. Now a bell in the lift was pinging in accompaniment to the closing doors. 'Better go, Nelli,' he said. 'I enjoyed knowing you.'

'Me too,' said Nell. 'I mean knowing you.'

Mort tried to block the doors with his body one last time but they were persistent now and kept opening

341

and closing on his shoulders and the sides of his legs and feet. As he reached out for Nell the doors seemed to sense their opportunity and rushed forward to close him in. He just had time to pull Nell to him and rub his cheek against hers before the steel doors closed and whooshed him downstairs.

CHAPTER THIRTY SEVEN

After Mort left, Nell went to the window and watched for him to make his way across the courtyard. She wanted to wave him goodbye. But the small square of cobble remained empty except for the concierge's tom cat who had re-established his territory on the scrubby patch of grass under the plane tree. Mort must have gone into town to do some last minute shopping, Nell decided, and went to get dressed for her appointment.

When the time came in the cool early evening to put together an overnight bag and head for Claudine's château, Nell went back to the window and scanned the courtyard, but by then even the cat had gone inside. She picked up the pile of letters and tucked them into her bag, then she closed the shutters and the windows, switched on the automatic light timer and the answering machine and left.

Down in the entrance hall, she thought that if she had a taxi to wait for she would have an excuse to linger in the dark cool shadows, but she intended to drive Luc's Citroën. Of course nobody else needed to know that she had a car at her disposal, she told herself. She could wait for a few minutes, perhaps even a quarter of an hour, and let them, whoever they might be, think that she was, indeed, waiting for a taxi. They would assume that with the return of

Parisians to the city, taxis were more difficult to come by.

Nell waited exactly fifteen minutes. She timed it on her watch. When those fifteen minutes were up and nobody had entered the building, left the building or even appeared on the courtyard to throw out their rubbish or collect summer mail from the concierge, Nell picked up her overnight bag and walked to Luc's car.

When she arrived at Claudine's château, there was still enough light and, for the first time, enough solitude for Nell to examine the building in detail. Claudine was right, she now saw: the place was falling apart. Now that her envy and resentment was gone, now that Luc was no longer beside her, describing all that they could have done with a place like this, Nell saw that, apart from the few rooms where Claudine had squatted, the château was a crumbling ruin. She saw the damp that the first rains of the autumn had brought to the main bedroom; she ran her finger along a deep crack on the wall in the bathroom, and recoiled in disgust from a grey mould that had spread across a wall in the pantry. She was astonished to find a dead mouse in a trap under the kitchen sink and another one at the foot of the bed in the room where Claudine slept. The cheese in the traps was a runny, pungent Pont L'Evêque that Claudine had bought on a spring trip to Normandy with Nell.

After she had collected some clothes for Claudine and disposed of the contents of the mouse traps and some rotten food in the refrigerator and gone through a pile of bills, Nell lay down on the crumpled sheets that Claudine had left in her latest bedroom and pulled out her stack of letters. She obeyed Mort's orders and read them all. At first, she jotted down addresses so that she could reply to the writer, then she reached for the phone to call a long forgotten colleague but found that it had been cut off. After half a dozen letters, she rummaged around for a paper handkerchief and wept because she felt guilty at having ignored these people and because she was amazed by their kindness.

Next morning, as she locked the kitchen door and climbed into the Citroën, Nell heard a plane overhead. At first she thought a mechanical professional thought, that the wind had changed and the flight paths had changed as a result. Then she looked up at the sky and wondered if by insisting on going to her friend she was slipping back into the old familiar mould of 'work and duty'. But as the plane climbed above her and she noticed that it had a Japanese insignia and was not headed for the US at all, she hoped desperately that, perhaps for the first time in her life, she had taken the right path. Perhaps this time she *had* understood life and *had* understood that she was not acting out of duty to her friend but out of love and loyalty.

She didn't look up at the next plane but looked instead at the weedstrewn driveway of the château. She thought to herself that ahead of her lay the blankest, emptiest path she had ever known. She thought of Luc off somewhere in his DC3s, and she smiled.

This symbolically blank, empty drive that lay ahead of her was right under the flight path, Nell now realized. Try as she might, she could not ignore the planes that were passing overhead. She didn't start the car for a few minutes but sat staring up at the 747s as they took off for all those cities she knew so well and which she also knew could no longer bring her any comfort. She thought of Mort making his myopic way through the airport and wondered how different her life might now look if she had been able to relax enough to have that cup of coffee with him all those weeks ago. She imagined herself going into the awful café across from her flat and eating a second-rate ice cream with the American, who didn't worry and who had taught her that, in between the pain and the loss, life might still hold something to be enjoyed. The idea of descending from the heavens in one of her beloved jets in the knowledge that she had a friend like Mort waiting below enchanted her.

I've learned to relax now, thought Nell, and wanted to say as much to the passenger in the charter plane that would soon fly overhead. I've stopped making lists, I've stopped worrying . . . and it's too late.

The headmistress who resided in her head reminded Nell that Claudine was waiting. Nell continued to stare up at the sky and wondered if she could make a sudden romantic dash to the airport, but the clock on Luc's dashboard said ten o'clock and Nell knew that the airport was two hours away and that it really was too late. But at least I wanted to go, she told herself. For the first time in my life, I *wanted* to do something as wild and feckless as running after a relative stranger at an airport. And not a cruel, distant, falsely romantic stranger but someone as kind and happy as Mort. Nell decided that that brief moment when she had almost abandoned all her duties, when she had *wanted* to abandon them, would have to suffice her for the rest of her life. Averting her eyes from the skies, she turned the key in the ignition and drove down the weed-strewn drive towards the clinic.

Early that morning, as he knelt down to slip his card under Nell's door, Mort noticed that in grabbing the brass door knob for support he had left fingerprints all over its polished surface. He wiped it clean with his shirt, winked at the blank closed door and returned to his flat to pick up his bags. Marina insisted on coming down with him to the front entrance.

'You forgot your paints,' she said, pointing to his sketch pad and colouring materials in the corner of the room.

'You can have them – or you can throw them out,' said Mort.

'I'll give them to Sofia,' said Marina.

She went down the stairs before Mort. He looked up at Nell's shuttered windows. On that September morning, Mort Engelberg was also quite sure that because of his brief acquaintance with admirable, difficult Nell he had understood something more about life. He was trying to form this understanding into a sentence when Sofia's window opened and the country song echoed once more across the cobbles: 'My life is at a railroad crossing.' The concierge stepped out of her lodge and yelled up at the window in Portuguese. The music stopped and Mort realized that a taxi had drawn up and that Marina was waiting to bid him farewell.

He hugged her, made a hasty promise to write when he was settled back in the States, and climbed into the cab. As the taxi pulled away from the kerb and he waved goodbye, Mort was caught in the crawling traffic of the morning rush hour. He found himself in the embarrassing position of waving farewell to Marina while he moved just three feet. They waved and winked and smiled at each other for almost ten uncomfortable minutes before the driver found a gap in the traffic and accelerated suddenly, throwing Mort backward, his hand still poised in the air, a fixed farewell grin on his face.

Out at Roissy Charles de Gaulle airport, the main runway had ruptured at about the same moment that Mort stepped into his cab and Nell drove off towards the clinic. An El Al pilot, about to take off for Tel Aviv, was the first to notice the baffling cracks and the sinking tarmac that stretched almost the width of the runway. The airport was closed immediately.

In the first moments of panic, as flights were cancelled and aircraft sent back to their gates, airport officials suspected terrorists of mining the runways. On closer inspection, when a team of important men drove out in a Land Rover and stared down into the cracks, one of them suggested that the extreme heat of the hottest summer on record was doing to the runway what it had done to so many of their houses. 'Subsidence,' they muttered.

A Senagalese aircraft cleaner, who spent more time on the runway than any of the important men, pointed with his broom to the hundreds of burrowing rabbits that none of the men had noticed before and said: '*Les lapins*.' But nobody heard him and they hurried off in their Land Rover to oversee the closure of the airport while further investigations took place. The airlines would provide hotel accommodation for delayed first class passengers and seek to transfer both them and economy class passengers to flights departing from Orly or the provinces.

In the ensuing confusion, stranded charter flight passengers were left to fend for themselves.

THE END

THE SINGING HOUSE
Janette Griffiths

'IT MUST BE RARE TO FIND A BIG NOVEL THAT IS
UNASHAMEDLY ROMANTIC BUT IS ALSO CRISP AND WITTY,
ATMOSPHERIC AND WELL PACED'
Hilary Mantel

On the night before her wedding, Rose Lorenzo (half Spanish but
properly raised in North London by a respectable English mother)
found a pleasant but eccentric stranger pressing a ticket for Covent
Garden into her hand. The opera was *Tristan and Isolde* and Rose,
with her wedding dress in a carrier bag by her legs, sat breathless
in the squashed-up amphitheatre for five hours. Next morning she
cancelled the wedding. She was thirty-nine and she realised that
grand, splendid, tragic romance was what she really wanted from
life, not a last-hope marriage to suitable Martin.

Within a short time she had thrown in her lot with the two middle-
aged twins, Otto and Eva (it was Otto who had given her the ticket)
and set off in their ramshackle, unheated car to haunt the opera
houses of Europe. For Rose had fallen in love – with the huge,
wonderful, romantic Leo, one of the greatest operatic basses in the
world.

Amidst the snows of a European winter, Leo and Rose pursue their
grand passion – exactly what Rose had always been searching for –
but behind Leo lurks the misery and tenuous pull of his elusive
and unstable wife who lives alone in their villa on an Italian lake.

Filled with witty, abrasive, and unforgettable characters, *The
Singing House* is an outstanding first novel that is both wildly
romantic and acerbically funny.

'A REALLY GALLOPING GOOD READ WITH A STRONG
INTELLIGENCE'
Clare Boylan

' A ROMANTIC, FUNNY, HUGELY ENJOYABLE NOVEL'
Choice Magazine

0 552 99610 6

BLACK SWAN

THE GOLDEN YEAR
Elizabeth Falconer

One enchanted summer in Provence and its aftermath.

Summers, to Anna, had always meant the Presbytery, the mellow old stone house in Provence where her mother, the formidable Domenica, lived. Now that Anna's marriage to Jeffrey was all but over, she thought that she had herself well organized, dividing her time between her riverside home in London, her two teenage children and her career as a gilder and restorer of antiques. And then there were her summers in France – a chance to eat and drink magnificently, to sit in the sun and to recharge the batteries. She hardly realised how narrow and lonely her life had really become.

But one summer her brother Giò, an antiques dealer in Paris, brought down a new friend to the Presbytery. Patrick, a handsome television director, suddenly opened up Anna's life in a new and wonderful way, offering her a wholly unexpected chance of happiness. But she did not immediately see that others might not share her joy, and that her beloved brother Giò could have quite different ideas about Patrick and the future.

'A delightful evocation of the sights, sounds and flavours of life in Provence'
Family Circle

0 552 99622 X

BLACK SWAN

HOLY ASPIC
Joan Marysmith

A delightfully funny and poignant novel of provincial
life.

Fenn Meadowcroft, beautiful, vague and a wonderful
cook, is battling with a crisis of faith. Somehow her
conventional beliefs no longer seem enough: why is her
ineffectual schoolteacher husband so dull, life so
unsatisfying, and the vicar's weekly sermon so
nonsensical? Her daughter Damaris, having failed her A
levels, is off to Australia on a worryingly disorganised
trip with Marie, the daughter of Fenn's next-door-
neighbour Dodo. By contrast Doug, Fenn's louche and
entrepreneurial cleaner, boasts of his son's success in
gaining a place at Oxford. For Fenn, life seems empty
and unfulfilled.

Small wonder, then, that she falls easy prey to Dodo's
enigmatic new lodger Lex, while Dodo, her own eye
firmly on Lex, fails to notice that her other neighbour,
frail and elderly May, is losing her grasp on reality.
Initially reduced to hiding in the fishmongers to
avoid the vicar, Fenn discovers other ways of filling her
time . . .

0 552 99688 2

BLACK SWAN

A SELECTED LIST OF FINE WRITING
AVAILABLE FROM BLACK SWAN

99588 6	THE HOUSE OF THE SPIRITS	*Isabel Allende*	£6.99
99564 9	JUST FOR THE SUMMER	*Judy Astley*	£6.99
99618 1	BEHIND THE SCENES AT THE MUSEUM	*Kate Atkinson*	£6.99
99716 1	RANGE OF MOTION	*Elizabeth Berg*	£6.99
99648 3	TOUCH AND GO	*Elizabeth Berridge*	£5.99
99537 1	GUPPIES FOR TEA	*Marika Cobbold*	£6.99
99622 X	THE GOLDEN YEAR	*Elizabeth Falconer*	£5.99
99488 X	SUGAR CAGE	*Connie May Fowler*	£5.99
99656 4	THE TEN O'CLOCK HORSES	*Laurie Graham*	£5.99
99610 6	THE SINGING HOUSE	*Janette Griffiths*	£5.99
99685 8	THE BOOK OF RUTH	*Jane Hamilton*	£6.99
99392 1	THE GREAT DIVORCE	*Valerie Martin*	£6.99
99688 2	HOLY ASPIC	*Joan Marysmith*	£5.99
99649 1	WAITING TO EXHALE	*Terry McMillan*	£5.99
99709 9	THEORY OF MIND	*Sanjida O'Connell*	£6.99
99696 3	THE VISITATION	*Sue Reidy*	£5.99
99608 4	LAURIE AND CLAIRE	*Kathleen Rowntree*	£6.99
99672 6	A WING AND A PRAYER	*Mary Selby*	£6.99
99607 6	THE DARKENING LEAF	*Caroline Stickland*	£5.99
99650 5	A FRIEND OF THE FAMILY	*Titia Sutherland*	£5.99
99130 9	NOAH'S ARK	*Barbara Trapido*	£6.99
99643 2	THE BEST OF FRIENDS	*Joanna Trollope*	£6.99
99636 X	KNOWLEDGE OF ANGELS	*Jill Paton Walsh*	£5.99
99673 4	DINA'S BOOK	*Herbjørg Wassmo*	£6.99
99592 4	AN IMAGINATIVE EXPERIENCE	*Mary Wesley*	£5.99
99639 4	THE TENNIS PARTY	*Madeleine Wickham*	£5.99
99591 6	A MISLAID MAGIC	*Joyce Windsor*	£4.99